PRAISE FOR
OCEANSONG

"*Oceansong* has it all! From the sassy heroine Angie, the devastatingly sweet and handsome merman Kaden, a brutal war between their people, and their forbidden yet undeniable romance, C.W. Rose's debut will speak to anyone whoever wished to share a dialogue with the sea itself."

— KASSIDY COURSEY,
AUTHOR OF *SINS OF THE MAKER* TRILOGY

"A poignant and delightful debut about unexpected love, community, and the importance of compassion for the earth and all of its creatures. An atmospheric and compellingly modern take on Romeo and Juliet, with two soulmates from entirely different worlds who find common ground in their mutual love for their families and the sea."

— PAULETTE KENNEDY,
AUTHOR OF *THE WITCH OF TIN MOUNTAIN*

"Take the plunge into the mesmerizing depths of *Oceansong* by C.W. Rose, a tale where forbidden love and perilous adventure intertwine. With razor-sharp wit, heart-pounding twists, and characters that will leave an indelible mark on your heart, *Oceansong* promises an unforgettable journey that will keep you on edge from the first splash."

— CHANTAL GADOURY,
AUTHOR OF *UNTIL THE LAST PAGE*

"*Oceansong* is a story that strikes the whimsical side of the heart that believes in mermaids while appealing to the worldwide issue of environmental impact. It's rare to find a romance that incorporates the bigger picture of real-world problems, particularly those which are environmental, with take-your-breath-away love, and seeing this in C. W. Rose's book is a breath of fresh air. Placing this gorgeous story into the Alaskan coast and its cold waters is such a new and exciting perspective you can't help but fully fall in. C. W. Rose's writing will leave you laughing, your heart aching, and your body swooning for more in this amazing debut novel."

— ERICA ROSE EBERHART,
AUTHOR OF *THE ELDER TREE* TRILOGY

"With prose as entrancingly sharp as her iconic protagonist's beloved Alaska, C.W. Rose shines an invigorating new light on familiar folklore in this beautiful debut. *Oceansong* is rich in atmosphere, mystery, and all the different forms that love can take—from the romantic, to family bonds, to affinity with the land. This is a brilliant and moving addition to the fantasy genre, each page brimming with all the rhythm and depth of the Bering Sea."

— THEA GUANZON,
NEW YORK TIMES AND USA TODAY
BESTSELLING AUTHOR OF *THE HURRICANE WARS*

"Against the stunning backdrop of the Alaskan landscape, C.W. Rose paints a tale of romance persevering despite impossible odds, weaving in Asian culture, real world environmental issues, and the senseless brutality of bigotry and war."

— DESIRÉE M. NICCOLI,
AUTHOR OF *THE HAVEN COVE SERIES*

"Explore forbidden love in *Oceansong*, as Angie and Mer-Prince Kaden form an alliance amidst a battle for peace in her famine-stricken Alaskan hometown."

— NEWINBOOKS.COM

"*Oceansong* by C.W. Rose is a uniquely gritty modern fairytale so beautifully written that you can practically smell the sea breeze from the pages. If you find yourself daydreaming about what it would be like to live deep in the sea you're in for a magical treat. Kaden and Angie's star- crossed story is wrought with the excitement of first love as they navigate the consequences of falling in love during a tumultuous war between Mer and humans."

— MARIET KAY,
AUTHOR OF *BORN OF STARLIGHT*

"Be ready for this top-tier East-meets-West action-packed debut. An unputdownable mesh-up of family duty, bloodshed war and forbidden love in the sagacious retell of *The Little Mermaid* and *Romeo and Juliet*. That questions our stand on compassion and necessity."

— DEBORAH WONG,
AUTHOR OF *ME IN YOUR MELODY*

"An enchanting read that is perfect to enjoy on a sunny day, preferably at the beach. *Oceansong* is a magical story filled with strong familial ties, merfolk, and steamy romance in frigid waters. This contemporary fantasy is one you won't be able to put down!"

— MELISSA KARIBIAN,
AUTHOR OF THE *A SONG OF SILVER AND GOLD* DUOLOGY

"A story for everyone who's ever gazed out upon the ocean...and wondered who may gaze back. Readers are compelled not only by Angie and Kaden's forbidden love, but by greater themes of ecofeminism, greed, and motherloss. The escalation of both a secret romance and polarized violence makes this book a page turner."

— COURTNEY COLLINS,
CO-AUTHOR OF THE *Vows & Valor* TRILOGY

"Splashing onto the scene with her debut novel, C. W. Rose's *Oceansong* explores the environmental impact of humankind on the world it shares. Creating a world that feels both familiar and fantastical, with relatable characters and vivid descriptions, Rose weaves a tale that readers are sure to dive into."

— BENJAMIN BISHOP,
AUTHOR OF *The Valley of the Angels*

OCE

BOOK ONE
ANSONG

C.W. ROSE

OCEANSONG

Copyright © 2024 by C. W. Rose

All rights reserved. No part of this book may be reproduced, stored in a retrieval system, or transmitted in any form or by any means—electronic, mechanical, photocopy, recording, or any other—except for brief quotations in printed reviews, without the prior written permission of the publisher.

All characters are fictitious. People, events, incidents, descriptions, dialogue, and opinions expressed in this work are products of the author's imaginations and are not to be construed as real.

First Edition 2024

ISBN: 979-8-218-43034-4 (print)
ISBN: 979-8-218-43412-0 (eBook)

Cover Designer: Jeanette Barroso, *J20Graphics*
Cover Illustrator: Gianni Vazquez
Editor: Caitlyn Hall

OCEANSONG

C.W. ROSE

For the women who have had to choose between duty and their heart. For the feminists and feminist allies, and the romantics and ocean children at heart.

For my family and especially my brother, Kevin, my oldest best friend, who supported me in chasing my publishing dreams and indulged my never-ending love for the ocean.

This is for you.

"And to the ocean I go, to lose my mind and find my soul."

— *Unknown*

ONE

NICK BOLTED TOWARD ANGIE AS THOUGH the docks were burning behind him.

"Angela! Hey, come here!"

Angie cringed at the sound of her full name. Figures the jerk called her *Angela* despite repeating to him over and over how she hated it. She'd only been home two weeks and already she felt like throttling him.

Nick was drawing closer.

Too tired to deal with him now, Angie lowered her head and turned the corner around the warehouse, blending into the evening crowd as they left the docks for the day, and lost him.

One last task to finish.

Stretching her fatigued legs, she walked to the dock's edge to wait for the last fishing ship to arrive. She smiled as a cool breeze swiped her nape. She spied the forty-foot-long boat approaching, in awe at how its modest size so easily sliced through the thick waves.

Summers in Creston, her southwest Alaska hometown, were always her favorite time of year. Late May brought highs only reaching the upper forties, and the cold invigorated her and awakened her senses.

Beneath the deck's wooden planks, the Bering Sea's gentle lapping waves created a hypnotizing *splish-splash, splish-splash*, carrying balmy, aromatic salt air into her nostrils.

So refreshing and calming.

The ship docked, jolting her from the moment of calm. Angie helped the sailors and fishermen moor it, grabbing ropes thrown to her and tying a round turn and two and a half hitches knot around bollard posts.

She itched to go home, doff her heavy boots and baggy pants, hit the shooting range for an hour, grab dinner with Bàba, and take a long, hot bath at her childhood home where she lived for the summer.

Workdays were long and physical. They weren't doing her energy levels any favors. She was such a worn out twenty-four-year-old.

A group of fishermen stepped off the boat, dragging their trawler behind them. A red-bearded fisherman addressed her as he walked past. "Hey lady, help us sift through this? We're running behind, and we still have to take weight and record everything." Then under his breath: "Dying for a hot shower. I smell like stale shit."

Angie chuckled. Had she been out at sea for three straight weeks, she'd feel the same.

She hesitated before answering. There was no need for her to stay. Yet, going through the catch would give her practice identifying fish. As an extra bonus, Nick would have to keep waiting. That didn't bother her one bit. "Sure." She followed them to the weigh station.

"How much today?" the red-bearded fisherman asked.

Angie half-listened to their rambling as she pulled out a pen and clipped a piece of paper to her clipboard.

"Half as much as yesterday," his colleague replied.

"Same as the last two weeks, then. I don't like this at all." The red-bearded fisherman stroked his chin. "Where the hell are all the fish lately?"

Jotting the weight down, Angie frowned.

Not good. Less fish meant business would suffer, and so would her job. Then there was that issue of her tiny, self-sustaining fishing village not receiving their daily fish supply and not having enough to eat.

She would have to investigate.

A shiny, sea glass-studded bracelet fell from the trawler.

Rosie, her young niece, would love this deep-sea treasure, as she liked to call them. Angie's gaze lingered on the bracelet before palming it. "Mind if I keep this?"

The red-bearded fisherman nodded without glancing at her.

Once they no longer needed her assistance, Angie said goodbye, fish report in hand, and scribbled down her daily duties to hand to Bàba.

Before she reached Bàba's office, Nick Richelieu called out again, a raucous "There you are!" followed by a "Goddamn, woman! You're hard to track down."

"And yet, you managed anyway," she spoke through clenched teeth.

He was within eyeshot, strawberry blond hair flopping at his forehead. His steps were heavy and clumsy, arm swing stilted, his forced smile lopsided.

What did Mia, her older sister, see in this overconfident, obnoxious man? It beat her.

Nick stopped beside her, panting. "Angela," he drawled.

"You know I don't like being called that." With her arms across her chest, she faced him.

"I know." His lips widened into a toothy grin, too fake for Angie's liking. "You told me. Because your parents and teachers called you that when you got in trouble."

So, he did listen, but clearly, he didn't care. No need to remind him yet again. "What's up?" She plucked the thick gloves off her hands and shoved them into her coat pockets, keeping her distance and angled her body away from him.

If she were lucky, he would get the hint that she wanted to go home, not be stuck here longer than she already had.

No luck. "Well, Miss Angela Song." He paused, still not telling her what he wanted.

Angie winced, but forced a smile.

Stay calm. Don't piss him off or you'll piss off Bàba, too. Can't have that. Nick was his right-hand man. The son he never had.

This was her dream job for the summer. She could be with family, save enough money for graduate school. And work near the ocean, her happy place, where she could dive and explore the undersea world in her free time.

And more importantly, get enough work hours to meet her future graduate school's requirements before starting her PhD program in the fall.

Nick continued despite her non-response, his voice grating. "You have today's duty report?"

"You want my duty report? That's why you were running at me like your ass was on fire?"

Her sarcasm might as well be a shooting star over his head. "It's the end of the day, and I need to get them from sixty of you. So, hand it over." The phony grin stayed on his face, and he extended his arm.

Angie pushed past him. "I'm giving it to my dad."

"No, he asked me to take it from you." Nick's outstretched arm blocked her path, and Angie sighed, dropping her papers into his grubby paws. "Oh, and Mia's looking for you. She's here with Rosie. They're coming this way now."

Angie's irritation subsided, and she beamed.

"She's picking you up?" She never broke stride, hoping to get to Mia and Rosie before Nick did.

Private time with her older sister and her daughter without Nick was a luxury. Not waiting for Nick's answer, she waved to Mia and swept Rosie—named for the female lead from *Titanic*, Mia's favorite movie—into a hug, before embracing Mia.

To this day, she didn't understand Mia's hopeless romantic views, or why she loved that movie so much.

How could you fall in love with someone in a matter of days? The thought of falling for someone who was her complete opposite just seemed like more headache than it was worth. Why should love be hard?

"Angie *āyí*!" Five-year-old Rosie's hazel eyes were alight.

"I see you've been learning Mandarin." Angie grinned. "Look what I got you!" She held out the bracelet. Rosie burst into excited chatter, taking it from her hands.

"Yay thank you!"

"Yes, we started teaching them Mandarin and French last year," Mia added, grinning.

Rosie offered up a greeting in a foreign language, hands on her hips and chest puffed. "That means 'hi, Auntie Angie' in French!"

"I love it. I don't speak French, but you sound perfect." Angie glanced at Mia, who stood with her arms loosely folded over her chest. She held her full figure rigid, keeping an eagle eye on her daughter. "And Nick is French? Like, French-French?"

"French-Canadian. He's from Montréal," Mia replied. "I've been with him eleven years and you never knew?"

"Nope." Angie pursed her lips. Why did that still surprise Mia? Angie didn't care for the man—outside of him treating her sister well.

"He's part of the family, you know." Mia's tone became cutting. "But if you hadn't gone to the lower forty-eight for college, you might see he's not such a bad guy."

Angie reeled in a sharp response. She wanted to spend quality time with her family in the few months she was home, not cause friction. Especially not over Nick.

"This came from the sea?" Rosie squeezed in between them, waving her bracelet at Angie.

"Yes, the fisherman got it with their catch." Thankful for the interruption, Angie knelt to slip the bracelet onto Rosie's wrist. "I'm glad you love the ocean as much as I do."

"Oh, she'd come every day if she could. She must have been a fish in a past life. Or a mermaid, from Bàba's stories," Mia said.

"Mermaids dropped this?" Rosie's hazel eyes widened with wonder.

Angie met Mia's gaze which pointedly told her to play along.

"They might have," Angie kept her tone neutral. Once upon a time, she was just like Rosie. Wanting to believe fairytales were real as she fell asleep to Bàba's bedtime stories of how merfolk with healing powers once frequented the waters around the Last Frontier but inexplicably vanished over three hundred years ago. She could keep Rosie's mermaid dreams alive until she found out about their nonexistence for herself. "Maybe one day you'll do what I couldn't and find them."

"Yay!" Rosie exclaimed, then looked to the side, eyes lighting up. "Papa!"

Angie moved aside when Mia walked around to greet her husband with a quick kiss before asking Angie, "Walk with us to the car?"

"Sure." They made the ten-minute trek out of the docks, idly chattering about their days, the way they did after middle and high school. Nick walked ahead of them, holding Rosie' hand and asking about her summer camp.

They crossed the threshold into the parking lot, the crisp, fresh air giving way to a leaden, brisk scent. Mia put a hand on Angie's arm. "Tell Bàba we're coming for dinner?"

"Sounds good."

"And." Mia stopped, letting Nick and Rosie walk ahead of her. "If you and Nick could try to be civil tonight, I'd appreciate that a lot."

Angie gave her sister a tight nod, and caught the slightest shake of Mia's head as she turned and joined her family.

She planned to be polite with Nick for her family's sake, but he could make it so tough.

Once they were out of sight, Angie returned to the docks to grab her belongings. As she strolled, she reached into her pockets for her phone to check if Bàba had texted or called her.

"Damn it."

They were empty.

The phone must be in her locker. She purposely kept it there to resist checking her texts all day to see if her sort-of college boyfriend had texted her back.

It was a half hour before the next ferry to her village came. She could make that work.

Angie dashed back to the waterside and into the nondescript building that was the staff's locker room. Most of the staff had gone for the day, and she hurried to enter the code.

As the long metal door flew open, a glint appeared at the corner of her eye. Angie glanced out the window at the ocean, where calm ripples trailed over the brackish seawater, a reflection of the overcast skies.

She leaned against the windowsill. Against the larger-than-life backdrop of towering mountains and majestic glaciers, a lone fishing boat coasted by. A tranquil, everyday sight.

When it sailed past, the glint reappeared. A long, slender maroon fishtail, unlike any she'd ever seen, broke the water's surface.

Angie staggered back, her next breath catching in her throat.

In a blink, the fishtail disappeared.

TWO

ANGIE SAT GLUED TO HER MACBOOK the next evening, fingers moving over her mouse scroller and keyboard, scouring her pre-downloaded e-textbooks for information on the mysterious fishtail.

The house was unnervingly quiet now that it was just her and Bàba in the spacious five-bedroom home. As it did at times in her childhood, the isolation was getting to her. The feeling that the rest of the world, including her old friends who left Creston, moved on while her little village was frozen in time. Back then, she eventually grew used to her own company, that of her family's and their handful of school friends, and select workers and residents in her secluded village with a population of just over two hundred.

That sentiment changed when she went to Wasilla to work at a marine animal rescue center after high school, followed by Washington for college. Having people around all the time stifled her at first, but she soon began to enjoy meeting new people, especially in bustling Seattle.

Now it was just her and her thoughts, and occasionally, the isolating feeling still jarred her, as it did now.

Her mind stayed focused on the blood red tail shimmering under the sun's glow. It wasn't a whale's tail. Nor a dolphin's or porpoise's.

So, what the Hells was it?

It had flickered over the water so quickly, as if the tail's bearer had come up for a brief glimpse of the world beyond the surface and abruptly changed their mind. The size, color, and shape didn't belong to any fish native to Alaska.

Angie scratched her head. Scouring through her pre-downloaded e-textbooks turned up nothing.

A hesitant mewing broke the silence, followed by a brush of soft fur against Angie's shins. "Lulu! I didn't know you were in here." Her black and white cat curled around her ankles and rubbed her cheek on her leg, whiskers tickling her skin.

"Coming out to explore?" Angie leaned down to scratch the fur between her ears. Lulu ducked away from her hand and meowed again, louder this time, and Angie took it as a cue that she was shouting for breakfast. "Okay, okay, coming."

Lulu scurried toward her food bowl on the opposite end of the sizable home, and Angie's feet creaked the floorboards to keep pace.

Her cat stared with unblinking sapphire eyes as Angie grabbed a can of dry food from the countertop, taking her time in scooping out the kibble and ignoring Lulu's attempts at pressuring her.

The bell above their front door jingled, signaling that someone had entered, and she tossed the empty can into the trash.

"Bèibei?" Bàba approached, calling her by her childhood name, "precious girl." Angie walked into the foyer to say hello, in time to see him leave his boots by the door. He slid into his house slippers.

"You were at the docks? I didn't see you leave."

"Yes, I was called in at zero five hundred," Bàba replied.

Angie's lips pulled into a half smile. Bàba was a retired Chief Petty Officer of the U.S. Navy, and she always thought that though he left the military ten years ago, the military never left him.

He walked across the living room to wash his hands at the kitchen sink with a distant gaze.

Angie knew the look, where he spoke to her but his mind was elsewhere.

"I received some interesting information, and I needed to see for myself."

"Really?" Angie leaned against the wall, folding her arms.

"Other docks have started shutting down because of the lack of fish. Some of those workers are coming to us, so we'll have fifty new workers starting tomorrow."

Angie raised an eyebrow. Bàba was always generous with his time and resources, but–

"How are you going to afford paying fifty new workers' salaries?"

"Beau and Emily are footing most of their pay." He referred to Creston's mayor and his wife. Beau had served with Bàba in the Navy, and the two had remained friends even after they returned to civilian life. "One of the transplants is their son, Luke." He reached into his pocket. "Second thing, divers and boaters in the area have reported seeing animals appearing to be human from the waist up and fish from the waist down below five hundred feet." Bàba's eyebrows came together, his expression thoughtful. "Quick glimpses, nothing more."

"Are–are you sure?" Angie sputtered, rubbing one eyebrow. "That's ridiculous."

Her mind flickered back to Bàba's stories of old legends passed to him from his parents, and their parents before. Yet without proof that they had existed in the first place, they were nothing more than fishermen's tales.

There had to be a rational explanation. Maybe they had seen manatees or their cousins, the dugongs.

She also knew they didn't swim this far north, or at those depths.

"Maybe there are more predators in the area driving the fish away. Or there's something poisoning them." If they were dead, the waves would have pushed their floating bodies ashore. Another thought occurred to her. "The tides might be changing, and they're seeking refuge elsewhere."

Or, could merfolk be the predators? She pursed her lips. The notion went against every book she read on them and every drawing she'd seen, against her town's old legends that the fish-folk were kind and patient creatures who healed ailments with their hands and once lived in peace with the sea's children and humans before their disappearance.

"I didn't believe it at first, either. Asked them to stop making things up. Merfolk haven't been seen around here in over three centuries. But they showed me this." Bàba offered his phone to Angie. A frozen clip displayed on the screen.

His hand shook as Angie took the phone and hit the "Play" button, bracing herself for what she might see. A blurred and grainy recording started. Muffled breathing came through the phone's speakers, the unmistakable, hollow-sounding inhales and exhales through diving regulators. Through the soft green night vision, coral formations appeared and a leatherback sea turtle glided by, darting into the dark when the camera moved closer to it. Angie squinted, waiting for the supposed merfolk to come into view.

Five seconds later, a long, scaly tail brushed by, and the camera shook as if the person holding it nearly dropped it in shock. Another tail followed.

What the Hells?

At first glance, it appeared to be a large fish slicing through the water. Then she saw human-like hands held at their sides, webbing reaching halfway to their fingers' first knuckles.

The camera tumbled out of the diver's possession, and they reached to grab it before it disappeared into the depths.

Her arm tingled as she handed the device back to Bàba. "No way."

"Told you." He stuffed his phone back into his pocket. "I'm sending out a group of divers tomorrow afternoon to take another look around, see if they can find anything else. If this is real, and if it truly is—" He stopped, taking a deep breath before continuing, "Merfolk taking our food supply, we will need to deal with them directly. I'll let you know what they find."

"Wait, Bàba." Angie grabbed his arm before he left. "Let me go with them."

"Tomorrow is Sunday. Don't you want the whole weekend?"

"No, I want to go. I haven't done a dive since I came back home, and I miss it." She struggled to process what she'd seen on the video, and wanted to see for herself in person. Angie admitted, "Makes me think of Māma." At the mention of her, Bàba's shoulders dropped, a forlorn shadow crossing his face. He pushed his glasses further up his nose and rubbed his five o'clock shadow, wrinkles forming around his eyes. "Okay. I will look at the conditions of the sea tomorrow and plan a quiet time to go out. But expect to be there around thirteen or fourteen hundred."

Angie nodded. "You got it."

———— ⏏ ————

The next morning, she gathered her scuba gear from her closet: flippers, drysuit, hood, BCD vest, booties, snorkel mask, and fins. Before leaving, she double checked her gear to ensure she didn't forget anything.

Her chest tightened, and she sucked in a gulp of air, hands hovering over her mesh diving bag. Behind their portable UV lights which they used to simulate sunlight for winter's unending dark, a chest full of her childhood belongings sat in partial view. Angie reached for it, pulling out a drawing of merfolk she made when she was eight. A school of them, swimming without a care in the world, complete with raggedly drawn green stripes she hoped depicted seaweed.

She held the picture close to her heart. It was a simpler time. Her family and friends didn't understand her interest in mythical fish-creatures, as they dubbed merfolk, but she didn't let them deter her from believing. Her ten-year-old self was so sure mermaids still existed somewhere in the deep blue sea, and she would prove everyone wrong. Of course, over a hundred dives later, she never found a trace of them. She continued diving in Alaska and Washington's lakes and oceans over the last thirteen years, but lost interest in mermaid hunting and stopped believing in their existence after entering high school, preferring to focus on her studies and friends.

Shaking the memories away, Angie put the drawing back in the chest and slammed the closet door shut. Intrigue and fury and anxiety played a three-way tug-of-war in her mind.

A pull came from deep inside her, a speckle of hope sprouting that the divers were wrong, and the video was fake.

So many years of failed searches. *She* had failed. If merfolk had turned up some years earlier, and if they truly had healing powers, she could have saved Māma.

A swell of resentment rose, and she pinched her lips together and zipped her dive bag closed. She caught a finger in it and hissed, jerking her hand back.

When she was thirteen, she scuba dived to search for mermaids. Now, she was twenty-four and about to go diving for mermaids again.

The irony wasn't lost on her.

THREE

AT ONE-THIRTY, ANGIE STOOD AT THE docks' edge, fidgeting with her drysuit and obsessively checking that it covered her wrists and ankles. She shivered in anticipation of forty-degree water that would soon meet any exposed patches of skin.

Their last diver—and her dive buddy—was running several minutes late from an unexpected traffic jam crossing the bridge into the harbor. Other divers chatted in a small group beside her, and their boat bobbed in tune with the waves, seemingly unfazed that they were to go searching for merfolk, of all things.

Angie's leg kept bouncing in anticipation, only stopping when her phone pinged and distracted her. The guy she was seeing from college had answered her after two weeks of silence with a vacant,

> hey, wanna come over tonight?

This was followed by the slanted-eye, coy smile emoji. The message was in response to her last text asking his plans for the weekend, and an inside joke. After four months, he hadn't asked her to be his girlfriend, expertly dodging the question when she brought it up.

Thinning her lips, she blocked and deleted his number without a response then put the device away and strapped her diving knife to her ankle. The final diver arrived, suited up, and was now gesturing at her with frantic motions.

"Hey, Angie." He jogged to her and retrieved his Heliox tank before tying his wavy hair back into a neat man-bun.

"Hey yourself, Stefan." Angie watched him don his booties, depth gauge, and rebreather. Stefan was well into his fifties, yet Angie thought he passed for ten years younger. His hair was still a vibrant, glossy ebony, with skin like porcelain and a lively spark in his whiskey-brown eyes.

It must have been the cold water diving he did. He jokingly called it a preserving agent.

"Mermaids, huh?" Stefan snorted.

"Right? But my bàba wants to see if the footage is real. I kind of do, too." Angie swung her pressure gauge and inflator hose over one shoulder. "Either way, maybe we'll see what in the Hells kind of creatures were on those videos. Or where the fish are going. I mean, the fish that we actually eat."

"What do you mean?" Stefan stopped in his tracks. "Only the fish we eat are going missing? Others aren't?"

"I came in earlier today to look at the reports from the last month, try to find a pattern of what kinds of fish we were getting and how many." She set her jaw. Their catches normally had an abundance of safe, sustainable king salmon, rainbow trout, and pollock, but lately— "We had a shit ton of bluefin tuna and rockfish, much more than usual." Fish that her village tended to avoid.

"The mercury-drenched, prickly stuff that nobody around here really wants to buy." Stefan finished for her.

"Maybe we'll see if mermaids are really doing this." The word *mermaid* hitched and broke as Angie spoke.

It still didn't seem real to her that they were actually doing this.

"Alright. On the off-chance we find them, I want to tell Ken I saw them first. I'd like to know where the fish are, too," Stefan remarked. "But fish matters aside, it's good to see you. Been a minute since you've come out with us."

She gave him a tight smile. He didn't need to know that losing Māma was the reason she stopped diving.

The captain cupped his hands around his mouth, amplifying his voice so Angie, who was in the back of the group, heard it loud and clear. "All aboard! Let's go!"

Holding her flippers steady, she followed the group onto the boat.

"You still diving out here on the reg?" Angie performed a final check, ensuring her dive computer was functional and felt for her flashlight resting snug in her upper pocket. Relief draped over her, and she relaxed against the boat's bench, knowing everything was in place.

"Ken and I try to get out here every few weeks. I have to say, I've dived a lot of places, but I haven't found anywhere as satisfying as here. We can't get enough." Stefan kept his eyes on the horizon, where the water line kissed the sky.

"Hubby's at the dive shop?"

"He agreed to run the place today so I could come out. He's trying to close on time. We have the grandkids and Ken's entire family is here." Angie caught the smallest of eye rolls from Stefan, even if his soft smile remained. "They came all the way from the Philippines, so we'd feel terrible if we didn't entertain them every hour."

The two chatted until the boat hit a bump in the water. Angie yelped in surprise and threw her hands forward on instinct even though there was nothing to stabilize herself with. She dug her feet into the deck so she wouldn't topple over.

Had they hit a rock? Was the boat damaged, and their search was going to be over before beginning?

The other divers settled back into their seats and chattered amongst themselves, their nervousness palpable.

Angie looked around. No rock to be found.

Yet the seawater rippled with angry waves. A strong wind gust barreled through and walloped her face.

"Hey! What's that?" Stefan pointed to the water. The other divers crowded around them.

A dark streak of scales appeared with two flowing, transparent caudal fins. The boat rocked again, a violent wave smacking the hull, and Angie clung to the sides to keep her balance.

The waters calmed once the tail vanished from sight.

Angie drew her head back, covering her mouth with her palm. The other divers chatted in low murmurs. She sat, resting her hands on her lap and took a deep breath so she wouldn't still be anxious when she started diving and burn through her oxygen too fast. The bumpiness and waves appeared when the—merman? Mermaid? Some other strange creature? —appeared, and calmed when it disappeared. As if it carried the turbulent waters on its back.

She'd never heard of such a phenomenon. The sun and moon controlled the tides. Not sea creatures. Curiosity and bewilderment rose.

The boat slowed to a stop, and the captain killed the engine. Standing, the divers donned their tanks and congregated at the side of the boat.

"Guess if that was a mermaid, here's our chance to find out," Stefan muttered from beside her.

Here we go.

At the divemaster's signal, they rolled backward and tumbled into the icy sea. Angie cracked the surface with a loud splash, screwing her eyes shut as icy hands surrounded her head and neck, squeezing with brute force.

The ocean was an icebox surrounding her for the next several minutes, until her body acclimated to the deep freeze.

Hanging weightlessly, she drifted sideways in tune with the current, and bobbed with her breaths.

They made the slow, uneventful journey into the depths.

A brush of freeze seeped through at her nape and grasped her entire body, and she clenched her jaw. The gentle splashing overhead faded into stillness, until the only sounds surrounding her were the rhythmic, soothing whoosh of air when she inhaled and exhaled.

It was quiet, tranquil, peaceful.

She reached out to brush through the algae beds stroking her belly and legs as she swam by and brushed away stray plastic fragments and the occasional cigarette butt and chunk of fishing gear floating about.

How she wished the ocean could return to its pristine majesty, without the pollution. The desire to take action was what drove her to pursue marine biology.

She checked her dive computer after descending further. It registered that they were at four hundred fifty feet, close to the depth where the divers allegedly saw mer. She made a sharp turn, trailing Stefan, and jotted down another mark on her dive compass so she knew how to return to the boat. Her heart fluttered at the marginal possibility she'd see a mermaid.

A seabed lay ahead, and nestled within the sand, a school of halibut flitted about. Curious eyes at the top of their heads peered at Angie and Stefan. A salmon shark sailed overhead, its silver and ivory body lithe and graceful, a floating dancer moving in tune with the flow and currents.

More concerning, other fish were scarce: salmon, whitefish, pikes, arctic chars.

Her shoulder hit a hard bump, and with numb fingers, she fumbled around to turn her flashlight on. It illuminated a gorgeous, deep sea coral formation, untouched by ocean acidification and warming. It showcased vivid oranges and pinks and reds, fitted like a jigsaw puzzle. Thankfully the coral was smooth. She would have hated to knock off the branch of a spiny one. It would have hurt like hell, and she didn't want to contribute to Alaska's collapsing coral reef population.

Tapping her, Stefan gestured in front of him. Humanlike flesh zipped by, with broad shoulders, slender fingers, and a strong back. A tail followed, the shape similar to what she saw in the video and at the docks, its color indiscernible in the crushing blackness.

The creature turned around; a flash of maroon caught in her flashlight's soft glow. Angie froze as her mind caught up to what she was seeing.

A merman.

What.

The.

Shit.

Mer were real. She gawped. He looked so human, at least, his top half. All those years she searched and searched, and now, a merman floated mere feet, or perhaps more aptly, tails away from her.

If the rebreather wasn't stuffed in her mouth, her jaw would have dropped to the seafloor.

After she signaled to Stefan that she was going to follow, Stefan gave her the "OK" hand symbol. Angie pedaled her finned feet faster keeping her gaze trained on the strange mer.

She couldn't take her eyes off him. Wanted to keep staring, studying. Admiring. With enough distance between herself and him, Angie lagged behind but kept the merman in sight.

He stopped.

A school of arctic char lounged ahead, and Angie went as still as the rocks surrounding her when a mermaid appeared from the dark, passing through her flashlight's beam. Her face was golden tan and beautiful, dark hair tied into elaborate braids crowning her head. Stacks of pearls wrapped around her chest and neck like a jeweled turtleneck crop top.

She was breathtaking: a mermaid as depicted in the various fairytales Angie enjoyed reading as a child.

The mermaid's glittering brown, doe-like eyes caught Angie's, and Angie pumped her arms to scramble backward.

The creature motioned to the merman beside her. As if by some magnetic pull, the arctic chars followed, and the group picked up speed. Angie followed, but couldn't get close even if she wanted to. They propelled like darts with each swish of their tails.

No, no, no. She couldn't look away, but she was going to lose them any second now.

They plunged downward and vanished into the watery void. No matter where she looked, she found no trace left of them, or the school of fish. Her face slackened. They had to be here somewhere. They couldn't just disappear, could they? Angie stared blankly into the unending abyss.

One thing for certain, the mer were hoarding fish. The big question was, why?

She gathered herself and swam back to Stefan, who gave her a thumbs-up, indicating they should head back to the surface.

Her skin tingled, and it wasn't from the arctic waters. A pulsing shiver crawled down her spine as she held onto Stefan's D ring, and they made their gradual ascent.

In the aftershock of the cold and seeing the mer, her extremities still hadn't regained sensation. She needed time to wrap her head around what she witnessed with her own eyes.

FOUR

"BEIBEI." Angie shifted her weight on the living room couch, lightheaded with images of the pearl-studded mermaid and her companion. She straightened at Bàba addressing her, her mind bursting with words she had been waiting to tell him. "I know you just got back, but when I was diving, we saw mer-"

On his way to the kitchen, he stopped short next to Angie, and peered down at her. "You saw what?"

Angie formed her next words in her mind before speaking them aloud. "The divers were right. We saw a mermaid and a merman."

"Are you sure?" Bàba dropped his hand and cleared his throat. "Mermaids?"

"I know it sounds crazy. Then there was a school of arctic char over my head and right in front of us. The mer herded them away from us. After that, they all disappeared." Angie's voice dropped to a murmur. "I can't believe I'm saying this."

"So you found them," he said under his breath. He began to pace, scratching his jaw.

Angie waited to see how he would react next.

He stopped pacing. "I'll have to think on this. For now, come help clean up. Your *jiějie* and her family are coming over."

"Oh, sure." Angie's chest and shoulders deflated as she walked to the kitchen as if she were on autopilot, and put the clean dishes into their cabinets. She would tackle Lulu's litter box afterward. After telling him the news, she was dying to know what went through Bàba's mind.

He wouldn't tell her until he had gathered his thoughts, and he always claimed that the more he moved and did, the clearer his mind.

"When you're done, take the compost out. I'm getting the garbage." Bàba called over his shoulder, holding a large black bag, filled to the brim.

Angie threw up her hands. She quit.

After tying the compost bag closed, she jumped at a black and white face peering at her from behind the bin, whiskers and tiny pink nose twitching. Running underfoot and almost tripping Angie, Lulu mewed as she scuttled away to find her next hiding place. "Lulu! You scared the shit out of me." Angie let out a loud yelp of surprise, and Lulu stopped, turning her head to one side, her mouth opening to release another "Meow?" This one sounding more tentative. The cat returned and wrapped her tail around her ankles, headbutting her.

"Oh, now you want cuddles after nearly making me fall?" She sat cross legged, and Lulu climbed into her lap, kneading her jeans. Then she curled into a furry ball, turning over to expose her belly. It was the softest part of her, but Angie knew better than to scratch it. She could switch from cuddly and loving to swiping at her in a blink with all eighteen claws.

When Lulu decided she had enough and left, Angie resumed her duty. The trek to the compost bin was a three-hundred-foot walk across gravel, and she grunted, struggling to keep steady while holding the bag firm.

Balance was never her strong suit, and the last thing she needed was to trip and drop the bag, spilling five gallons of trash all over the impeccably kept driveway. Her rubber boots crunched on packs of loose pebbles, the path dotted with puddles from the morning rainfall.

The bag made it to its bin, and she dusted off her hands while squinting at two figures in the woods, a quarter mile away. They held plastic bags, and the man squatted to pick up something, inspecting it before dropping it into their shopping bag.

Huh. What were Dave and Jenny doing here?

Were they foraging? Angie had grown up with them, and they had never given off the impression that they were struggling to feed themselves and their kids.

Angie hiked over to them. "Hey, what are you doing?"

"Oh, hi, Angie." Jenny shielded her eyes with one hand and gripped the container in the other. Her face scrunched as if it would repel the sunlight. "Looking for food; Peter's hungry."

Angie's posture stiffened.

"Got a couple huckleberry and lingonberry handfuls and broccoli," Dave added, motioning to their shopping bags. "I was out all morning at the pier. Got a couple of them pink salmon, enough to feed us for a day or two."

"We have some tuna and rockfish," Angie tried. It was normally the type of fish her village shied away from, but it was still food.

"I can't be eating all that mercury." Jenny shook her head. "I'm pregnant. We went through all our stored food already."

"I'll eat them," Dave said, with a grunt.

Jenny's gaze darted to him in a look that Angie couldn't read. "Alright. We'll bring some over to your place tonight."

Dave nodded, appreciative.

"And congratulations on the new baby," Angie offered weakly.

Jenny gave her a despondent smile. "Thanks. The Ngos, Estrellas, and the Davises have been out all day and night at the pier and on their boats. We were hoping to get some of their extra catches, but even they don't have enough."

"Took that long-ass ride downtown with a couple others to Amy and Carol Lum's shop. Everything's twice as expensive and they were running low on a lot of meat and veggies," Dave added. "Something about demand being too high for how fast they can resupply. It's bullshit."

This situation was getting worse and worse.

Dave furrowed his brow. "What's going on with your dad? He was so good about bringing us fresh seafood, supplemented whatever our anglers were getting." Dave smiled, seemingly to himself. "Still have no idea how he got away with bringing all those fish back."

"Well, he owns the docks, so he can do whatever he wants. And there's been a shortage of fish." Angie forced a chuckle. "The catches have been getting smaller. You're not imagining it." She didn't want to divulge merfolk to them just yet—no need to send anyone into a panic until they confirmed what was happening.

"But what's going on? We're not the only ones who're hungry," Jenny spoke up, her voice rising. Dave rested a hand on her shoulder, and she calmed.

A truckload of resolve smashed into Angie's gut.

The villagers relied on her family's weekly deliveries of salmon, halibut, cod, and shellfish to survive. Their littoral village was surrounded by water on three sides and dense forest on the fourth side. Its cold soil yielded a limited number of crops, adequate to feed the villagers if they were coupled with a healthy supplementation of seafood. Their scarcity of crops was not conducive to raising livestock. The next town was over fifty miles away by air.

If even their tiny grocery store downtown—a ninety-minute trip away and where new stock was airlifted in once every two weeks and mostly served the downtowners—was spiking in their prices and running low, her villagers would begin to starve. How long did the merfolk intend to hoard the fish? It had only started three weeks ago. The ocean's ecosystem would be upended. It was a horrifying thought on both ends.

The young couple stood before her, their expressions silent and pleading. "I'll talk to my bàba," Angie said, voice resolute. "Promise."

— ෴ —

Angie didn't get the chance to talk to Bàba again before Mia, Nick, and Rosie arrived.

He hadn't lost his perfect, host touch, that was for sure. She admired his handiwork.

That night, the sprawling dining room was lit wall to wall with dimmed lights shaped like flowers and leaves. Bàba and Māma had wanted the dining room to be lodge-inspired, the walls and triangulated ceiling appearing to be made of stacked logs.

A long, solid wood table sat in the middle, seating ten, reminding Angie of the days when her parents hosted get-togethers for the villagers and threw surprise birthday parties for her and Mia.

Once, she couldn't wait to get out of Creston and move away for college. Four years later and she now relished the comforts and memories of her childhood home.

The fireplace roared in the living room, spitting out tiny chunks of crimson and jet-black embers, warming the space like a cozy blanket. Angie rushed over to drop aromatic dried herbs and cinnamon sticks inside, keeping the pleasant, fruity, peppery, and earthy scents circulating and drifting into the kitchen.

Tonight, Mia and Nick brought a crockpot-sized meal of homemade bison chili, enough so they would have leftovers for the next two days.

Lulu made sporadic appearances and delighted Rosie who waved a laser pointer around.

Nick stood from the table, leaving a portion of his food uneaten. He moved into the living room and play-wrestled with Rosie while she shrieked in laughter, spooking Lulu, before Bàba called him back to the table.

The night was going off without a hitch, and conversation flowed.

Until after dinner.

Nick stayed sitting while Mia, Angie, and Bàba cleared the table.

"You going to help or just sit there?" Angie faced Nick once Mia and Bàba disappeared into the kitchen. She wasn't sure if her biting tone would get Nick's attention, or if, as usual, he would ignore being called out.

"You go ahead. I'm watching Rosie." Except Nick was turned away from Rosie, who ran around and shouted for Lulu. Plates and cups stacked in her arms, Angie walked to the kitchen, shaking her head. She left Nick's dirty dishes in front of him.

Clean your own plates then, prick.

"I'm still not used to this house without Māma," Mia was saying when Angie joined them. "I miss her."

Bàba set his lips in a tight line and gave a nearly imperceptible nod. He didn't meet Mia's eyes for a beat. Hanging back, Angie's heart ached at the mention of Māma, with memories of how she made delicious recipes passed down from her own mother–Angie's *wàipó*, still in China–many of them involving their favorite food, rice, in some form. Angie, Bàba, and Mia would affectionately call them *fàntǒng*, meaning "rice bucket."

"Thank you for the food," Bàba said, finally meeting Mia's gaze.

"Of course," Mia said. "We were able to get Amy and Carol's last two pounds of bison. And the prices definitely went up, on *everything*."

"I heard." Angie stepped into the kitchen. She turned the sink on and ran the hot water over the plates and mugs.

Bàba raised an inquisitive eyebrow. "Beibei, I was thinking about what you said. About the mermaids."

"Wait, what?" Mia cut in. "Mermaids?"

"*Gōnggong! Gōnggong!*" Rosie rushed to Bàba. "Papa told me to say thank you for inviting us for dinner. So, thank you!" Then she stopped short and spun around to face Angie and her mother, her mouth agape. "You found mermaids?" She bounced up and down and clapped her hands with glee. "I have to go tell Papa!" She dashed back into the living room.

"Great, she's never going to leave me alone." Mia cursed, and then groaned. "Angie, did you actually see mermaids? Because it's nuts if you did."

"Angie āyí! Did you see the mermaid that dropped my bracelet?" Rosie had returned, waving her bracelet at Angie and Mia.

"Okay, that's enough about mermaids for now. Let's go find Papa." Mia rubbed her face and took Rosie's hand, leading her from the kitchen.

Folding her hands behind her back, Angie twiddled her nervous fingers where Bàba couldn't see them. "What were you thinking about, with the merfolk?"

"I think we should find out what they're doing." Bàba's voice rang flat and even.

Angie stood straighter. "And where all the fish are going."

He gave an absent nod, dark brown eyes trained on the floor. "Yes. I will arrange to have deep sea cameras placed around where you found them. See if we can follow their path."

Dave and Jenny flashed in her mind. How many other villagers were also suffering? Her thoughts were a jumbled mess. "I'll help."

"Good." Bàba nodded, still not facing her. "But, the mer have seen us lurking in their area. They could be dangerous. We don't know a thing about them." His tone sounded unnaturally stilted. "Be ready for anything."

FIVE

ANGIE STEPPED DOWN FROM BÀBA'S BRAND new Toyota Tundra and shook her hands. They cramped from death-gripping the steering wheel after off-roading twenty miles in the rugged wilderness to get to the closest shooting range and after Bàba's thinly veiled threat that she'd be fully responsible for any damages she incurred to his brand-new pickup truck.

Fortunately, she got here without incident. After settling in, she loaded the magazine of her Glock 19X, pointed it downrange, and turned the safety off.

Bàba's words, "Be ready for anything," blared in her mind.

After her and Bàba's talk yesterday, Nick texted asking her to come in for today's afternoon shift.

She had a free morning, and she was going to take full advantage. Brilliant sunlight beat down on her, glinting off her targets. She gripped the barrel with both hands, index finger hovering over the trigger. Crisp, cool air filled her nostrils, carrying the nearby woods' natural fragrance. There was one other young man at the range firing a shotgun, leaving behind the metallic scent of gunpowder. The pungent and ashy smell reminded her of home.

Her parents had insisted she and Mia learn to handle a gun for self-defense when they were young girls. The loud bangs and violent kickback used to terrify her and make her cry. Later, Bàba and Māma took her and Mia on weekly shooting range trips, and when she was proficient, Bàba gifted her a handgun as her high school graduation present.

She let the bullet fly, the grip digging into her palm when it recoiled, and she held firm.

Bullseye.

Angie aimed again, going for a second one.

A muffled voice slipped past her protective earmuffs.

"Nice Glock!"

Tiān, who was bothering her? She had to keep her focus. One wrong slip of the finger could mean a potential injury, or worse, for her or the other person.

Another shot, an inch away from the bullseye. Adrenaline flowed. The muffled voice came back, but this time, it was unintelligible.

Angie cast him a side-eye and gave a brief nod. Maybe if she acknowledged the pest, he would leave her alone.

The voice came again. "Hey, you're Angie, right? From the docks?"

He knew her?

"Yeah. And you?" Angie removed her ear protection and flipped the safety on her Glock, pointed it downrange, and straightened up.

A coltish, redheaded teenage boy approached her, bright-eyed and energetic. He gathered his ammo boxes, moved to the shooting stall next to her, and held out his hand, his wide grin lifting her spirits. "Luke. Just started at your dad's docks last week. It's great there."

"Oh! My dad mentioned you. You're a big deal around here. The mayor's son, right?"

"Yeah, I mean, it's not that big of a deal." Blushing, he ran a hand through his hair and looked at his sneakers. "Didn't think I'd see anyone else here. Actually, wait, hold on." Luke jogged downrange to set up his targets, scattered colored circles with numbers on them, and then ran back up range to stand beside her. "I like it here. Nice village you all live in."

"It's homey. Where are you from?" Angie aimed the Glock at her target and turned the safety off.

"I was working at the port in Unalaska."

Angie lowered her gun, flipping the safety back on. "How come you were out there when your parents are here? Do you have family there too?"

"When I finished school, I thought about going to stay with my big brother in Tacoma for a while, work there. But then my aunt and uncle offered for me to stay with them for the summer in the Aleutians, and I love it there. So I couldn't say no." Luke's eyes danced with excitement as he spoke.

"Your brother's in Tacoma?" Angie perked up. "I went to school in Seattle."

"What for?" Luke stepped closer.

"Got my marine biology bachelor's. I'll be going back in the fall for my PhD."

"Right on." Luke gave her a buck-toothed grin. Angie turned back to her gun, about to pick it up, but Luke lingered. Clearly, he wasn't ready to end the conversation. "So I guess you know what happened there, and a few other ports."

"A little bit. What happened?" She was enraptured and gave him her full attention.

"Fish gone missing, so they shut the place down while they have, like, the military and government investigating. Heard it's similar in even bigger ports like Anchorage." He lowered his voice, even though Angie didn't see anyone around who could possibly overhear them.

The fish problem stretched all the way to Anchorage? Tingles danced over her skin.

Luke spoke again. "Are you going to work later?"

"Not until twelve. You?"

"Well, I have to go to the docks in an hour. And then I'm heading out with some of the guys and girls on the *MV Castaway* tonight. Hopefully, we can bring back some fish."

Luke returned to his stall and laid out his ammo boxes in a neat line in front of him. "Then I'll get some time off once we return, so I can start getting my things ready for college. I'm headed to Anchorage in the fall."

"Congratulations! You must be so excited." A flush of happiness washed over Angie, and she faced him. She just met this boy, and she liked him already. "They have you working the cargo ships, huh?"

"I am! Steward's department." Luke shifted his weight and slipped on his protective eyewear. "And thanks a lot, Angie." Angie couldn't mistake the light in his eyes as they turned back to their targets and resumed practice.

Fueled by the thought of her fellow villagers starving and the anxiety of what the deep-sea cameras might pick up, she pointed the Glock at her zombie target's bullseye, hitting two in a row.

She pointed her eyes heavenward, grinning to herself. Now, she'd be a quicker, more accurate shot in the event she'd have to defend herself, whether she held her Glock, or a speargun.

After going through one more ammo box, she waved goodbye to Luke.

"Luke, be safe, alright? I'll see you at the docks. Heading home for a bit."

He said goodbye, and Angie packed up, heading home to drop her things off before work.

"Today's catch was a quarter of the usual." Bàba looked deflated. "*Tāmāde.*" He muttered the curse under his breath. Angie bowed her head, balancing her clipboard in one arm, rising from the waveguard she was leaning against. The clipped papers with cargo inventories fluttered in the incoming breeze.

Days had passed with no mer sightings since she, Stefan, and the rest of their diving group had placed the cameras. Angie took a deep breath before asking her next question. "What kind of fish were in the catch?"

Bàba furrowed his brow. "Mostly tuna. Green and white sturgeons. A few king salmon, arctic char, and cod. Enough to feed a few families." He stiffened.

"I heard it was like that for the last few weeks." Angie drew her shoulders together, posture wilting in confusion. She'd give the measly amount in her savings to find out why the mer were so intent on starving them.

"There's not nearly enough to feed everyone. I heard the other fishers have gotten similar catches." Bàba crossed his arms over his chest, his square jaw set. Sporting a faded mustache and the shadow of a soul patch, Angie figured he hadn't shaved in a few days. "They will blame me, more than anyone else."

"I saw Jenny and Dave the other day picking berries and mushrooms," Angie said, her voice low. "Nobody's going to believe us when we tell them about mermaids. I didn't even believe it until I saw them." She set her lips in a tight line.

"I saw that video from the divers, and you told me you saw the mer, but to see them in the flesh is something else."

"What are you talking about?" Angie drew her shoulders back and looked at him with wide eyes. "In the flesh?"

"Two were killed earlier today, and the divers brought one to the surface. It is here now."

"Dead mer? Here?" Angie nearly choked on her own words. "Can I see?"

"Yes, when you are done with taking inventory, come find me or Nick, and we'll show you." Bàba left, and Angie checked her watch. Lunch break was over, and she carried on looking over the last of the inventory on the *MV Arctic*. The next ship to leave would take Luke with it.

"Got everything written down?" the ship's captain asked.

"Yup."

Luke crept up behind her and tapped her shoulder, a sparkle in his bright blue eyes. "Hey, I'm gonna go see the mer they got. Want to come with?"

She nodded and followed Luke.

What would the merfolk look like up close where she could see every detail of them? What could she learn and, more importantly, what kind of insight could she get as to why they would need so much fish? Maybe they were strict fish-eaters and couldn't sustain themselves on anything else.

Angie and Luke found Bàba and Nick amongst a throng of other workers by the east fishery, the murky waters barren of life. From the back of the crowd, Angie could see a limp tailfin hung off a table. Angie squeezed her way past them to get a better look.

A merman lay flat on his back, a sunburst of blood coated his chest. The end of his iridescent fishtail and long caudal fins brushed the smooth, slippery floor. One rugged hand lay on his chest, the other arm like a pendulum at the table's edge.

Angie couldn't tear her gaze from him. The mer had been killed hours ago, and somehow, the blood on their chest was still wet and red? How? It should have browned and dried by now.

From beside her, Luke sucked in a sharp breath. "Woah. They're real. They're actually real. Wait until I tell my brother and my parents! They're going to want to know. Probably come see it for themselves. Wonder what they'll do about it."

Angie kept her eyes trained on the merman, Luke's words drifting in one ear and exiting the other as she replied with a breathy, "Yeah."

Her gaze trailed to below the mer's torso. A serpentine, bisected dorsal fin reached from his waist to just beneath where the knees would be on a human, slack and faded, as lifeless as its owner. A dim overhead light gave off an ethereal, canary glow to the room. His skin was hairless, and her gaze trailed to the half inch of webbing between his thick fingers.

Obscure markings of faded brown semicircles and wavy lines wove together in an intricate pattern across his arms and chest, their meaning and symbolism foreign to her.

A glance behind his ears and at his neck revealed four closed gill slits, nearly imperceptible to her eyes.

His teeth revealed a similar structure to her own. So, her hypothesis about them needing to eat fish wasn't correct.

Two divers stood at the corner of the room, one man and one woman, beaming at their handiwork. A small group headed by Nick surrounded them, congratulating them and shaking their hands.

Luke bounded off to join them, and Angie slowly followed. He squeezed in between the group to talk to Nick and the divers, making excited gestures with his hands. Nick broke into a bright, toothy grin when Luke approached him, and they slipped into their own conversation.

"When did you find him?" Angie looked at each of the divers. "Where?" A pang of envy struck that she wasn't the one to find the merman laying before her.

She certainly wouldn't have killed him. Not before trying to understand him first.

"We found two of them when we were out scouting." The female diver's gaze slid toward Angie. "Crazy that they're real, right? I could hardly believe it, myself."

"But why is he dead? Can they not survive outside the water?" Angie struggled to piece together how the merman was found in the water and was now dead on land. "We could have tried to see if he could speak."

"We brought it back alive like Zixin and Nick wanted. Tried to talk to it, but it just spouted unintelligible gobbledygook." The diver pointed an accusing finger at the merman. "But the minute we put it on the table, it lunged at us, so we had to put it down."

Angie shuddered at the diver calling the merman "it." They were still part human to her eyes. "He was probably terrified."

The female diver shrugged. "Maybe. I didn't want to take a chance that it would kill me, though."

Angie supposed she understood the diver's point.

"How'd ya get the son of a bitch?" one dockhand asked, eyes wide with wonder, never taking his eyes off the merman. "I heard they hear real good and are awful squirrely."

"Easy. You don't hear a damn thing with the rebreather on," the male diver said. "Swam up real slow, didn't make a sound, circled the area to create turbulence so they wouldn't know where I was. But she got the final blow. I just restrained it. Easy to grab it by the tail when it isn't looking." He held his gloved hands up. "I brought extra grippy gloves today."

Their gloating at murdering a merman made her feel ill. As if they found it fun.

"Why did you only bring one back?" Another dock worker yelled out. "It's not the male we want to see!"

"Does it matter?" Nick piped up, turning away from his conversation with Luke. "These heroes did you a favor, and all you can do is ask for more?

Greedy little shits." He rolled his eyes. "Who knows why Dad entertained the idea of talking to them. Primitive fish."

Angie glared at him, letting out an exaggerated sigh.

"Fair question," the same dock worker stated.

"They're not light, you know. We caught the male first, and by the time we had secured him, the female had escaped. It probably bled out," the female diver said.

They kept talking and poking and prodding at the merman, and Angie slipped out of the fishery. She was feeling claustrophobic with the crowd in the small space, and the damp, heavy air within the fishery was a heavy weight on her shoulders.

When seven o'clock came, most of the other workers had gone home, leaving Angie alone at the harbor and Bàba and Nick making their final rounds.

Once this last fishing boat, the *Odyssey* came in, she'd be free from work for today.

The *Odyssey* had missed her scheduled return time almost three hours ago with no word. Angie knew the small group of boaters that had gone out. They were constantly wary of the time and always gave their supervisors updates each hour.

Still, boats could miss their return for any reason, and if they didn't show in the next thirty minutes, Angie could officially report them missing and call the Coast Guard.

Twenty minutes passed.

She reached around to her backpack and slid her phone out of the side pocket.

Baba, where are you? Odyssey still hasn't returned. May need to report missing.

Bàba replied right away.

> In the control room. Meet me there.

A brief pause, and ellipses popped up from his end.

Angie didn't take her eyes off her phone as she walked to the control room, bemused as to why he was there. Normally, he let the dock operators have the run of the space and relay information to him as needed.

He texted back,

> Just found out what happened to the fishers on the Odyssey.

Shit. Angie picked up her pace, finding him inside the small building with Nick and two operators at his side, surrounded by monitors focused on various spots in the docks. Two large radios flanked either side of the monitors on the central desk, and Bàba was looking through his phone.

"What's going on? You found them?" Her words rushed out.

Bàba nodded. "They sent distress calls. But we did not receive them until several minutes ago." He sighed. "I called maintenance to update our older radios."

Angie's gaze slid from Bàba to Nick, to the two operators, and back to Bàba, holding her shoulders tight with anticipation.

"I took a recording. Listen to this." With visibly trembling fingers, he tapped on his phone. Voices came through, distorted and crackling.

"Mayday, we…help!"

"Storm surge, came…nowhere…controlled for now."

A chill snaked down Angie's spine.

"Tails…water…what the fuck?"

Static.

"…rfolk!"

"Boat rocking…can't hold–"

A broken scream followed. "Fuck! They're dead, they're all d—"

Deafening silence.

With cold hands, Angie gathered her hair into a bunch and then let it back down while staring at the radios, now eerily silent.

Bàba put his phone away, his voice monotone. "Six of them. Gone."

The operators were as pale as freshly bleached sheets. Nick looked as if he were restraining an outburst, lips clenched and cheeks puffed, eyebrows drawn together. Angie's heartbeat slammed in her ears.

Bàba crossed his arms over his chest, speaking through gritted teeth. "If those creatures are going to hoard our food supply, have everybody starve," he took in a sharp inhale, "and kill our people, then we will hunt them down. This is war."

SIX

*T*HIS IS WAR.
 She couldn't stop thinking of what Bàba said.

As Angie left work the next day, a loud splash from behind jolted her, as though a wave had slammed headfirst into a bed of rocks. Her grip tightened around her backpack straps. It sounded like somebody had cannonballed in. Or a boulder had fallen and broken the water's surface.

Her body was turned toward the dock entrance, but one leg stayed planted, as if she were being pulled in two different directions.

Must be hearing things. She should just go home.

On the other hand, someone could be behind her. Or fell into the water.

The shrubbery behind her crackled and fluttered.

Someone was definitely here, and better she get the jump on them or help them if they were hurt.

Hackles raised, she checked the time on her phone. Twenty minutes until the next ferry came, but if she caught the following ferry, she could still make dinner on time.

Might be a few minutes late, but she'd take her chances.

So much for her plans to go for a quick round of shooting.

Angie reached into her bag, fingers sliding around the roughshod grip on her Glock. She crept toward the source of the sound, sliding the gun out.

She followed a winding pebbled path to where land joined the ocean. Another loud splash, this time directly in front of her.

Angie held her breath and peeked out from behind a white spruce tree, hands shaking.

A man rested face down ahead of her on shore, the lower half of his body in the water. His head was turned away, covered with thick hair reminiscent of ravens' feathers, and his torso was exposed, sunbeams reflecting off smooth, light olive skin. Angie furrowed her brow.

Who was this man? And why was he topless in forty-five-degree weather?

Must have been drunk and passed out, the only sensible explanation. Angie took one step forward on the graveled ground so she could lean in closer without losing her balance.

Propping himself on his hands, elbows fully extended, the man gawked at her. A lengthy, maroon fishtail flicked up behind him.

Angie staggered back, agape. The merman hadn't moved. He appeared unarmed, staring at her in return with an equal expression of shock.

She didn't know what to do. Images and words flashed through her mind. Of the dead merman from earlier. The diver claimed that he had lunged at her. Then, listening to her colleagues on the *Odyssey*'s screams on the radio as the mer massacred the entire crew. They were all dead.

To her, there was no question about it. The mer were dangerous.

She drew her gun, aiming the barrel between his eyes. Her index finger trembled while inching closer to the trigger.

The merman held up his hands, tail curling to support his lower body. "Wait, stop!"

SEVEN

"Y-YOU TALK?" ANGIE SPUTTERED, HER AIM unwavering. He spoke, and she understood him. Her mouth slackened.

His eyes caught hers, and he lowered one hand. Angie stepped back, muscles twitching.

If she had to shoot, she prayed her aim would be true.

Nodding, he lowered the other hand, his body still tensed. He hadn't blinked once, long, thick eyelashes wide open and framing bright topaz-brown irises.

Angie hadn't blinked either. Her eyes were starting to dry, but she couldn't blink and have him flee, or strike at her.

"I understand you," she whispered.

"Evidently I've learned to speak your language, landwalker."

"B-but how?"

"On second thought, I could be making nonsensical noises you happen to understand." The merman's upper lip curled into a disdained sneer. "Did you think I communicated with bioluminescence, like jellyfish? Or perhaps

I use echolocation like a whale. We cannot possibly be intelligent enough to form words!"

Angie held her body taut, containing the fury threatening to burst forth. "I get the point. You don't have to be an ass."

His tail relaxed, resting beside him. Luminous maroon flickered beneath the sun, brightening each scale down to the silver tips of his dorsal fin. "Why haven't you killed me yet? You've killed several of us already." His silvery voice took on a hard, jagged edge.

"What?" Angie's tone became as tight as her eyebrows she'd drawn together. Her legs ached from keeping them in a wide base with knees bent, and she straightened.

Her brain hadn't processed the fact that she was staring a merman in the eye, and that they were communicating.

If this passed for communication.

The merfolk were stealing food, starving her fellow villagers. They weren't the cutesy, pretty creatures she grew up thinking they were.

She had been so wrong about them.

"You just killed two of ours!" His fingers gripped hard at the sand.

"I didn't kill any of your filthy kind." Angie spat the words through gritted teeth.

Shoot him now and think later, Angie.

Her finger wouldn't cooperate.

"Perhaps not you, but one of your two-legged kind." He sneered at the last word, voice mocking.

Maybe it was because he hadn't tried to assault her. Then again, he appeared unarmed, and she had a gun pointed at his face. Her thoughts were a dark cloud in her mind, jumbled like tangled knots in her brain.

Their standdown hadn't ceased, each waiting for the other to make the first move.

Angie inched forward.

His shoulders tensed.

"Mocking me is a really good look for you." Her finger grazed the trigger. "Give me one reason why I shouldn't shoot."

The merman stared her dead in the eye, challenging her. "I'm not stopping you."

Angie's grip faltered. "You know what? You all are hoarding fish, sea life, the food we need to survive. Why?" An explosion of fury rose from her chest and reached her mouth. "We're forced to eat fish that are unsustainable and unhealthy for us, and now we're decimating the fish populations even more!"

"You humans need to be taught a lesson about the damage you've done to the ocean." The muscles in his neck became tightly coiled cords.

"Oh, give me a break. When people are hungry and about to lose their livelihoods, you really think they're going to sit back and think, 'Wow, it's because the mer want to teach us a lesson?'" Angie's ears pounded. He opened his mouth to say something else, but she cut him off. "No, they're going to do whatever they need to survive."

"Extremes may be needed to force a change," he deadpanned when she was done.

"I disagree. People need time to adjust to change." The pounding in Angie's ears subsided. "So, you're going to starve us, then." She stepped closer, gun still aimed to his forehead.

Half his lips curled into a taunting smile. "Maybe you greedy humans deserve it."

Angie shook with rage. She was a breath away from pulling the trigger when he pushed off from his hands. His muscular tail curled and swept the sea's surface, stirring up a roaring wave crowned with a thick film of seafoam before he disappeared beneath.

The wave rushed in her direction, a bat-of-the-eye away from crashing over her with glacial brine. Thinking fast, Angie scrambled out of its path. The wave's edges gripped her legs, icy liquid seeping through her long cargo pants and clinging to her calves.

Her lower leg muscles clenched, each droplet a tiny knife driving into her skin.

The water calmed when the merman left. Angie flipped the safety switch on her Glock and shoved it back into her backpack, shivering.

Once she was far enough from the shoreline, she sucked in another shallow, trembling breath, her nerves firing haphazard jolts and making her skin tingle.

Angie flung the backpack over her shoulder and stormed toward the dock entrance, the merman's words playing in her mind–"Maybe you humans deserve it."

Her face tightened, and her nails bit into her palms.

Asshole.

——— ☳ ———

Angie's cheeks still burned hours later, fuming about her encounter with the rude merman.

Who did he think he was?

How the Hells did he know he was in danger when she pointed a gun at him?

And how the fuck could he speak and understand English?

She polished off her second glass of Pinot Noir of the night.

The rest of her family was gathered in the dining room of Mia and Nick's single-family house in the more populated southeast Creston and were enjoying a small bowl of egg fried rice, two slices of reindeer sausage, half of a fry bread, and a cup of berry cobbler. It was a far cry from the plentiful, elaborate meals Mia and Nick prepared when their families visited. In Chinese culture, food was love.

Some of her favorite foods were on the table, but she hadn't left the comfort of the toasty electric fireplace, sitting on the gray couch closest to it. She couldn't eat when she was so deep in thought.

"Angie āyí." Rosie pulled at her sleeve. She peered at her with those gold-flecked, hazel eyes that Angie adored. "What are you doing?"

"Just thinking about some stuff." Stashing her phone in her pocket, Angie beckoned her to sit next to her, and Rosie climbed on the couch. "What's up, love?"

"Are you sad?"

She reached over to ruffle her wavy brown hair, the alcohol shooting straight to her head when she moved her arm. When had she become such a lightweight? She'd spent a good part of junior year in college partying with her dormmates and their sororities. Then her world tilted on its axis after getting news of Māma's passing, swept away in a freak scuba diving accident. At the time, she had come home for the funeral and left the next day, unwilling to return to the hometown where she and Māma had shared so many happy memories. When she returned to school, she drowned her grief in studying and alcohol. She stopped when senior year started, attended therapy, and hadn't touched more than a single glass of wine in one sitting since.

It was as if her body didn't know how to handle the second glass, but Angie resolved to stop after this one.

"Why do you think I'm sad?" She flashed a smile at her, and Rosie returned it with a gap-toothed one of her own.

"Cause you're not talking to anyone. You're sitting here by yourself when everyone else is over there." She pointed to Mia, Nick, and Bàba, their necks bent forward in conversation, a second bottle of Malbec opened before them. "They must be talking about something serious. None of them are smiling."

Angie's face fell, and she groaned while rising to her feet, her head swimming while she regained her balance. "You're right, I should stop being antisocial."

"Yeah, don't be antisocial! And you'll come play with me later?"
"Of course."

Leave it to a kid to tell her to get off her ass and go spend time with family.

Rosie ran off, and Angie walked to the dining table, stopping for a glass of water. Mia brightened when she saw her.

"Look who decided to join us again. More wine?" Mia waved at the second, half-empty bottle, their three wine glasses half full.

"Ah, no thanks." Angie plopped into an empty chair and sipped the water. Refreshing and cooling, it slid down her throat.

"Yeah, you have that Asian flush going." Nick leaned back in his chair and grinned like a fool.

Angie faced him and didn't say a word.

"Nick, stop." Mia put her palms to her cheeks and squeezed them together, muffling an exasperated groan. "Angie, are you okay? You looked lost in your own world there. I wanted to go talk to you, but it didn't look like you wanted to be bothered."

Before Angie replied, Bàba spoke up. "I meant to tell you all. We killed another merman today." Until now, he'd been quietly sipping his wine and staring at his phone like it held the secret of the missing fish.

"What? When?" Angie dug her short nails into the plastic navy-blue tablecloth. Could it have been the same merman who mocked her and lashed a stream of salt at her earlier?

"After you left. That's why I didn't get to tell you once it happened." Bàba gave her a sympathetic nod, refilling his wine glass.

Angie set her lips in a grim line. She wavered between gladness that there would be one less fish-creature to take their food supply, and a sense of loss that maybe she could have found some use for him, the only mer who was known to have spoken to a human.

She had to know. "Wh-what color was the tail?"

"The tail?" Bàba furrowed his brow, thinking. "I believe it was green."

"Turquoise, to be exact," Nick added, sounding a tad too smug. "Maybe now that a few of them are dead, they'll start getting the hint and give us our fucking seafood back." Her face drained of blood, Mia put a warning hand on her husband's forearm, but he continued. Angie heard enough stories from Mia about his ramblings when he had too much to drink. "Because if they don't, we'll hunt them down. Right, Dad?"

Angie hated it when he called Bàba *Dad* because it reminded her that she was related to him through marriage. Bàba nodded, silent.

"Oh." Her chest deflated.

"Why did you ask about the tail color?" Bàba's eyes narrowed, facing her.

She cleared her throat and her head. "Before I left today, I heard a loud splash. So, I went to investigate. And I saw one."

"A merman?" Mia's jaw dropped.

Even Nick listened during her confession. Bàba's eyes burned a hole into her head. Nick put his wine glass down. "Why didn't you kill it? Or did you?"

She shook her head, squeezing her hands together. It was a good question, why couldn't she finish him? "He got away before I could pull the trigger," she fibbed.

"Don't hesitate next time. They're just fish." Nick flashed her a sly, drunken smile. "Or, if you're too scared, you can call one of us men to do it for you." He sat back and draped a lazy arm around the back of Mia's chair, using his free arm to sweep an arc over the table. "You don't see one chunk of fish, or crab or lobster meat, or even one single clam here, do you? They're killing us off slowly. I say we round them up and execute them."

Angie flinched, thinking back to Jenny and Dave. Yes, they had enough food for now, and their own stores could last them another month if they ate half of what they normally did. But many of her fellow villagers didn't.

Nick continued. "The fishing nets are sitting empty right now. Why not use those to catch more mer, eh? Angela? Mia? What do you girls think?"

Angie flinched at Nick's words and calling them *girls*.

Patience, Angie. Don't snap at him in front of Mia.

She thought back to the way the merman spoke to her. Thought of Jenny and Dave and the others she grew up with, outside scouring for food. Seeing the fishermen and women come off their boats with their nets a quarter full at best.

Without regarding Nick, Angie looked at Mia and Bàba and squared her shoulders. "I'm happy to help."

EIGHT

A RAINSTORM RAGED OVERHEAD, AND A TALL, angry wave barreled in, the gangway shaking beneath Angie's feet. She pulled the hood on her rain jacket over her head and stepped forward to keep her balance, her other arm tight against the clipboard with the incoming ship's inventory. She wiped away rainwater clouding her vision, and her work boots squished into puddles on the ground.

Thankfully, she wore brand-new, expensive water repellent work boots today, a college graduation splurge. If there was one thing she despised, it was the feeling of wet socks.

What she would do to get back the pleasant, cloudy skies of the last three days.

Damn weather app had lied. It had forecasted moderate rainfall, not a raging thunderstorm. She set her jaw, turning away from a gust of wind threatening to blow her over.

Her gaze trailed out to the sea, where fierce currents rose and fell.

If only the employee break house was within sight of the dock, where she could shelter from the storm. For now, she was stuck outdoors until the ship came in, her misery compounded by the unrelenting storm. A globe of rainwater from her hood plunged down her throat, and she coughed.

Ten more minutes passed, and the *MV Castaway* hadn't appeared yet, not even as an amorphous shadow on the fog and mists which crushed the ocean's surface. They had radioed in earlier that they were returning early because of unusually rough seas. She put her hands on her hips and lifted one foot at a time to stretch out her tight calves from standing so long on her feet, then walked to the edge of the gangway and back.

Anything to take her mind off how cold and drenched she was.

Still no ship another ten minutes later. They were thirty minutes late.

It was the ship Luke was on. If something had happened to the *Castaway*, to Luke and the crew...

No. She refused to think of negative possibilities.

Angie smoothed out the stack of paper on her clipboard, original copies of inventory from the past week. As per Bàba's instructions, she had to keep these papers until they input the numbers into their systems tomorrow. The aforementioned papers were sopping wet.

Why did she have to be the one who got stuck out here in inclement weather?

Still, she sucked it up, already having waited this long. Angie yawned, not bothering to cover her mouth since she was alone. Time slowed to a crawl, and walking in aimless circles was the only way to keep somewhat warm in the torrential rain. The time on her phone read six-thirty p.m.

Another overtime day, her fourth in a row, taking over the missing workers' duties. She was running on five hours of restful sleep, where she normally needed at least seven to function properly.

The holstered gun at her hip created extra weight with each step. After they started losing dock workers, Bàba insisted everyone carry their guns to shoot at any mer who dared come near.

Stay patient. Once the ship arrived, she could leave.

Any minute now.

Any.

Minute.

Another breaker rattled the gangway, and Angie lost her footing, catching herself before tumbling headfirst into the waves below. She fell onto her buttocks.

The clipboard rolled over the edge and landed with a *splat* into the water. "Oh no. No, no, no! Shit!" Grumbling to herself, she climbed back to her feet and lowered herself off the gangway and onto the shoreline below. She raced to the clipboard, retrieving it with a sigh of relief once it was safely in her arms, and stepped out of the water line with one foot. Before she recovered her balance, another wave came, this one nearly as tall as her five-foot five height.

Moving into a guarded position, Angie ducked and put one arm over her head, a futile shield against the wave's weight as it bore down on her.

She fell to her stomach with a gasp, the wind knocked out of her once her body met the sandy ground. Pointy pebbles dug into her chest and legs, and she grimaced at the sharp pain. She groped in front of her, pulling herself onto the clumpy, rain-drenched sand. Icy seawater rushed into her mouth, tasting of liquid salt and grime from whatever junk the wave dredged up.

Angie gagged.

The winds accelerated. Hands grabbed her ankles, pulling her deeper, deeper, the cold wrapping her in a chilly embrace.

Mer hands.

She jerked her foot away, but the grasp remained. Her heart was a flying fish desperate to escape her chest.

Angie yelled, the sound an unintelligible gurgle as soon as her head dunked beneath the roaring surface. Salt stung her eyes. Her legs flailed and kicked behind her, and another pair of hands gripped at her ankles, one pushing, one pulling. Her hands fumbled to her sides.

Her mind raced. Think fast, Angie. Or you're a dead woman. She was descending lower, lower. Light began to fade, her head and ears thrumming with pain and pressure.

Her Glock was still intact and sealed in its holster. After unbuttoning it with quaking fingers, she whipped it out, aiming behind her and firing a shot when the barrel pressed into flesh.

A muffled *boom* made the water ripple behind her.

NINE

BOTH PAIRS OF HANDS RELEASED HER.
Sweet merciful Buddha.

Still clutching the gun, Angie broke into a flutter kick, her legs in hyperdrive until she touched the shoal, and breathed in the sweet, sweet air.

She crawled back onto the beach, coughing up globs of seawater. Saltwater exposure blurred her vision. Gritting her teeth, she swiped at her eyes with the backs of her hands and screwed them shut to expel the scratchy, salty liquid. Her hair, which she normally curled at the ends to give more volume, now lay pin-straight and stuck to her back like an adhesive.

She spun in a one-eighty direction after hearing furious splashing behind her. A familiar maroon tail came into view, the mer leaked streams of blood resembling tiny, crimson snakes wriggling across the sea's surface. A tuft of dark hair emerged like a flash.

The mer struggled, movements in the water sudden and jerky, fighting the small currents.

Good. He was hurt, but Angie couldn't unearth much more than a shred of empathy for the son of a fish. Especially if it was that rude merman who had spewed a lungful of venom at her. She stopped in a half-kneel position when ashy triangular shapes appeared from the horizon, coasting along like toy sailboats.

Sharks.

Three, no, four of them circled the struggling mer, who thrashed and flopped about like an injured fish desperate to survive, which, she supposed, he was.

The sharks were familiar to her. They were a species she learned about for her final project for her bachelor of science degree, a presentation on lesser-known shark species.

Two, short, brown fins belonged to blue sharks, and two, long, gray fins were from salmon sharks, and their curious and aggressive natures would drive them to poke and prod until they had their fill.

The sharks closed in, and Angie clambered to the shoreline and then watched the scene play out. One shark struck, biting the mer's tail. Another followed, but the mer dodged it and jerked his torso and arm away from the sharks' jaws.

Angie flinched. As averse as she was to the mer, her heart constricted at the thought of one suffering a slow, drawn-out death by sharks because of her.

She cupped her hands around her mouth and yelled. "Hey! Come back!"

Of course he couldn't hear. His head was submerged.

Damn it. Angie chewed on a nail, gaze zeroing in on a pile of rubble in front of her. Another shark attacked, and she grabbed her gun, aiming it for the fins darting and zigzagging around. She couldn't get a clear shot.

Stuffing her gun back into its holster, Angie instead reached for a rock the size of her fist. The sharks hadn't relented. Even if she scared one away, others would soon follow the scent of blood.

More fins appeared from the horizon.

The mer's dorsal fin appeared, and Angie reared her arm back and chucked it in the mer's direction.

The rock bounced off him, breaking the water's surface with an audible *plop*. The merman's head jerked out of the water.

Angie waved her arms. She didn't know if he would understand her meaning, but she had to try.

He ducked underwater, tail wiggling and thrashing beneath the glassy surface as if his life depended on it. It did. Once he was closer to shore, the merman faced the encroaching sharks. Angie grabbed his tailfins with both hands and gave a forceful pull.

He pushed himself onto the seashore. He was the same one from the other day. The merman clutched at his arm, falling to one side, breaths coming out in long, wheezing heaves. He curled up and tucked his slender tail underneath him, coiled like a muscular snake. Deep crimson scales glimmered beneath the emerging sun while the rainstorm passed. Angie eyed him up and down, chest heaving with worry. Rivulets of thick, red blood trickled down his biceps, forming a spider web around his elbow, and sliding toward his forearm.

She swallowed a gulp, eyes trailing to the gunshot wound at the front of his shoulder.

"Ugh." The merman put a strong, rugged hand over the wound, applying pressure. The sharks lingered, but did not move too close to the shore.

She slipped off one boot and pulled off her long sock. "What are you doing—" His eyes were as wide as two shiny globes of Tiger's Eye.

"Stopping the bleeding. I know the sock is wet, but you know, you live in the water. So it should be fine." She tied the sock tight around his arm and made a knot. "Wait here." The makeshift gauze would hold temporarily, but blood was starting to seep through the gray sock.

"Where are you going?"

"Getting something that will hold a little better!" she called back. After a quick look around to make sure she was in the clear, Angie ran to the nearest storehouse a five-minute walk away and grabbed a blanket, waterproof bandages, and gauze, and a packet of antiseptic. She could do the bare minimum, at least: patch him up, throw him back to the sea, and quell her guilty conscience that at least he hadn't died a long, bloody death by her hand. When she returned, he was on his back, tail straight out, tapping his caudal fins on the ground in a staccato rhythm.

The two semicircular fins bordering his hips fluttered with the breeze, a dividing line between his fleshy upper half and scaly lower half.

"I don't need your help." Was the first thing he said when they made eye contact again. His shoulders were elevated and arms tensed in a defensive posture.

Was this merman an idiot? She gritted her teeth. "Oh?"

He gave no indication of catching onto the sarcasm lacing her tone.

"Yes, I'll wait for the sharks to lose interest. Then I can make my way back home." He rolled to his side, propping himself up with his good arm. "I've been cut by coral many times, bitten by *kuiyu* and *shayu* with teeth like knives when I've accidentally entered their territory. I will survive and don't need help from a landwalker."

"Great for you. I'm assuming you're talking about viperfish and sharks. Guns are a little different from them. Why come back when I threw the rock at you?" Angie tucked her chin. "You could have stayed out there, tried to survive by yourself."

"I seized the opportunity. It was better than being torn apart by sharks," he said, voice softening and eyes downcast. "But I will take my leave now." He braced his tail as if he was about to launch himself into the sea.

"Uh, no you can't. You have a giant hole in your shoulder, which I assume is going to affect your ability to swim. You're bleeding profusely, and you're shark bait. There's more coming." She pointed to the horizon, where two more fins had appeared. "Also, I want my sock back. Let me bandage up your shoulder. Then you can go back, and we can pretend we never saw each other, alright? So, we'll both be happy."

The merman cast his gaze over the water and pulled a long face. "Fine."

She removed the sock and pressed a cotton ball to the wound. "Hold that there?" He did, and she returned her attention to her sock which was now soaked through with thick, dark blood. She wrinkled her nose and turned the sock inside out before bundling it into a ball and shoving it deep in her coat pocket.

Once, she thought of becoming a physician so she'd have an excuse to move out of Creston, but volunteering at a local hospital during her gap year changed her mind. Blood made her squeamish. The metallic smell, its odd viscosity, the way it wouldn't stop coming out when skin was lacerated.

Her stomach roiled with nausea.

Throwing the blanket around herself to keep warm, she went to work on his arm and held her breath so she wouldn't have to smell the blood. "Why the Hells did you try to drown me? That was you, right?"

"Yes, it was me, but I didn't cause the waves to do that. Another merman did, and I was trying to pull you to the surface."

She didn't want to meet his eyes, as she dabbed antiseptic on the wound and plastered one bandage over it. He flinched under her touch.

"You could have let him drown me."

His shoulder twitched when she dabbed alcohol on the wound. "There is no love lost between us, now that your people have started a war with mine. I hope I don't come to regret what I did for you."

"Makes the two of us." She wrapped another layer of gauze over the bandage, finishing it with a waterproof wrapping. Then she sat back and cocooned herself in the blanket so her head poked out, bringing her knees to her chest. The warmth invited her to stay nestled in the blanket forever.

"Thank you." He rolled his arm around. "The stinging is subsiding."

"Why did you push me to the surface?" She steeled herself for his answer.

"I can sense you're not out for our blood."

"Mer can read minds?" Angie cocked an eyebrow. "I shot you. And I almost shot you before. In the face."

"No. It is something about you, I suppose. I cannot describe it." He sat upright, taking in a deep breath and rounding his broad chest.

"I see." Angie didn't see, but she let it go. She kept her distance, and he seemed content to stay where he was as well. "What about the merman who dragged me under? Won't he know you helped me?"

"No, in the rough turbulence, we were thrashing, the waves haphazard. It was a mess of debris and tails and hands. He fled when you fired your weapon, leaving me as your target. He does not know it was me who was helping you."

"Appreciated." His explanation was feasible enough for now. "So, you can manipulate the seas?"

He looked away without answering, staring at some invisible sight over the waves. His face was impassive, but Angie caught a twitch feathering along his jaw. It drew her attention to the side of his face, and his full, sea-kissed head of dark hair. His skin was smooth and hairless, to ensure easy movement through water, she knew, without the impedance of body hair. The newly emerged sun highlighted his pert nose, not much larger than her own, and angular jaw and high cheekbones. A breeze blew his hair back, revealing his gills.

So human, and yet so foreign.

The question of why he was hairless except for his head and eyebrows interested her. She said nothing, not wanting him to have any inclination that she was looking at his body. Even if it was for scientific reasons.

Angie didn't know if the mer thought the same way, but she had had enough young men misinterpret her friendliness and curiosity for interest.

She looked back down at her feet before he could catch her staring.

"The sharks are dispersing. Thank you again," he said, and rolled onto his belly, tucking his tail beneath his hips. He cut his gaze to her. "I come ashore every few days. I may see you again."

What was it about this merman, and the thought of seeing him again, that intrigued her? "What's your name?"

A pause before he answered. "My name in your language is Kaden."

"My language? So, what is it in your language, then?"

"Also Kaden." A twitch appeared in one corner of his lips, but it disappeared as fast as it appeared. "In Renyuhua. Yours?"

He spoke slowly enough that she made out the sounds of his language, and it sounded like "merfolk speak." Yet, the tones were off. Angie had picked up local tongues from her family trips to Taiwan and China as a child and preteen, but this sounded like a strange Chinese dialect. "Angie Song." She flushed.

"Why do you have two names?" Kaden's tail relaxed, followed by the rest of his body.

"My first name is Angie, and Song is my last name, uh, my family name."

Kaden cast a sideways, inquisitive glance at her. "Ah, we do not have family names. We distinguish ourselves by colors. When two mer join, their tail colors meld together to signify the forming of a new family." He thinned his full lips. "What shall I call you, then? Angie? Or Song?"

"Angie."

"Okay. Angie it is then." Kaden offered the tiniest hint of a smile, making his face light up. Then it fell, and his shoulders went rigid. "The sentinels will be looking for me." Angie gave him a small nod as her goodbye. He pushed off his tail into the water, and then he was gone.

TEN

KEEPING THE BLANKET WRAPPED AROUND HER, Angie looked to the ground when she stood. There, a tan corner peeked out underneath a patch of shrubbery. Her clipboard, thankfully with all pages intact. Angie held it close to her, refusing to let it out of her sight until she got it into Bàba or Nick's hands.

She thought about what Kaden said.

The sentinels will be looking for me.

It begged the question of who exactly he was, and why there were sentinels seeking him out.

Angie made it back to the gangway, fanning the clipboard and drying the papers attached to it. The ink bled on the page, but it was legible enough.

An impending shadow loomed, and an ocean of relief splashed over her. The container ship she had been waiting for, the *MV Castaway*, finally pulled into port. The anchor dropped, and the engine died, the ship rocking with the waves. Sailors departed, each greeting Angie as they rushed past. She stood by, waiting to step aboard and take inventory.

Finally, Luke appeared at the entryway and waved her in, a jovial smile on his pale, freckled face. Angie returned his smile, following him aboard as he walked her through the ship's interior.

"Glad to see you're okay. I was getting worried when your ship was delayed by—" She checked her phone. "Over two hours."

"I know." The boy's tone dropped low and dull. "We hit a giant swell coming in and lost half our cargo. We recovered whatever we could, though. Sorry, I'll explain everything to your dad, I don't want you to get in trouble."

"It's fine, I'll explain. Besides, my bàba won't get mad at you."

"It's late, I get it." Luke nodded his head in agreement. "And yes, he will. Or that dickhead Nick will." His cheeks grew scarlet. "Oh, sorry. I didn't mean to curse in front of a lady."

"Apology accepted." Angie patted his shoulder, and caught him blushing under the dimmed cargo hold lights. "Where was the swell?"

"About five nautical miles southwest of here. Strange. I mean, we hit some choppy waters coming from the Aleutians, but this came out of nowhere. I heard," Luke cleared his throat and started walking her back to the ship's upper level, "that it's merfolk doing it. A few sailors fell overboard, and we couldn't save them. Had to turn around."

Angie eyed Luke, choosing her next words carefully. Did she want to confirm the rumors and possibly jade him? The boy was young and innocent. Warning him would be the better idea. "That's the rumor." Her voice cracked. "But be careful, alright? Try not to hang around the coastline. I'll talk to my bàba about getting you some more work inland."

"I like being by the sea." Luke folded his arms across his chest, tight enough to make his small pecs pop.

Stubborn, the way she was at his age. For his own good, she had to try to get through to him.

"I know, but just for now. You could have been thrown overboard. Please listen to me on this."

Finally, Luke relented, dropping his shoulders and arms. "Okay, I guess that's everything for today. I'll see you tomorrow or the day after? Well, I mean, you know, if you're going to the ferry, I'll come with you."

"Yeah, sure." A gentle smile formed as she waited for Luke to grab his things. They walked to the ferry terminal, a short walk outside the docks, together, talking all the way there. Angie kept her conversation with Luke on point, but she couldn't stop thinking of Kaden and whether she should look for him again.

If he was willing to talk, then other mer might be, too. She could try to coax information out of him. Why were they hoarding fish, how many, how were they doing it? Use him to find out who and where their leaders were.

Luke's voice cut into her spiraling thoughts. "When I come back to work the day after tomorrow, can I talk to you a bit about marine biology? I think I want to major in that in college."

"Oh yeah, sure. You decided on that already?" Angie thought back to how she had an undecided major for her first two years of undergrad.

"I want to own my own dock one day, be close to the water. I don't care where. As long as I can hear the soothing crashes of waves on the shore, the seagulls circling the skies, and breathe in the salty breeze." They reached the small ferry terminal's waiting area, where two other dock workers waited. "Even though it was only for a short while, working with you inspired me to chase my dream." He spoke such touching words.

"How about we meet for breakfast? I'll bring some coffee and breakfast sandwiches?"

"Sounds delicious," Luke replied. "I promise I'll pay you back. I can't wait."

"Don't worry about it, Luke." Angie returned to her thoughts. The debate still raged when she boarded the ferry.

ELEVEN

ANGIE CHECKED HER PHONE TWO DAYS later, waiting at the spot that she and Luke had agreed to meet, in front of the employee break house.

He was nowhere to be found, and no text or call from him, either. They were supposed to meet fifteen minutes ago.

The coffee and egg and cheese bagels were getting cold.

She texted him, but no response.

This wasn't like him. She and Bàba hadn't known him long, but in the short time he was here, he was always punctual. It was a trait that Bàba praised.

Something wasn't right, and she walked away from the break house, keeping her eyes and ears open for him.

She stepped onto the gangway, the coffee and bagel bags feeling heavier and heavier in her hand.

Overhead, smoky clouds loomed against an ashy backdrop and grazed the sea line, creating a gloomy, somber setting.

An amorphous lump lay on the gangway's end, and when she reached it, she froze momentarily, her knees weak.

The bags slipped from her hand, and the drink carrier and disposable cups tumbled out, creating a coffee puddle around her feet. The bagels followed, one rolling off the gangway's edge, tumbling into the sea below.

Her hunger dissipated, and food was the last thing she cared about now.

Luke lay before her on the gangway's end, a jagged-tipped spear through his chest, pierced through with deadly accuracy.

"Luke? No, no, no! Oh, tiān."

Angie stood over his body, numb and fighting back tears.

His arms and legs sprawled out, his face serene and pale. Bright red blood pooled on his chest around the spear protruding from his heart.

It sickened her to see him lying murdered and exposed. A bitter tang coated the inside of her mouth.

A low vibration of pain thrummed while she called Bàba, who was still at home, and told him what happened. After a strangled noise, he hung up the phone. He'd be heading there now.

She dialed the Creston Police Department to report the murder. Once they confirmed her location and that they were sending an officer, she put her phone away.

"Luke, what happened?" she whispered, kneeling beside his body. "I asked you not to go near the water. You promised." She wiped tears gathering at the corners of her eyes and rose to her feet, bowing her head. "Why did you come all the way out here? Did you see something? You were supposed to have met me at the break house."

So many questions, none of which she could venture an answer for.

Regret squeezed her chest. If she had told Luke about the danger of mer instead of dancing around the issue, he might have taken her warning more seriously. She berated herself for not being more forthcoming.

Now she'd never know if that would have saved him. Her stomach knotted.

A flicker entered her peripheral, capturing her attention. In the distance, a maroon tail rested around mossy rocks protruding from the sea. She couldn't see the mer's body, but she already knew.

Kaden.

Her heart weighing heavy, she retrieved a spare blanket from storage and laid it over the teenager, and waited for the police officer to arrive, keeping Kaden in her peripheral vision.

A stocky, mustached officer came after twenty agonizing minutes, and after a short chat of what she found and when, he thanked her.

Thoughts of the boy gripped her mind while she trekked to the merman.

Possibly, Kaden was the one who killed him. Fueled by the notion, she pressed her lips together and quickened her pace, hands balled into tight fists.

Their gazes locked when she approached.

He pushed himself up on his palms, facing her. "What are you doing here?"

"I saw you out of the corner of my eye. Didn't seem like you were making much of an effort to stay hidden. Thought we could have a little chat, you and I." Angie widened her stance and folded her arms across her chest, holding him in a challenging stare. His eyes shifted back and forth, as if caught off guard.

"Okay, I suppose I can oblige. You patched me up, after all." He pushed off his tail and hands so he landed back in the water. He swam to and climbed atop a lower rock closer to the seaboard. Closer to Angie and out of the gangway's view.

She stepped back.

"You 'suppose you can oblige?' I suppose I should be flattered. I'm not. Did you kill that boy back there? Put a spear through his chest?" Her voice emerged rough and demanding, anger seeping from her throat.

"What? No! I haven't killed any of your disgusting kind!" He drew his shoulders closer to his ears, adopting a defensive posture.

"It's too much of a coincidence that I happened to find his body and then see you right after. You seem to be the only mer hanging around the surface lately. I can't decide if you're brave or stupid." Angie thought again of Luke. A gust of fury swept through her, quickly followed by heartache at his untimely loss.

"It's none of your concern why I 'hang around the surface,' as you say. And I swear on the Sea Goddess' watery embrace that I haven't killed anyone. There were patrols in the area recently. Looking for the humans that killed four of ours."

She studied his face. Somehow, the earnestness in his tone, the softness in his gaze, and his body language reflected hints of remorse, asking her to believe him. For now.

Kaden's shoulders relaxed in tune with this tail, which he kept wrapped around the rock in a loose hug. "Two of the dead were royal sentinels. A male and a female, a joined pair."

The fine hairs on Angie's arms stood on end, a chill shooting through her veins. "Did they have markings on their bodies?"

"Yes. The royal guard wear paintings on their bodies and faces to mark them as such. How did you know?" Kaden's eyes narrowed.

Angie pressed her lips flat, shoulders sagging. "They were captured and brought back as trophies. The divers were celebrated for outsmarting and killing them. The first mer I ever saw that close."

"Humans gloating about catching unsuspecting prey. Typical," Kaden sneered.

Just when she thought they might be getting along, he had to make a jab. Angie's jaw and facial muscles tensed.

"And just how the Hells would you know what's 'typical' of us?" Her body was a hodgepodge of emotions. Fury and irritation at Kaden. Lingering horror and sadness, a dizziness in her head that wouldn't go away from seeing Luke. "What are you, some kind of expert on humans? A spy?"

"Do you think I'm the only one who comes to the surface? You don't think any other mer have had that curiosity and sated it? Caught sunlight, get a change of scenery? Observed your two-legged kind and shared stories? We just make sure you don't see us."

"Until I did." Angie tapped her foot on the ground and checked her phone. No word from Baba yet, but it had only been forty minutes since she called him. He wouldn't get here so fast.

"I was careless."

"Believe me, I don't always agree with the way people act." She locked in his hard stare with one of her own. "But if you didn't hold the fish hostage, then maybe nobody would have died."

"You started this. Don't be upset that we're finishing it." Kaden's words bit at her.

"The seas are practically empty of life. The more of us you kill, the more we retaliate." Angie swept her arms out to her sides in a gesture of frustration. Typical male, who didn't listen to anything she said. Seemed like that was one similarity both their species had. "You want to stop this? Release the fish, wherever you're hiding them. Or are the mer so ravenous that you're eating them all?"

"Why?" His voice raised to a thunderous roar, jaw set and eyes blazing.

She refused to back down under his death stare. "You would know if you had heard a word I said. Or is your hearing not so good on land?"

"I heard everything you said. I asked why you want the sea life back. Tell me, what do humans do with them? You take much more than you need, trap them in tiny tanks, content to let them suffer until the day they're cooked and eaten. The smarter animals are imprisoned for your entertainment." He paused, a wave crashing onto the rocks and splattering it. Seafoam coated his caudal fins, curled downward and held stiff, though his upper body looked relaxed. Angie recoiled as if he had hit her.

What the Hells was he going on about? Surely, if he knew anything about human life, like he claimed he did, he would have seen that not everyone was as terrible as he thought.

He continued his rant before she had a chance to rebuff him. "Your kind overfishes and destroys entire ecosystems, affecting those who call the sea their home. You pollute the oceans with plastic and waste and trash, and your loud, obnoxious watercraft disturb and kill all who dare to swim at the surface. Entire species of sea life are becoming extinct. Apex predators are over-hunted and prey species are overrunning the seas, destroying swaths of plant life and coral."

The sarcastic response Angie had prepared withered away and died.

He didn't give her time to reply, even if she wanted to. "Nothing to say? Good." He spat out his words. "We've seen people kill *haituns* by the pods and capture the most docile ones for entertainment. *Hujings* are caught for the same purpose, dooming them to a life of misery and loneliness in plastic prisons no bigger than them. *Longxia* are boiled alive, an atrocious way to kill someone. Never has there been a species so cruel as yours. And you believe you are entitled to these precious animals? You do not deserve them." His death glare turned into a fireball searing a hole through her body.

Once Angie figured out the animals he was talking about—dolphins, orcas, and lobsters, respectively—her immediate thought was to smack him, even if he made many valid points. If there was something she hated more than wet socks, it was being talked at. It made her feel as if like she was being treated like an emotional trash can, or in this case, a verbal punching bag.

She took a deep breath to calm herself before responding. She wouldn't give him the benefit of knowing he had flustered her.

"What does this have to do with us? We don't do those things. We don't even have an aquarium." She was genuinely perplexed. "Like I said before, we only take what we need. We're not doing most of the things you're complaining about."

"But nobody is stopping those people who are." He looked at his hands, still planted flat on the rock.

"We're trying. Besides, don't you eat fish, too?"

"No, most of us primarily eat sea fruits and vegetables and only eat animals when we must. We never take more than is needed for survival. And we ensure that their deaths are quick and merciful."

Angie's chin trembled with resignation. "I know. In other countries and towns who depend on fishing for survival, commercial fishing has cost so many small-town fishermen and women their livelihoods." Her voice dropped a .ch. "My point is, I know about overfishing and what happens when people take more than they need."

"Human greed truly is the root of all evil." Kaden slid off his rock and cut through the water until he reached the beach. "No other species has wrought the destruction that humans have."

"We're still figuring things out." Angie sat and crossed her legs. "Undoing our mistakes. People are fighting back for animals' and oppressed groups' rights, and protecting the environment. So many good people want to do the right thing and dedicate their lives to it." She interlaced her fingers together. "I know how big a problem the trash in the sea is. I went on ocean cleanup trips with my sister when we were younger. And once I go to grad school, I want to start a project to advocate for less pollution in the ocean." She wet her lips.

"I wish we had come across more people like you. But we have to save our home too. I hope those groups can push for true change." His countenance softened, eyes wide and clear underneath his thick lashes.

"Same." Angie shifted her weight, her hands falling onto her lap and shoulders relaxed. "But it'll take time." She cleared her throat. "Some people survive on seafood, and it's all we have. We, and other fishing villages only take what we need. Why should we suffer collectively for the greedy actions of a few?"

"You make a fair argument." He gave her a halfhearted shrug and punctuated his words with an audible sigh. "I will see what I can do. Speak with my family."

First sentinels, now apparently an important family. She arched a dubious eyebrow. "You can stop the war? Your family can make a difference? You all must be really influential in mer society."

"I might be able to help release the fish, but the war started because you killed some of us first. And yes, erm, we are influential." He said no more and avoided eye contact with her.

A beat passed, but he didn't elaborate. Angie let out a long, slow exhale. "All right. I'll take your word for it." Another look at her phone which revealed a message from Baba, saying he would be there in ten minutes. "While I have you here, why would the patrols kill that boy? He was minding his own business." She choked on her words. "Right?"

"I don't know. I wasn't there when they found him." He thinned his lips.

Angie stared at the ground, shifting her weight from foot to foot. "Okay. I should get going, then." She jumped to her feet.

"Meet me here in three tidesdays. My family will be due back by then. I hope to have an answer to your earlier request." He gave her a single nod and disappeared beneath the waves.

Angie jogged to the main warehouse, where Bàba asked her to meet him. "Where did you go? I was worried that something happened to you, too."

"By the coast." No sense in lying to him, but she didn't have to tell him the whole truth, at least, not until she figured out what she could get out of Kaden.

"Why would you do that? Luke just died so near." He studied her for a moment. "But I'm glad you're okay." He put an arm around her shoulder and squeezed. "Thank you for calling the police."

Crime scene tape had been put around Luke's body, and Angie stood outside of it. A second cop had joined the first.

Bàba put his phone back in his pocket. "I contacted Beau and Emily." His voice sounded thick with Luke's parents' names. "They will inform us of the official wake and funeral date."

She swallowed hard and bowed her head.

A week passed, and Angie stood slumped like a dolphin in captivity in Creston's small cemetery. She shouldn't have been attending the funeral for a seventeen-year-old boy today. Her shoulders were tight and her knees touched. Anything to look away from Luke's polished wooden coffin, adorned with pearly honeysuckles for him to receive positivity and love in the afterlife. The flowers were bright, beautiful, and alive, a stark contrast to the peacefully sleeping boy inside. She hadn't wanted to see him during the wake, afraid she wouldn't be able to stop from crying.

Bàba and Emily, Luke's mother, had told her he was buried with his favorite video games, fantasy and science fiction books, and his trusty wetsuit.

Emily and Beau closed out the service with a short, emotional speech, thanking everyone for coming. Angie stood shoulder to shoulder with Stefan, her full attention on them. Their voices quivered and their emotions were raw, their vulnerability and grief overshadowing the confident, affable personas they usually displayed at public appearances.

Beside them, Bàba stood impassive, face neutral. Outwardly, he appeared like his usual, calm, coolheaded self, a cover for the turmoil he hid beneath the surface. The slight tremble in his lower lip he tried so hard to keep still, eyes squinted just enough to hold back tears. His hands were held in a seatbelt grip at his waist. Like he was holding in the tension, his emotions. Angie didn't blame him. Luke was becoming his little protégé, right after Nick.

Angie's gaze trailed to Nick. He stood on the other side, shifting from foot to foot, his face holding contorted rage. His lips were pursed, like he was dying to speak, but stayed quiet.

After Emily and Beau finished, Angie did her duty and offered her condolences, and they responded to her with a single nod of acknowledgment and mouthing, "Thank you," before they were swarmed by others wanting their turn.

Nick approached and put a hand on Beau's shoulder, bowing his head. "Sir, what happened to Luke is a damned tragedy. He should be here with us today, not in there." He motioned to the coffin, now being carried away to a hearse parked outside. "I promise you. We'll find and kill the savage fishes that murdered your son. They've already taken too many of us, and now they've killed a boy on the cusp of manhood. An earnest and hardworking boy who did no harm. This is the last straw."

"I hope you're right," Beau murmured, holding Emily close and rubbing her shoulders. He looked to Bàba.

"Chief, you and Nick just let us know if you need funding, or manpower. We want every last one of those monsters dead."

Bàba shook his head. "Call me Zixin, please. You don't serve under me anymore."

"Okay, Zixin." Beau forced a tiny smile. "I'm still not used to calling you that. Eight years of habit is hard to break."

Angie turned away, feeling as if her heart were full of rocks instead of blood, and she tucked her hands into her jacket's pockets.

"Beibei." Bàba's hand came down on her shoulder, and she met his eyes, wet with unshed tears. She put her hand over his.

"I'm so sorry, Bàba," she murmured.

"It's a shame we lost him," Bàba said. "He will be remembered. But come, let's go home. I could use a rest. Think of what we will do next."

Angie followed him to the ferry station after they made their rounds to say goodbye.

Kaden better be able to get some answers for her.

TWELVE

THE DOCKS WERE STRANGELY EMPTY WHEN Angie got into work. The caution tape still hung between the wooden beams of the railing. Except for the two police officers who were searching the area where she found Luke two days ago. Her heart dropped when she thought of him, plunging further as she dreaded and anticipated what Kaden would have to say.

She yawned; the three extra shifts she picked up the past week were catching up to her. Her body ached for a restful night, and she rubbed her eyes.

Come to think of it, exhaustion was her default state since she came back from college. She unfolded her to-do list for the day, which had been folded into a nice square in her pocket: Check and record inventory in the warehouse, boathouse, and supply rooms. Then sweep the walkways, gangways, and ship loading and unloading areas for debris and trash.

Essentially, her work area today was the entirety of the docks. Her mind fogged, dreading the day ahead. No wonder she was exhausted.

A woman brushed past her speed-walking, turning Angie's attention from her piece of paper. The woman's dark ringlets were piled in a high ponytail on her head, bouncing with each step.

It was Eva, a woman who had been working at the docks for nearly two decades. "You going to the meeting? The boss and Nick are waiting for us!"

She hadn't heard about any meeting, and she wrinkled her nose. "What meeting?"

"You didn't get the memo this morning? Said it was urgent. C'mon. Boss' daughter can't be late."

"Clearly, the boss' daughter didn't get that email."

Eva snorted with a half-smile, and Angie followed her to an empty outhouse at the dock's far corner, by the water's edge. "Had no time to check it."

"I know. Can barely scrape up enough energy to have dinner with my daughter. I want this shit to be over already," Eva grumbled. "I'd hate to see how much worse it'll get."

"You and me both," Angie muttered. "How's Celia doing?"

"I'll show you." Eva flashed her a toothy grin and pulled out her phone. It was a photo of mother and daughter standing in knee-deep crystal-clear water on a white sand beach, arms wrapped around each other with broad, mirthful smiles. The sunlight in the photo winked off Celia's nose ring, creating a ball of light on her cheek. "We went to Cabo when she graduated high school last year. Get away from the cold a bit, you know?"

"You two are beautiful!" Angie exclaimed. Eva's happiness rubbed off on Angie, and she was glad to talk about something else other than the mer, for however brief a time. "Is she in college now?"

"No, she decided against college. She's working for Creston General Hospital as an inpatient medical assistant. Comes here every weekend to scuba dive." Eva ran her thumb over her phone screen as if caressing her daughter's cheek. "Feels like yesterday I brought her home from the orphanage. How time flies." She put her phone back into her jeans pocket, her next words spoken under her breath, but still clear enough for Angie to overhear. "If only Adrianna could see us now."

Angie laid a hand on Eva's forearm. She remembered her story, what felt like a long, long time ago. How Eva's wife, Adrianna, had left her because Eva wanted kids, and she didn't.

Eva cleared her throat. "Anyway, you should come by for dinner sometime so I can re-introduce you ladies." Her smile vanished. "If we have enough food for more than our family, by then."

"You're feeling the fish shortage, too?" Angie couldn't hide her surprise. Eva and Celia lived one hour southeast of the docks, where there was adequate farmland.

"Yup," Eva's voice pitch dropped, her shoulders following. "Since we don't have fish, we've been going through our crops faster than we can grow them. We also went to the Lums', but we haven't had much luck. Seemed like once the new stock came in last week, the downtowners and rich folks snatched it all up. Doesn't leave much for the rest of us." Grim creases lined Eva's eyes as she pushed the creaky wooden door open. The room filled with the susurrations of a hundred dock workers, boaters and divers, gawking and pointing in front of them.

What interested Angie was a small group of divers gathered around a long rectangular table, and she sidled her way in. The smell of warm saltwater, pungent fish, and metallic blood filled her nostrils. She gagged at the fetid stench.

Three mer lay side by side, like fish being organized after a catch. Two mermaids, one smaller than the other, and one merman, dead by spearfishing. Angie scanned them, their tails an equal shade of brilliant, eye-catching viridian.

A family.

Angie held her breath until she grew dizzy, her clasped fingers tightening and draining the blood from her knuckles. She stepped closer, looking for markings on their bodies. There were none.

The door behind her flung open, and she jumped back. Nick and Bàba strode in with two senior dock workers in tow. Not a semblance of a smile to be found on their stoic faces. None of them looked at her when they walked past, and Angie fell into formation with the others.

Starting the meeting, Bàba produced a folded piece of paper from his pocket. First, updates to dock's buildings and fortifying the shorelines with traps in case any wayward mer happened to wander too close. Then, he warned everyone not to approach the shoreline alone, even if armed.

Angie leaned in to murmur in Eva's ear. "If I were still in Washington, the mer would be all over social media. And that video would have gone viral."

Eva gave a dry laugh. "You know how us Crestoners are. We like our privacy."

She nodded, knowing all too well. Privacy was one of the reasons their mayor turned down any request to implement a wireless network, and only a single cell tower served part of the docks and downtown for Crestoners to keep in touch with each other, and the outside world. "I downloaded some of those apps in college, but I didn't see the big deal. And I couldn't keep up with everyone, so I deleted them a week later."

"I never encouraged Celia to use it. I'm actually surprised she hasn't asked about it like all my friends' kids have. I mean, we got along just fine without it, growing up."

Creston was an insular community, and it seemed little had changed since Angie had been gone.

Bàba reached for the water flask around his waist, drawing Angie's attention back to him. "I'm sure some of you have heard that other docks are also experiencing a massive fish shortage. The Coast Guard has been deployed to investigate." He sipped. "In terms of us, the Creston council and mayor is assisting us with funds and recruitment."

Then Nick jumped in, and Angie would have sworn Bàba shot a glare at him for interrupting. "Yes, Dad, thank you. They can kill them or take them alive."

"Why would anyone want to keep them alive? As a pet? Like we'd want to stare at those things all day. Well, maybe the females," a male dock worker retorted from beside Angie, cackling after his last sentence.

Angie flinched at the thought of them imprisoned and made to suffer for human satisfaction. Still, she held her tongue.

"Do what you want. For all I care, they're just a bunch of good-for-nothing fish." Nick's voice grew louder, carrying through the entire room.

"We will not stand by and let them starve us out, run us into destitution, kill us slowly!"

Gross. Nick was even more sadistic than Angie thought. His confident proclamation ignited something in the workers, riling them. The dissonance of their blended words crashed into Angie's ears like old family gatherings, where her parents, uncles, aunts, and grandparents tried to one-up each other by who could talk the loudest.

"Yes!" Another female dock worker exclaimed, throwing up her hands. "Where else are we going to get food? The grocery prices are insane now!"

"I'm killing more farm animals than I can raise so my family can have enough to eat!" Another worker's strident voice pierced the room, and Angie startled.

"Not to mention, those fishes' natural predators will also die out. And the fisheries will go out of business," another chimed in. The room erupted into outrage, and Angie shrunk back, mind racing with endless convoluted thoughts. She wanted to counter them, but couldn't find the words.

"They killed the mayor's son! And the whole crew of the *Odyssey* and some of *Castaway*!" another worker chimed in. "My friends were on that ship."

The rabble wasn't dying down, and finally, Bàba's voice boomed over the rest. "Enough! And Nick, you've made your point." He held up both hands, shaking his head in disdain. Nick's mouth snapped shut, darting a furtive glance at Bàba. He appeared ashamed, if the man was capable of such a feeling. "Settle down, everyone. We will ration out what fish stocks we have left." Another angered glance in Nick's direction, and Nick shrunk back an inch.

Angie itched to speak, but she wanted to wait until Bàba finished.

"Yes, the mer have committed some unforgivable acts. We cannot let that slide. But, do not make any rash decisions without me." Bàba took a deep breath. "In other news, as I said earlier, other ports are starting to feel the effects of sea life shortage, too. Namely, Anchorage, Ketchikan, Kodiak, and Kenai. The currents have also become rougher lately, and we must decrease the number of fishing boats we send out."

"Right, because a lot are going out right now," Eva grumbled from beside her, arms folded tight across her chest. "We barely have enough to eat as it is."

"I know," Angie said, voice soft, thinking.

"But the boats we do send will go further. So, they will be in less danger. And we may catch the mer before they are aware of where we're going next." Bàba turned his paper over. "They are obviously close to, if not equal to us in intelligence. They can strategize, organize."

Angie looked out the window behind her. On a normal day, the sight of still, blue waters beneath a clear sky would have greeted her. Today, the waves appeared disarray, churning and splashing and entwining with each other, watery soldiers running amuck without orders to fall in line.

"Wait, I have an idea!" she called out, raising her hand.

"What idea could the new girl have? Just let us go. We'll kill the mer if needed. They won't get anywhere near the shore," a stocky-framed dock worker grumbled, but loud enough for her to hear him. He stood with his arms folded over a bulging belly, his thick unruly eyebrows slanted downward, his wrinkles and salt and pepper hair standing out beneath the ceiling light's yellow cast.

Angie's eyelids twitched. She held seniority over many dock workers, and he was certainly aware she wasn't new. The condescending smirk on his face, and the way he didn't even face her when he spoke didn't escape her.

She had always had a baby face and was the youngest in the family, and it happened far too often for her liking that someone older had brushed her off and treated her like she didn't know what she was talking about.

Her face and neck flushed with heat. She was sick of being treated like this.

"Hey, boy." Angie's stare shot flying daggers at him, fists clenched. "First, I'm a woman, not a girl. Second–"

Ian cut her off. "How about I call you whatever I want? You don't tell me what to–"

"Stop!" Bàba yelled. "Ian, you will not talk to her like that. Let her speak."

"But–"

"She's my daughter." Bàba maintained an unwavering glare, as if daring Ian to challenge his decision.

Ian's lips thinned, but he said no more. Angie stole a glance at Bàba.

"Beibei, please." Bàba motioned for her to go ahead, his eyes soft and warm when they faced her.

Angie's breath hitched. He had never called her that at work. "Why don't we catch some and study them? We could learn a lot about their speech patterns, their behavior. We should know our enemy, right?" They had so readily agreed to blindly slaughter the mer, and she had a strong feeling her suggestion wouldn't be received well. Still, she had to try to buy Kaden some time. If they started killing them by the masses, the mer would never agree to peace. Couldn't have Kaden killed before she found out what she needed from him. He was the only mer foolish enough to stick his head and body above water.

For a drawn-out moment, silence befell the room, and Angie looked to Eva, Bàba, and Nick.

Bàba regarded her, brow wrinkled – his expression when he was thinking of something.

Then the room erupted into boisterous, mocking laughter until Bàba slammed his fists down on the table, and once again, the room went silent.

"No way." Eva spoke up, shocking Angie. "They killed too many of us already, including Luke. They clearly have no interest in talking to *us*."

"Agree," Ian said, the dock worker who sneered at her earlier.

Angie's chest deflated in defeat.

"Angela, why would you mention something like that?" A knowing smirk was plastered across Nick's face. "They may look half-human on the outside, but they're animals. What's there to understand about them?"

Angie clenched her jaw and rubbed her brow, trying to mitigate the headache of Nick's voice.

Another older man spoke up, this one not looking much younger or healthier than Ian. "Know your place, *woman*. Let the men speak."

"So, speak, you condescending male prick," Angie shot back. "I don't know how you or Ivan could chase down any of the mer without collapsing."

"It's Ian–"

"I wasn't done talking."

Bàba gritted his teeth and walked over to the two men. "Ian, Marc. Get out. Don't come back until I call you. You do not disrespect anyone who works here." The order came crashing down on them, and they left without a peep of protest. Bàba turned to Angie next, his glare shooting icicles at her. "That goes for everyone." Angie flinched. She knew she shouldn't have fought fire with fire, at least not with men like them. Yet, she didn't regret her outburst.

Bàba rubbed his face and ran his hands through his thinning hair. Then he nodded at Angie to continue.

"Look, Bàba. If one of the mer was willing to talk, would you consider hearing what they have to say? We could bring in marine biologists who specialize in marine animal communication. Maybe even find one that can speak our language."

"I would have. But we've lost six of our men and women. Luke is dead. And it's because of them." Bàba murmured, rubbing the newly-sprouted small patch of hair on his chin. "Speaking of which, the Coast Guard recovered the missing boat. But no bodies. As for the mer, shoot them on the spot. Nobody is to get any ideas, understood?"

"Yes, sir," the dock workers said in unison. Angie only mouthed the words.

"We need to get the day started," Nick said while Bàba walked back to the middle of the crowd. "There are a handful of fishing boats left that we can send out. Scout the area and capture whatever fish are available. But not enough to attract the mer's attention. They are slow, quiet, and hardly make a ripple in the water." He paused for a breath, looking around at the workers with an air of importance. Angie rolled her eyes. "We need volunteers to go out on the boats."

A few hands shot up instantly, and several hesitant others followed. "We need one more." Bàba said, after counting. Angie raised hers too.

"Absolutely not!" Nick's voice exploded over hers. "Does Angela even know how to man a boat?" The question was snide, and his nose upturned.

"Yes, I do." Angie met his glare, keeping her gaze level. "I learned the ins and outs of driving a boat since before you ever laid eyes on one."

Nick shut up.

"We will send you out in a day or two, when we figure out the schedule." Bàba's inflection was confident, assertive, but Angie caught a wobble of trepidation below the surface. He rolled up the piece of paper. "Meeting dismissed. Get back to work, all of you."

Thirteen

ANGIE STOOD AT THE SHORELINE, STARING with revulsion at the sight before her.

What in the eighteen levels of Hell was wrong with these people? This was positively barbaric and archaic. The early evening breeze carried the stench of ammonia and the heaviness of death. It made her sick, and her stomach squelched in agreement.

Three mer captured this morning were strung up on poles by the seashore, a crude warning to any of their kind who dared approach. The sight of them marred the harbor's usually lovely view, full of lush, green vegetation.

Since she and the workers got the order to shoot mer on the spot, tension wove through her muscles and nerves, a rain cloud of negative thoughts following her every move. Bàba had gone home without her after she told him she had some things to take care of. He hadn't questioned what kind of work she supposedly had, appearing deep in thought while making his way off the docks. Angie's patience wore thin as she paced up and down the coast. Her heartbeat quickened, yet weighed heavier with each beat each time she saw the strung-up mer. She willed Kaden to appear so she could warn him away from the area.

Except he was nowhere to be found. Angie wrinkled her forehead. If he was smart, he would have stayed far from here.

Or, he could have decided he no longer wished to meet her and decided that gallivanting with a human was too risky. That particular notion put a bitter smile on her face.

Minutes passed. Still no sign of him. She let out an indignant huff.

Footsteps shuffled in the distance, and a deep voice called out behind her. "Hey!"

A male worker strolled by on the top of a hill, where she stood at the bottom. He peered down, his eyes two, wide, azure orbs.

She waved weakly.

"Whatcha doing down there? Little late to be wandering around by yourself, isn't it?" He grinned like he knew something she didn't, making the mole on the upper right corner of his lip more prominent.

She didn't recognize him. He looked young and bright-eyed, and must be a new hire.

Frantic, invisible hands racked through Angie's mind. "I'm sweeping the area before I head home."

"Oh, okay. Me too." He laughed. "Hey, you be careful if you see any of those crazy fish!"

"Yup, got my trusty Glock." Angie patted her side pocket hard, making a point to him. Her hand met with her filled holster, her palm molding around the comforting lump.

He walked away, disappearing into the distance. A minute later, it hit her. He had asked why she was hanging around so late, but she never thought to ask him why he was still around by himself, when everyone else had gone home. She made a mental note to ask if she saw him again.

Angie walked down the shoreline, watching out of her peripheral vision for mer in the vicinity. Her vision closed in on a set of footprints, looking to have been made with boots larger than hers. Someone, perhaps a dock worker had been here recently. Maybe they were still nearby.

"Kaden." She got to one knee. She kept her pitch low, hoping he alone heard her and not anyone else. As she expected, no answer. Her lips thinned. She called his name again, louder. Nothing, not even a ripple of water to acknowledge her. He had five minutes, and if he wasn't here by then, she was leaving.

Five minutes passed. Still no merman, but as she walked away, a bottle jumped from the water and rolled across the wood planks, stopping when it touched her feet. "Of course. More trash washing up."

Grumbling to herself, she picked up the bottle and turned back toward the docks to drop it in their single recycling bin. While walking, she turned it over in her palm. A hastily scrawled "A" on a rolled-up sheet of viridian algae inside gave her pause.

"Message in a bottle. Cute."

She slid the algae sheet out into her hand, a thick sheet of kombu kelp. Perplexed, she found scratches on it, appearing to form a pattern. She looked closer.

A simple message.

Follow where the currents shift westward.

Angie pursed her lips. She pulled out her phone to check the Maps app compass, and followed where it pointed west.

She found Kaden a three-minute walk away, waving to her and sitting in between two gray boulders. A wave rose behind him and crashed into the rocks, creating a liquid fan capped with snowy seafoam.

"Sorry to have you come all the way down here," he said as soon as she was within earshot. "Humans found our meeting spot, and it was too dangerous for me. Especially after I saw—" Kaden visibly swallowed, an air of panic clutching at him.

"I figured." Angie waved the kelp-directions at him. "The bottle was a little cryptic. It was about to go right into a recycling bin."

Kaden's lips quirked into an amused smile. "Pray tell, Angie, how I would have made it more obvious without sticking my head out of the water and screaming your name? I threw a bottle at your feet. Is that not obvious enough?"

"All right, whatever." Angie raised her hands in surrender. She wanted to get to the point, not linger around and give someone a chance to see them. "I get it. I know there are other people around." Also, she was sure it didn't help to see three of his people impaled.

"I saw what your people did to mine." His nostrils flared, and his eyebrows drew together, his jaw tightening. His gaze pointed where the dead mer hung, fingers curling tight around the rock he sat on. His countenance flickered to reflect some hidden rage mounting inside him. By instinct, Angie took a step backward, keeping him in her sight.

His fingers relaxed and his expression collapsed, lips falling into a frown.

"I'm sorry you had to see that." A sorrowful note spiked her words.

After all, she couldn't forget the sensation of fear and despondency when she saw Luke, and she hadn't been forced to see his decaying corpse each time she came to the seaboard.

"I am too." Kaden's chest heaved with heavy breaths, as if something in the air affected his respirations. "They were old friends of my family." He let out a quiet cough and bowed his head. "But you're not here to hear me lament."

"I wasn't, but I feel awful that happened." Angie found herself at a loss for words. "That is horrible."

The bottom third of his tail emerged from the water and curled at the end, caudal fins draping like an upside-down fan. "Agreed. But I know we agreed to meet for another reason. I spoke with my family of your proposal, to release the fish back into the seas to feed your people. See if we could come to an agreement. They would not hear it."

Angie's next breath caught in her throat, her eyes feeling as if they were popping out of their sockets. "They wouldn't listen at all?"

"I tried to convince them to see my side." His voice became more strained with each word, and she crept closer to hear him clearly. "They said it's too late. Your people keep killing ours, and now mocking us with that tragedy at the shoreline. They refused to keep talking about it and said landwalkers brought it on themselves."

Defeated, she slumped and covered her face. "Thanks for letting me know anyway."

"I apologize for not being able to do more, or deliver better news." He peered toward the water's surface, and then back at her again. Still, he kept his head slightly turned away from her, his gaze darting back and forth.

"Are you expecting someone to sneak up behind you?" Angie followed his gaze. Before he answered, more footfalls sounded behind her. She jolted and Kaden hid between two taller rocks.

A man walked past without a second glance, whistling to himself and picking up garbage and debris from the floor with a reacher. Part of the evening cleanup crew, but they didn't come this far out. Her chest tightened. Then again, things weren't normal these days.

The man left, and Kaden reappeared from his hiding place. "Kaden." She took another cursory glance around. "I should go. If they're sending people further out here, it's not safe for us to keep meeting."

Kaden narrowed his amber eyes, nodding slowly. "Agreed. And Angie?"

"Hm?"

"If we ever see each other again, I promise I will not strike at you. But, I will not be coming ashore anymore."

She gulped, her next words tumbling out breathy and cracked. "Me neither."

What was she supposed to do now?

With a flick of his tail, he dove back underneath the sea. She made her way back, pulling her jacket tighter as the cold and heavy winds howled.

She struggled to think of a plan B, but she had nothing.

FOURTEEN

A FORTNIGHT PASSED BEFORE BÀBA CALLED ANGIE to go fishing since she had volunteered at their last meeting.

"We found a safe route, and we're using smaller, quieter boats to hopefully not draw the mer's attention," he said as soon as she arrived at the boat dock. "I know you've been counting the days until you could go out, and we already lost two boats. But the past week has been quiet."

Angie knew, and she dreaded what the mer might be planning. If she and Kaden hadn't agreed to part ways, she may know a thing or two. If he even knew, or would have told her, that was.

"I know, and I understand." Heart thumping with excitement, Angie took the keys from him and stepped aboard the midsized, single-decked open hull boat with a center helm. Despite the danger of mer, she still wanted to be out in the open water instead of being stuck at home and on the docks day in and day out.

"Be careful. If you see anything, don't hesitate to attack. I'd rather you—"

"Impale a random sea creature than risk merfolk following us," Angie finished.

He pressed his lips together. "Yes. Exactly."

"You've told me three times this morning already." She gave him a knowing smile and moved to the helm.

"I worry about you; that's all."

"I know what I'm doing." Angie started the blower before turning on the engine, and it roared to life.

This was it. It had been years since she helmed a boat, but she wouldn't let Bàba see her nervous. Yet, putting her hands on the throttle and steering wheel jogged her memory.

With a heavy sigh, Bàba turned and waved to the two women who walked toward the boat.

One looked to be Angie's age, her hazelnut hair tied in a long braid down her back, expression open and eager, and she introduced herself as Abigail. The other looked middle-aged, and spoke with a quiet reservation, a fishing rod steady in her hands.

"And this is Elise. She's a seasoned spear fisher. Also, Abigail has been fishing since she was a young girl. So, you're in good company," Bàba said. "And both of you know my daughter, Angie. Take care of yourselves, okay? Call the command center if anything happens. And I mean anything." He pointed the last part of his statement at Angie, and she raised an eyebrow, folding her arms over her chest.

"We will, Zixin," Elise said.

Angie drove them out to the open sea, making conversation with them as they moved further away from land.

Even though it broke the monotony of her days, she felt even less safe. It was mer territory, but the waves' gentle lapping and swaying of the boat put her at ease for the time being.

Their hour out was uneventful, and Angie killed the engine twice at two spots where Elise and Abigail could fish. In the first hour, they hadn't caught more than a handful of pacific cod and two halibuts. Another hour passed, and they had filled a small fishing net.

"You two okay back there?" She stayed close to the steering wheel and scanned their surroundings, making sure all was well before starting the boat up again.

"Yeah. It's a little quiet for me, but it's alright." Abigail hooked fresh bait on her fishing pole and dropped it into the water.

"Think we have time for one more?" Abigail was eyeing their small catch.

Angie checked the time. "We have another hour before we should start heading back. We can stay if you ladies are alright with it."

Elise gave her an "OK" sign with her thumb and index finger.

To Angie's surprise, the next hour yielded another small net full of fish, and she pushed the throttle into gear and spun the wheel, steering them back to the docks.

A wave hit the side of the boat.

Then another.

"What's going on?" Abigail held one hand to her forehead, shielding her eyes from the sun. "Is there a storm coming?"

"It's supposed to be clear today," Elise murmured.

"Then how come the waters are so choppy?" Abigail directed her question at Elise. Then her voice softened. "It can't be the mer, can it? Zixin said they've never been seen out here—"

"Must be a rough patch. I'll get us out." Angie hit the toggle button on the dash to trim the boat, trying in vain to quash her fears that mer had discovered them. Luckily, she faced away from the women so they wouldn't see her hands shake. "Hang on. Making a sharp turn."

She hit the throttle, boat churning toward the calm waters on their right. The choppy waters followed, and then Elise raised her voice.

"Mer spotted!" She grabbed a lance from the pile at the back of the boat. Angie's grips and forearms tensed. Mer with opaque, teal, and stormy gray tails darted in and out of view underneath the boat.

Behind her, Elise leaned over the side of the boat, aiming her lance at the water, gaze and arms tracking them. A quick rearing back of her arm and carefully placed aim later, she struck the lance downward, and Angie winced, imagining it impaling a mer's body. Another look back revealed her and Abigail pulling a dead merman aboard, Elise's spear through his neck.

"They're surrounding us!" Abigail's voice heightened in pitch and cadence, scrambling to the marine radio at the boat's stern. "Angie! We have to go!"

The sea's agitation swelled as the winds spun to tropical storm-like speeds. Choppy waves broke at the wind's crest, smacking against the side of the boat like watery fists pounding on a door that would not open. Angie struggled for a deep enough breath, her head growing light with her hyperventilation.

Focus! Get us out safe.

The boat shifted to its starboard side, and Angie reduced the speed, turning the boat into the wind at a forty-five-degree angle, a desperate bid to maintain control. Her heartbeats raced quick and shallow like the waves assaulting them, her hands breaking into a cold sweat as she struggled to steer away from more oncoming waves.

Behind her, Abigail yelled for help into the radio, words coming out in sputters.

She sucked in a frantic breath when a funnel of water rose like a sea creature emerging from the depths. Angie's skin shivered and crawled. The howling winds tore against her face and made her eyes water and burn. The water funnel's apex crashed down, knocking the boat over with a violent slam and throwing the three of them into the unforgiving waves.

"Abigail! Elise!" Angie shrieked, punching down the raging waters to keep her head afloat. She was a strong swimmer, but she was no match for the relentless waves threatening to pull her under. Faint screams came from the other side of the boat, and she paddled toward them.

"El—" Saltwater rushing into her throat cut her off, and she coughed, her throat burning. She forced herself to paddle and to kick her feet in a furious freestyle, shoulders fatiguing and calves cramping under her exertion. Their screams were gone, cut off midway. Raw panic sunk in. Another mighty wave rose, muffling her cries and pulling her into its raging undertow.

She dashed for the surface only to be yanked down again by two arms wrapping around her legs, pulling her deeper, deeper. Angie flailed and kicked in desperation, but the hold was too tight, making her a statue sinking to the bottom of the ocean.

A tailfin struck her across the cheek, and then another. A thick, strong tail swept past her, wrapping itself around her waist like a serpentine corset, squeezing her stomach in tandem with an arm around her neck, tightening over her jugular.

Stupid her. In her excitement and rush to get on the boat, she forgot to grab her gun and diving knife out of her locker.

Then the hold loosened, and through her blurred vision, a combustion of colors came into view. Mer tails. She couldn't tell how many. Their tails blended together, a paint palette whose colors had conglomerated.

Something wrapped her underneath her shoulders, and she was being sped away. Her lungs were about to burst, her head spun and made the world around her a dizzying kaleidoscope.

A miracle happened, and her head burst through the surface. She swallowed air as though she were starving and oxygen was her first meal in months. Exhausted, Angie shut her eyes. She didn't care where she was, but she was alive and could breathe.

Nothing else mattered.

FIFTEEN

ANGIE LAY ON DRY GROUND WHEN her eyes fluttered open. The hazy sun glared back at her, and she squinted. She was on the edge of a small island on the rocky shoal before it transitioned into the actual beach a few yards away, but how?

Pushing up on her arms, she slumped forward and coughed out a lung full of seawater, searing her throat.

Where was she? Where were the mermen or mermaids that nearly drowned her? Surely, they hadn't just let her go so easily.

Glassy, calm waters surrounded her on all sides. Across from her, a mountain range shrouded in fog. Behind her, a thick forest of spruce trees loomed over her head, imposing and mysterious.

Nothing looked familiar. No land masses, no landmarks that she could place.

The hair on her nape and arms rose as she imagined the worst-case scenario. That the mer didn't kill her because they chose to leave her alone here, isolated, to die slowly.

She patted her pants and jacket pockets. Her phone was gone too. Nobody would find her here, and her chest ached at the thought.

As she continued scanning the area, she froze.

"What the f—"

Kaden's upper body bobbed up and down in the water, amber eyes wide like orbs. He didn't swim closer.

Just stared.

Angie scooted backward. As soon as she moved, nausea and dizziness hit, and she dry-heaved. Tears blurring her vision, she rubbed her eyes.

Finally, he paddled forward and rested his arms on the island's edge. The ends of his tailfin peeked out from the waves. "Are you alright?"

"Wh-what happened?" Angie rubbed at her temples and folded her legs, settling into a more comfortable position. "Why in the eighteen levels of hell were you just floating there, staring at me? It's creepy."

His biceps twitched, and he bit his lower lip, failing to keep one side from pointing upward. "Apologies, I did not want to be practically on top of you when you awoke, and scare you."

She blinked, processing what she just heard. "Why would you be on top of me?"

"To ensure you were still breathing?" He stated it as if it were an obvious fact, and his smile grew into a full-blown one that reached his annoyingly breathtaking eyes.

She didn't find that notion funny at all, and didn't return his smile. "So, I would have been forced to see your giant face when I opened my eyes because you were, and I quote, 'on top of me?'"

"Well, yes, I'm a decent being who didn't wish to see you drown." Kaden's eyes rounded, and for a moment, he looked as innocent as he sounded.

"I suppose I'll try and be flattered," she said, sotto voce.

"You can feel however you wish. That mer who was slowly cutting off your air supply? I distracted him and then grabbed you when he wasn't looking."

"You didn't have to save me, again. I mean, I almost killed you, and almost turned you into shark dinner after shooting you." She searched his features, trying to pinpoint what it was he could possibly want from her in return for the rescue.

"You nearly put a bullet between my eyes. Then you shot me anyway the next time." His tail swished from side to side, creating drag. "But you saved me. So, consider the favor repaid."

"Yeah, yeah, I remember," Angie grumbled. "Shit. My dad is going to wonder what happened to me." Bàba was going to be worried sick that they hadn't come back on time. Hopefully Abigail's radio message had gone through. Were there people searching for them? How much time had passed since the waves swallowed their boat, and Abigail and Elise?

Thoughts of the two women sent a wave of sadness crashing over her head.

Without her phone or another way of telling time, she had no idea. She also had no idea how to get off this island, and a sudden and overwhelming sense of dread cloaked her.

She couldn't get Elise and Abigail out of her mind. Maybe they were still alive, somewhere, somehow. "Did you see what happened to those women I was with?"

Kaden's voice took on a melancholy timbre. "The two mermaids likely drowned them."

Angie's throat tightened and she wove her fingers together. "How did you know where I was?"

"I heard three royal sentinels say humans were approaching on a small boat." Kaden shifted his weight.

"But how? We were so far from the usual places." Angie's voice dropped to a frightened whisper. "That area was specifically picked because humans and mer hadn't encountered each other. And the boats were quiet."

"We hear vibrations rippling when watercraft approach, even if they sound quiet to humans. There were more patrols sent out and in a wider swath, to watch for divers and boaters. I followed them, not believing humans would come this distance. They never do." He swallowed hard, his Adam's apple rising and falling. "I sensed something was wrong, and then I saw you on the boat."

"Thank you." Angie faced him, and he gave her a nod of acknowledgment. "Where are we?"

"About one seamile from where we found you." His eyes shifted away from her for a beat. "Angie, you asked me earlier, why I saved you again. I know you were not responsible for killing any of my people. I would like to work with you, convince our leaders for a ceasefire."

Angie thought about Elise and Abigail, and her lower lip quivered. Earlier today, she was on a boat with them, about to bring fish home. She also thought of Luke. He was going to be a marine biologist because of her.

Now, the fish were gone. Elise and Abigail and Luke were also gone. His devastated parents would be the most difficult to persuade, but if Kaden hadn't come on time, she would have died, just like them. She set her jaw and clenched her fists tighter, her fingertips digging hard between the bones in her hand.

"Okay. I can get on board with that." Her voice surged with renewed fervor. "But I need to get home, somehow. I should have been back; I don't know how long ago. And I need to figure out how to explain why I'm still alive, and the others aren't. I'll think of something," she added, mostly to herself, a chill running through her bones. "I have to talk to my dad. Feed Lulu."

"Who's Lulu?" Kaden perked up.

Angie took a string of deep breaths to re-orient herself before answering him. "My cat."

"What's your cat like? I am unfamiliar with them. Except hearing about them from the mer that encountered them. Described them as little terrors with cute faces, sharp claws and sharper teeth who strike fear into the hearts of my people."

Angie brightened when she pictured Lulu's sweet, mischievous face. "They're curious, they want to see what glowy and shiny things are, like mer tails. Lulu's loved shiny things since she was a kitten. Used to steal my jewelry and hoard them next to her bed. I think she was a barracuda in a past life. Or a literal cat burglar."

"Intriguing. I'd like to see this mysterious creature myself," Kaden mused aloud.

"I adopted her as a kitten. Her previous guardian hoarded cats, so she was neglected. For the first few months, she'd only come out to use the litter box," Angie continued.

"The poor creature." Kaden thinned his lips. "She must have trusted you eventually?"

"Yeah, after a lot of patience. I had to wait and feed her under the bed every day. Now she's my spoiled girl."

Another cough wedged out of her throat, and she lost her balance, throwing one arm out to keep from falling to her side.

He caught her, long fingers curled around her upper arm, and pushed her back into an upright position. Jolts of electricity fired through her nerves, originating from where his fingertips met her skin.

Angie put a hand on him to steady herself. His skin was warm to the touch, the high body heat likely an adaptation to living in arctic waters. He felt firm and lean. The sunlight winked off his broad shoulders, strong chest, and back. His stomach was flat, and his waist seamlessly transitioned into the transparent fins hugging the start of his tail.

He was a beautiful, ethereal merman, and it was hard to take her eyes off him.

Kaden seemed to have noticed the twitch in her bicep causing her to pull her hand back. "What's wrong?"

"Nothing." She glanced away, cupping her hand on the back of her neck and snapping out of whatever trance she was in. "Clumsy me. Can't even keep myself upright with a stupid cough."

Kaden lifted a single thick eyebrow and cocked his head, blinking.

Collecting herself, Angie looked around her once more.

After a stretch of silence, Kaden spoke again. "If you are feeling better, I will take you back to the main island." He reached out as if to touch her arm, but stopped before it made contact.

"Thanks. So much for not seeing each other again, huh?" She forced a small smile.

"I wasn't planning on it until this happened. But, come. You can jump on my back. I'll make sure you stay afloat." He slid into the water, face-first, and she followed, trembling when the water rose to her mid-shin. She straddled his lower back, keeping her knees tight against his narrow waist, sitting upright and keeping her hands between his shoulder blades like a kickstand.

Angie didn't want to get closer to him than she already had, and especially not as intimate as pressing her chest to his back.

Creston Harbor came into view within fifteen minutes, and Kaden picked up his speed, staying level beneath the surface, his back and side muscles contracting into her legs. His body heat kept her warm for most of the trip. Angie focused on the landmass ahead.

Once her feet met the sand, she shivered. Kaden surfaced again, facing her, his breathing shallow, face flushed, and he clutched the sandy ground as if it were a life preserver.

Angie quirked one eyebrow. "You good?"

"I will live," Kaden replied with an audible inhale. "If you would like, I'd meet you again. And perhaps devise a plan. The usual spot? Three tidesdays from today?" His brilliant eyes shone even brighter at his request.

"Sure, okay."

Kaden gave her a nod before making an abrupt turn and disappearing under the sea.

Angie made her way back to the docks, walking as fast as her feet were willing to move. The cold of the sea stung at her when a breeze swept by. Goosebumps covered her arms and legs. She quickened her pace while clearing her raspy throat. Once she arrived, she headed straight to the locker rooms and changed into spare clothes before any dock workers spotted her. She would see Kaden again in three days and anticipation simmered, a small burst of heat emanating beneath her skin. Was her heart, once hardened like a stone in winter at the thought of seeing a mer, slowly thawing?

She frowned, perishing the doltish notion. Whatever warmth fluttered in her stomach was only her body recovering from shock and regaining her senses after a near-drowning.

That had to be it.

SIXTEEN

ANGIE FELT LIKE BÀBA's TOYOTA TUNDRA ran over her. Twice.

The day after she left Kaden, her throat itched. It took one more day for it to turn into a sore throat and runny nose. Chest congestion and repeated sneezing arrived soon after.

Her blackout curtains were pulled shut, not allowing a sliver of sunlight through. She would do anything to stay in her bed the rest of the day.

Working overtime, swallowing seawater, and freezing her ass off in forty-degree weather was a very, very bad combination.

Just as Angie was drifting back into deep sleep, extra weight appeared on her bed coupled with an effortful chitter. Twitching whiskers tickled her nose, followed by a furry paw on her cheek.

"Lulu, not now." Lulu's large eyes searched her expression while sniffing her face, pink nose twitching, tapping her forehead like Angie was a small rodent she was coaxing closer.

The cat's mouth opened, and she mewed into Angie's face, cat breath prominent. She gently nudged Lulu toward the edge of the bed. With a meow of protest, Lulu jumped off and returned to her window perch, throwing Angie one last, haughty, "I-won't-forget-this" look over her shoulder.

"Beibei!" Bàba's booming voice drifted up the stairs into her room. "Breakfast is ready! If you're not going to work for the second day in a row, the least you can do is eat something!"

Angie groaned into her pillow.

"Coming." Leave it to her father to make her feel guilty for not going into work or eating his meals while she was sick. Bàba, the man who would only put his life on hold if he were on his deathbed.

Angie pulled herself out of bed and wrapped a robe around herself. She slid into her soft, velvety slippers, shuffling down the stairs and sniffling every other step.

If she could muster up an appetite for anything, that would be great.

Bàba stared at her, holding a mug of steaming tea. "Feeling better?"

"Slightly. Thanks, Bàba," Angie grumbled, moving to the kettle and turning on the switch to boil water. She reached overhead for a cylindrical container of dried chrysanthemum flowers, wincing at the stretch, and filled her tea steeper with them. "Probably stress. And falling into the freezing cold ocean." The kettle gave off a *pop!* Signaling the water inside had come to a rolling boil. She filled her cup, inhaling the soft scent with honey undertones.

"You still haven't told me what exactly happened."

Angie swallowed a proverbial rock. Carrying her tea to the table, she stirred in a tablespoon of raw honey from their local apiary. "I'll tell you the whole story once I feel better."

"I'm holding you to that." Bàba sat and pushed a plate of deer sausages and toast with watermelon-berry and crowberry jam toward her, half the portion that they normally ate. It would sate her in her ill condition. Her belly protested as soon as she laid eyes on the meal, mouthwatering steam still drifting from it. She undertook the Herculean task of forcing herself to reach for her fork.

Having enough food on the table now was one of those times she appreciated her father's near-neuroticism about keeping the fridge, freezers, and pantries overstuffed to the point where they barely closed. He grew up in a poor family in rural China, where they didn't know when or where their next meal would come from. When he immigrated to the States with his family at eighteen, and joined the Navy at nineteen, he had vowed to make something of himself. He had vowed that his family would never be without food or have to suffer the way he did as a child.

She pulled out a chair, a subtle scritch following it. Bàba narrowed his gaze at her.

Angie sat, lifting the chair with her in it and walking it under the table before setting it back down.

Bàba returned to his breakfast. He was protective of the hardwood floors he'd installed himself and made it clear that whoever damaged the floors would be responsible for coughing up the cash, or time, to fix them.

Salmon jerky was noticeably missing. Bàba always loved a serving in the morning before the fish had disappeared. Angie had a taste for it herself, but after what Kaden had sneered about how humans treated marine life, she wasn't sure she could bring herself to eat seafood again.

Bàba fixed her with a glare like cold steel. "Beibei, is there something happening I should know about?" His voice took on a hard edge, and she stopped chewing her bite of toast.

Angie knew where the pointed comment came from. She and Mia were rambunctious as teenagers, missing curfew numerous times to be with their friends, and Bàba had taken it upon himself to punish them, by grounding them or worse, locked outside the house for every hour they missed curfew by. Then at sixteen, he'd caught her sneaking alcohol because her friends were drinking after a school dance. His quiet disappointment when he found out was enough to keep her from alcohol again until she was twenty-two and found out Māma had passed. He never yelled. He never had to.

Bàba was in his late fifties now, and even with deeper wrinkles around his brown eyes and more gray hairs, he wasn't any less intimidating when he glared at her like she'd done something horribly wrong. Even now, the hardened look on his face resulted in instant obedience. A trait that Angie both envied and feared.

And yet, she couldn't bring herself to tell him about Kaden.

She swallowed, moisturizing her dry throat. "I-I'm just stressed, Bàba. There's always so much work to do." She forced down a chunk of sausage, smooth and firm and rich on her tongue, and wished she could savor each bite.

Bàba grunted and polished off his own plate.

"Have we lost anyone else?" she asked.

"Not since Elise and Abigail." Bàba shifted his weight in his chair, visibly uncomfortable. "I've been talking to some friends in Sitka and Whittier, and I've talked to Beau and Emily about this too. They also cannot make enough catches and worry about losing their livelihoods, feeding their people. If only we knew where the mer were coming from. We need to strike where they live." He shook his head sadly and moved to the sink to wash his dishes and ceramic tea mug.

Angie hung her head, thinking the same. They could be anywhere in the mysterious sea, the least-explored place on Earth.

"But I have to go to work. Take care of yourself, okay? I'll see you tonight."

"Bye, Bàba."

Half a sausage and toast remained on her plate, and she resolved to eat it. After all, there were people starving in her village, and she'd be damned if she didn't at least give it her best effort to finish her food. She'd need the strength to recover and return to the docks. There were fish that needed to be found.

She was supposed to meet Kaden tomorrow, but she wasn't sure if that would happen.

The guilt that previously jabbed at her now swallowed her whole.

"I brought you soup," Mia said. The evening came quicker after spending most of the day sleeping. Mia and Rosie made a surprise visit, Mia with a small container of creamy and salty roasted carrot and potato soup. "There's not much, but we can share."

Angie lay stretched out on the couch, finding comfort in front of the fireplace, her thick, childhood fuzzy blanket wrapped around her. Where it once bundled her up like a cocoon, now it only covered her torso down to her ankles, but she didn't mind.

Across from her, Lulu prepared to pounce, watching one of Rosie's bracelets. Angie let out a loud, sharp hiss of air, and Lulu backed down. The cat pawed at the end of the bracelet dangling from Rosie's small wrist, tilting her head to study it. With big questioning eyes, Rosie looked up to Angie.

"It's okay. She won't scratch." Angie sat up and reached for the soup bowl in front of her, taking a ginger sip.

Lulu lost interest and galloped to Angie before hopping on her lap, curling into a fuzzy ball, contented purrs sent soothing vibrations down the tops of her thighs.

"How are you feeling?" Mia sat on the couch angled by Angie's feet.

"I've had better days. But this soup is amazing, thank you, jiějie." The warmth and salt coated her insides and filled her with deep relief, however fleeting it would be. One nostril unblocked, and she took in the aromatic steam with notes of ginger and thyme. "Where's Nick?"

"I asked him and a few of the boys and girls to stay late. Make sure the docks are cleaned up," Bàba interrupted, walking in and sitting across from Mia, who quirked an eyebrow.

"What were they cleaning?" Angie held her shoulders rigid, anticipating his answer.

"Mm. This I want to hear, too." Mia reached for a butter cracker topped with a slice of reindeer sausage and smoky pepper jack cheese from the charcuterie board on the living room table. There were four slices of meat and cheese on the table accompanied by eight crackers, less than they normally set out. Angie watched them in envy. When her appetite returned, she vowed to eat an entire tray if there was an entire tray to be had by then.

Rosie nibbled a cracker, sitting on the floor next to Mia's chair. Bàba left to refill his whiskey glass. Seeing the whiskey gave Angie an idea, and she walked to the kitchen to whip herself up a hot toddy. She followed Bàba back to the living room, and she and Mia turned their ears to him.

"We found traps buried in sand by the shore. Some of our workers were caught, leg traps, tripwires, even quicksand, which I don't understand how that's happening. Two of them escaped, thankfully, but Paul Bay didn't make it. Dragged underwater before we got to him."

"Paul, the maintenance worker?" The glass stopped before it reached Angie's lips.

"Yes." Bàba sipped his whiskey, his expression vacant. He looked at the charcuterie board for the second time that evening, but still, he didn't touch it. "Now we will need to find somebody else for the job. But who will want it?" Bàba dropped his head back against the armchair.

Angie wasn't about to volunteer for that.

"So, what's going to happen?" Mia squeaked. Angie thought she knew why. If she knew Mia, she didn't want Nick to be called in for the job and work even longer hours. Mia hadn't wanted Nick to take the dock job in the first place, knowing it meant irregular hours and unpredictability, things Mia despised. She had protested until Bàba promised her Nick would keep regular hours, putting Mia's mind at ease about childcare and household chores.

"I'll try to pull in a few favors to fill the position. Speaking of missing people. Beibei, you never told me how you got back to the coast by yourself." Bàba pointed his gaze directly at her. "And where your phone is. I must have tried calling a hundred times."

"My phone is at the bottom of the ocean somewhere." That answer was easy enough. As for the other…

She swallowed a bit too much of her drink, choking on the whiskey and lemon juice. After a cough, she cleared her throat, breath hitching. "A-a lifeboat happened to be in the area and took me b-back."

Bàba slanted his eyes at her, and even Mia looked at her in disbelief. Before either of them uttered a peep, Rosie shrieked. "I'm so happy the lifeboat found you, Angie āyí! And you didn't get killed by those fish people!"

Angie swallowed hard and nodded, the motion a little too exaggerated. "Nick told me what happened," Mia chimed in. "I was so worried. My blood pressure went back to normal after Bàba told us you were okay."

Angie took another sip of her drink. Another awkward silence passed, and Bàba set his glass on the table with a loud *clink*.

"Well, it's clear she doesn't want to talk more about it. Rosie, I just noticed your bracelet. Looks like sea glass." He sat back in his chair and took another sip of his drink, giving his full attention to his granddaughter. "Where'd you get it?"

"Angie āyí gave it to me from the ocean." She beamed.

"Did she now?" Bàba asked.

Angie slumped back onto the couch. Thankfully Bàba dropped the subject.

SEVENTEEN

ANGIE NEVER THOUGHT SHE WOULD BE thrilled to be pulling on thick, frayed rope. It dug into her palms. She hated this part of the job, the fiery pain when her hand slid and the loose fibers lacerated her palms. Today, it signified that she was back at work after another two days of suffering and lying in bed and that she was feeling well enough to return to her usual routine.

Most of all, she hoped to see Kaden after her shift ended, who she was supposed to have met two days ago.

Even the usual, jovial, easygoing mood of the docks had taken a dark turn. These days, tension and anger and fear hung like an oppressive fog over the docks, and it wasn't lost on Angie.

"Good to see you back, Angie!" Eva remarked once they'd pulled the empty fishing boat ashore. "What happened to you, anyway? You never call out. Thought you kicked the bucket."

"Eva, don't joke!" A young female worker cried from beside them. "It's not funny. Abigail's gone. She was—" The woman choked on her words. "She was my friend."

Angie winced and slid her gaze to Eva.

Eva's face fell. "I'm so sorry. Just, you know, trying to lighten the mood a bit. Poor joke." The other woman's face puckered, as if she were holding back tears, and said nothing. Eva looked back to Angie. "But seriously, are you okay? Boss said a lifeboat saved you. You're lucky the mer didn't go after them too."

She nodded. "Had an awful cold. Felt like shit."

Angie dusted off her hands and thumbed off the small streak of blood on her palm's center, lips twisting into a grimace. Damn it, she should have grabbed her work gloves from her locker before coming to help tie the fishing boat to the posts. She was on administrative duties today, and when she got the call from Nick to help Eva and the younger female worker, she didn't want to run across the docks to the locker room and keep them waiting and hanging onto the boat's rope until she arrived.

"Welcome back." Eva fist-bumped the first couple of fishermen, and Angie stepped off the gangway to make room. Nick's loud, obnoxious voice drifted in her direction, and she rolled her eyes so far back that she strained the bottoms. Eva craned her neck in his direction. "Oh, there's Nick. Let me go tell him the boat is in."

She strode to join him, and they walked together. He passed by without acknowledging her, but it was Eva who gave Angie goosebumps.

An invisible fist curled around her innards and squeezed, and she blinked away tears pricking the back of her eyelids. Eva had straightened her usually curly hair in a way that looked like Māma's, and she had a similar willowy build. Angie hadn't noticed when she was in front of and beside her.

Memories came of the past, and Angie turned away. Her feet became dead weights.

―― ෴ ――

When her shift ended, she walked to the spot in the harbor which also served as a scuba diving entry point, shallow waters quickly feeding into the deep sea. Stefan usually took groups out from here, Angie had been on a few back in the day. It was also the last place Māma was seen alive.

Angie sat on the creaky wooden boards, hugging her knees to her chest and resting her chin on the tops of her hands, bracing for the onslaught of sorrow that would inevitably hit as memories of Māma came flooding back. Contemplating why she wanted to dive when she was so ill.

Invisible rocks weighed heavy on Angie's body, her breathing shaky, and tears pooled in her eyes. Sniffling, they flowed freely, salty on her lips.

Memories came, of the stories Māma told of her eventual arrival to Alaska from Taipei when she was thirteen. In her family, it had taken her the longest to assimilate and learn the English language. She met Bàba during her freshman year at the University of Alaska at Fairbanks, and he was twenty years old and on shore leave. When he retired ten years ago, they moved to Creston with Angie and Mia, and as she was finally growing comfortable with life in the States, she was diagnosed with metastatic breast cancer. It didn't respond to treatment.

In Angie's mind, she heard Māma's voice ringing gentle and melodious, yet harsh and strained when she was angry. At least, before the disease affected her brain and speech, and then her voice was subdued, feeble.

It wasn't fair. Māma was a good woman, taken much too soon.

A calm voice jolted her out of her reverie, and she swiped at her eyes, wiping away her tears.

"Are you okay?" Kaden swam to her, gaze soft and face holding an expression of care.

"Uh, yeah. I'm fine." Angie cleared her throat, thick with longing. She threw a quick glance behind her to ensure they were alone. The coast was clear.

"People who are fine don't sit by their lonesome and cry." He tilted his head to one side and arched an eyebrow.

"I guess you have me there." Angie pursed her lips, her cheeks tight as dry streaks of tears clung to them. She supposed she could confide in him. He had saved her life, after all. "I was remembering my māma—uh, my mom. She was here last, before she passed away in a diving accident and was swept out to sea. I wanted to come here. Think about her."

"A diving accident? I'm sorry." Kaden inched closer to her. "Were you close?"

"We are. I mean, we were. We used to do everything together, including diving." A wistful smile broke over her face when she thought of happier times. "But now she's gone. Being home reminds me of her. It was easier when I was away at school." Angie sniffled. Kaden was still watching, his undivided attention clear. "My dad had the Coast Guard and divers and boaters all over searching, but nobody found her."

He didn't meet her gaze. "What was your mother's name?"

"Song Ning. I mean Ning Song."

Kaden appeared East Asian, but she wasn't sure if he knew Chinese naming customs.

Five heartbeats passed. "I know why she wasn't found."

Angie blinked away the spots that had appeared in her vision. "I don't understand."

"My people and I found her floating lifeless at eight hundred feet. She had drowned. We found an identification card with her name and photo on it hanging from her waist. We did not want to engage with the humans, so we took her to be buried in a traditional mer ceremony."

"Wh-what?" Angie rubbed her eyes. "How could she drown? She never dove unprepared. Especially deep-sea diving!" Her mind scrambled for answers, for possibilities, anything explaining Māma's intent.

"She must have had her reasons." Kaden stumbled over his words.

The mer's intent was unexpectedly touching, but—

"We worried for years! All we wanted was closure. I almost wish you left her there so we could have found and buried her." Her jaw clenched.

"I am sorry. On behalf of my people, I apologize. We respect the dead too much to leave them there to decompose, or to be nipped at by scavengers until someone finally finds their remains."

"Your people bury humans often?" The irritation seeped through Angie's tone.

"Yes. The few we have found dead are honored as if they were mer. We all live together on this planet." Kaden's tail flicked behind him, sending droplets of icy water flying into the air and splattering on the top of her head. "Something your species should keep in mind." The freeze seeped through Angie's skull, and she threw him a frosty scowl.

"You had no problems leaving humans dead on the beach the past month." Angie took back her biting words as soon as she spoke them. She didn't mean to be so snippy. He was listening and showing genuine concern, and he didn't intentionally take Māma from her.

Kaden's eyebrows slanted downward, his expression visibly strained. "We were not at war when we buried your mother. We don't show the same respect to our enemies. Particularly not ones who brutally murder us and leave us strung up as a show of mockery! Your kind never wants to understand, only to destroy."

Angie flinched. "We're not all like that—" Her defenses spiked. "I tried to make them see, but they wouldn't listen to me, either. I'm still trying to get through to my dad."

"I know. Not all of you. But enough of you want to see us dead." Kaden's shoulders deflated. "But thank you for trying. I hope you continue to do so, as I am."

Kaden shifted toward the sunbeams piercing wispy white clouds. His handsome face carried soft, gentle features reflecting care, respect, and loyalty.

She looked away from him lest he caught her gawking.

"Angie, I meant to ask earlier. Have you been feeling well?"

He couldn't have known she was sick. "Why do you ask?"

"You did not show yesterday. I was on the way back to the same spot today and happened to see you here." He looked at his own reflection in the calm sea, closing his eyes.

"I know. Sorry." She covered her face with her hands. "After that whole ordeal where you pulled me out of the water, I got terribly sick. Brain fog, fatigue, sniffles, body aches—I had it all. It's like my immune system overreacted after having no illnesses to fight off for years."

"No, don't apologize. If you weren't feeling well, you did the right thing resting and letting your body heal."

"So, you thought I didn't show up because I was sick? Not because I didn't want to see you?" One side of her lips curled in a playful smile.

"Well, I would have given it one more day before coming to that conclusion. But at the moment, I thought it might be the case." A flash of hurt appeared in his eyes. "You are rather pale in the face. I'm unsure if it is similar for humans, but whenever we recover from injury or illness, we tend to be pale while we heal."

"I'm functional enough. My dad and sister took care of me."

A spark appeared in his eyes. "You seem close to your family, even though your mother is no longer with you. It's touching to hear." A brief pause. "You know, the mer have tight-knit families, as well. When a member of the family passes, no matter how old or young, they are forever honored in our homes, commemorated so they will never be forgotten."

Their kinds may not be so different after all, and the knowledge brought Angie some small comfort. "In my family, we have a shrine for my mom and my grandparents, and we honor our ancestors every new year."

He leaned in, eyes sparking with interest. "So, we are similar in that way. You said your mother was the one who took you to the sea for the first time?"

"Oh, yeah. I loved being near the water, even as a kid. So, you can imagine how happy I was that my mom shared her passion with me." Angie kept her mind trained on happier thoughts.

"It is a beautiful place to be, and there's much to see and learn." He flashed her a cheeky smile. "But it is my home."

"It's where I truly feel at peace. But enough of that. You already caught me crying, you don't need to hear more sentimentality from me." Angie rose to her feet to return home. "I appreciate the chat and your asking after me."

"I understand, and it was my pleasure. I wanted us to speak of stopping the war, but it didn't appear as if today was a good time. But, I should be getting back." He looked over his shoulder to the rippling sea. "May I see you again in one tidesweek, at low noontide? The mer are becoming suspicious of my frequent trips to this spot. We can go someplace else if necessary. I haven't had a chance to speak with my parents, but will do so before we meet again."

"A tidesweek?" Angie raised an eyebrow. She took that to mean seven days, but she had to be sure. "Low noontide?"

"Yes, after seven phases of the moon and sun's passing. And yes, low noontide. Around the same time of day as now."

Now she understood his meaning. "You tell time from the shifting in tides."

Kaden nodded, and Angie thought on his proposal. See him again? Which was what she wanted. Or say no and detach herself, and spare them both should they get caught speaking?

Her dilemma.

She put her palms together and cracked her knuckles. He was fascinating, much as it bothered her to admit, and he gave her the closure she so desperately sought about Māma. The more she learned about the mer, the more she could find some angle to appeal to Bàba.

Mind made up, Angie gave him a brief nod.

EIGHTEEN

WITH TENS OF THEIR WORKERS GONE, it was all hands on deck.

Angie returned from maintenance duty toward the end of the next day with Eva and another of their colleagues, and approached Bàba at his office.

"Everything okay, Beibei?" He slid his reading glasses down his nose, peering at her.

"I was just thinking. Why don't we shut the docks down to focus on the mer so the employees would stop getting burnt out and more importantly, stay alive?"

He sat back, crossing his arms. "What brought this on?"

"Because everyone's exhausted and scared for their lives. Including me."

He appeared to think on it for a moment, before shaking his head, to Angie's disappointment. "No. I don't think that's wise."

Angie's face pinched. Why wasn't he listening? This was the only solution that made sense. Pull back and regroup. He was the one who taught her it was the best way to boost morale. She thought again about Elise, Abigail, and Luke. With the docks shut down, even temporarily, they could stay safe from the mer and discuss strategies that didn't involve blindly killing them. And it could keep Kaden safe from human attacks.

"But you could still shut it down and strike at them, right? Then nobody else will be at risk." Angie tried again.

Bàba shook his head, his expression mournful. "The docks are our best point to strike. We don't know where they're coming from. Beau and Emily are trying everything they can to keep us running. To abandon that post would be like letting them win, and we still don't have what we need—business and fish. If that wasn't bad enough, more workers quit."

Angie didn't blame them. She was tempted to do the same, if her boss wasn't her literal family and if she didn't need her work hours and money for school.

The door swung open behind her, and Angie whirled around to look. Nick strolled in, hands behind his back.

Tiān, this man was everywhere. Like a cockroach.

"I couldn't help but overhear your conversation when I was coming in." Nick clasped his chin and put one finger on his lips.

"You just happened to hear, or you were standing outside, listening?" Angie widened her stance and tapped a foot on the ground.

"Does it matter? I have good news that I came from across the docks and paused my duties for." Nick's tone became sharp, but once he turned his attention to Bàba, his voice became boisterous, and he leaned in to talk to him. "Dad, I think you'll like this."

Ass kisser.

Bàba beckoned to Nick. "Go on."

"We haven't lost anyone this week, thanks to our workers who volunteered to watch the coast. Finally, police patrols arrived at the beach this morning. We're well armed, so the mer haven't come near us. No new traps. We even have divers down searching for their base, so we can end this once and for all, and they've come back alive." He put his hands on his hips and widened his stance, taking up more space than he needed to. Angie didn't move, even as his elbow brushed her arm, and she took a step toward him, forcing him to shift another inch. "See, Dad. I told you it was a good idea to get the cops involved. Good thing I had Beau and Emily's backing."

Angie thought he was gloating, but for Nick, it was nothing new. She couldn't imagine how many cops their tiny police department actually spared to help them fight merfolk.

"They gave us three cops. Not nearly enough," Bàba said, sotto voce. "We've had to get some of our own to help hold the shore. Which, thank you, Nick, for finding people willing to patrol."

Angie glanced back to Nick again, whose shit-eating grin widened. It made her biceps and fingers twitch.

Bàba continued, two fingers on his chin. "We must remain on guard. I wish I knew what they were thinking. It might not be a bad idea to capture some and question them as you suggested before, Beibei. If they can even survive above ground." He muttered the last sentence, before walking away and leaving Angie and Nick alone.

Not wanting to speak to him, Angie left at Bàba's heels, her neck flushed and her intestines corkscrewing over each other from simply being in his presence. Somehow, she had a sinking feeling that if they did catch mer, they wouldn't be merciful to them.

Angie had the next day off, and she spent it at home.

She sat at her desk, a pre-downloaded e-textbook open about the diversity of fishes in the ocean.

The lighting was perfect, her room overflowing with an abundance of warm sunshine, and through her cracked window, a slight breeze came in lifting a lock of hair as it brushed her neck.

Angie forced herself to concentrate. The book's contents were exciting and lively, with colorful pictures and flowing, easy-to-read text on a topic that interested her. Yet, she couldn't keep her mind focused; a pounding sensation emerged behind her eyes and tightness constricted the inside her skull as she fought off an oncoming migraine.

Angie reached for her tumbler full of black coffee beside her laptop, the second pouring of that morning alone. The bitterness coated her mouth with the first sip. She should drink water, but she also wanted to stay awake and get some reading in.

The shrill landline downstairs blasted through the house, and Angie jumped out of her seat.

She dashed for the phone and picked it up before it cut off on the last ring. "Hello?"

"Hey." Mia's voice filtered through the phone, broken by static. "Can I ask you a favor and pick up Rosie after camp?"

Angie struggled with her answer. She wanted to see her niece, but at the same time, she coveted her full days off.

"I—" she started, but Mia interrupted her.

"I'm sorry to ask, I know you're tired, and it's your day off. But I got a last-minute client."

Well, when Mia put it that way. As a patient flow consultant for Creston General Hospital, she was able to work remotely most days, but Angie knew that on the days she was in the office, she often stayed late.

"No worries. I'm happy to get her. Camp's done at four, right?"

"Yes, thanks so much. I owe you. See you later, okay? Love you sis." Mia hung up, and Angie checked the clock. It read eleven in the morning, and she had to be at Rosie's day camp by four. If she left by two thirty, she would get there in time.

The headache persisted, and she rifled through the medicine cabinet beside the kitchen for painkillers. A sweeping gaze through the shelves revealed none to be seen.

The closest pharmacy was downtown, more than two hours by ferry and bus. In the opposite direction of Rosie's camp.

Where were the damn painkillers? She swore they still had a bottle when she looked into their cabinet last.

There was one other place they could be. She passed a sleeping, purring Lulu on the living room couch as she headed into Bàba's immaculately kept room with its abundance of natural light.

The small bottle that would be Angie's savior was on his nightstand, between a framed photo of him and Māma on their wedding day, and one of Mia and Angie when Angie was a year old. So his daughters and late wife would always be close to him. He still slept on the left side of his king-sized bed, because the right side was always for Māma.

She marveled how there was not a speckle of dust to be found. How all his shirts and pants atop his dresser were perfectly pressed, resting in neat stacks underneath two rectangular canvases with Chinese calligraphy. One with the words *Xīn jìng*, for tranquility of mind or calmness of heart, and the second with *Yǒngqì*, for courage.

Angie swiped the painkillers and took her leave, stopping when two new medication bottles caught her eye.

Lisinopril: Take 1 tablet once a day for high blood pressure. Prescriber: Imani Thompson, MD.

Right beside a bottle of Ambien. When did Bàba get blood pressure medication and sleeping pills? To her knowledge, his pressure was always under control.

With an arched eyebrow, she left the room and made a mental note to ask him later.

Almost three hours later, she sat at the docks with Rosie chattering nonstop at her side. After downing two pain pills, she gave herself a face mask and took an hour-long nap after having a tall glass of water.

For now, she was the epitome of bright-eyed-and-bushy-tailed.

Nick was nowhere to be found, and she was content to wait patiently until he showed. Angie took Rosie to a quieter spot, far enough from the shore so the mer couldn't reach them if they came by, but close enough so she could still see it in her peripheral vision. "How was camp?"

She was supposed to meet Kaden, and she wanted to stay within his line of sight if he swam by. Angie especially wanted to see him today, find some explanation to why the mer had been so quiet, and if she should worry.

"I drew this," Rosie announced, rifling through her bookbag and pulling out a crumpled piece of paper. "See? This is me. And Mommy and Daddy. That—" She pointed to a smaller stick figure next to Mia, with large eyes covering half her face and long dark hair down to the floor. Eyes that were much bigger and hair longer than her true features, but Angie smiled, appreciating the effort. "Is you, Angie āyí. That guy," she moved one finger over to the taller stick figure next to her, with hastily drawn on spiky hair and thick rimmed glasses. Angie's smile grew even wider at stick-figure Bàba. "Is Gōnggong."

"I love it." Angie put her arms around Rosie, giving her an affectionate squeeze.

A splash in the distance caught her attention. Kaden stuck his head above water, but as soon as he saw Rosie, he ducked underwater again. Rosie followed her gaze, leaning forward with eager, curious eyes. "What happened, Angie āyí?"

"Sorry, Rosie. Thought I saw something, but it's nothing. Don't worry."

Breathless pants and heavy footfalls approached, and Rosie perked up. She jumped to her feet and rushed to greet her father. "Papa!"

"Hey kiddo." Nick knelt, ruffling Rosie's hair and then pinching her cheeks. His jovial smile vanished when he faced Angie, and he rose to his feet. "Angela, why would you leave my daughter by the shore? People died here!" He hissed out the word *died* through a clenched jaw.

Angie poked a tongue to the inside of her cheek and breathed deep. "She's fine. We were nowhere close to the water."

Rosie looked from her to Nick, and then back to her again, her bright eyes wide with befuddlement.

"Still. Don't endanger my kid. But I wouldn't expect you to understand since you don't have any." Nick shook his head, a condescending frown stuck to his face.

She knew he was needling her, and she refused to take the bait. "Please. You know I see her as my own." Her voice remained steady. "She was safe."

"Okay, whatever." He took Rosie's hand. "I got it from here. Come on, Rosie. Let's go home."

He turned abruptly as Rosie said goodbye to Angie. Angie glared after him, hands on her hips. Not even a thank you, huh, Nick?

She wasn't sure why that still surprised her.

Nineteen

"My family has been working here all their life, and no matter how many times I've been here, I never got so close to the lighthouse." Angie looked up beside her from Creston Harbor's northernmost point, nearly three miles from the docks, where its lighthouse sat unused and quiet, like a ghost beacon.

"It's a desolate area. The bright lights used to draw me to it, until the light vanished one day. I have always wondered why." Kaden followed her gaze to the defunct structure, still standing proud.

"It stopped working a couple years ago, I heard." She crossed her legs, into a position of comfort. "Rumor has it the last keeper vanished one day, and his body washed ashore a few weeks later. Nobody knew what happened. It's been abandoned ever since." Angie peered at the top of the lighthouse, imagining a keeper there, watching for incoming ships. Another thought occurred to her. "How did you see it from so deep down?"

"As I said some time ago, I come to the surface every now and again."

Angie gave him a sideways glance. "You come to the surface often? As far as I know, nobody's seen mer. Except when I saw you a month and a half ago, when I was diving."

He frowned. "You saw me underwater?"

"Yeah, you and a mermaid with a white tail." She scooted forward an inch.

"Oh, no. That was my brother, Cyrus, and his lifemate." A playful smirk formed and two dimples emerged.

"Lifemate? Then how come they have different tail colors?"

Kaden's caudal fins curled and drew messy lines in the sand. "It can happen anytime during their life together. If not when they were first joined, it could happen with the birth, or adoption of their children."

"I see. Is he older or younger than you?"

"Older." He dragged his gaze to her. "Do you have siblings?"

"Older sister." A brief thought crossed before she uttered Mia's name. But, he had told her his brother's. "Mia."

"We're both the babies of our families," he said. "And yes, I occasionally observe the goings-on of the surface world, from afar. Human and land animal behaviors and patterns fascinate me. Life up top is so different than it is undersea."

"And I feel the same about all of that. Except change land to sea." Angie grinned.

Speaking of the sea. Angie's thoughts of her recent, failed attempt at studying were fresh in her mind. The last chapter she started reading was about deep-sea creatures, but her fatigue won, and it remained unfinished. Kaden stretched out his tail beside her. She asked, "You ever see strange creatures in the deeps?"

Kaden pursed his lips, tapping his smooth chin. "I have, in the rare times I explore that deep."

He proceeded to say something she couldn't understand at all. "What?" Angie scratched at her temple. Kaden explained, and she brightened. "You're talking about a goblin shark and barreleye." Angie thought of the rarely seen deep sea shark, its snout shaped like a blade. "Not sure I'd want to run into one of those. Sharks I mean."

"It probably wouldn't hurt you. Unless you get in its way." Kaden smirked. "They're partial to ambushes rather than a chase. But, imagine this." He rotated to face her. Angie sat at attention. "You're minding your business. You sense something coming toward you in the dark, slow, methodical. You see a soft pink body, a blue-tipped fin. Then the nose. It glides right by you, and you think you're safe, until it stops. And then..." He leaned in.

"It strikes like lightning and chews your head off?" Angie wiggled her eyebrows.

"Close! But no. They circle you for a torturous moment, and before you know it, their jaws shoot out, and you're dinner." Kaden put his hands in front of his mouth, wiggling his fingers at her and mimicking the shark's jaws protruding out. Angie flicked at one of his fingers, half smiling.

"Top notch impression!" She put her hands to her chest and gasped in an exaggerated, mock show of awe. "If you swam around like that, those poor little cephalopods wouldn't be able to tell the difference." A soft chuckle escaped her.

"I tried that once, but they weren't fooled." He winked.

"That is amazing, though," Angie said with a wistful sigh. "I'd love to get myself into the deep sea one of these days. Like the Mariana Trench, even the Challenger Deep. I wish I could visit your world."

"There is a lot to see."

Angie gave him a playful nudge with her elbow. "Aren't goblin sharks mostly in the Atlantic Ocean? And Oceania? And barrel eyes are way south of here."

"Yes, thank you for the geography lesson," Kaden laughed. "I know where they live."

"Ha, ha. Those are animals I've only ever read about, seen photos of. But to see one in real life." Goosebumps grazed her neck as she imagined the sights Kaden had seen. "You must have traveled far and wide."

"Up and down the Pacific, and I once swam to the Indian Ocean two tidesyears ago. I went with Cyrus, a trip for him before he was to be bonded." Angie grinned to herself at the thought of a merman bachelor party. Kaden propped himself on his forearms, ventral fins waving in the breeze. "Afterward, we almost crossed the Dead Sea. I wasn't prepared for the waters to be so warm, or to see so little marine life. It was eye-opening. To see territory and cultures so different from here. Took us more than a tidesyear." He leaned in close enough for Angie to catch his scent, carried on the gentle gust of wind. He smelled of a fresh sea breeze, crisp with a hint of salt, or maybe that was what she was actually smelling. "Eventually, I would like to see other oceans and seas."

"I'd be lying if I said I wasn't envious." Angie surprised herself when her voice lowered. She sat back upright, putting her hands on her lap. Kaden mirrored her.

"But, enough about me. Have you been to places other than here?"

"I didn't see the exotic places you did, but I dived in the Caribbean, and the islands around Vancouver between high school and college. Otherwise, I haven't been anywhere else, really. Except Washington. Now I'm back home."

"Travel is something we both enjoy doing." A glint of approbation crossed his features. "What of your plans now? Will you stay here?"

Angie couldn't infer the meaning behind his question, if he was fishing for information or if he asked simply out of curiosity. "I'm here for the rest of the summer. Living with my bàba. I'm going back to Seattle for grad school in September."

"Do you and your father live close to the main island?"

"No. It's an hour and a half northeast by ferry and a bus, both of which come once every hour or two." Angie hedged before saying more about where she lived.

Kaden didn't press it. "It sounds like quite the ways to travel. What brought you here, if your school is not near?"

"Work experience and money for school. I also promised my bàba I'd help him when I could. At least, that's what I wanted. But with this mess now, I've been working way too much. Wondering if I'm going to get drowned or speared if I dare get too close to the water. I just want to live through this, if stress or your people don't kill me first." Angie stared at the base of the lighthouse, watching the breeze stir up a small tornado of sand. She never thought she would have to add the last caveat.

"I wish this was not happening, either," Kaden murmured, "that there was more I could do. I know I asked to meet you to discuss how we could stop this bloodshed. My leaders will not hear of any request for a ceasefire. They believe that you landwalkers started it, then taunted us with the strung mer at the shoreline, and believe you must pay." A despondent chord struck in his voice. He slid one arm out to his side to shift his weight, his fingertips touching hers. A tiny jolt buzzed to her hand, a surprising visceral reaction to such a minor touch. Neither of them moved.

"I suggested that we speak to the mer. Instead of killing them. But since our ship, uh, the *Odyssey* sunk and your people killed everyone onboard, and then killed our leaders' son, they're out for revenge, too." Angie shuddered. She thought about what he said, and her heart sank. "What's happening with the mer now? They've been quiet, and it's a little unnerving. If you can tell me. Or want to."

Kaden's fingers shifted away from hers, the sand crunching under his fingers. " I cannot say much more because I don't know, but we are deciding our next move. We have noticed the same silence with your people, though they lurk in our waters sometimes." His voice dropped to a whisper, choking out his next words. "We await news from leadership. And we are to keep a lookout for divers and sea vessels. We were told not to attack for now unless the humans strike first."

Angie brightened with a sliver of hope. "So, if we stop attacking, you'll stop too?" Hopefully, Bàba and Nick would listen to reason. Then she furrowed her brow, thinking. It would leave them at a stalemate. They still needed fish. "Never mind." She pulled her knees closer to her. "I'm afraid. Afraid my family will be caught in the crossfire." Her words shook as they left her lips.

"I understand. I am afraid for my family, as well." A forlorn glint flashed in his eyes as he stared over the horizon. "But, on the topic of family. The child with you earlier. She is yours?"

"Oh, no, she's my sister's." The words came out faster than Angie intended.

"She appears very attached to you. I respect that you value family."

"Always have."

He leaned in, eyes sparking with interest. "Yes, family is important, whether blood or found."

At eight p.m., the sun still beat down on them, and Angie soaked in the warmth.

They had inched closer so their shoulders were touching, and the tiny jolt from her fingers moved to encase her arm, his presence electric.

In the distance, a humpback whale breached toward the skies and fell back into the sea with a mighty splash, a marvelous sight to behold.

She wouldn't squander this rare moment of peace. Or the feeling that if their two species weren't at each other's throats, all would be right.

TWENTY

SEEING THAT BÀBA HAD MADE IT home before her, Angie froze momentarily. He had been staying late at the docks, and by the time he got home in the past few days, she had been asleep.

A smile spread across her face, and she wanted to spend some time with him this evening.

He sat at the dining table, with a hardcover military thriller and his rimless reading glasses poised over the bridge of his nose, and she recalled the Lisinopril and Ambien in his room.

He didn't notice her right away, and she left her boots at the door, sliding her feet into her pink velvet house slippers. "Bàba."

He turned his head a fraction. "I didn't hear you come in."

"You got home early today. Except for work, I feel like I haven't seen you in days."

"Grace and I are splitting the time since Everett quit." He referred to his junior managers. "She was able to take his entire shift today, but I'll have a lot more late nights and early mornings coming up."

"Let me know if I can help at all." Angie moved to sit beside him.

Stretching his legs, he sat back in his chair. "Keep doing what you're doing."

"Is that a new book?" She leaned forward with her elbows on the table and crossed her legs.

"Yes, the latest in this series I'm reading."

The question she had been wanting to ask burst forth. "I went to look for painkillers in your room, and saw that you had blood pressure meds and sleeping pills."

Bàba blinked and put the book down. "I'm not sleeping well. Speaking of which, can you bring it to me? If you're going into the kitchen." Quiet and reserved, the Bàba she always knew.

"Sure." She stopped halfway to the kitchen. "Why didn't you tell me you were back on your meds?"

Bàba jolted as though he'd just been electrified. "It has been a lot."

"I understand. I just wish you—"

"I don't want to talk about it. I don't want to think about the docks. The war. The mer." His sharp tone cut her off, and he turned away, effectively closing himself off.

Angie's head lowered as she entered the kitchen. From the overhead cabinet, she swiped her bottle of multivitamins and Bàba's sleeping pills.

She swallowed two vitamins and then gave Bàba his medication. The pills sat on the table in front of him, but he didn't touch them. Angie breathed in the scent of earth and tobacco, and her heart jumped. They came from the cigars he favored when he was younger.

Māma hated his smoking and the woody, mossy aroma, so he finally kicked the habit to keep her happy a decade ago.

Angie didn't blame him for smoking again. After all, she wanted a drink each time she worked late or fretted over the odd feelings she was developing for Kaden.

Speaking of Kaden. Were they becoming friendly? And what did that mean for them, and for this war they waged?

She would deal with her emotions instead of burying them under a drunken stupor, even if the latter would be easier.

Bàba scratched his stubbly chin. "We also found two of our men and women, drowned and speared. Their dead bodies were thrown back to the coastline." His voice pitch dropped, somber and low. With a listless swipe, he closed his book without bothering to mark the page he read.

Angie's upper lip curled in disgust, reminded of what Kaden said, that the mer would not attack unless the humans did first. The temporary peace was short-lived. "Wait. Were there more mer killed? Before that?"

Bàba sat his book down. "Yes, Nick told me that he and a small group caught another merman, who he said tried to attack them. So, they shot him."

Angie bristled. Unable to stomach anymore talk of dead mer or workers, she put a hand on Bàba's forearm. "Want to get a little fresh air?"

"Mmm, why not." Swallowing his pills, Bàba stood, chair scraping against the floor as he pushed it back. Angie winced at the grating noise. Now she knew he was discombobulated. He wouldn't be caught dead scratching their hardwood floors.

She followed him to brew tea, a cup of strong *pu'er* for him, and hot, white tea with a dash of fresh honey and a sprig of mint for her.

"If you're trying to sleep, that won't help." One of Angie's eyebrows moved into a high arch, and she pushed the porch door open.

"It's either this or bourbon. I'll wake up in a better place if I drink this," he replied, voice gruff.

They sat side by side on rocking chairs, facing the beach and watching the sun cast a golden halo over scattered foam-capped peaks. Since she first became entranced by the sea, the view from the porch was Angie's favorite part of the house.

During her childhood, she and her family would gather on the spacious porch after dinner for conversation and games or movie nights during warmer months. A pang of nostalgia struck of how their gatherings used to be, and a sense of closeness to her Bàba overtook her, knowing she only had a month left in Creston before she returned to the lower forty-eight for school.

At the corner of her eye, Bàba rolled a Cohiba cigar between his thumb and forefinger, staring at it like it held the answer to ending this war, as if contemplating whether or not to light it. He stuffed it back into his pocket.

Angie sighed with relief. Bàba certainly didn't need more detriments to his health with all the stress at the docks and with the war. She crossed her legs and sipped her tea, subtle apple notes and sweet honey rolling smoothly down her esophagus, followed by the aftertaste of cool mint. Beside her, Bàba quietly sipped his own tea.

"Emily and Beau asked to meet me on Friday. They're coming to the docks. Said they wanted to talk about the mer." His voice cut through the silence a moment later.

A thought rolled through Angie's mind. Today was Tuesday, and to her knowledge, the mayor never stopped by on such short notice, except when their son was found dead.

Then again, there were no rules in war.

"Can I come to the meeting, too? I'd like to hear some updates for myself."

Bàba nodded. "Sure. They will be there around zero eight hundred." He rocked his chair back and forth, creaking against the boards. "Are you ready for your PhD program? You worked hard to get here."

"I hope so," Angie murmured. "Haven't had much time to research, there's been too much going on. I guess I'll have to go on the first day of class and wing it."

A long silence followed. Where Angie normally found such silences awkward, now it felt natural and relaxing.

"I will miss you when you go. I hope this situation with the mer will be resolved by then. If there is something I can do to end this without any more deaths, I will. For your sake."

"Thanks, Bàba. That means a lot." A smile pressed against her cheeks. At eleven thirty p.m., the sun was fading, leaving a sky full of deep violet streaks against a navy-blue backdrop, the hazy glow of the leftover sun slipping through cracks in the dark colors.

Bàba's next words chilled her. "Even if I have to make sure every last one of them is dead."

Biting her lip, Angie stared into the horizon. The remainder of the sun vanished, violet and blue blending into obsidian night. Glittery stars filled the sky, clouds parting to unveil the silver moon. Flowing water and frog and insect sounds surrounded them, their soft breathing chiming in harmony with the biophonic chorus.

The air had become a lot colder.

Kaden met her as planned. His tigerseye-hued gaze was fixed on her. "You're looking refreshed today."

"I feel better. Finally got a good nights' sleep, but I still feel like I could sleep an entire day." Or, more apt, she could hibernate like a dormant squirrel or bear in the brutal winters.

Kaden straightened up, his tail flexing. "How about a change of scenery? Here." He pointed to an empty rowboat some feet away from them. Angie had seen it when she passed by to meet Kaden earlier, but she hadn't paid it much attention.

"Here, what? The rowboat? Where did that come from?"

"It appeared abandoned on a nearby island. Nobody seemed to have claimed it for tidesdays, so I guided it here."

"Convenient." Angie scrunched her face.

"I thought so, too. The place I have in mind is some miles from here. You can use that. By swimming under you, I'll use the waves to propel you in the right direction." He gave her a self-satisfied grin.

"Aww." Angie gave him a mock-pout. "No more merman-back rides?"

Kaden stared at her. "What? No! I was exhausted after the first time." He leaned onto his forearms, his lower body still underwater.

"Not used to giving people aquatic piggyback rides?" Angie quirked an eyebrow.

"Well, typically, the most that mer carry while swimming are their children. And parents carry their babies at their fronts up until they're about a year old, so we're not built to carry anything more than about thirty pounds for long distances. Especially not on our backs." Kaden motioned for Angie to get in the boat, and heart thumping from not knowing what to expect, she took her chance and boarded.

He pulled the boat into the water before ducking under it. From beneath her, she caught glimpses of his form. Sunlight winked off each scale on his tail, a brilliant crimson lightshow. The beach disappeared behind her. His grace and agility in the water was a marvel to her, the smooth way he cut sideways, under and over to avoid rocks and buoys.

Minutes later, a mass came into her field of vision. Sheet ice, floating innocently on top of the water. Her boat was moving too fast, and she was going to crash, while Kaden could just duck underneath it.

He probably didn't even see the ice. The boat's nose was inches away, and they were showing no sign of slowing.

Tāmāde!

Instinctively, she climbed overboard and threw herself into the icy seas with a yelp. Everything below her neck numbed in an instant, and her teeth chattered.

To her chagrin, the boat cut sideways and made it safely onto the other side of the thin ice, and stopped. Kaden stuck his head out of the water, questioning her with his eyes. "What are you doing?"

He directed the boat back to her, and with icy blasts still firing through her nerves, she climbed aboard until they reached a tiny island one more mile out.

"You all right?" Kaden used his tail to muscle his way onto the surface after she stepped off the boat. She swore he was fighting back a smile, and she glared at him.

When she found enough breath, she spoke through a clenched jaw. "I thought my stomach was going to fall out of my body after jumping off."

"I would have gotten you around safely, as you saw." Kaden's shoulders shook, a short laugh sputtering from his lips. "But you decided to, quite literally, jump ship."

"You're laughing?" Angie clenched her fists and narrowed her eyes at him, her face scrunched. "Not funny! I didn't know you were going to do that, or if you even knew the ice was there. That was like a water ride from the deepest level of the Hells."

"I knew. But I'm sorry that I could not warn you earlier." Kaden's smile faded, and he pursed his lips. "I've been thinking of what you said. About your mother."

She shivered. "I'm listening."

"I would like to show you her final resting place. It's the least I can do after we took her body from you and denied you peace."

"You would?" Angie sat straighter. "Where is she?" After she asked, it struck her that even if he told her where in the vast ocean it was, it wouldn't hold any meaning for her.

"Over two hundred fathomspans below and—" Kaden stumbled over his words and cut himself off. Angie did the math in her head, converting what she assumed to be fathoms to feet. "In my queendom." He spoke as if forced to reveal something he didn't want to.

Angie's stomach fluttered, and she jerked her head back. "Did you say *queendom?*"

"Well." Kaden rubbed his neck. "It's my parents' queendom, not mine. The mer-king and mer-queen."

The admission rendered her speechless. "So, you're, what, a mer-prince? That's why you kept saying you can talk to your leaders. Why didn't you tell me?" The sun emerged overhead, and she used her hand to shield her eyes from the luminous onslaught.

Kaden tucked his tail on the opposite side of him, basing with one hand on the ground. "At the time, I could not trust you with the truth, could not have your people coming after me to use us for their ends. Obviously, royalty would attract more attention."

Damn him for making sense.

"But if you're a prince, shouldn't you be, you know, spending more time at court? Doing princely things? You're at the surface an awful lot." Angie scratched her chin, thoughtful.

"I do not wish to be at court," he swallowed hard, "nor do I have much desire to be near the mer-king and mer-queen these days."

His fingers tapped his forearm with nervous energy. Angie moved closer, gazing at him with laser focus, and put a hand on his bent elbow. "Kaden?" He swept a fleeting glance over her hand, and she retracted it.

"They have started talking marriage prospects for me, since I am of age. The queendom buzzes with excitement." He said the word *excitement* dripping with disdain.

A jealous pang burned her chest, and Angie forced herself to smother it, failing to understand where it came from. "S-so your parents pick out a wife for you?"

"Yes. When we are old enough, it is customary for our families to go to a seer, who foretells a union and presents them with a list of appropriate mates. In my family, it happens during an engagement ceremony, where the princes and princesses are to narrow down the list to one." Kaden paused for a breath. "I do not wish to attend the event where my family would present me with prospects. They have been actively searching for the seer's recommended mates for the last year. When my parents are in mate-hunting mode, I have no desire to listen to them bombard me with this mermaid name and that one, names that mean nothing to me." His back and arms became taut. "Cyrus is doing his part. He is bonded, and he has agreed to take over once my parents are gone, or should they abdicate the throne."

"Do you ever want to rule?"

"Not unless it were imposed on me. The rest of my family make much better leaders. Simply because they want that power."

"I guess. But if you lead, you can help change things." Angie had always liked the idea of being a leader and having the power to make changes.

"It's something you aspire to?"

"There's a saying, 'be the change you want to see in the world.' I can do that by leading and not always following." The notion of leading one day, whether it was the docks, a research project, or coming up with an innovative product made her flush, exhilarated. "I want to see change happen in our environment and advocate for healthy seas. You can't sit and hope that someone else takes the lead."

Slowly, Kaden nodded. "You've given me some things to think on. Thank you for sharing your perspective."

Another silence befell them, and Angie thought back to what Kaden had said about his parents finding marriage prospects. "Earlier, you said you were of age to find a lifemate. How old are you?"

"Twenty-three."

"Is that old or young in mer years?"

"Young. We live to about a hundred tidesyears." A brief silence.

Ah. They had similar lifespans.

"So." She swore his voice's timbre had lowered, sounding huskier. Angie spun on her backside to face him, crossing her legs. "Humans find their own mates, yes?"

A bundle of nerves inexplicably unraveled. "It depends, I guess. Some people's families pick a partner for them. But yeah, mostly we look for our own."

"You look for your own partners?" Kaden ran one finger along his defined jawline. "How?"

Angie tucked her chin. She never had to explain the concept of dating, and she was worthless with impromptu explanations. "Well, you go on dates, and if you like each other, then you bring it to the next level."

"And what's that?" Kaden closed the distance between them and brought his tail closer to his body.

"Well, if you'd let me finish." Angie chuckled and nudged his shoulder with hers.

"Apologies, do continue."

"Depending on what both people want, they can agree to a committed relationship. They can make it purely physical. Or they can live together. Or get married, and if they want, have kids." She thought of what else to say. "If they later decide they don't want to be together, they break up."

He relaxed his pose, his torso falling away from her. "So, it is courting, then. We court our potential mates, as well, when we've chosen a match during our engagement events."

"Can't imagine having my life chosen for me."

"This is our tradition," Kaden replied. "I just choose not to partake in it."

"Don't blame you. I wouldn't either. Oh, and I just wanted to let you know, our mayor—uh, our leader—is coming on Friday. They're meeting with my bàba, and I'm going to join them."

"That's good news. What are you planning on saying to them?" Kaden had pulled his shoulders back, rapt.

"My family seems pretty set on shooting you all on sight. And my bàba is close to our leaders. If I can talk some sense into them, something might actually come of it. I'll let you know what happens." A cold, passing breeze greeted her, and Angie shivered, despite sitting beneath the evening sun's rays. She tightened her light jacket around herself and brought her knees closer.

"You are cold?"

"What gave that away?" Angie grinned and shook her head.

"You don't have much body fat, except for your chest." He pointed at her jacket. "No wonder you have to wear layer upon layer to stay warm. What is that part underneath the waist called?"

"My hips? You're saying I have big hips?" She sat ramrod straight, crossing and uncrossing her legs as she waited for his answer.

"Not big. They look, erm." Kaden flushed pink. "Well rounded. Healthy. Like the rest of you."

"I can't tell if you're insulting or complimenting me!" Angie exclaimed with mock-incredulity, dramatically putting a hand over her chest.

"It was meant as a compliment."

"Alright, wisecracker. How do you supposedly have so much body fat keeping you warm in zero-degree waters?"

Kaden's lips twitched before he cracked a small smile. "We have smaller organs. Hence why we do not appear as if we have much body fat, but we do have a thin layer beneath our skin. Helps keep us warm."

"Makes sense. But how do you breathe underwater with your nostrils open? And see without the saltwater burning your eyes?" Angie hadn't meant to stare and examine him like a specimen for one of her marine biology classes, but she couldn't help herself.

Kaden flared his nose as if to prove a point. "My eyes are covered with a protective lens when I'm in the water. And my nostrils close as well. I don't need them to breathe."

"Ah! So, similar to a sea lion. Or a walrus." She was proud of herself for how much she remembered from her college courses.

"You—uh, those are the first animals you would compare me to?" Kaden blew out an amused huff.

"I'm not saying you look like them!"

"Right. I believe that. Now, are you done critiquing my appearance?"

"If you're done critiquing mine," Angie fired back with a smirk. "You may have all those special adaptations to live in the sea, but at least I have legs and can walk on land."

"Oh!" Kaden doubled over, shoulders shaking with hearty laughter. "And yet with all the grace and speed you may have on land, you will never be as so in the water. Or be able to breathe without your bulky contraptions."

"The downfall of having legs instead of a big old fish tail and no gills." She clucked her tongue, cheeks practically pushing against her eyes while she laughed with him. It felt good, the lighthearted tone their conversation took. Her spirits lifted.

"We adapt to our environments, yes? Except your hair. Does it not get caught on things around you? What is the advantage to having hair so long and unbound?" Kaden's eyes roved from the top of her head down to where her hair ended at her waist.

"I don't make it a habit to whip my hair around in places where it might get snagged." Angie scooped up a small handful of cold sand and flicked it at his chest. "And I like the way it looks. It also keeps my neck warm."

He brushed the grit off, his face still upturned. Then he flicked the sand back at her, bouncing off her nose, and she wrinkled it. "Long, loose hair like yours can attract the attention of *qisainman*. Or *liuyeyu* if you're deep enough. They could mistake stray locks of hair for delicious fish. I would know."

He slowed down when he said the fish names, and by piecing together the words, Angie got "lampreys" and "lancetfish."

"Why, you used to have long, flowing hair too?" She tried envisioning him with waist-length locks, like hers, and the vision made her chuckle to herself.

Nope, it wouldn't suit him. She preferred him with his short, full head of hair.

"Nearly had my hair ripped off my head once, when I grew it past my shoulders. Almost got sucked in by a giant *zhangyu*. I'll never forget how scary its eight tentacles looked." Kaden drew his shoulders to his ears, then dropped them.

Angie jumped in her own skin at the notion. She imagined being dragged into a web of tentacles eager to make her their owner's dinner, and she jutted her chin forward, pressing her lips together. "How did you get out?"

"A lot of thrashing, prying the suckers off, then using a stray piece of coral to jab at it until it released me. Never swam so fast." Kaden's nose crinkled. "Learned my lesson to keep my hair short. Most of us do, or tied into tight braids or whichever other style they desire. Coral and rocks and their rough edges are a danger too. You never know which way the currents will take you."

She brushed leftover sand off her pants. "What's the point of having hair on your head, and eyebrows?"

"Blunt with the questions, are we?" Kaden had moved even closer so his tail touched her legs. "Sexual selection among the mer. Thicker hair and eyebrows are more desirable in a potential mate. For us, it signals health and fertility." His face was inches from hers, and she sucked in a short breath. His eyes gazed at her lips, and she parted them to take another breath of brisk air.

Silence descended, her senses zeroing in on him. His nearness and clean scent, the warmth emanating from his skin, breaths deep and relaxed, clear eyes hooded.

His nose bumped hers, but he stopped and appeared paralyzed by indecision. Still, she wanted to know what their lips meeting would feel like.

No, she couldn't. Whatever would happen would lead to nowhere good.

Walruses singing in the distance drifted to her, chimes and hoots riding on gusts of wind spurting by.

She turned her head away before his lips touched hers.

Kaden broke eye contact with her and pressed his hands to his temples. Angie stole a glance at him, the disappointment in his expression clear.

When she stepped foot onto Creston Harbor's soil, Angie picked up her pace, boots clacking against the wooden planks while she ran to the ferry terminal.

"Next time." Kaden spoke before she moved too far from him. "I'll show you your mother's resting place."

She stopped, and turned to face him. "How? She's underwater. Is she buried under the sand, or something?"

Kaden wiggled his eyebrows at her. "We have burial grounds. I will show you. But you must promise me one thing."

"What's that?"

"It's for your eyes only. Please do not speak of it with anyone."

She thought about it, sure she would want to take pictures, but she didn't want to squander this opportunity. Angie gave him a brief nod and smile before continuing toward the terminal. Excitement and anxiety warred within her at the prospect.

Her nerves tingled, spreading a toasty sensation through her body, despite the wind's chilly ribbons winding around her. The sun transitioned from luminous golden to radiant orange-crimson.

New feelings bubbled to the surface, veering from intense magnetism to hesitation and caution. These had lain dormant until now, wiggling out to smack her across the face.

She brushed the tangled feelings away and would sort them later. Still, her heart fluttered with anticipation at possibly seeing Māma.

For now, she had one hour to get home on a trip that normally took her two.

Twenty-One

THE DAY SHE WOULD SEE MĀMA arrived. Angie met Kaden, her diving equipment at the ready. She sat at the end of the small pier where he had comforted her the other day while she cried. It was the perfect place to begin a dive. "Wait, how far down are we going? Do I need Heliox—" She was breathless and tingling all over, a tangled web of nerves. Hope and try as she may, she couldn't suppress it. They were much too close to the docks proper for her liking, but Kaden appeared unbothered, swimming back and forth in front of her. A quick glance revealed the space around them was empty.

"Not at all," Kaden said with a knowing smile. The waters were clear and calm, inviting her to jump in. "I can give you sight and breath, so you will be able to see and breathe as I do. Should we encounter other mer, you will be able to understand our language."

Angie blinked. "How?" She scanned the endless sea imagining where Māma could be. "What is this—this magic?"

"A blessing from our Goddesses and God, for the intention of protection, and to promote harmony between humans and mer."

"How long will it last?" Angie asked in awe. She struggled to wrap her mind around what he just said, and narrowed her eyes at him. "How do you give it to me? And how are we going to avoid other mer?"

"Okay, one question at a time. It will only be trouble if we encounter a sentinel, or palace workers. I will take you to where it is most desolate, so the chances are lessened. And the gift lasts for a full tidesday. As for your other question." He paused, resting his hands on his tail. "I would press my lips to yours and give you breath."

"We have to kiss?"

"Only briefly. Mere seconds." His forehead wrinkled. "Or I could just let you stress me out until I release it inadvertently, but I'd rather not go that route."

"Uh, I can dive. It's-it's not a big deal." Her heart leaped around her chest, and she thought if she suppressed the warm and fuzzy feelings long enough, they would quench.

Kissing him, even for a second, would pull those feelings to the surface.

"All that gear would slow you down, and the mer are on high alert for divers. Are you interested in my offer?" Kaden leaned in, his tailfin tensing and curling upward. "No hard feelings if you are not. We can come back when you are ready. Or if you prefer to dive."

Angie racked her mind. She did want to see Māma, more than anything. If what Kaden said was true, and she could be in the sea unburdened…

"Okay, fine. Give me a minute to get my drysuit, at least. I don't want my clothes to get wet. And my flippers to help me swim."

"You won't need flippers. You'll see what I mean," Kaden assured her.

Angie stepped into her crushed neoprene drysuit and zipped it up with hurried hands. She pulled out the last lock of hair stuck inside the collar.

"Ready." She sat cross legged in front of him.

He put a hand on her face. She closed her eyes and parted her lips.

Kaden pushed his mouth to hers, exhaled deep, and pulled back. Quick and passionless, a simple transaction. Angie clutched at herself, rubbing her elbows, her heart feeling like it shrank into a small ball.

She forced herself to ignore the sensation. No, she hadn't wanted him to really kiss her.

Had she?

Then a calming warmth bloomed in her, flowing through her blood and lungs. "What is this feeling? The magic? I feel hot. How does—how does all this work? What is it doing to me?"

"That's normal. The magic will affect your lungs so they essentially act as gills, and shield your eyes from the salt. Just breathe normally when you're undersea. Your blood will be warmed, and it will soon travel to your vocal cords and ears—"

As if by cue, her throat and ears heated, and her hand flew to her neck.

"So you can speak and hear unhindered."

"Okay, got it." She wanted to ask more about the magic, but she didn't want to waste time on land. Māma was waiting for her, somewhere down there.

"Let's go." He took her hand and used his tail to push himself off the ground. She followed suit and attempted to mimic his form, his back and tail arched into a perfect semicircle. They landed into the water, slicing through the waves like two knives. Angie caused a light splash where Kaden didn't make a noise as they broke the barrier between air and sea.

Damn it, she should have put on a hood or her flippers and gloves. Why did she listen to Kaden about not putting on flippers?

She hovered near the surface, and tried taking a breath through her nose. It felt like breathing on land, and not even bubbles escaped her lips when she exhaled.

Okay, so the magic worked, and she shook her head slowly and in disbelief.

Her drysuit did its job of keeping her body warm, but most shocking, she didn't feel the glacial water's sting on her exposed skin. Nor did it feel warm. The temperature was neutral, comfortable. Her hair fanned out around her head, flowing with the sea's constant sway.

Kaden leaned into her. "Next time, make sure you tie your hair back. We're going deep."

"I can hear you perfectly." She gasped, and then surprised herself when her own voice came out clear as if she were projecting it through thin air. It wasn't muffled, and she could articulate clearly, and her body vibrated with her words. "Is this because of that magic?"

They moved toward the ocean's twilight zone, and Angie stopped several feet down, preparing to equalize; however, there was no pressure in her ears or sinuses, so she kept swimming with Kaden. Her arms circled before her in a broad breaststroke, and she flutter-kicked behind her, breaking through the water's resistance. Even without flippers, she felt more streamlined and smooth when swimming.

Kaden paused before the sun stopped illuminating the world beneath. Finally answering her, he confirmed her suspicion. He winced, his hands flying to his chest.

"What's wrong?"

"A slight ache in my lungs. It's where we store our magic, and it happens when we grant landwalkers the gift. The pain will fade."

Her eyebrows creased with concern. "I just don't want you to die while I'm down here. I'll be lost and wouldn't know how to help you."

He took her other hand and turned her around to face him, his grip tightening. "I'll be fine."

Angie nodded, and her neck tipped back as she took in her surroundings. Her eyes didn't sting from the salt, and she saw as well as if she had her scuba mask on. At least, before it fogged.

Still, the seas were unnervingly devoid of life.

Save for a stray sea lion who passed through, stopping briefly to assess them before moving on. The seabed started sloping downward, and when Angie peered over, Kaden's tail kicked up a large rock, sweeping it down the slope. It bounced and dropped into an endless abyss.

Angie gulped. It was a reminder of just how vast, how deep, and how mysterious the sea was.

A forceful current barreled into her and swept her out. She grasped Kaden's forearms to stay in place, and he reached around her waist, pulling her flush against him.

"Kaden." His name came out breathy and gentle. Their noses brushed together, and his long, thick lashes fluttered with a quick blink. Her head swam like a gallivanting fish, and she pulled back. A beam of sunlight filtered through, bathing him in an ethereal light. His eyes lit like they held a sunset within. He looked so natural—of course he did, this was his home—and she hated to admit, he was stunning.

The waves swept back his thick, jet-black hair, and his cheeks glowed under piercing blades of sunlight. His eyes roved over her face, as if taking in and memorizing each of her features. His muscles tensed as he slid one hand to the base of her skull.

"I—" Angie struggled to find her next words.

"Is something wrong?"

"I'm afraid if we do this, I won't be able to hold myself back anymore. I'm already feeling things I don't want to feel."

"What makes you think I'm not feeling the same?" Kaden reached behind her and ran a lock of her hair through his fingers. "I have been wanting to do this for a while. If you would allow me, I would like to kiss you. An actual kiss, this time."

She had hardly finished saying, "Okay," when a small noise of pleasure escaped her throat once he lowered his head and locked her lips with his. Her eyes drifted close, and she wrapped her arms around his neck, deepening their kiss. Blood rushed into her ears, pounding inside and making her feel as if she temporarily lost her senses, all but her sense of touch. Kaden's skin was pearl-like under her fingertips, his lips sensual and pillowy as they moved with hers.

As they floated in the water, he wrapped his tail around her legs, keeping her close. Her mouth opened in tandem with his, tongues searching until they entangled with one another. Kaden pulled back, purportedly for a breath. Even though he breathed through his gills.

Wanting, no, needing more, Angie cupped his cheeks and pulled him to her again. He tasted of sharp salt, burning and puckering her lips, but she couldn't get enough.

She put one hand on his neck, and he jerked his head back, wincing.

Her finger poked one of his gills while it opened. "I'm sorry! Are you okay?"

"I will live." A chuckle rumbled through his chest. "It's, ah, sensitive there."

"I'll—well, I'll put my hand…" She fumbled around the base of his neck and his shoulders. He took her hand and interlaced her fingers with his.

His free hand slid up to her neck, his fingers tangled in her hair, and he kissed her again. Blissful delirium overtook her until she had to take a breath, panting when their mouths parted, their bodies pressed flush.

"While I want to do this all day," he whispered against her lips where a contented smile played, "I promised to show you to your mother."

"Yeah, let's g-get going." Her tongue was no longer tangled with his, but she found herself tongue-tied all the same. He methodically unwound his tail from her legs.

A Dungeness crab skittered by, its large claw narrowly missing her face, and she twisted her torso to the side. She clung to his hand as they descended deeper, deeper, deeper.

A new sensation emerged. She smelled everything around her: whiffs of the salty tang of the sea and the earthy aroma of sediment. The scents were a welcome change from her rubber scuba mask.

The uneven edges of emerald and crimson seaweed blades brushed against her, soft whispers tickling her bare hands and feet. The sensation was acute and so close on her skin, and a thrill raced through her limbs.

The seafloor became sparser, her surroundings ever darker as they plunged further into the midnight zone.

Thank goodness she trusted Kaden, and didn't use her equipment.

And then from the suffocating darkness, golden light emerged. She tightened her grip on Kaden's hand, and she observed and soaked in the sight before her. The light brightened, spotlighting a magnificent, gold and silver multi-tiered pagoda-like structure on the seafloor, its height and width rivaling a sea knoll. The ground level hugged an open archway, and each level above it had rocky balconies protruding from the sides. Stone pillars lined the eaves, wrapping around the structure's outer walls. A grand courtyard, with a floor of smooth sea glass stretching for days, lay sprawled before the palace's sweeping entrance, elaborate coral in the shape of a tree adorning its center. The building was flanked on two sides by carved coral and stone.

She had seen pagodas when she was younger, but to see one of this scale, and underwater, no less, stunned her into awe and reverent silence.

Smooth coral puzzles climbed the rock walls at her side, and she flinched as it snagged a lock of hair.

She was definitely tying it back next time.

"What is this place?" She glided over it alongside Kaden. "It's beautiful!"

"My family's queendom and towns. And that is our palace. Once they were visible to all, welcoming sea animals to live among us. But as landwalker exploration became more widespread, threatening sea life and us and our home, we made the decision to shroud our lands from the human eye. You are the first to see it in over three centuries."

Angie went completely still. "That's why the mer seemed to disappear."

"Yes, we have lived among you all this time."

She turned her attention back to the palace. "How did you shroud it?"

"There is an invisible barrier that surrounds it. Magic maintains it." He pointed above her head. "Like that mermaid is doing. She's one of the five oracles who protect the palace."

Angie looked up. A single mermaid with a metallic blue tail swam high, and stopped. She put one hand to her lips and reached upward, a golden flicker of light bursting from her palm, and disappearing in a second. Then she darted off.

"How often do they maintain it? If it surrounds all this." She motioned to the palace with her hand. "It must be huge."

"There are ten oracles per tidesday for this region, and they rotate daily." Kaden made a noise, as if he were going to say more. He didn't.

Angie looked back to the palace. Mer swam in and out of the structure, their tails a rainbow in the dark. Splotches of green moss decorated the structure's sides, and curious, vibrant fish and a stray octopus zipped about.

"I've thought about what you said. About being the change you want to see in the world," Kaden admitted. "I agree. I would rule if I had to. But I still don't desire it."

"Not everyone wants to lead. That's okay." She put a reassuring hand on his forearm.

Another pod of mermen and mermaids came into view on the palace's side, their tail-ends pointed to Angie and Kaden. They swam around a stone formation reminiscent of undersea mountain ranges, decorated with lively corals and emerald-hued sea moss, and partially shadowed in the deep sea's gloom. One by one, the pod swam into a grotto and disappeared.

"Will anyone see us?" She bit her lip, hesitant to draw closer.

"No. We will not go into the palace proper, and I know where we will not be spotted. Or, where there are mer I can trust not to utter a peep. Your mother's resting place is not far from here." He gave her hand a gentle tug when she stopped to gawk at an oblong, sandy brown fish with a scaleless, limp body, slithering by without a care in the world.

A ragfish. Angie counted her lucky stars. If only she had a camera to capture this once-in-a-lifetime moment.

"We have towns and villages scattered throughout the region, and our territory stretches from north of here to three thousand nautical miles south."

"That's a lot of land. Or water? It looks like Atlantis," she said once they were out of earshot of the mer. "Or maybe, Pacifica?" She angled her head and caught the teasing grin tugging at Kaden's full lips.

"It could be the Pacific Ocean's version of it." They circled around the back of the palace.

"Does Atlantis exist?" His comment piqued Angie's interest.

"I've heard stories, but I haven't been there yet, myself," he replied. "These." He turned his body around so they faced each other, his long tail circling her. "Are the burial grounds. Your mother is this way. Come, look down."

Beneath were rows upon rows of long coffins, each brushed with golds and silvers and embellished with characters she didn't recognize. A tombstone and coffin in the same structure, packed together with an inch of space between them.

Of course, the mer didn't need to walk between coffins.

Kaden slowed down once they hovered above the burial grounds, and Angie followed, slowing her steady kicking.

"The royal sentinels and their family are tucked in this corner." He gestured with one arm to a blocked off corner to their northeast, boxed in with dense, clear material. His voice cracked. "Some of our sentinels' bodies were never retrieved after we lost them."

She squeezed his hand. "I'm sorry."

"You were not responsible for their deaths." Kaden slowed to a stop. With quick flicks of his tail, he descended upon a coffin lining the burial ground's easternmost border. It looked no different than the rest, but Angie's heart filled to the brim, overwhelmed with emotions.

Her wide-open eyes met with Māma's closed ones, and she jolted. From the shoulders up, she was visible through clear glass, a window to her peaceful, eternally sleeping face.

"Māma." She laid a flat palm on the window. The tears she'd been holding back sprang forth, swept away by the sea's watery grasp.

Kaden tugged on her hand, bringing himself closer to her. "Do you need a moment?"

"Yeah." Angie sniffled. Kaden bowed his head and let go, leaving her to float alone. She relished the stillness, the silence, the peace. Māma looked exactly as she did when Angie saw her last, and after two years, her lovely face was still intact.

"Māma," she whispered again. "Why did you let yourself go? What were you thinking?" Angie reached down and laid her hand over Māma's cheek once more. "I miss you so much. I'm glad you're resting where you're happiest." With a quick breaststroke of her arms, she moved down head first and grabbed the sides of the coffin to pull herself closer. She pressed her lips to the glass where Māma's forehead was.

Her mind leaped to alerting Bàba. He would be glad to have closure.

Then she'd have to tell him how she found Māma, and she wasn't ready to have that conversation with him.

Still, she'd bring it up at the right time. She hated the thought of disregarding the promise she made to Kaden, but Bàba deserved to know.

She calmed and folded her arms over her chest, her feet paddling in quick, small motions to keep from sinking or ascending.

"Māma, I hope wherever you are, you're not hurting anymore. That you reincarnated into something beautiful." She bowed her head, mouthing a silent mantra of peace and wishing her well in the afterlife. Or in her new body, wherever her spirit may be, and wishing for her ancestors to continue taking care of Māma.

When enough time passed, she called for Kaden.

"I'm here." He reappeared from the dark and stopped beside her, their arms brushing. Angie wanted to get closer, given the passion of their kiss earlier, but he was busy looking at Māma. "I can see the resemblance between you two." His gills opened. "This row is due for their renewal ceremonies. I have to let my family know."

"Renewal ceremony? Will my mom get one too?"

"Absolutely. When we entomb those who have passed onto the next realm, their family gathers before the coffin is closed. If they had no family, seers and oracles will come with their acolytes instead, and invite any mer who desire to join. They perform a traditional song and dance to allow the soul to depart into the afterlife." He reached for her hand again and stroked her palm with his thumb. The motion sent excited tingles running to her wrist and up her forearm. "Every few years, the bodies are re-dressed in traditional burial garb, and the song and dance are performed again. Though the body is an empty vessel, they are still respected and honored as they were at the time of their passing."

"Must be time-consuming. There are like hundreds, if not a thousand tombs." Her lips thinned, thinking of going through each coffin one by one, performing a ceremony over and over. Her head spun.

"We limit the number of coffins at a single burial ground to ensure adequate participation in our ceremonies and prevent the oracles, seers and acolytes fatiguing. This town is smaller, and larger towns have larger burial grounds, and more seers and oracles."

"Thank you for showing me. I appreciate it more than you know." Another surge of emotion brought more tears to her eyes, and she swept her fingertips along his cheek. He placed his sturdy hand over hers.

"You are welcome." He brushed underneath her eyes, even though the seawater stole her fallen tears. She wanted to go home, sit alone with her thoughts and memories for a time.

"Can we go back to the surface? I want to stay, but I have to get home."

Kaden nodded. "Follow me."

When they broke the surface, Angie had no idea what time it was. She recognized the dock's main gangway, a blurry speck down the coastline. Kaden sighed blissfully and touched her face, running his other hand down the length of her back, and then she climbed ashore. "Angie." Her name from his lips was a sweet, thrilling sound. "Same time, same place, tomorrow?" His voice rose with hopefulness. Kaden leaned in, flashing her what she assumed to be his most winning smile. It was gorgeous and enticing, but it didn't sway her.

"Not tomorrow. I'm off, but I have plans with my sister, and she took the day off to spend with me. How about the day after?" She sat on her knees.

"Ah, fine. The day after it is, then." His chest deflated, and he propped himself up on his forearms. "You asked me once why I kept going to the surface. I didn't tell you the entire reason why."

"Because you didn't want to be engaged to a mermaid you didn't know?" Angie raised one eyebrow. Where was he going with this?

"Partially. I also hoped to see you. I found you beautiful, if not off-putting from the moment I met you." He jerked one shoulder back, as if anticipating her reaction.

"What? Off-putting?" Angie folded her arms across her chest, throwing him an I-dare-you-to-keep-talking look. He didn't take her signal.

"We didn't start off on the best of terms." Kaden pointed to his now-healed shoulder, where she'd shot him previously. "But!" He raised his hands as Angie gasped and made a sudden movement toward him. "That feeling has long passed."

"Two tidesdays." Before she could say something else, he flashed her a sly, mischievous smile and dove back into the ocean.

Twenty-Two

Enjoy your day off.
Don't focus on the eleven-hour shift awaiting you tomorrow.

Angie repeated the two thoughts to herself, over and over.

Three more workers quit out of fear yesterday, and Bàba and Nick were growing desperate.

She forced herself to focus on the rest of today as she stepped off the bus, making the ten-minute walk to Mia's apartment.

The late afternoon brought golden sunlight on her head, the warmest day of the summer so far at sixty degrees.

The memories of the underwater world, seeing Māma again, and kissing Kaden came upon her. A hot flush crept over her cheeks at the memory of his mouth moving over hers and the taste of his tongue for too brief a time. His sturdy hands had cupped her waist and pulled her close so they were chest to chest, his tail wrapping around her to stop her from floating away with the currents. Never had she felt so safe, so content, and so warm in subzero waters.

She rang Mia's doorbell, and immediately, her sister flung the door open. Mia reached around Angie's shoulders and squeezed. Angie returned the hug before removing her shoes and stepping inside. "Glad you made it!"

"Yeah, almost didn't make the bus here. It came five minutes early and was about to take off on me," Angie grumbled. "But glad I made it, too."

Unlike their roomy and airy family home, Mia and Nick's Parisian-style, cosmopolitan house in downtown Creston felt so constraining and sparsely decorated. Mia said Nick lived a simplistic lifestyle, and over their years together, she followed suit. White walls and tall windows surrounded her, making Angie feel small and exposed. The couches, ottoman, and circular coffee table in front of an electric fireplace sat too close together.

Still, their sparkly, unique chandeliers always stood out to Angie. Most notably, the one appearing to be of four discs held together by three cords. They had picked it out together.

A simpler time. Angie had been on the cusp of twenty, and Māma had gone with them. The last time the three of them were together before she left for college.

Because it was Mia's home, Angie considered it hers too, by extent. They kept the place impeccably clean, not a speck of dirt to be found despite their young daughter living there.

"Want a cup of tea? Rooibos?" Mia smoothed out her sea-green terry cloth robe, slippers shuffling along the parquet floors in the foyer.

"Sure, I'm not picky." Angie helped Mia grab the box of tea in the overhead cabinet. Dark circles swelled beneath Mia's eyes, and her hair was tied back into a short ponytail. Not a trace of makeup on her pale face, and she yawned while brewing two cups of vanilla rooibos tea.

She seemed tired. Not much different than Angie felt at the weeks' end. They sat a foot apart on the living room couch, their teacups resting on small porcelain plates. "Mia."

"Hmm?" Mia rubbed her eyes.

"Is this a bad time?"

"No, I'm the one who asked. I'm glad you made it. Wait, I already said that, didn't I? I really am glad."

Angie cocked an eyebrow. Her words came out slow, pitched with concern. "Is everything okay, though?"

A pause ensued before Mia answered. "Nick took Rosie to his parents' for the weekend. I wanted the house to myself for a bit. Spend some time with you." She shifted her weight. "I'm beat. Can't this shit with the mer to end already? Drop a bomb on them or something, just wipe them from existence." Her fingers pinched around the teacup handle.

Angie stopped breathing for a moment, and her chest tightened in response. "I hope we'll never have to go that far."

Mia shook her head. "Don't you feel it, working there? It's getting worse. I barely see my own husband anymore, and Rosie misses her dad. He's always working, and when he's finally home, we're lucky if he can sit down for dinner and stay awake long enough to hold a conversation. I can't remember the last time we went on a proper date." She choked on her last words, her voice thick.

Now Angie understood. "Believe me, I want this to be over too. But we can't give up now. Otherwise, we'll never get our fish back. The docks will go bankrupt, and our village will starve." Her thoughts turned to Kaden. The mere thought of Mia's suggestion becoming reality sent her into a panic.

"I want my husband back. I'm sick and tired of worrying about him. He isn't eating properly, and he's on medication. He's so angry all the time, talking and cursing in French and walks around like something's brewing beneath the surface, and he'll blow any second. All he talks about is the mer, and he hates them with a passion I've never seen him have for anything in over a decade of being with him." She clenched her teeth.

Angie paled. Did Bàba know Nick was getting like this? She would ask him later. "I'm sorry he's acting like that. He always came off to me like—" Angie wrinkled her nose, tried to think of the proper words. "Annoying, sometimes insensitive. Like he always has to one-up you. Macho. But never explosive." She side-eyed Mia. "Was he?"

"No! It's like getting a taste of power has turned him, I don't know, ambitious? If ambition was on steroids." A thunderstorm reflected in Mia's features. "He mentioned once that he felt like he didn't have much say in his family, growing up. He was the second youngest of five. Not that it's an excuse." She buried her face in her hands. "I go to work, come home, take care of Rosie. Then on top of that, I worry about Nick. I had to be away from them for a couple days to settle myself. Feel like I'm going nuts."

Angie set her lips in a tight line and moved to sit next to her.

"I feel like he's a shadow of the man I married, like we're drifting further apart. At least he's still trying to be a good dad." Mia twisted her wedding ring.

The concept of shitty husband, but good father stumped Angie. Māma and Bàba taught them and exemplified that part of a parent's job was to teach their kids how to respect and love the people in their lives. She held her tongue. This was about Mia's feelings, not hers.

"Thanks for listening. Helps to get it out." Mia still fiddled with her diamond. "But how are you holding up?"

"Well, Bàba and Nick have me working overtime by default now. Some days I can barely remember what I just ate, and I can't think straight half the time."

"You can say no, you know. They can't force you." Mia sat back and folded her arms over her chest. "Bàba would work all day and night if he had to. That's how he is."

Bàba believed in hard work over play and rest which would happen post-retirement.

"Just because he works fourteen-hour days doesn't mean you have to. Well, I guess now it's sixteen-hour days since Everett quit, right?"

"I know, but I'm here to help Bàba and get experience. Sometimes there's too much work for me to finish in eight hours. How would it look if I kept leaving on time while he's forced to stay until past dinnertime, or go in before breakfast?" Angie lamented the thought.

"I suppose. You're a grown woman, it's your choice. Remember you can say no." Mia sat back upright, her features hardening again. "The mer deserve whatever awful thing happens to them. You're at the forefront every day. Promise you'll be careful and never let those fishes get you, okay?"

Angie nodded, mute.

Mia draped her arm around her shoulders and pulled her close.

They sat in silence. Angie mulled over Mia's words, her chest tightening with dread.

TWENTY-THREE

THE ELEVEN-HOUR WORKDAY ARRIVED, AND ANGIE stepped out for her lunch break much later than normal. She sat alone on a bench overlooking the shoreline. Close enough to take in the calming, rhythmic roll of the waves, but far enough away to stay out of sight of any passing mer.

Despite the serenity, the absence of squawking gulls and terns circling the blue struck a discordant chord in her. The skies were as silent as the seas.

She unzipped her light jacket, taking another bite of her steamed bun, the soft, fluffy texture hugging salty, chewy pork and leek inside. She made a small batch last night, just enough to tie her over for a day, using Māma's classic recipe, and after a quick reheat this morning, it was still fresh and delicious. Where she normally had two buns per meal, today she had one, supplemented with a handful of pickled cucumbers.

Angie tried her best not to think of the tasks awaiting her after lunch. Not only did she have to help inspect all the perennially docked boats and take inventory in their many warehouses, now the task of organizing and maintaining their file systems fell to her as well.

Stop it. Focus on your break or you'll drive yourself insane.

She looked out to the seaside, where much of it was blocked off by ropes to prevent workers from wandering too close to the water. She grimaced.

A demanding squawk came from a gray and white herring gull who landed at her feet, cocking its head. Angie pursed her lips, and ripped off a piece of her only bun. The gull opened its yellow beak and eagerly snatched it. It looked upward, loud squawks belying its minute size, and seemingly out of nowhere, more gulls appeared.

Angie smiled to herself. Gulls' ability to smell food from miles away never failed to surprise her. "Alright. You win." She picked off the bread from her bun and tossed them to the birds, leaving her to eat only the filling. The gulls dispersed, leaving the skies silent once more.

"Hope you don't mind the company." Stefan plopped down next to her. Angie took too big of a bite and swallowed quickly, coughing and swallowing hard again to get the meat lump down. Stefan reached out to slap her upper back. "You okay?"

"Ate too fast." Angie coughed again and took a big swig of water.

"Don't go dying on me now."

"Hah. Trying not to. What's going on?"

"I was taking a walk and got a whiff of those steamed buns. Something about it is uniquely yours and your dad's. Figure chatting with you beats walking around in circles." Stefan winked at her. Angie side-eyed it as she finished her lunch, her stomach growling. "Was that you or me?"

"Me." Angie pulled out a tissue from the travel pack in her jacket and wiped her hands. "Why were you walking around in circles?"

"Beats thinking about how hungry I am. We're being conservative with what we still have in the house. So we're skipping breakfast and lunch." Stefan leaned forward, resting his elbows on his knees. "Since we don't go out for dive lessons anymore and business has been slow at the shop, Ken and I were thinking of going for our own dive today. See if any boats were going out, since there haven't been any mer attacks in a while. Thought it might be safe. But, there's that." He gestured to the blockade by the shore. "Could be why they haven't attacked. Anyway, we stayed and enjoyed the beautiful day. Ken went to chat with Nick and some of the guys."

"Beautiful day?" Angie raised a dubious eyebrow. "The sky is a giant cloud, and it looks like it's going to rain any minute."

"Hate sunny days! It bothers my eyes, and I burn like crazy. We get way too much daylight now as it is. This keeps up, and I'll turn into a lobster." His words carried a scornful intonation. "The first one we've seen around here in months."

Angie chuckled, acknowledging the sad reality.

Stefan rubbed the stubble on his jawline. "The seas are looking rough." He motioned with his head toward the choppy, scattered waves merging into one another. Angie twitched at the mention, but said no more. They both knew its meaning, that mer were likely lurking.

"Yeah." She cleared her throat. Though they were obscured from the mer seeing them, she asked, "Should we move farther away?"

Stefan stood and she followed as they relocated at a safer distance.

"How are the grandkids?"

Stefan followed on Angie's purposeful tangent without missing a beat. "They flew back to Juneau. Speaking of the no-lobster problem, they said seafood prices were too high there. Looks like they're feeling the shortage, too."

Angie's muscles went rigid. "It's getting worse, isn't it?"

They slipped back into a tense silence. A breeze passed, plastering a lock of hair on Angie's face. She brushed it off.

Two dock workers walked near the blockade, picking things up from the ground and shoving the contents into a large bag.

Stefan spoke from behind her. "What's going on? Why are they so close to the water?"

"My dad and Nick are sending out a lot of cleanup crews. They found traps around. One of the maintenance crew ladies got caught on caltrops made from coral. It blended in with the sand. She was going with her crew to fix up the gangway."

Stefan stared, riveted. "So, what happened?"

"Her crew was quick enough to get her out. Then they bailed."

Stefan let out his breath in an audible *woosh*.

Returning her attention to the two dock workers, Angie noted they were getting too close to the blockade and into the danger zone.

"Angie—"

"Hold on." Angie had taken five steps in their direction before they changed course and moved away from the blockade. Her shoulders dropped.

The other worker stepped forward, her leading leg sunk beneath the sand. She screamed, dropping her bag and clawing in front of her, a futile attempt in staying above ground.

Angie broke into a full-on sprint, nearing the end of the dock when wood met ground and eventually sand. She was so close, so close.

A tidal wave twice as tall as Angie roared upward, and as if pushed by an unseen force, sped toward the coastline and crashed over the stuck worker, drowning out her cry for help.

The mer were here. One navy blue and one storm gray tail arched above the water before disappearing again. They looked much too close to the shoals.

Her colleague flailed his arms and bolted to where the stuck worker had been. The water receded, and she was gone, dragged into the ocean's depths.

"No, come back!" Angie cupped her hands around her mouth and shouted as loud as her lungs would allow. The male worker skidded to a stop, eyes wide and mouth agape.

To Angie's relief, he ran in her direction, toward the docks.

A jagged lance ripped through his chest, and with a choked gurgle, he fell facedown. Angie dropped to her hands and knees, breaths coming out in quick huffs, arms shaking and leg muscles tightening so much they cramped.

"Angie!" Stefan yelled behind her, pulling her to her feet.

What had come over her? It wasn't the first time she had seen her colleagues fall to the mer, but this was the first time she'd seen someone killed in front of her.

She wasn't prepared for the visceral reaction it invoked. Her heart hammered, mingled with a high-pitched ringing in her ears that temporarily deafened her.

And Kaden was the murderous mer's prince. The gentle, handsome mer with sturdy hands and velvety lips and skin and a sleek, beautiful maroon tail.

She loathed to think that he played a part in ordering the attack. The notion sickened her and made her retch, bringing tears to her eyes. Stefan shouted into her ear. "We have to go! We have to tell your dad and Nick!"

Angie snapped out of it, short tremulous inhales and exhales making her hyperventilate. "O-okay. Okay. Okay." She kept repeating it. If she believed it enough, she might eventually feel the same.

When she turned her gaze toward where her colleagues were felled, a white ship with a red stripe sailed past them.

A Coast Guard ship.

It sailed toward the horizon line, and disappeared.

Her initial shock subsided by the time Nick and Bàba arrived. The men had carried the dead worker to the edge of the deck, closer and safer inland. Bàba crossed his arms over his chest, shaking his head, a glint of disgust in his eyes. Nick stood with his hands balled into tight fists, knuckles drained of blood, his upper lip curled into a disdainful sneer. Like Angie earlier, his shoulders and legs trembled, but she suspected it was out of anger, not shock. Or a mix of both.

Bàba knelt by the dead worker, pressing his hand onto his forehead. "I asked him to show Marisa the ropes." Angie wasn't sure if he was talking to himself, or to her and Nick. "They didn't deserve this." He stood. "How did they get past the blockade? It was meant to be out of the range," he said with measured words.

"They have traps outside the blockade range. Must have army crawled up the beach between rotations or something." Angie stood closer to Bàba. "I'm guessing when Marisa triggered the trap, it alerted the mer." Bile burned in her throat when she thought back to what happened. "The seas were choppy. They must have been nearby, watching."

"I will have their heads strung along the seaboard. They've gone far enough." Nick growled his words, cursing under his breath as he stormed off, footfalls loud and deliberate and slamming onto wood and concrete ground.

"We'll contact their families and call the coroner to come pick his body up. All our people they've taken. We'll get them back. Find them," Bàba said, downtrodden.

"The Coast Guard hasn't found anyone yet? I just saw a ship go by, and it didn't even stop. I don't know how long it was there for, but it must have been close enough to see them die." Angie's pressure rose thinking about it.

"Beau and Emily told me that if we see ships here, they're probably going to the bigger ports to investigate the fish issue." Bàba kept looking at the ground and rubbed his temples. "If you want to know more, you can ask them yourself tomorrow." Turning on his heel, Bàba began to walk away.

Angie trailed behind him, and he walked ahead without waiting for her to catch up.

To her left, a pearly glint under the sparse sunlight caught her eye, and she craned her neck and stood on her tiptoes.

Then, a splash.

Bàba was out of sight now, and Angie leaned onto the railing until she nearly toppled over. Squinting and searching side to side.

Before the horizon line, a dark-haired head appeared above the water. A mermaid.

Her hair was gathered into tight braids winding around the top of her head, and sunlight gleamed off honey bronzed skin. Something about her rang familiar, but Angie couldn't make out enough of her features to place her. The mermaid ducked underwater, but her dorsal fin stayed visible. She patrolled back and forth, as if searching for something beneath. Then she stuck her head back up, eyes locking on Angie.

Angie stepped backward. The mermaid held her gaze, but Angie couldn't tell if it was a challenging or curious one.

The mermaid ducked underwater again and didn't resurface. Was she swimming closer to her, watching her still? The thought gave Angie goosebumps.

She turned and ran after Bàba.

TWENTY-FOUR

AT EIGHT O'CLOCK IN THE MORNING, Angie sat in Bàba's office, waiting for Beau and Emily to show up for their meeting. They arrived five minutes later, and after a brief greeting to Angie and Bàba, they took their seats to Angie's right. She didn't have her chance to talk until twenty minutes had passed.

Bàba gestured to her. "Beibei, was there something you wanted to ask them?"

Emily tilted her head, her expression soft, urging Angie to go on. Beau had his chin resting on his fist, lips pursed, his focus like a laser beam.

Angie jumped at the chance, having both Beau and Emily's attention on her. "The Coast Guard situation? Two of our colleagues died yesterday, and I saw one of their ships pass by. It looked like it was just leaving, so they had to have seen what happened."

Beau let out a slow exhale.

Emily sat straighter, and spoke. "We don't know. The feds won't send us help. Said they need to prioritize the bigger ports, but I can't shake the feeling they're hiding something."

"What do you mean?" Bàba cut in. "Hiding what?"

Emily shrugged. "I don't know. It could be anything. Secret experiments, protecting someone important—" Whatever she was going to say next trailed off as Beau shot her a wide-eyed look.

"Thanks for your time, Zixin. We should get going." Beau stood. He put a hand on Emily's shoulder, and she did the same.

"Wait, one more question. Please?" Angie couldn't let them leave now, not without doing what she promised Kaden. To her relief, they paused at the door. "Would you consider stopping killing all the mer? At this point, I think we need to try diplomacy. We've lost so many people already." Her voice shook as she asked, suddenly self-conscious of appealing to her town's mayor for help. Though they were friendly with Bàba, Angie still saw him as an out-of-reach leader. She forced herself to continue. "They're highly intelligent beings and not just animals. We could come to a truce. Make a deal."

"We've tried to talk to them before, but if there is a way we can understand them, I'll consider it," Bàba said, and Angie gave him a grateful, relieved smile. "The more we keep this up, the more people we lose, too."

"No, absolutely not." Emily folded her arms across her chest, her countenance hardening. "How could you ask that? Zixin, you know as well as anyone why we're doing this. Them killing us is exactly why we need to hunt them down. What makes you think they'll stop if we will?"

"We can just catch one and learn how to talk to them." Angie was repeating herself from their staff meeting almost two months ago.

"I agree, and—" Bàba started, but Beau cut him off.

"You forget what they did. They killed my boy. My teenage son was fucking *impaled* by those bastards." His voice cracked at the word *son*, and Angie's heart dropped. "If they hurt or killed one of your daughters, would you not want the same? What, you would just talk to them, and everything will be okay?"

Bàba paled.

Beau continued. "And Angie, who's side are you on?" His cheeks flushed. "Speaking of which, where were you when my son was murdered? He said he was meeting you that morning."

"Don't question her loyalty," Bàba cut in. "I'd trust her if I were you. She'd never go behind my back."

An invisible razor drove itself into Angie's heart.

"I was going to meet him. He wanted to have breakfast together, and we planned to talk about my school. But, when I got to the docks, he wasn't there. I found him." The memory made tears well up behind her eyelids, and she swiped at them.

Beau studied her as if searching for cracks in her story.

Emily touched his arm, and he slid his gaze to his wife. "We should go," she said, her voice hardly above a whisper.

The door shut quietly behind them, leaving Angie and Bàba sitting in silence.

When her shift ended at seven p.m., Angie waited at the same spot she saw Kaden last. Bàba and Nick were holed up in the central meeting room and showed no signs of coming out anytime soon, no doubt planning their retaliation.

Her skin crawled thinking of what they were discussing.

Minutes passed, and Kaden didn't show, but a familiar rowboat approached her from the horizon. She fixated on it as it moved closer to her, until it finally wedged onto the shoal.

Kaden peeked over the surface, and angled his head toward the boat. Angie's shoulders collapsed in relief, and after ensuring she was alone, she climbed aboard.

He took his time, meandering underwater, back and forth, back and forth. Angie's hackles lowered. She'd expected a rough ride not unlike when she nearly hit floating ice, but now, the gentle bobbing and swaying and soft breeze melted the tension in her body.

She stretched out her legs and her eyelids fluttered close.

The boat slowed to a stop. Jolting awake, Angie rubbed her eyes and ran a finger over a deep vertical indentation in her forehead.

Great. She must have fallen asleep with her forehead on the rowboat's edge.

Her hair was a tangled mess from the wind messing it up, there was a dent on her forehead, her eyes were bleary, and her lips were dry.

They stopped at a remote piece of land nestled within a fjord. Landmass surrounded them on both sides, bases for towering granite walls dotted with bright greenery. In the distance were mountains nestled within a blanket of fog, the epitome of nature's masterful craftsmanship. Angie's fatigue vanished as she took in the awe-inducing sight.

Kaden climbed ashore first and held out his hand as Angie stepped off. She lost her footing when the boat rocked with the waves, landing into his waiting arms.

"You planned that, didn't you?" Angie grunted, sitting back up and dusting sand off her jacket and out of her hair. The sight of him set her aglow, sitting coyly and with hooded eyes, one arm draped casually over where his waist transitioned into his tail.

"Perhaps." With a tender sweep, he brushed a strand of hair away from her face, his palm lingering on her cheek. His gaze trailed to her forehead, and his playful smile returned.

"Wait, that stupid dent is still there? Damn it." Angie rubbed her forehead. "I was tired, and I fell asleep. Okay?"

"You're still beautiful, and I doubt I will ever stop finding you so."

She rolled her eyes, her cheeks flaming. "Flatterer."

"Is it flattery if it's the truth?" Kaden stroked her cheek with one hand and let his fingers slide behind her ear. He smirked. "No gills to worry about jabbing my finger into."

"Oh, stop." She laughed and gave him a light shove on his bare shoulder.

"But please, don't worry about your appearance. I can tell you've worked the entire day."

"More than worked. I talked to the mayor this morning."

He tensed. "Good news?"

"No," Angie said, glum, and recounted the meeting's events. "I don't know what else to do. I don't even know if there's anything my bàba can do."

"I'll keep trying on my end." Kaden tapped his smooth chin. "Have you been eating enough?"

"Barely." Her lips thinned. A spark of irritation flared. "We're rationing out what we still have at home. Been eating a lot less."

Kaden reached behind him, the movement drawing her attention, and Angie tilted her head. "I worried about that, and brought you a few things. I hope you'll like them." He opened his palm, unveiling a full handful of dried black seaweed. "Snacks?"

"Nori? I love this!" Angie plucked two from his palm and chewed on them. They were crispy and light and mildly salty, exactly the way she liked them. "I bought these in bulk from Korean supermarkets when I was in college."

"They're all yours." Kaden pushed his palm closer to her. She took him up on his offer, brushing his soft, warm hand when she took the last one.

"Thank you." She put her free hand over the proximal part of his tail, solid and cold and smooth under her touch. He glanced at where her hand was, and a tail muscle twitched under her touch. The seaweed's mild bitterness danced on her tongue. "How did you dry this to be so crisp?"

"It's not wet everywhere all the time." She didn't blink while mulling over what he said. Kaden clarified. "In the palace and mer dwellings, there are airy parts. Mostly for keeping things dry."

She nodded, trying to visualize it. He reached behind him again, but froze.

"Wait. Where did it go?" He planted his hands flat and tensed his tail, using a powerful force to push off.

To Angie's astonishment, he launched himself a good fifteen or twenty feet ahead, swiped at something, and then returned, landing with such grace that he hardly stirred the loose rocks and soil. One hand flattened on the ground, his other holding something within.

Her eyes rounded. "Can you do that again?"

Kaden stared at her with an expression of disbelief.

"No. It's an extremely inefficient way for us to move on land, and it uses too much energy. Energy I would much rather spend on you." He pressed a thick bracelet into her palm. "And this is also for you. Thought I lost it. Must have dropped it when I came ashore."

Speechless, she turned it over. It looked to be solid gold and dotted with pearls, wrapped inside a soft, romantic design, curved and dreamlike. A gold hallmark was etched into the bracelet's inside, beside the letters and numbers "10K" and "1902." The quality of the gold and the year it was made. Not a single spot of rust to be found. "This is over a hundred years old!"

"You said you wished to explore the deep. Until I can take you with me, I wanted to find something for you."

"Where did you find this?" Angie slipped the bracelet over her wrist. Slightly loose, but it held on tight enough.

"In the trenches. I swam through some schools of *pipayu* and *denglongyu* who eyed me like I was about to steal from them. Or perhaps they wanted to eat me." His lips quirked into an amused grin.

He spoke the fish names slowly, and she mouthed it to herself, his language that sounded like a strange Chinese dialect to her. Anglerfish and lanternfish, respectively.

"You didn't have to bring me anything. But I appreciate it." She scooted to him and pulled him into a tight hug. He returned it, pressing his face to her neck.

"I wanted to." His lips on her skin sent a burst of warmth racing down her shoulders and up her jaw. Angie pulled away, giving him a gentle tug onto the smooth ground of dry, packed sand, and snuggled into him. His arms were a comfortable safety net around her. The brisk breeze caressed her cheeks, carrying with it the refreshing pineapple-like notes of sea buckthorn, mingling with the neighboring leaves' musky-sweet scents.

This was Alaska, her home. Four years away, and now here in the natural beauty of her childhood town and snuggled up with the alluring, kind merman she was slowly falling for.

If only the humans and mer weren't fighting, this would be her nirvana.

On the rocks ahead, harbor seals with their pups rested and stood guard, their faint barks filling the air.

"I wish I could stay here forever." She closed her eyes, enjoying the feel of the light wind on her neck and face. "I don't know where we are, but wherever it is, I love it." The sounds and smells of the island melted her stress away like invisible hands massaging her body.

She knew the feeling of serenity was fleeting, and she'd eventually have to return to real life. For now, she was content to stay in her little, stress-free bubble.

Kaden squeezed her shoulder. "Do you enjoy being outdoors?"

"I go stir-crazy if I'm stuck in the house for too long." She laid back down, on her side. "There's so much beauty in the world, and I want to see all of Mother Nature's marvels and creations."

Kaden laughed, a hearty, deep sound. "I would agree." His face fell, a shadow falling over it and temporarily marred his attractiveness. "But one or both of us may not live to see tomorrow. I am happy to steal whatever time I can."

"Well, that got morbid quick." Angie frowned. There was truth in his words, but she didn't want to think about that now. She leaned in close, brushing the tip of her nose against his. "But, me too." He exhaled, his breath warm and delicate.

She pressed her lips to his.

Kaden circled one hand around the back of her head, pulling her in deeper. Angie was a pool of liquid warmth in his arms, and she gasped when he laid her on her back. Her breaths trembled.

Tenderness and desire flashed in his eyes. His strong arms framed her, forming a protective shield as he leaned down to drop soft kisses on her forehead, eyelids, and cheeks. She parted her lips, a starburst of warmth rippling outward where his mouth landed. One hand slid down to her waist, and a pleasurable, fuzzy tingle sparked at her bellybutton, shooting downward.

His kisses trailed across her jawline and neck, stopping at the corner of her lips. He moved his head back and tilted her chin upward. Angie's heart beat like a black marlin sailing at top speed, breaths shallow and ragged. Then he lowered his head, their lips crashed together in an explosion of passion. Their mouths parted in tandem, tongues finding each other and joining. She wanted him like she'd never wanted anything, or anyone else, like they were two opposite poles of a magnet refusing to be pulled apart.

She wanted more. Wanted Kaden to give her everything, and she'd do the same. The scorching fire ran wild and untamed.

"Angie," he rasped in between heaving breaths. "How in the Sea Goddesses' name do you taste so good? I will never get enough of you. You taste more intoxicating than the sweetest of candied sea peaches."

Her lips lifted into a coy smile and pulled him back into another kiss. Kaden draped the end of his heavy tail over her legs. A sensuous growl escaped his throat when they had to come back up for air, both gasping, his lips flushed maraschino-cherry red. "You make me crazy. I cannot think straight when I'm this close to you." His gaze slid southward. "I would see you every day, if it were possible."

"I wish I could, too. But there would be too much suspicion." The thought was an unhappy one, and she tried to shake it. "If there isn't already."

"Yes. My family have been inquiring where I've been disappearing off to." He moved away from her, leaving one hand clasped in hers. Angie searched his eyes, waiting for him to continue. "I tell them I check on the fish in the sanctuaries, and they do not question me further."

"The sanctuaries must be huge if they believe you're checking on them for so long."

Kaden straightened. "Would you like to see for yourself?"

"Would I?" Angie's eyes rounded until they bulged out of her. Seeing the Arctic and Northern Pacific Ocean's life in one place? An absolute dream. "Yes!"

"What was that you said? That you wanted to visit my world? You have already seen some of it. Now I will show you more." Kaden fidgeted with his fingers. "Would you like to see the palace, as well? Where I live?" The words tumbled out of his mouth, and he watched her expectantly after he asked. "A change of pace?"

Angie chuckled at his awkwardness in asking, though she found it endearing. Then she wrapped her head around his question. She wet her lips and squeezed her eyebrows together. "Sounds dangerous."

"I'll ensure your safety when we're there. The palace is shielded, remember? My people don't expect any landwalkers inside, so it's not heavily guarded. I would not propose this if I thought we would be in danger."

He sounded so earnest, so sure, and it begged her to believe him. After all, who would know the palace better than someone who lived there? She gave him a firm nod. "How about four days from now? I'll have time off."

"Great!" He stroked her cheek. "I look forward to it."

She elbowed him gently in his shoulder. Glad the moody atmosphere had lightened, she kissed him again.

Twenty-Five

Her second trip under the blue sea was more exhilarating than the last. This time, she wasted no time acclimating to her new senses and remembered to tie her hair back. Today, she donned a deep green monokini, anticipating that the magic would keep her warm, and left her jacket ashore. Kaden had given her the cheekiest grin when she dropped the coat, and she caught him stealing glances when he thought she wasn't looking.

The swim to the sanctuaries felt like it zoomed by. Kaden informed her they'd moved two tidesmiles and were now more than two thousand feet underneath the surface.

Angie took in the sights. Colorful corals surrounded her. The sands shifted as camouflaged animals darted within. Jade and ruby seaweeds undulated with the currents.

"We're here," Kaden gave her one more pull toward the abyss of the sea floor before letting go of her hand.

First there was only darkness. Then resplendent colors came into view. Reds, silvers, blues, and oranges blended together like an underwater rainbow above her head.

"It's gorgeous," she whispered to herself, eyes wide so she wouldn't miss a single thing.

How she wished she could photograph this.

Well, if she still had her phone. She didn't own a camera.

Kaden's earlier words came back to her, that this was for her eyes only, and not to be spoken of to anyone else.

The sea life stayed within invisible confines, and Angie's gaze slid upward. "Some of these are shallow-water fish. They can survive with the pressure difference?"

Kaden flashed a knowing wink. "There is a barrier enacted to prevent them from being crushed by the pressure, similar to what's around our palace. We have sanctuaries all over the seven seas, mostly to rehabilitate injured animals. We leave a lot of room in case we ever need to take in more. Out of reach from humans."

Once the initial sense of wonder wore off, Angie trembled. She was on cloud nine, surrounded by schools of fish swarming her and creating soothing waves. Seagrass tickled her feet and legs, and she gasped when a king crab skittered past her, its mighty claws out, a warning. She obliged, watching the fish play and eat and explore, living free without a care in the world, swimming and skittering and sliding side by side. Vibrant corals were abundant, playgrounds and homes for the life surrounding them.

Massive schools of arctic char, salmon, pacific cod, and pollock surrounded her. A stark reminder that fish here were fish that her village and docks were not getting. If only she could bring some of them back with her.

Kaden appeared to read her mind. "I know what you're thinking. You want to feed your family, your people. You see us selfishly keeping them here."

"I do want that." She kept staring at a ratfish moving along the floor, the cartilaginous fish's rodent-like tail wiggling behind it. Her throat briefly constricted. "They look so happy here."

"They are well cared for."

Angie hung her head, and Kaden put his hands on her shoulders, turning her to face him. "I thought I'd be happier to see this, and I am. It reminds me that this is what we're fighting over, dying over. All this, right here."

"If this is upsetting you, we can leave." Kaden's features were an expression of earnestness with a flicker of regret. "I would not have brought you here if I knew it would trouble you."

She shrugged, pushing the despondent thoughts out of her mind. "I asked you; though, I'm ready to go."

Her gaze lingered on the sanctuary until they were out of sight. She was torn. The fish deserved their lives and freedom–every living thing did–but her village also deserved to eat. Businesses relying on seafood also deserved to make a living and feed their families and themselves. Didn't they? Still, human greed was a beast to contend with. Some could hold the world in their hands, and it wouldn't be enough.

Angie sucked in a quivering breath. She'd worry about that later, when she figured out how to broach the subject to Bàba again. Kaden's voice alerted her. "Did you still want to see the palace? I am happy to take you back if not."

"Sure." Angie followed him away from the sanctuaries, moving with the currents.

Something flashed in her peripheral vision, catching her attention.

A red light flickered, and it appeared distant.

Then, it vanished. The only thing in front of Angie was a rock pillar dotted with starfish and corals.

"What's the matter?" Kaden asked.

Angie studied the darkness, waiting for the red light to come back. It never did. Maybe she had imagined it. "I just thought I saw something," she said. "Did you see anything?"

He shook his head.

Several more kicks ahead and glittering metal flashed into her vision. She slowed her pace. Gold and silver plates were buried beneath the sand, and she swam toward them.

"Buried sea vessels," Kaden explained. "The same barrier around the sanctuaries is around our queendom. Anything non-biological attempting to pass will be repelled, and missiles will ricochet back to the vessel it came from. Hence, those."

Angie tilted her head to one side, wanting to look closer. The vessels must have been over three hundred years old, if that was the last time humans and mer had contact with each other. What could she learn if she could unearth those wrecks?

She shook away the thought. The last thing she wanted was to be caught poking around in mer territory, studying the vessels they destroyed. "I see. Let's keep going."

"Of course." Kaden gave her a gentle tug.

"Before we get there." Angie pulled back, rubbing the back of her neck and swallowing hard. "Wh-what are you expecting?"

They were underneath a mossy arch, surrounded by smooth rock. Two translucent moon jellies drifted by, sweeping over her ponytail.

Soft wrinkles formed on his brow. "I wished to show you where I call home, and have some private moments with you. But I promise you, nothing you do not wish as much as I." One eyebrow shot up. "Why do you ask?"

"Because uh, when someone asks you back to their place, they're expecting you to, well, have sex with them." She grew uncomfortable at explaining that to him. "Sometimes they get upset if you don't want to."

"I expect only what you're fully willing to give. If it is enough for you to see the palace and then leave, I will oblige right away, as I've said before." The tip of his tail curled loose around her ankles. A comforting gesture, telling her he would never hold on too tight.

Angie had heard those words from the occasional young man she'd dated in college, but none of them said it with the open sincerity Kaden had. "My culture does not allow us to act any other way. We are only to give ourselves to one another when two, or in some cases, more than two mer have decided to join for life."

The butterflies in Angie's stomach settled, and she dropped her shoulders, accepting his answers.

Away from the sanctuaries, the seas were barren of life again. The seafloor's only companions were scattered rocks and sand and the occasional coral reef, resting still like statues against the constant shifting of the tides.

They moved into an area dotted with sea knolls and guyots, tall and short. Angie twisted her upper body away to avoid a jagged piece of rock wall much too close to her face.

The palace came into view, a golden beacon in the midnight seas, the sudden onslaught of light overwhelming her. Seeing so many mer in one place, though they were far away, was a truly dazzling sight to behold. Kaden led her around its confines.

"Come, stay close to me. I will not let anything happen to you." A little burst of happiness popped in her, and she pulled him close, pressing their foreheads together. She half-expected to feel his breath on her skin, but it was impossible since he used gills. His lips brushed her skin, and a dulled spark feathered across her forehead. "This is the way to my private quarters. We will pass by the throne room, but keep swimming flush with me and you will not draw the King and Queen's attention."

Kaden rested his hand on a makeshift handle on the rock wall, pulling it open and revealing a wide tubular hallway. He pulled the door closed again when they passed through.

The mer-prince stopped when they moved through the hallway and into the next room, circular and empty. Angie looked around, noting nothing of interest, until he tugged at her hand. "You had asked me how we keep foodstuffs and other items dry." He gently pulled her so she was beside him, looking to the left wall.

It wasn't a wall. It was a glass pane leading to what looked like a cavern behind it, and what seemed to be hundreds of air bubbles floating about, a hypnotizing sight.

Kaden spoke up again. "Here. We have several rooms like this around the palace. This is one of about twenty drying chambers."

Angie watched each of them float by, some empty, others with various dried fruits, kelp, and seaweed inside. The bubble sizes ranged from as small as her pinky nail to as large as her head.

"This is amazing," she murmured, putting both palms on the glass pane. "I guess that answers my question, then. But why have dry food at all?"

"For emergencies or if there's a scarcity of fresh foods. It also provides easy access to food without having to constantly swim to the surface to harvest the sea fruits and vegetables."

"Oh, that makes sense. Like how we preserve and can foods." Another thought came. "How did you keep the nori dry when you gave it to me?"

"A simple matter of guiding bubbles toward the surface. I used a little of my magic to keep the currents moving in the right direction."

Now, she understood. Angie took one last look at the bubbles before they left the room.

They moved through quiet halls, passing each room with ceilings and windows with vibrant clear, crimson, and cobalt hues. The floors were made of stained glass, depicting rocks, seamounts, sea caves and corals, and various fish species.

Kaden stopped.

"Shouldn't we keep going?" she whispered.

"This is the princes' quarters. The servants are on break, and Cyrus is at court. We'll be alone for a few moments." He motioned with his head toward the stained-glass ground. "These are the stories of my people." They continued onward, and he pointed out different pictures to her as they carried on.

The first was of two groups of mer on opposite sides of the mural, facing one another. "This is when my parents traveled to this region and settled here thirty-five tidesyears ago, and the first group of mer that joined them."

He pointed out a second drawing in the next room, of three regal, elegant merfolk. "This is Iarra, one of the mer Goddesses." He motioned to a golden beige-skinned mermaid with flowing chestnut hair down to her waist. "Another Goddess and our primary deity in the Pacific queendoms, Sanyue." The second Goddess' straight raven hair was swept into a neat updo, her skin pale and nearly translucent. "And this is Aruna." He pointed to a depiction of a merman with umber-hued skin and wavy jet-black hair. "The mer God. They represent the tidal cycles."

The third illustration, beside the second, was of mer and humans shaking hands by a shoreline. "This was over three centuries ago, when your people and my people were still cordial and had an alliance." Kaden shook his head slowly. "The last time we were."

Angie set her lips in a tight line and bowed her head. "But what happened? Our stories say that you suddenly disappeared."

Kaden beckoned her to keep following.

"This is what happened." The fourth drawing he pointed out to her was of a group of humans standing over dead mer, with muskets, pistols, and swords in hand. "At one time, mer lived in harmony with the humans, and they would give them our magic so they could join us in the seas. But, a large group of humans used that ability against them and besieged them in the seas and at the surface, killing mer by the thousands." His voice lowered. "There were so few of us left to fight back. The remaining mer decided that humans couldn't be trusted, and closed their queendoms off from the surface world."

"Oh, tiān. I'm so sorry. I didn't know." Angie's hand moved to cover her mouth. "That's horrible."

"It was, yes." Kaden thinned his lips. "Since then, we've learned to use our Goddess-granted ability to manipulate water, and help us in battle with landwalkers. It is our second gift from them. The first being able to give you breath underwater. Let's keep going."

The throne room was next, situated to her left when she passed it, and she peeked over Kaden's shoulder. The thrones, in the shapes of pillars, were carved of pink, white, and orange corals, surrounded by fish who made their homes there. They sat on a bed of trimmed seagrass, and Kaden's mother and father were upright, their tails wrapped around the pillars. They faced ahead, another mahogany-tailed merman floated beside them.

Given his resemblance to Kaden, he must be Cyrus, but where Kaden's features were soft and gentle, Cyrus' appeared harder, sterner, reminding Angie of Bàba's austerity. Three mermaids and mermen were before them, gesturing wildly as if pleading a case to their superiors.

The mer-queen was lovely, her hair of ebony and silver tied into a single large braid surrounded by threads of smaller ones. Her skin was iridescent pale, her eyes creased with deep lines, and she sported jewelry of pearls and shimmering gems covering her neck and breasts. The mer-king had moved upright and was speaking to the small crowd, the tip of his tail flicking back and forth. Possibly a gesture of annoyance. His hair was silver, his chest and arms strong like his sons' were, and rough edges lined his face. On his right wrist was a thick, brass bracelet full of inscriptions. Cyrus wore an identical one, except his was bright silver, bordering on white gold.

Kaden didn't wear one. Was that for the father and eldest son, the same as in her own culture, where tradition dictated the eldest son became head of the household when the father passed?

Despite her insides quivering, she couldn't look away, fascination taking over.

Cyrus turned his head in her direction, and she lowered herself so she sank below Kaden's level. "Angie, come on. If they spot us, they'll have us imprisoned or exiled." His voice grew urgent as he tugged on her wrist.

"Okay, okay. Sorry." She followed him down another hallway, and then another, stopping once to allow a mermaid to swim by far ahead of them.

They reached his private quarters several kicks later. The room was more cavernous than the rest of the palace, or at least, the little she'd seen so far, and she took it in. Kaden swam to the oval mirror across from them and shuffled away his floating trinkets and personal care items into small nooks inside a rock ledge.

"Sorry for the mess. I put everything away before I came to you, but the currents must have gotten to them." Kaden rubbed at the back of his neck, looking sheepish.

Angie thought it was cute. She returned her attention back to her surroundings. A bookcase embedded in rock sat on the other side of the room, filled with what looked like thin slabs of stone. Beside it, two hooks kept a stack of thick, square-cut kombu kelp in place. Underneath the stacks were what looked to be a handful of thick, pointy rock cylinders and shells, anchored to the rock wall with sturdy, fibrous rope.

Must be writing utensils, given their proximity to the kombu stacks.

She looked closer at the first piece of kombu, with writing on it. The words *ocean* and *hello* were scratched in neat lettering, and three symbols were above them. The symbols looked vaguely like traditional Chinese characters, but she couldn't make out what they said.

"It's the first piece of translation I learned when I was a child. I kept it as a memory." Kaden swam up beside her, resting a hand on her elbow.

"I kept one of my old childhood drawings of mermaids, too." She performed a gentle sidestroke so she was closer to him. "How did you learn modern English, anyway? I thought you've all been closed off from us for three centuries."

"Well, the royal families sent sentinels to the surface to observe and keep abreast of human behaviors and speech. As a way to keep an eye on and understand their enemy. Mostly, they watched ships and sailors, but some would venture closer to shore or through rivers. They were very careful in staying out of human sight." Kaden's hand slid around to her waist and pulled her so they were flush. "They would report their findings back to our royal and noble families. All royals and nobles and their families are taught human languages, of the land regions they are closest to. Some non-nobles and royal mer may speak your languages, too, but most do not."

Angie nodded, absorbing what he told her. He kissed her temple before moving away from her. She returned her attention to her surroundings, taking in everything she saw.

Violet seagrass atop a sandy, ridged seabed dusted underneath the bookcase and beneath his dressing ledge. The sides of the room were of frosted glass embedded with seashells, pebbles, and preserved bright sea grasses and seaweeds.

The room was lit of pale greens, blues, reds, and aquamarines from a glass ceiling, though there was no natural light this deep in the ocean.

Angie looked closer at the lights, lips pursed. They were thousands upon thousands of tiny lights of varying colors, from bioluminescent deep-sea critters.

Utterly fascinating.

A small grouping of cylindrical rock protruded from the ground, its tops flat and sloped.

"What are those for?" She pointed to them.

"For us to sit on. It's sloped so we don't crush our fins." He was still across the room, rearranging the stone slabs in his bookcase.

Angie let herself float in stillness, looking for something to grab onto so she could relax for a moment. Her sights settled on a large, thick, and gelatinous hammock, held in place at two adjoining walls.

Kaden swam behind her and pulled his turquoise, frosted, sea glass door shut, and with a hungry glint in his eyes, he zipped to Angie and pulled her into a hard, desperate kiss, his lips parting, and his tongue finding and entwining with hers. Kissed her like he hadn't eaten in weeks, teeth playfully dragging on her lower lip, a sultry groan escaping his throat. She kept her arms tight around his neck, wanting to savor every tingle, every pleasurable ache flooding her.

"Do you want to stay longer?" He moved his head back and cupped her cheeks.

She hovered her lips inches from his. "I'd like to stay here. With you."

He responded by swimming upward with her and laying her inside the hammock, which shifted and molded around her, preventing her from floating away.

"What's this made of?" She tapped it and stretched out.

"Seaweed and seagrass fibers of the highest quality. I could lay there for hours on hours and feel no need to leave."

"Sounds like me every morning"

Kaden's laugh made his shoulders shudder. "It's hard to leave the arms of comfort."

Angie wiggled her eyebrows, then pointed at the ceiling. "Those lights. They're from fish?"

"Yes, jellies and anglerfish and sea worms."

With the mer magic, she didn't struggle to understand Kaden's words in Renyuhua for marine animals, and she was grateful.

Kaden kept talking. "When we need light, we give them enough food to provide us with however much light we need." He swam to the ceiling, opened a small hatch and stuck his arm through, and pulled out a thick, empty bowl made of rock. "It's a symbiotic relationship."

Instantly, the lights flickered off, one by one, like stars disappearing into the night. For the first time, in their inky surroundings, the absence of candescence on his body struck her.

"The mer don't glow," said Angie. "I just realized."

"No." Kaden's voice sounded far. "To light up does not serve us. We see well enough in the dark, and it makes it harder for predators, humans, to find us."

The room lit up again, and Kaden returned from the hatch on the ceiling. "They needed a refill."

He returned to her in the hammock and kissed her again. Her pulse thrummed in her ears, heartbeat sounding like it had been magnified and she was hearing it through earbuds with the volume turned to its max. He trailed kisses down her neck and sternum, cradling her to him.

She swung her legs over his hips and straddled him, keeping her knees close to his tail, and he let out a surprised gasp before their lips joined again. His hands ran over her legs, hips, and back, setting her aflame. She craved more when his hands moved to her shoulders.

"Angie." He stroked her hair, his eyes locked with hers. "You make me lose my mind."

"I could say the same about you, Mer-Prince." She sat upright, holding onto the side of the hammock and keeping her knees tight against Kaden's tail to keep her sitting balance. "To think that two months ago, we got off on the wrong foot. Or tail."

"If it led me to you, here, I would have taken that chance again, but without the part where you left me as shark bait."

"I did pull you back out."

"That you did." He gathered her into a warm hug. Then he whispered into her ear. "You've seen me in my full glory. May I see you, if you are of mind to show me? Now that we are here alone, no distractions, no intruders."

Angie sucked in her breath, ruminating.

To her family, she had always been too skinny or put on too much weight, and though she was a healthy weight now, she hedged at the notion.

But this was Kaden, and he had never given her cause for worry.

She pulled her tight ponytail loose and let her hair fall around her shoulders.

Holding his intense gaze, she moved one hand over to one strap of her swimsuit, and then the other, slowly peeling it off. His jaw slackened, fiery desire burning in his eyes. He didn't touch her until she tossed her swimsuit to the side.

When she fully disrobed, he scanned her body, stopping to linger at her breasts and legs. He reached out a tentative hand and stroked her left leg, and then her right. Then parted them and touched her with gentle, curious hands, his eyes darting back and forth, up and down in tiny, quick motions.

Angie jerked her knees toward her chest, and he stopped abruptly, eyes wide like he was caught in the middle of committing a crime. She gave a nervous chuckle. "I feel like I'm under a microscope."

"Apologies, Angie. It is wondrous to me what humans use to walk. Each part of you is tantalizing." He lowered his head, dotting kisses on her lips, her neck, her breasts, her stomach. Greedily, his hands roved over her skin as if he wanted every inch of her for himself. "Tell me what pleases you. Or show me." Her nerves became a bundle of live wires sparking each time he touched her. When he dragged his lips down to her legs and moved between them, the cautious flick of his tongue made her arch her back and gasp.

He stopped. "Did I hurt you?"

She ran her fingers through his hair in assurance. "What? No, no, that felt good. Really good."

"Mm. Okay." He returned his attention to what he was doing before and focused his mouth there, each stroke of his tongue and lips making her jerk with blissful spasms. She whimpered his name, grabbing his hand and holding it tight.

"Please don't stop."

Her breaths came out faster, shallower. When she crept too close to the edge, he slid two fingers inside her, stroking and pushing until he hit a spot that made her shiver and her legs shake. Angie's fingers clung to the hammock's ropes, her core and arms and legs tensed as she pushed into him, a desperate plea for release. She wanted it, and yet she didn't, wanted him to make her wait and tease her until she felt like she would implode.

He worked in perfect harmony, never pausing until the pressure built and built and boiled over, sending waves of ecstasy crashing through her and a thousand tiny stars bursting into her vision, the climax almost drowning her. She gasped for breaths and rode out the smaller waves that followed, until only a gentle, comfortable warmth radiated within her. A blanket of oblivion splayed over her as she fully relaxed, her senses returning to where they were undersea.

Kaden's kiss on her neck brought her back to reality. "How are you feeling? I hit the right spots, then?"

"Like I had an out-of-body experience." Angie cocked an eyebrow at him. She closed her eyes in contentment. "How did you know where to touch?"

"Knowledge and rumors circulated among us, in secret. You think I am the only mer who's had clandestine relations with a human?" Kaden replied with a knowing grin.

"Is there anything I can do for you? I want to make you feel like I did." Angie opened her eyes and looked him up and down.

Kaden shook his head no. "Not at all. I am content simply being in your company. Seeing you pleased excited me just as much. It is an experience."

"A good or bad experience?" She snuggled closer to him so they were chest to chest, her legs and his tail intertwined.

"A wonderful experience. But, we typically do not physically join until we're bonded. If I join with you, it will bind me to you for life."

"Oh." Angie hadn't expected that. "So you're like penguins? Well, most penguins."

"Now I'm a penguin." Kaden teased.

"You're a very handsome penguin." She gave him a playful poke on his solid chest. "I respect your decision to wait. I'm not ready for that level of commitment yet."

"I understand. I have that desire to join with you, but I can't act on it. Not until we are both sure." He put his hand on her thigh, hiking it up so her leg was underneath his hips. "I am sure of one thing. That what I feel for you is beyond describing. A foreign feeling, but I only know I cannot stand to be apart from you. You bring me such fulfillment, and if you are the last person I would ever have the pleasure of kissing and caressing, I would have lived with no regrets." He grazed the back of his fingers over her cheekbone. "When I am with you, it feels as if all is right, despite the hostility between your people and mine." The words were sweet sounds from his lovely, soft lips.

Angie pressed herself closer to him, speaking into his chest. Then, before she could take them back, she said, "I feel the same way."

He put his hand on the back of her neck, running his fingers through her hair. Her happy hormones lit up collectively like tiny flares, and she shut her eyes, letting dreamy sleep take over. Kaden stilled next to her with his chin resting over her head. Though he breathed with his gills, his chest still rose and fell in a soothing rhythm in tune with her own breaths.

She wanted him and cared for him and desired nothing more than to call him hers.

Yet in the back of her mind, she knew confessing their feelings would damn them both.

Twenty-Six

While Angie slept, she was acutely aware that he awoke partway through the night. Kaden left her grasp for a moment, returning with a weighted blanket that felt to be of the same material as his hammock.

Her heart swelled at the mere thought of his name, and she became hyperaware of her body whenever he was near. A sensation of emptiness arose at the possibility of being without him, a feeling new to her.

She loved the way he molded with her, like they were two missing pieces of a puzzle. Kissing him made her head swim with pleasurable, delicious waves.

The crass sound of glass grinding on rock drifted into her ears. The blanket moved to cover her head, and muffled voices followed, sounding a mile away. Glass moved over rock again, and then it was quiet.

The sounds she heard sounded so clear before were now muffled. Why—

A cool, fuzzy sensation spread through her chest, turning into pressure. Angie jolted awake, one hand flying to her breastbone.

The pressure built, and her vision blurred. It became harder to breathe. She purposefully inhaled and exhaled slow, conserving oxygen, trying to make sense of what was happening.

The voices, the rock and glass noises, they weren't a dream. Kaden was gone.

How long had it been since she'd fallen asleep? How long since he—

"Oh no. No, no, no." She scrambled out of the hammock and grabbed her swimsuit, slipping it back on.

The mer magic was fading, and she needed to get out of here, fast. She thought quickly.

Oxygen. She also needed oxygen. Without it, she would never make it to the surface in time.

What was that that Kaden showed her the day before? Right, air bubbles.

Angie held her breath, and swam to the glass door. After a quick look around to ensure no one was outside, she tried to pull it open, but it was heavier than she thought. She couldn't manage enough force while floating, and trying resulted in her legs floating out from behind her.

Angie wedged her feet against the roughshod edge by the door and put both hands on the handle. Kicking off with both feet and giving the handle a hard push, it opened. She swam out with a slow, cautious breaststroke and flutter kicks, listening for aberrant sounds.

Only the gentle rustling of water in her ears surrounded her. Angie thought back to the directions.

Turn left at the corner. Keep going against the wall, then make a right.

She followed the directions, or so she thought. When she made the last right, there was no glass pane with air bubbles. Only a solid wall greeted her.

Shit. Where was she? This place disoriented the crap out of her. The hallways all looked the same, reminding her of when she became vertically disoriented during a wreck dive in college, and couldn't tell which way was up. She had a group to help her then.

She was alone now. Knowing up from down wouldn't help here. The space enclosed her.

Her heart raced, and she breathed in, slow and controlled.

Stay calm.

She retraced her paddles, going back to Kaden's room, and tried again, swimming slower and against the wall.

The soreness in her chest became a sharp pain. Her surroundings grew blurrier.

She was going to make it. She had to. This couldn't be how she was going to die, not after having the night that she did.

This time, she found the room she searched for. Angie reached the glass pane with the bubbles behind it and felt around the edges, her finger curling around a notch at the sides. The door slid open easily, and she made for the first bubble she could find. More water shot to the back of her throat when she tried to take a breath. She put her lips around an air bubble and breathed it in, and then another, larger one. Angie made a U-turn and made her way out of the cavern, back toward the palace.

The tip of a maroon fishtail appeared in her field of vision, and she let out a sigh of relief. About to ask Kaden just where in the Hells he had been, she looked up at him.

Fear seized her entire body.

The merman in front of her was decidedly not Kaden. The angles on his face were sharper, his whiskey-gold eyes hard and unblinking as they focused on her.

Her eyes trailed to the white-gold bracelet around his wrist.

It was Cyrus. Kaden's older brother.

The look on his face twisted from utter confusion to positively murderous.

"Landwalker!" Cyrus' voice sounded of thunder booming through open skies. "A spy?"

Tiān-fucking-damn-it to the eighteen levels of Hell!

Her heart all but stopped. She could still hear his words, though they remained dulled. Whatever mer magic remained in her and with her new-found oxygen, she had to take advantage.

He lunged for her, a venomous sea snake about to strike at its prey.

Angie scrambled for the nearest rock face, banging her knee against a large stalagmite-like sea erosion pillar below her. Shooting pain burst at the area of impact, and she grimaced, her teeth clenched together so hard that her gums hurt. She continued swimming, fluttering her legs as fast as she could, and clung to the corals with trembling hands, climbing them to the top.

She had no plan and didn't know where she was going, only that she couldn't let him reach her. Angie didn't stand a chance against Cyrus. He was bigger, faster, and in his element, but she did have the advantage of a head start, and she intended to use it. She would never outswim him, and had a better chance if she traversed the rock walls.

"How did you get in here?" He approached her quickly.

She didn't answer, and kept crawling along the cave, gripping onto rock protrusions and ledges. Where the walls were smooth, she latched onto sea stars, and after a brief hesitation, she used soft, smooth corals. Angie didn't want to damage the corals' health, but she had no choice if she wanted to keep moving.

Her arms and legs were growing sore from her constant moving, and fighting the water's resistance.

Stalactite-like erosion pillars hung above her, and her breath hitching, she grabbed for the closest one, burying herself in between a grouping of them.

His fingers grazed her ankle, and she drew her knee up to her chest, barely out of his grasp.

Angie's breathing came out quick and shallow, and she curled herself into a ball in the gap between the rocky icicles. A pillar piece broke off when she pressed her feet against it, and she grabbed it, holding it in front of her like a makeshift weapon.

It wasn't much, but she would take anything in a feeble attempt to defend herself. A miniscule chance of survival was better than none.

She didn't know whether it was better to die by drowning, or die by Cyrus' hand. Or tail, whichever he chose to end her with.

"Stop, please." She hugged the stalactite in front of her, like a seahorse clinging to a stone for dear life. Her words still came out clear enough. "I'm not going to hurt anyone! I just want to leave and go back to the surface."

Cyrus looked her in the eye, and shook his head with a look of contempt. "I don't believe you. How are you able to speak?" His eyes narrowed. "You have our magic?"

"I–I–" Angie didn't know what to say. Her mind raced in so many directions that she couldn't keep track of her thoughts.

He swam underneath her feet, quick as a marlin, and grabbed them, pulling her out of safety.

"Cyrus!" She thrashed her feet, the force mitigated by the swirling waves, and she found herself losing control of her legs.

Cyrus' hand closed around her neck. He darted forward, slamming her back into a rock wall. "How do you know my name? How long have you been spying on us, *human?*"

Angie winced as the rocky nodules drove into her spine, causing an explosion of agony. Sharp pain followed from her skin dragging upward against the roughshod wall as Cyrus forced her to meet him at eye level.

"I'm not a spy." Her voice came out strangled as he tightened his grip. The muscles in his neck popped, the heat of his glare searing an Alaska-sized hole through her.

She kicked again, tried to pry his fingers off her neck, to no avail.

This was going to be the end of her.

Angie was going to haunt Kaden in her afterlife until she reincarnated for leaving her to die at Cyrus' hands, and there would be no trench deep enough for him to escape from her.

Bright spots flashed into her vision, and her head pounded.

Cyrus released her, and she gasped, racing for another air bubble before figuring out why. She breathed in one some feet away from her, and turned her head, making herself as small as possible in the cavern's corner.

Kaden had Cyrus's shoulders gripped in his hands, and moving like a torpedo, pinned Cyrus onto a jagged piece of wall. Starfish and large barnacles dislodged from the rock and drifted around them like floating debris, until they were swept away by the currents. "Brother! What are you doing? She's harmless!"

"Landwalkers are far from harmless." Cyrus retaliated by raising his tail and pushing it against Kaden, forcing Kaden to loosen his grasp. Cyrus then wrapped his arms around Kaden's shoulders from behind, his tail rising to curl around his younger brother's, placing him in a chokehold.

Angie had to help him somehow. She would deal with why he left her alone, later. For now, she had to do something. She breathed in another air bubble, this one holding a handful of nori, and it scattered around her, floating out of her sight. A quick scan around the space revealed two more air bubbles in her immediate vicinity. One small and one larger the size of her closed fist. She made a mental note of them for when she would need air again.

After kicking off from the rock wall, she swam for Kaden and Cyrus.

Before she reached them, Kaden grabbed Cyrus' elbows, giving a hard upward push. He escaped Cyrus' chokehold.

"Kaden, what in the gaping trenches are you doing?" Cyrus' voice came out as a low, slightly muffled growl, the currents carrying his words to Angie's ears.

The brothers darted around, over, and under each other, each trying to grab and maintain their hold on the other. By grabbing Cyrus' wrists and locking them behind his back, Kaden ended their skirmish.

Angie gasped for air again, and she turned, sucking in a large air bubble floating by her right temple. That would buy her some time.

Kaden wrapped his tail around Cyrus, effectively immobilizing him, both their gills flaring. For a moment they floated in stillness, like a statue of two mer entwined in a deadly embrace. Passing currents brushed through their thick hair like a soft breeze, lifting strands from their heads.

Cyrus' lips tightened into a line, exasperation twisting his features. "Let me go. Now."

"If you promise to stay your hand, brother," Kaden replied. "And keep your silence about her."

Cyrus' shoulders tensed and drew forward, and Angie kicked backward, prepared to swim for her life again in case he broke from Kaden's clutches.

"Why would I do that? You're putting us all in danger," Cyrus spat.

Angie hadn't been counting the minutes that had passed, but her lungs were protesting for air again. She had one hope left, the small air bubble, and she swam for it.

Behind her, Kaden spoke again, his voice harried.

"I'll take responsibility for any trouble that she causes. If she harms any of us, punish me in whatever way you and the Queen and King deem fit. I will not run, and I will not resist."

Angie turned and faced them. Neither of them looked in her direction, their softening glares locked on each other.

Cyrus snorted and squirmed in Kaden's iron grasp. "You truly trust her so much?"

"Yes. Please, look at her. She's half your size and unarmed. I wouldn't have brought her here if I thought she was going to be a danger."

Angie's chest tightened again. Each breath grew shallower until she felt like she was choking.

She willed Cyrus to listen. To believe his brother. The silence stretched, Cyrus' lips thinned, still trying to loosen Kaden's arm around his neck.

Her head grew light and stars flashed in her vision.

Tiān, Angie. Everything is going to be okay. She didn't believe it, but she had to stay calm.

Kaden glanced in her direction, and then back to Cyrus, panic flashing in his eyes.

She backed against the rock wall behind her, her hands flying to her chest, and she could do nothing but stare at the two mer-princes as she slowly drowned.

Kaden twisted Cryus' wrist until he winced, nostrils flaring. Sneering, he gave a curt nod.

Kaden released him and bolted to Angie, pressing his lips to hers, and breathed out.

Her vision and hearing cleared, and magic warmed her lungs. She could take full breaths again. Angie's body slumped, her muscles relaxing.

Cyrus floated before them, eyes roving from one to the other, his tail swishing side to side and eyebrows so close together they formed a thick, jet-black line.

Before she could say a word, Cyrus spoke up. "The mer-queen and mer-king finally let you go? And after all that time I spent looking for you. Worrying about you, and thinking something terrible had befallen you. Only to find that you had been swimming off with a landwalker."

For the first time, Angie noted the dark circles hanging beneath Kaden's eyes, his face marred with residual worry mixed with fury.

Kaden put both palms over his face. "Son of a triggerfish."

Angie would think the swear was cute, if it wasn't in the context of Cyrus discovering them.

"You didn't get enough of a verbal lashing from the King and Queen? You already missed your own banquet. If they find out you were with a landwalker, they'll cast you out and kill her." Cyrus threw his arms out.

Angie pulled her shoulders tight, her body racked with fear. "I'll leave. And never come back," she whispered.

She turned to face Kaden, who searched Cyrus' face with desperate, pleading eyes. "I care for her. I swear on the Goddess' name that she will not hurt us. Please, brother. Stay your tongue, even to Adrielle."

"She doesn't look like she's in a position to hurt anyone." Cyrus looked to Kaden, and then back to Angie again. He gritted his teeth, his hands becoming tight fists by his waist. In the strained stillness, Angie was afraid he had imploded and would lunge at her, strike her down like a moray eel.

Another stretch of silence.

Then Cyrus rubbed his face and ran his hand through his hair. He held his tail in a rigid set, and his gills flared open and close with exaggerated movements.

Angie caught a flicker feathering along his jaw, and to her relief, he finally spoke again.

"Fine, because you're my brother, and I love you. But," he pointed an accusing finger at Kaden, "do not make me regret this. I cannot be harboring your secrets and putting Adrielle's and my life in danger."

The tension in Angie's chest made her pulse throb.

She wanted nothing more than to go home, be away from the two of them.

Kaden held out a tentative hand, and Cyrus gripped it tight. Cyrus leaned in close, lowering his voice. "We meet for dinner tonight. You tell me everything about her, and everything about the two of you. Going forward, you will hide nothing." A golden-brown flame lit Cyrus' eyes. "If you withhold anything further, you will feel the queendom's wrath upon your head. If I don't kill you first myself, and then I'll kill her."

Kaden swallowed hard and nodded his agreement.

Cyrus let go and scowled at Angie before brushing past them to leave the cavern, speaking plainly for her to stay put. She didn't take her eyes off him until the tips of his caudal fins had disappeared.

Kaden returned to her. "Angie—"

"What happened? Is that where you went, to talk to your parents? I almost died." Angie flung her words at Kaden, unable to hold her anger in any longer.

"I'm sorry. It was so sudden. Cyrus came into my room to find me. The Queen and King wished for an audience with me. They were on their way to come looking for me themselves." Kaden's gaze pleaded with her, his voice softening. "I thought you would be okay. You still had some time before I would have to replenish the magic. My intention was only to tell them why I missed the banquet, and then leave."

"So why didn't you leave? Did they hold you hostage there?" Angie's tone came out bitter and rough, and she immediately bit back her words. She didn't mean to sound so harsh, but the adrenaline and unbridled terror still raged in her from her near-drowning and near-death because of the elder mer-prince.

Kaden blinked, looking down at his clasped hands in front of him. "They did. Had sentinels at the door to ensure I didn't leave until they were done with their tirade and threats to punish me if I continued to embarrass our family." There was no force in his words. "I'm glad I found you on my way back to the room. I feared I'd find you drowned in there."

"I'm sorry they did that." Angie's voice cracked. "I didn't mean for what I said earlier to come out so, you know, mean."

Kaden gave her a one-shouldered shrug. "I understand. What you had just gone through, it would have put anyone on edge." He swam closer to her so they were inches apart. "If I had awoken where you lived, and you'd left without explanation, and then if I was bested to an inch of my life by your sister, I would be angry as well. So, I don't blame you for feeling the way you do."

Angie stayed silent, taking in his words.

"I'm so sorry for what you endured today, and that I couldn't protect you until it was too late. This should never have happened." His voice thickened with regret and pain, and Angie put a hand on his forearm. He didn't reciprocate, brushing the tips of his caudal fins back and forth against the palace floor. "Let's go back to bed? I swear I'll never leave your side again when we are here together. No matter what anyone wants with me."

"I know it's not your fault." She let her fingers hang loosely from his palm. The thought of staying here any longer shook her to her core. Where she normally found every opportunity to be in the water, now she craved being back on dry land. She peered at him. Fear and shock still held her hostage, the beautiful night with Kaden ruined. "But I should go. C-can you take me back? Please."

His luminous eyes became downcast, and he obliged, motioning for her to follow as they made back for the surface. She made sure she never strayed too far from him.

Twenty-Seven

With locked knees and stiff steps, Angie left the sea, the happiness of last night sucked out of her. Her head swam with residual vertigo as she re-acclimated to being on dry land again.

On her way out, she scratched her bare arms on a nearby barnacle-studded rock, prickly bumps embedded in a blanket of deep emerald algae. She grimaced.

Cyrus was much more intimidating than Kaden. His eyes, darker than his younger brother's but just as mysterious and striking, burned with fury and hatred, and she truly believed she was going to die before Kaden stopped him. His hands and tail were poised to strangle the life out of her.

Angie couldn't blame him. She was an enemy and in their territory.

"Are you sure you will be alright?" Kaden's head and shoulders bobbed in the waves, a flicker of concern crossing his features.

She smiled weakly. "I'll be okay."

"But I don't want to leave you until—"

"No, no. I have to get to work, anyway. I'll meet you before the week's end." He didn't move, and she kneeled to clasp his hands in hers. "Friday. Uh, two days from today."

Kaden squeezed her hands, his shoulders sagging. "Please don't worry about my brother. He has a tough shell, but ultimately, he holds an open mind and heart. I will explain to him when I see him tonight and hope he will change his tune. He is very much my mother's son." He bit his lower lip, his eyebrow raised. "I am so very sorry about what happened. I shouldn't have brought you to the sanctuaries, or to the palace, knowing the risk."

"I don't regret it." She gazed into his eyes as she said the words, and stroked the tops of his hands with her thumbs.

With a forced nod, he pressed a kiss on her cheek before they parted ways. His words were of small comfort to her.

She retrieved her pack, right where she left it yesterday. Her body flushed warm with the mer's magic, though Kaden had said it would only last minutes once she broke dry land. She towel-dried herself and slipped into her long pants, plain shirt and thick jacket.

Her back and knee throbbed when she walked. The memory of her and Cyrus stirred, a proverbial dagger twisting in her gut. The helplessness and cold terror from those moments crashed over her head and encased her entire body. Shuddering, she wrapped her arms around herself and shook the feeling off. She had to focus on getting to work.

Angie hoisted her pack over her shoulder and trekked back to the docks proper, tying her hair into a loose ponytail so its dampness was less obvious, in time to see Nick walking in her direction holding a thick swath of rope in his hands and undoing its knots.

He never came so close to the dock's edge, and she deliberately lowered her head.

Nick stopped and looked her up and down, and zeroed in on her hair. Then he squinted and pursed his lips.

Angie stiffened.

"Angela," he said after the uncomfortable silence. "What are you doing here so early? And why are you wet? It's not raining." He pointed to the sky.

She sighed with relief, and then indignation overtook her. "I can see the sun. Didn't dry my hair after showering this morning."

"Why would you not do that? Won't your head get cold?" Nick deadpanned. "I'll never understand women."

You're married to one though, dipshit.

He pointed to her jacket and pants. "Change into your uniform. We have a lot of work to do."

"More than usual?" Angie grumbled, following him back to the dock's main hub.

"Yes. A couple other dockhands resigned, so the rest of the work is falling to us."

She held her tongue, holding her true thoughts back. It wasn't him the work was falling to. It was her and the other regular dockhands who couldn't resign.

He tossed her a rope. "A few boats are coming in. Anchor them." Then he ran ahead and out of sight.

She stopped by her locker and changed into her uniform, leaving her swimsuit by the cracked-open window to dry.

Bàba walked past when she exited the small outhouse. He rubbed his eyes, stifling a yawn. "Beibei? Did you just get in?"

She nodded. "Morning, Bàba."

He brushed past without waiting for an answer. She hadn't seen him so exhausted in a long time, where he asked a question and then walked away, as if forgetting he asked. Like his mind was someplace else entirely.

Angie followed his retreat, staying several feet behind as he approached Grace, his junior manager.

Grace checked her clipboard. "We caught two and killed two more armed mermaids lurking by the shore early this morning."

"Good." Bàba's gaze pointed everywhere except directly at Grace.

Angie stroked her neck and grimaced. She turned away from them and hoped they hadn't caught her eavesdropping. Had those mer been caught last night? She had been oblivious to it, all wound up in Kaden's arms.

The thought positively sickened her, and she walked away to regain her composure.

Twenty-Eight

The last person Angie expected to see when she walked into work the next morning was Celia, in front of the building with the staff locker rooms.

Eva's daughter.

Angie hadn't seen Celia here since the start of the summer, when she had come with some friends to go scuba diving. Before Angie had first glimpsed Kaden's tail.

The young woman had her hands wedged in her sandy hair while pacing back and forth, appearing flustered.

"Celia?" Angie began, once she was in earshot.

The young woman stopped and let her hair fall limp around her face, eyeing Angie up and down, as if trying to figure out where she knew her from. "Have we met before?"

"You probably don't recognize me anymore. I met you a couple times when we were younger, and your mom brought you to the docks." The same way Mia came with Rosie to meet Nick, and the same way Māma and Bàba brought her and Mia when they were little girls.

"Oh!" Celia's face flashed with recognition. "Angie, right?"

Angie nodded. "Are you okay? Waiting for your mom?"

A stream of tears slid down Celia's cheeks, and on instinct, Angie moved to comfort her. "I'm looking for her. She didn't come home last night, and she's not answering my texts or calls. I thought maybe she might still be here, and I don't know, but I'm so worried. Grace and a few others are looking for her now."

"I'll stay with you, if that's okay."

Celia's anxious energy rubbed off on Angie, and Angie held her arms over her stomach, dreading what news would come. Eva had to be okay, right? Maybe she had just worked overtime and somehow forgot to tell her daughter—

"Celia?" Grace approached them.

Celia stood at attention. Her face hardened. "I've seen doctors with that same look when they're about to give a patient's family bad news."

Angie's gaze darted between the two women, her next breath catching in her windpipe. Grace hung her head. "We found her, pulled her out from the water. She's unconscious, and the paramedics are with her now."

"What? No!" Celia began to push her way past Grace. "Where is she? Where's my mom?"

"Celia, wait!" Grace ran behind Celia. "You're going the wrong way!"

Angie followed as they changed directions, and they stopped in the middle of their main gangway, where two paramedics were on their knees performing CPR and a group of workers cluttered around them watching the seas, hands on their gun holsters. An ambulance was parked nearby.

"Mom!" Celia shrieked, wedging her way between the paramedics and dock workers, and collapsing at Eva's side, her body racked with sobs. "Mom? Come back. Please come back. Don't leave me all alone."

"I'm sorry, we couldn't save her," one paramedic said. "We tried."

With a roaring in her ears and a numbness in her cheeks and chest, Angie walked to Celia's side and kneeled beside her. Eva lay supine, bloated and pale, her lips blue.

Celia's wails and cries rang through the open sky, and Angie's heart broke.

——— ☪ ———

Friday evening came, and Angie waited for Kaden at Creston Harbor's lighthouse before the sun descended. She replayed her night with Kaden over and over in her mind, wishing she could go back in time and take back her confession. Though she meant every word, she should never have said them aloud.

She was moving back to Seattle in less than a month. If she made it to the first day of class. The thought turned her nerves into fireworks. She should be elated at what her future held. Instead, stress and frustration overshadowed whatever happiness may have been bubbling inside.

She checked off the other reasons in her mind: There was a war. Kaden was a merman. She lived on land; he lived in the sea.

Self-loathing festered in her knowing she was betraying her bàba and her people.

An impossible situation that could never be.

It was cruel to lead Kaden on, thinking they had a future together, especially given their circumstances.

Both of them would be better off if they parted ways now.

"Did you wait long?" Kaden approached the shoreline. He took her hands in his and squeezed. The broad smile faded as he studied her face.

"What's wrong?" Angie quirked an eyebrow.

"Your face. It's awash with pallor, and there is smoky puffiness under your eyes. Your lips are no longer that beautiful pink. You are sitting here, slumped as if holding up the weight of your body is too much."

"That's a really poetic way to say I look exactly how I feel. Exhausted." She covered her yawn.

Kaden curled the distal part of his tail and used it to give him a forceful push onto the seaside.

Tell him now. Cut the cord.

The words rose to her throat, ready to be vocalized.

But damn it. She cared for him, and it was much too tiring to fight the feeling. The look on his face, his smile, was so heartfelt.

"Sorry. I'm beat. I feel like my head is going to explode if it keeps pounding. This was supposed to be a fun, educational, relaxing summer. I feel like I aged ten years." The words tumbled out of her mouth in a single breath. Pausing to think through her words would overwhelm her fatigued brain. She straightened her back, and then collapsed again. She swallowed hard, blinking back tears. "More of our workers disappeared. One of them was Eva, someone I've known since I was fourteen. Found out about her yesterday, when I saw her daughter at the docks."

Kaden parted his lips, but Angie hurried before he could utter a sound. "Do you know what happened to her?"

"I—" The word stuttered.

"Please, tell me." A pleading note coated her voice.

Kaden's gaze was fixed on the space between them. The lower part of his tail tensed, as if hugging the sandy ground. He fiddled with something in one closed fist. He didn't look up at her. "I didn't see it happen, but the mer-king and mer-queen spoke of it and praised our sentinels for capturing and killing two humans the day before. The woman you speak of was left to drown, the sentinels striking her down when she attempted to swim to the surface. They watched her struggle until she no longer drew breath."

An uncontrollable shudder swept through Angie's core. "They couldn't at least kill her quickly? To think she suffered like that." Her hands curled into fists. She knew her own people hadn't shown mercy to the merfolk, but it tore at her innards to know Eva died a slow, agonizing death.

"I wished they had delivered her a merciful death, as well." Kaden wet his lips. "It makes me sick hearing the proud swell of the mer-king's voice when he praised them for their barbarism."

Angie drew her knees to her chest. "I know we've done terrible things to the mer, but still. It's awful. Her poor daughter had to see her, too."

Kaden visibly softened and put his hand over hers. "I can only imagine the horror she experienced. I hope she's able to take the time she needs to grieve properly."

"I called her this morning to check on her. Some of her friends and family are going to stay with her for a while. She'll have support." She rested her chin on the tops of her knees, thinking back to what Kaden said. It stuck out to her that he called his parents by their royal titles. She questioned him about it.

"Cyrus and I asked once why we could not call them Mother and Father like our peers referred to their parents. They shot the idea down. Told us they were our superiors and the rulers of their territory, and we would respect them as such. It's how we've lived." His tail swept across the sand, creating a gritty arc. He slid one arm around her, and she pulled in closer to him.

"Interesting. I can't imagine calling my mom and dad anything else besides Māma and Bàba." She changed the subject, "Boats aren't going out anymore, unless they're boats that can do some damage to the mer. They brought another merman back last night." Her words faded into silence.

"Your people sent a boat full of spear fishers. They came hunting us yesterday. I heard they found a family of wayward mer in the southern seas. They fled, but the father stayed behind to defend them and was killed. That was likely the one you saw."

"Did you know him?" Her voice lowered, blunting her words. Angie lifted her gaze to meet his.

Kaden shook his head. "Not personally, but he was of my queendom. Lived in a rural town far from the palace."

"I'm sorry." Angie pulled away from him, fingering her ponytail until it fell over one shoulder. "The people in my village are getting skinnier by the day. The docks are losing business, and soon my bàba will be struggling to run it." She stopped short. Was this too much information? Would Kaden take this and go to the king and queen? Her guilt was a dagger in her abdomen. Here she was, talking about how her people suffered, revealing how weak they were, while cozying up to the mer's prince.

Yet she didn't want to stay away from him.

"The humans do look skinnier," he agreed. "I think of you each time I go to the sanctuaries."

She cast a side-eye at him. "How do you get those fish to go there? It's like they willingly trap themselves."

"It's not a trap." Kaden sounded defensive. "We don't force them to go. They live in harmony with us and trust us because we treat them as equals." A distant, unfocused smile stretched across his face. "They know they are well fed and cared for when they are close to us."

A series of frenzied splashes emerged and faded into the distance, like someone pranced through a puddle, diverting his attention. Kaden froze, and Angie whirled around, eyes wide, her hand to her mouth.

Her heart jumped at the thought that they had been spotted. She tensed. "Y-you think there are mer here?"

Kaden's guard held strong, but he wanted to comfort Angie. He kept a lookout around them. "Likely not a mer. They don't usually come around this area."

Angie yelped when, from behind Kaden, a tall wave rose from the sea and rushed for them.

TWENTY-NINE

THEIR QUICK REFLEXES WERE NO MATCH for the wave's fury. Forceful water swept them off to the side, hurling them like two cannonballs back into the sea. Loose debris from the island followed, twigs and rocks and dirt assaulting and splattering onto them.

Grimacing, she plucked a plastic bag with a smiley face on it off her head.

"What in the black depths?" Kaden clutched Angie's wrist and led her back to the shore.

"What happened?" Angie exclaimed as soon as they were back on dry land.

A mermaid's head emerged above the water.

Oh, she was what happened.

The mermaid followed them, swimming like she was in a sprint, and caught up before they reached the island. The pearls around her neck and bust shone like they were brand new. Her ivory tail glistened beneath the sunlight, a tendril of dark hair falling on the side of her face while the rest of her long braid fell down her back.

Angie recognized her. The mermaid she'd seen with Cyrus while scuba diving, what felt like years ago. She seemed more familiar than that.

"Angie, meet Adrielle," Kaden said, his voice flat. "My brother's lifemate. Thank you for launching us into ice-cold water." His gills and nostrils flared as he faced her.

Adrielle swam closer to them and squinched her small face. She spoke through a clenched jaw, "Kaden," the *K* sound gravelly and harsh. Angie paddled nearer, but Adrielle backed away and held out her hand in a signal of warning. "Wait."

Angie obeyed and stopped where she was. "You were watching me the other day."

"I was." Adrielle tilted her head to one side, staring them down. "I had to see for myself."

"See what?" Kaden's skin tightened and the tip of his tail stiffened. "Did Cyrus say something?"

"Don't blame him, but now I know that Cyrus knew and couldn't be bothered to tell me, we will have words. I went to find you after you didn't show up for your engagement announcement ceremony. After you missed your own banquet!" Her voice rose with each word. "What is wrong with you? Are you trying to turn the entire queendom against you?"

Kaden paled.

"King Aqilus and Queen Serapha are already branding you a traitor, and rumors are swirling that you are abandoning us for landwalkers." Adrielle was positively seething, and Angie winced at her radiating ire piercing the cold around them. Her expression became pleading. "For a human woman?"

"There's nothing more for you to understand. I care for her," Kaden said, voice raspy.

"The engagement party," Angie whispered to him. "That was today?"

A flash of hurt struck her. A reminder that he was meant to be with another. A mermaid, someone more suited for him than she would ever be.

"It's not what you think." Kaden kept his voice steady and assuring.

Adrielle turned to Angie, her tone blunt and sardonic. "He is not to be bonded, landwalker, so no worries for you. Not anymore. The King and Queen are furious."

"It's an event where they present me with mermaids who they thought were suitable and who had shown interest in me. I knew it was today. I chose not to go." Kaden directed his glare back to Adrielle. "I resent it. Seeing mermaids corralled like they're nothing more than animals to be inspected and one chosen to be a trophy. Now they can spend their time on mermen or other mermaids who wish for their time and affections."

"I am a prized animal, then?" Adrielle's shoulders twitched, and she moved toward them, extending her torso out of the water. Her intense gaze dared him to answer.

"There was no contest, and the interested mermaids and mermen knew it. I envy the love that you two have, forever and true." He directed his next words to Angie, his expression softening and voice lowering. "I wished to only join with my true heart's desire. I never imagined it would burn for a human."

"Believe me, I didn't want this to happen either. Having feelings for him." Angie said to Adrielle, waving a hand at Kaden.

Behind him, Adrielle scowled and rested her chin on her hands, appearing crestfallen. "Kaden, if the King and Queen find out you were a no-show because you're romancing a landwalker, especially in the midst of what has been happening, they'll make you an outcast forevermore. You understand, right?"

Angie sucked in a sharp breath, her heart leaping to her throat and wedging itself there.

"Are you going to tell them?" Kaden's words were strained, breaths coming out like he'd swam a marathon.

"You're being reckless," Adrielle answered with a frustrated shake of her head, "but no. I won't tell."

Kaden's shoulders and chest deflated at her answer.

"Oh, stop looking at me like that!" She groaned. Adrielle raised her hands, bringing a stream of seawater with her, and then dropped her face in her palms. "I need to talk to you in private."

Kaden bowed his head and looked to Angie, who nodded at him while rubbing her hand over and over on her pant leg, still damp from when they were thrown into the water earlier.

The time that they were gone felt endless.

What were they talking about? Every possibility crossed her mind. Perhaps Adrielle was convincing Kaden to leave her, for his own good, she would guess. Or it could be as innocuous as her asking questions about Angie. Time passed and her mind wandered to darker thoughts. Persuading Kaden to kill her, even? She shuddered and squeezed the horrifying, uncalled-for thought out into the Mariana Trench where it could stay.

Finally, Kaden and Adrielle returned.

"Is everything okay?" she asked.

He scooted to sit beside her, wrapping his tail around the front of her legs in a protective gesture. "It will be."

"Angie?" Adrielle's voice joined theirs. Angie sat up to attention, listening to her. A raging storm brewed in the mermaid's eyes. "If you ever do anything to hurt him, or any of our people, I will hunt you down myself and kill you."

"You and my brother are truly two of a kind, even down to your threats," Kaden muttered.

Angie swallowed hard. So, Adrielle was worried she would hurt Kaden. "I won't. I promise."

"Good." She addressed Kaden next. "What am I supposed to tell the King and Queen?"

"You never found me." He took her hand and squeezed it.

"Whatever happens from this, it's on you." Adrielle set her jaw. She moved her hand out of his and ducked underwater.

"What did she say to you?" Angie asked. She had to know if she had anything to worry about.

Kaden rubbed his cheeks. "She believes you may have clouded my mind. Brainwashed me."

Angie jerked her head back, skin tingling and nerves firing icy shock through her system. The merfolk would really believe that humans had mind control powers?

It made sense to her that they were as much of a mystery to them as the merfolk were to the humans. Somehow, it made them seem more sympathetic to her. There might be hope yet, that if the two races could truly understand each other then a truce might be reached.

Kaden continued. "She asked me to look out for myself, that your people will show no mercy on me. As my parents would not." A heavy sigh from him. "She also offered to tell my parents and the queendom that you altered my mind."

"And what did you say?" Angie narrowed her eyes at him. Some feet away from her, a wave crashed on the shore, and she flinched. Her clothes hung heavy and wet from her skin.

"That I'm with you because I want to be." He sat up, his back ramrod straight with resolve.

Angie pursed her lips.

So much trouble just to be together. She could part ways with him, as she originally planned. Make it easy on herself and find a man whose people weren't actively murdering her colleagues and friends.

Kaden deserved better, too. The thought of him putting everything on the line for her made her heart ache.

"Is this worth it? You could be exiled. I could lose everything I worked so hard for. I could lose you."

Kaden's facial muscles went slack. "Is it for you?"

Was it worth it for her? She had to think about her answer for a moment.

"I'm not sure," she finally croaked. "I want to say yes. I don't want to stop seeing you."

"Then don't." His voice was soft, and he laid a trembling hand on her thigh.

"But knowing what we both could lose. I wish it wasn't this way." Tiān, she had never thought love should be hard. But this was hard. At the same time, she was drawn to him over and over, and didn't want to let him go.

"I wish it wasn't either. I told you I would keep trying. And I will." His grip on her thigh tightened to a firm grasp. "I'll show you that being with me is worth it."

"Then when are you going to talk to the King and Queen? They have the power to stop this, right?" Her tone grated like sandpaper and came out sharper than she intended. "Can't you do something? You're a prince; you must have some kind of power."

She didn't regret what she said; she was tired of waiting for Kaden to appeal to the mer-king and mer-queen.

"I do, but anything I rule or decree must be executed by the current rulers, and speaking of the King and Queen, I tried. Yesterday." His voice volume dropped a notch. "I approached them myself, without waiting for their sentinels to give me the go-ahead. When I arrived, two sentinels blocked me, told that they were not seeing anybody else."

"But you're their son." Angie folded her arms across her chest. "How could they not want to talk to you? Aren't they concerned at all?"

"I suppose they were mad that I've refused to find a lifemate. Though, the sentinels then told me they held court for the day, and they were not to allow anyone else in. So, I went for the doors myself. They blocked me. I went back later, and the King and Queen were nowhere to be found. Not in the throne room. Nor the bedchambers. Only for me to learn from Cyrus that they'd left to visit another part of the queendom." The more he spoke, the more his jaw clenched, his words emerging like spittle.

Angie pinched the bridge of her nose and closed her eyes. "I just, I don't know. Where is this going to go? Do we even have a future together?"

"I could ask you the same. If I commit myself to you, I am yours for life. I understand humans don't necessarily operate that way." Kaden gave her a pointed look.

Angie shrugged, defeated. "What choice do we have? Run away like teenagers?"

He bristled at her last sentence. "I want to be with you. Even if it means splitting my time between land and sea."

Angie's heart filled with joy at the notion.

"I'll be a marine biologist if we come out of this alive." She choked up and stumbled over the *if*, and a chill ran through her bones. "I'll be spending a lot more time in the water. I want to study deep sea fish and educate others on overfishing and its disastrous consequences."

Kaden leaned in closer so his breath swept over her ear. "I'll show you things no human will ever see. The greatest treasures in the deep, untouched by human interference." A coy smile played over his soft lips, drawing her attention to them, and he added, "As long as you let me steal you every now and again so I can have you to myself."

"Hmm." Angie sidled closer, brushing wispy bangs out of her eyes and moving in until her lips were inches from his. Her breathing quickened in anticipation, in tandem with his, and the air stilled between them. Her heart burst with adoration, and she put both her hands on each side of his jaw. Pulled him into a deep, passionate kiss. "I'd like that, but I'd like it even more if you took me for yourself now."

Kaden latched onto her, his hands tangling in her messy ponytail and running his fingers down her back. Whimpering, she arched her chest into his then pulled away just as quickly.

"Kaden, Kaden, wait." With desperate hands, he brought her close to him again, but she stopped him. Her eyes searched his face. "You made me feel so good last time, but I don't know how to return it. I'm sorry, I don't know what to do with a tail, and I want to make you feel just as good." Then she sat straighter, focused on the spot where his waist ended and tail began. "Where is your—?"

Kaden gave her an amused smirk. "My what? Come Angie, out with it."

Her neck flushed. Why was it so hard to say? She was a scientist, damn it. "Your penis."

That sounded decidedly clinical and dry, and she buried her face in her hands.

Kaden's smirk grew wider. Clearly, he was amused by her awkwardness. "It's internal. For now."

"For now, huh?" She dragged her gaze up and down his tail again.

"I can tell you're not satisfied with my answer." Kaden bit down on his lower lip, a nervous laugh escaping him. He rolled onto his back, fully exposing the ventral part of his tail. Between his small pelvic fins, a thickened section of scales and an extra fin atop it came into view.

"Oh." She could sense his discomfort, and a part of her hated that she might be ruining the moment with her insatiable curiosity, but she wanted to understand how he worked. All of him. "So, when you mate, it comes out of—"

"Must we keep talking about mer sex? I would prefer to enjoy you." Bewilderment strained his features.

Angie sat back. "Can I touch you, erm, there? I know you said intercourse binds you to me, but just touching you wouldn't cause that to happen, right?"

Kaden's cheeks tinged pink. "It won't, but I–I've never been touched there."

"Then, may I?"

The muscles in the proximal part of his tail twitched, and he scraped a hand through his hair. He nodded. "I would like to try. With you."

Angie perked up and kissed him again. Their lips parted, and her tongue searched for his until they became entwined. She grazed one hand tenderly between his pelvic fins, testing his reaction.

He gasped against her lips, and she took that as encouragement.

His scales parted, and he filled her hand, and she was surprised it was so smooth. His size felt similar to a human male's. She moved gentle and slow at first, listening to the way his body responded to her.

He clenched hard at her shoulders while they kissed, his body pulsing and breaths became ragged and hitched. The bottom half of his tail moved to wrap itself around her until she sat within it like a cushion. It tensed and curled, his caudal fins sweeping over and brushing the ground.

Finally, they broke apart for air. He struggled for breath, his head falling back and jaw clenched.

His fingers dug into her back, and he buried his face into the crook of her neck, his thick eyelashes fluttering against her skin in a gentle tickle. "I've never felt anything like this."

She grinned, though she knew he couldn't see her. "I try."

When his pelvic fins covered him again, he grabbed and pinned her down with a sharp, audible intake of breath, and his mouth crashed into hers again.

He reached beneath her sweater and shirt, inching up and cupping one of her breasts and moved his other hand down to the hem of her pants, and got stuck there.

Kaden leaned back, wearing a mask of puzzlement.

"Need help?" She grinned against his mouth. "They're buttons and a zipper. You pop them, like so."

He watched with fascination as she undid them, and she took his hand, sliding it beneath her clothes.

"Ah, first time I've seen such a thing."

"I imagine the mer don't have much use for buttons and zippers," she said with a light laugh. His expression was sheepish, his hand moving lower, lower, and she gasped, her gaze locked with his.

"Open your legs." His voice came out hoarse and breathy.

She did. His fingers met her damp heat and worked in slow, methodical circles.

A gasp emerged from her throat when he slid one finger inside her, and then another.

His mouth moved to her neck and her breasts, pleasing her desperately, as if today were the last time he would ever see her. It drove her to want more, need more from him. Her mind ran wild and again, her body thrummed.

She pressed her lips to his ear. "Kaden, don't you dare stop. Please, please, please."

He listened and kissed her again, a clash of tongues and lips, her body heat rising with his. She wanted to hold on to this feeling, to him, forever.

Under his arduous touch, the pulsing in her temples made her feel as if her head was going to explode into a thousand stars, clouding her vision and mind like a school of fish swimming around her in dizzying dances.

She unraveled with forceful pulls until she became undone, and a cascade of dull warmth spread from the top of her head to the tips of her toes. A cry escaped her, and she squeezed her legs against his arm while she buried her face in his neck, her body shaking. He enveloped her in his arms and kissed the top of her head. Her breathing gradually slowed to a normal cadence.

Neither of them spoke, but she was content to stay where they were. She didn't want to think about returning to the docks yet.

Instead, she nestled in his arms, fearing that if he let her go, their worries would become reality.

THIRTY

THREE—OR WAS IT FOUR?—DAYS PASSED SINCE Angie was with Kaden last, and still, her heart fluttered when she thought of him. The way he touched and kissed her made her feel like she could walk on water. A flush of heat emanated beneath her belly and dissipated over her thighs when the handsome, sturdy mer-prince made his way into her thoughts.

The perfect lover. And a mer, the enemy of her people. A fact she couldn't forget, much as she tried to tonight.

Cyrus's face flashed in her mind. The way he had nearly killed her, and her panic as she desperately searched for air bubbles. Her only hope at the time of staying alive thousands of feet under the sea. She shivered at the memory.

Beside her, Mia and Stefan laughed while setting up a long table full of plastic cups and napkins. Behind her, Bàba, their village physician Imani, and Jenny and Dave from their village prepared drinks. Kodiak Coffee—Bàba's favorite—dessert wines and Mamie Taylors flowed with abundance and soda, water, and hot chocolate topped off the rest of the table. Angie had invited Celia, but the young woman declined. Other villagers and dock workers milled around the patio, chatting and laughing.

All that was missing was the food.

Nick was also missing from tonight's festivities. Apparently, he was still at the docks, according to Bàba. Angie couldn't fight the feeling that he was up to something.

"So, Nick was the one who set up this whole celebration, and he's nowhere to be found?" she sniped to no one in particular. "Would be nice to actually feed everyone here."

"Last I heard, he was on his way. Promised good news," Ken, Stefan's husband, said, passing by and standing next to her.

Angie jolted. She hadn't seen Ken coming, and Nick promising good news made her stomach clench with unease.

An upwards of forty some people were in their sprawling backyard, including Jenny and Dave and a group of fishermen among them. It came alive beneath early August's midnight sun, like their summer family gatherings when Māma was still alive. Even Lulu came out for a peek, a tiny thing standing in the corner and staring at the new people with wonder in her round eyes.

Rosie tugged on Angie's shorts. She pointed to Angie's wrist. "Angie āyí, where did you get your bracelet from? It looks like mine, but nicer."

"Oh, uh." Angie looked down to Kaden's gift snug around her wrist. "It was a gift. But, tell you what. After I get out of school and I have a little more money, I'll get you an even nicer one."

Rosie's curious expression brightened, and her eyes sparkled with her smile. "Okay! And, um, I wanted to ask, but have you seen more mermaids?"

Angie acknowledged Rosie. She couldn't tell her about Kaden and Adrielle and Cyrus.

Adrielle was the type of gorgeous mermaid that Rosie dreamed of seeing. Angie knew, because she had once dreamed that too. She hated lying to her family, but she couldn't take the likely chance she would run off and tell her parents.

"Not recently sweetie, no."

"Aw." Rosie pouted. "But will you tell me when you do?"

"Of course I will. Did you have anything to drink yet?" Rosie shook her head. "Well then!" Angie stepped aside and handed her a cup. "Go get your māma so she can get something to drink in that cute little belly of yours until your dad comes."

"Okay!" Rosie seemed to have forgotten about mermaids as she ran to Mia, waving the cup at her.

Angie followed behind her to grab a Mamie Taylor for herself, bumping into Stefan when she reached for the ginger beer. She had been drinking more liquids lately, hoping to fill the void in her stomach.

Even though she tried not to look, she caught him leaning over to whisper something in Ken's ear, and they laughed. Each time she saw them, they had the energy of two new boyfriends with the familiarity and comfort of a long-married happy couple. She'd find it a blessing if she and her future partner were still so loved up after over two decades of being together.

Meanwhile, she couldn't figure out what she felt for Kaden.

"Ugh, where the hell is Nick? I'm starving," Jenny said from Angie's other side, putting a hand over her swollen belly.

"How far along?" Angie asked.

Jenny kept her gaze on her midsection, a forlorn smile tugging at her lips. "Sixteen weeks."

"I'd kill for some protein right now." Dave joined her, kissing the top of her head. He squeezed Jenny's shoulders, pulling her closer to him. "I've been giving her most of the food we get. I'll gladly starve if it means my wife and kids will live."

Angie exchanged a sad look with Mia who had joined their group with Rosie and Peter, Jenny and Dave's son. Dave did look skinnier than the last time she saw him, his T-shirt hung loosely on his upper body.

An urge struck to tell them that she'd seen the fish. That they weren't all gone. The fish were safe, and if they agreed to talk to the mer, maybe they would get them back.

No. She had to stay quiet. Couldn't betray Kaden's trust.

"We're so happy you all are here." Mia leaned back in her chair.

The sun had set, the skies lit with scintillating stars, and Angie zipped her jacket all the way up.

Then, Mia, Ken, and Dave looked up, and pushed their chairs back to rush toward two men who had just arrived, each holding one side of a one-hundred-and-fifty-quart cooler.

It was Nick and a red-bearded fisherman, the one Angie had helped when she first realized that fish were missing.

Angie trailed at Dave's heels.

"What you got in there, Nick?" He towered over the cooler when Nick and the fisherman set it on the grass.

A triumphant grin spread over Nick's face when he threw open the cooler top.

Chills trailed down Angie's spine.

Fish filled the cooler. Sea bass, salmon, arctic char, all the fish that hadn't been seen in months. Two lobsters and three crabs were tucked into the corners.

"Nick! Holy shit, where'd you get that from? You two are heroes!" Ken clapped them on the back, and Angie stayed back as more partygoers joined, including Rosie, Bàba, and Stefan.

"Where did you get these from?" Stefan asked. "Angie, come with me to throw these on the grill?" He handed her a cold, dead salmon. Numb, Angie held out a limp hand to receive it.

She didn't move, and felt as if roots had grown under feet and anchored her into the ground.

"Well." Nick pulled out a lobster in each hand and handed them to the red-bearded fisherman, and two crabs to Ken. "Help me unshell these, boys?"

"You got it, man," Ken said, following the fisherman toward the long plastic table next to the grill.

Beside Angie, Mia, Bàba, Dave, and Stefan fixed their gazes on Nick who seemed to relish the attention, with his chest puffed and a smug smile plastered on his face.

"We found where the mer were keeping them. Somehow those scaly bastards managed to keep all the fish in one place. Our cameras sensed movement, we were able to follow a trail straight to the site. I can't believe it." Nick paused for dramatic effect, turning his gaze to Angie and holding it.

"Took us a little while to pinpoint exactly where it was and then get enough fish for us, but we did it."

How did this happen? How did he find—

Realization stung her face. The flashing red light she saw when they left the sanctuary.

Her palms grew sweaty, and her head spun.

It was a camera, and damn her for not stopping to investigate. If she had, she would have seen it, could have gotten rid of the memory card before divers retrieved the footage.

Nick held her gaze for a moment longer, his expression impassive.

She waited for him to say something, to out her in front of everyone in typical gloating Nick fashion.

He said nothing to her and returned to his conversation with the group gathered before him.

An hour passed, and lowering her head, Angie turned away from him and nudged Mia, handing her salmon to Bàba. The fresh air around her had become stifling, and she needed to be anywhere but here. "Let's get another drink, and then go for a walk?"

Mia nodded and waved to Nick, who blew her a kiss in return, and Angie led her to the house and pushed the door open.

Once inside, Angie washed her hands and reached for a pair of wine glasses, and poured two glasses of demi-sec champagne and offered one to Mia.

"No thanks, Angie. I'll stick to this." Mia pointed to her can of black cherry-flavored seltzer, which she'd retrieved from the fridge. "I'm pregnant. Found out a week ago. Came as a surprise to Nick and I."

Angie's grip loosened on the champagne bottle, stopping short of dropping it. All thoughts of Nick finding the fish fled her mind as a deluge of emotion burst in her: worry for Mia's stress and health and fear about bringing in a new baby during a time when they warred with a race they once deemed mythical. But excitement for a new niece or nephew to dote on overshadowed all.

"Congratulations! Guess I'm having two tonight." Angie clasped her hands together as they strolled outside. "When did you find out?"

Mia put a hand over her belly. "Last week. I'm almost two months along. I'll tell Bàba when he's not so stressed."

"Or you could help him de-stress by telling him." Angie took a sip of her champagne, the sweet, cold bubbles racing down her throat.

"True." Mia grinned. "I'll tell him tomorrow morning. He's not working, right?"

"No, I think he actually took a day off. Or at least the morning. I had to talk him into it before he practically killed himself from the stress and lack of sleep."

They kept walking, away from the party and onto a wide swath of open land facing the single rough road bisecting the region. In the distance and out of sight, the roar of the shore drifted to them.

"Still sticking with the Titanic theme for the new kid?" She smirked.

"I've thought about this," Mia said, after another sip of seltzer. "Definitely Jack, if it's a boy. Or Margaret if it's a girl. There's lots of characters to choose from."

"I love both those names. And look, the lights are out!" They stopped at a cliff's edge, taking in the sight.

The Aurora Borealis lit up the night sky with soft violets, sea greens, and deep blues, sweeping across the horizon like mesmerizing, undulating drapes, shimmering as rainbow paint on a pitch-black canvas. Below, it illuminated the nearby ocean and canopies of fellow villagers' homes and the boreal forest in the distance with muted colors.

"This never gets old." Mia piped up after a moment of silence. "Remember when we were little girls and we'd lay outside and stare at them? Back when you were still in your mermaid-hunting phase? You'd bring all those mermaid books from the library with you."

That elicited a laugh from Angie. Now, not only had she found them, she'd become much too close to their prince. Again, her cheeks warmed.

"Yup, I remember." A wide grin stretched over Angie's face, and then fell as quickly as it appeared. "Is everything okay with you and Nick? You haven't seemed too happy lately."

"He's like a completely different man. One I don't recognize," Mia said. Her lips moved as if she were about to say more, but then she pressed them shut and looked to the ground. "I miss how we were. He used to prioritize us, and we were happy." When she looked up again, her eyes were red, and Angie put an arm around her. "I know he has his moments and isn't always easy to get along with. But he tries."

Angie started to refute her last sentence, but stopped herself. It wouldn't accomplish anything other than make Mia feel worse. "I'm sorry he's acting like that."

"Thanks." Mia wrapped her arms around herself. "But, that's mine and Nick's problem to deal with. You have enough on your plate." They began walking again. "I know you don't like him, but I appreciate you listening to me vent."

"Of course." The champagne had loosened her inhibitions, and Angie blurted out her next words. "He's never been nice to me, and he's even worse now that he's one of my bosses."

"I know he's a lot sometimes," Mia admitted. "But he's my husband. Has always been there for me." Then she added, "You went to Wasilla and then Seattle after high school, and then Māma left us a few years later. Bàba went into overdrive at the docks with her gone. Nick was all I had for a while."

Angie bristled. She knew Mia hadn't meant it that way, but guilt jabbed her core.

"I didn't know. I'm sorry. But you know Wasilla had the center I wanted to work at. I needed money for school. Bàba offered to help with the costs, but I couldn't put that pressure on him. Not with him taking care of Māma and all her medical bills."

Mia visibly softened. "You don't have to justify your choices to me."

"Still, I regret not visiting more in the last six years."

Angie focused on the mesmerizing Northern Lights, and put her head on Mia's shoulder, the way she did when they were kids. After a pause, Mia exhaled a plume of frost, then put her head over Angie's. "You ever want to get married? Start a family?"

Angie's shoulders twitched at the mention. Marriage or children had never been at the forefront of her mind. She never daydreamed of her wedding day like Mia had once she and Nick began dating. Even when "well-meaning" aunties and uncles grilled her about why she was still single.

That she needed to find a man before she became a *shèngnǚ*, or "leftover woman" which, to them, was any single woman older than her mid-twenties. And the best, when her aunties warned her not to be too successful or she would scare off potential suitors.

Notions Angie scoffed at in private.

She was content to be Angie āyí and marine biologist extraordinaire with her own office, aspiring to become head of the health sciences program at her graduate school while traveling during school breaks for research, and a house full of pets.

Kaden swam into her mind.

"I'm not sure." She picked her words carefully. If they did go down that path, was it even a possibility? Biological children would be impossible regardless of what either of them would want. If she were to spend the rest of her life with him—an idea that made her giddy and shaky—how would they merge their two worlds? Or perhaps this was simply a fling for them both. Then again, Kaden's words at their last meeting stated otherwise.

If I commit myself to you, I am yours for life.

It was all too much. He hadn't said he wanted to give himself to her. She didn't want to confront her own jumbled feelings either. It was a matter of weeks before they would be separated indefinitely.

"It's nice in theory," said Angie. "But I'm indifferent about kids. Besides, your kids and Lulu will be enough for me to handle. I don't have that maternal instinct like you."

"Well, I had Rosie when I was twenty-two. Everyone told me I was too young, but I knew what I wanted. If you know, you know." Mia sobered at her words. "You're leaving again soon. Your PhD program isn't short, you know."

"Depending on my schedule, I'll come back more often. I'll do my best." No matter what, Angie promised herself she would visit, if only for several weeks, during school breaks, more often than she did while in Wasilla and Seattle. Kaden paddled his way into her mind again, and she couldn't stop the starry eyes from coming on. "And I'll consider marrying a man who can add to my life."

Mia, perceptive as always, picked up on it right away. She gasped. "Is there someone special?"

"Maybe." Angie turned and headed back for the party.

"I knew that bracelet came from someone. I didn't see it when you first came back."

Angie dropped her head. Rosie likely ran and asked her mother for a similar bracelet.

Mia followed at her heels. "Whoever he is, I hope you two are happy together. As long as it's not one of those murderous sea creatures."

She detected the joking tone with Mia's last sentence, but still, an invisible knife poked at Angie's chest. She rounded her shoulders in response. "We're not any better than they are. They're not all bloodthirsty monsters."

Mia snorted her disbelief. "How would you know? Just because you've gotten lucky and haven't been hurt by one yet?"

Her words stung, and Angie fiddled with her empty glass and, with nervous hands, dropped it on the ground. It made a loud *clack* as the bottom of the glass made contact with the pebbled road. "Would you like to meet him?"

Mia's eyes brightened.

Angie picked the glass back up. "I'm seeing him tomorrow evening. Come without Nick, alright? It's okay to bring Rosie though. After work, seven o'clock."

Mia's face tightened, and one finger tapped at her seltzer water can as if making some sort of nonverbal point. "I'll be there. I know you're not telling me the whole story."

Angie nodded, enjoying the peace and quiet. Owl hoots and frog songs and coyote howls filled the night. A breeze swept past, carrying with it the sea's tangy scent, followed by the smell of fresh wood and sea air crispness.

Beside her, Mia's lids were drooping, and they made their way back to the house. The anticipation of tomorrow evening made something in Angie's chest jolt. She wanted Mia to see that not all mer were the enemy, but she hoped she hadn't made a grave mistake.

THIRTY-ONE

IN TRUE MIA FASHION, SHE ARRIVED with Rosie ten minutes before seven in the evening, as promised. Angie designated their meeting spot outside the storage shed, out of view of the seashore.

"Angie āyí! Angie āyí! Where's your boyfriend?" Rosie hollered. "Is he gonna be my new uncle?"

Angie laughed, drawing the attention of some passing dock workers. "Uh, I don't know." She stopped there. It was too strange to use the term *boyfriend* to describe Kaden. Despite their closeness, she had no idea what they were, or what she was to him.

"I wanna see mermaids!" Rosie exclaimed, jumping up and down and clapping her small hands, her bracelet jangling. Angie thanked her ancestors that Rosie hadn't yet seen the murdered mer, innocent to the death and carnage.

Mia shushed her. "A little quieter, please? Tiān, she has not stopped talking since I got her from camp. Must have eaten too many candy bars."

"Sorry, Māma," Rosie muttered.

"So, where's this mystery guy? You meet him here at the docks? In college?" Angie caught Mia's sharp eyes lasering in on all the young looking men.

"At the docks. And sorry Mia, we have to walk a little bit." Angie motioned with her head toward a desolate stretch of beach. Mia's eyes burned a hole through her back as Angie led them further from the busy part of the docks.

"Angie," she piped up after several minutes. "Where exactly are we going? Utqiagvik?"

Angie chuckled. Utqiagvik was Alaska's northernmost city.

"My feet are tired," Rosie whined.

Angie glanced over her shoulder.

"Just hang in there a little longer, okay, sweetheart?" Mia grabbed Rosie's hand.

After another ten-minute walk, she stopped where Kaden had asked her to meet him. "I was kidding about Utqiagvik, but maybe you did lead us there," Mia grumbled. She mumbled something else under her breath while fumbling around in her purse and taking her phone out. "One second. Nick's calling."

"Papa!" Rosie called out, turning around to face Mia, standing on her tiptoes and pulling down on Mia's tucked in blouse, rendering it untucked.

"Honey, wait, I can't hear you. Let me go somewhere with better reception." She turned and walked back the way they came, still on the phone, and Rosie bounded after her.

Angie rolled her lips between her teeth, watching after them. Leave it to Nick to ruin this moment.

A splashing and sloshing noise caught her attention.

Kaden awaited, partially submerged in the water so only the top of his head and shoulders were visible.

Her smile faltered when he didn't return it, his expression as frigid as the winter seas.

"Is everything okay?" Angie walked toward him, but he held up one hand. Why wasn't he happy to see her? Had something happened with his family, in his queendom? Or...

The image of fish at the barbecue last night came back to her.

"Tell me something," he started, moving toward her enough so she could hear him, but far enough so that she couldn't touch him from where she stood. His tone was abrasive, yet carried a doleful undercurrent. "The sanctuary was raided. The same one I showed you."

She sucked in a sharp breath, the punch of realization striking her and hollowing out her chest. "Kaden, wait." Her voice cracked with emotion under his unhappy visage. "It's not what you think. Hear me out for a second, okay?"

"There's no other explanation, though. You're the only person who knows their location. Did you tell your family? The dockworkers?"

"Kaden, I didn't say anything to anyone. My dad put—"

Before she could say *cameras*, Rosie's boisterous voice came from behind her. "Angie āyí! You have a mermaid friend?"

Angie drew her mouth into a straight line and bit her lower lip. Maybe this wasn't a good time for them to meet Kaden.

"Oh, no. No, no, wait, let's go back!" Angie whirled around and ran in their direction, but Rosie, smaller and more agile, zipped past her and ran toward the water where Kaden was.

Kaden's eyes widened, and he looked from her, to Rosie, and then back to her, and she took solace that he didn't leave.

Mia was at Rosie's heels, stuffing her phone into her purse, and when she was close enough, grabbed Rosie's hands to keep her from running. Rosie was staring at Kaden, open-mouthed.

"Sorry, Angie. Nick just wanted to know where we were and when we could—" Mia looked up to where Rosie stared and screamed. "There's mer here! Kill it! We have to get out of here!" Panic surged in her voice, and she reached into her purse and pulled out a pocketknife, unsheathing the blade and flung it in Kaden's direction.

His eyes became two bulging orbs in his face, and with quick reflexes, he disappeared underwater. The knife landed with a *plop* beside him, and sank.

Angie grimaced. She screwed up and should have warned Mia, but it was too late now.

Kaden resurfaced and shrunk back, putting his hands up, staring at Mia.

"Mia! Stop!" Angie rose to her feet, and fell flat on her face when Mia grabbed her arm and yanked her backward toward the tree line.

"We have to go. We have to go," Mia kept saying.

Rosie squealed something that Angie thought was French then, "a real merman!" She bum-rushed Kaden. "Can I touch him?"

"No!" Mia yelled. Her hands shot forward, grabbing her daughter's arms. "Rosalynn! I said come back!"

"Mia, it's okay!" Angie looked at each of them. "And Kaden, she's harmless."

"K-Kaden? It has a name?" Mia shot her a look that screamed shock and surprise. "What the Hells is going on here?"

"I'd like to know, too." Kaden's tone was as sharp as the razorblade Mia threw at him.

"I'm sorry, I should have said something sooner. Mia, this is Kaden. He won't hurt you or Rosie." Angie turned to Kaden. "Kaden, Mia, my sister. That's her daughter, Rosie."

"We'll finish our conversation later." Kaden eyed her.

She nodded. It seemed he'd put aside the sanctuary chaos until after their little meet and greet.

Mia and Kaden's strained poses relaxed, but only slightly. Angie pressed a palm to her heart and thanked her ancestors. It was a start.

"Are you real? Like real real?" Rosie cut in. "Can I see your tail?"

Kaden gave a nervous laugh. "Yes, I'm real." To make a point, he pushed himself up to sit on the shore, bringing his tail closer to him. Rosie yelped in excitement and rushed over to touch and "ooh" and "ahh" over it. He held out Mia's pocket knife. "This is yours."

Without a word, Mia took it from him, fiddling with it before stashing it back in her purse.

"I can tell you two are related. Your sister tried to kill me too when she first saw me. Twice, actually," Kaden said. Angie's face grew hot at the mention. He continued, "Mia, yes? Mia Song?"

"Mia Richelieu now. Nice to, uh, meet you?" Mia looked to Angie, silently asking for help on how to greet him properly.

Angie gave her a thumbs up.

"Why do you have a different surname? You are not sisters?" His eyes held questions for Angie.

"Well, that's her husband's last name. When people get married, they can take the husband or the wife's last name to signify the start of a new family. Or choose to combine the two."

He pursed his lips. "So, he is your lifemate?"

Something about watching Mia converse with Kaden warmed Angie's heart, despite him being upset with her.

This time, Mia gave him a soft chuckle. "Yeah, you can say that."

"Then I've learned a new word. *Husband.*" Kaden flicked a small stream of water at Rosie, who laughed and asked him to do it again, so he did. "So, you and Angie are no longer family?"

"Oh goodness, not at all!" Angie punctuated her words with a quick shake of her head. "Mia is my blood sister forever."

A spark of understanding appeared in Kaden's eyes.

About to say something else, Mia stopped and her eyes rounded again. Angie followed her gaze. "Is something wrong?"

Behind Kaden, two more heads poked out of the water. Adrielle and Cyrus.

"I didn't realize our meeting was going to become a family gathering." Kaden's gaze slid to Angie.

"I didn't either. I wanted to introduce my sister and her kid to you. Show her that your people aren't the bloodthirsty murderers she believes your people to be." Angie dropped her gaze.

"A noble intent. Except I assume my brother and Adrielle are not here to exchange pleasantries."

"Angie," Cyrus began, "and more humans." He and Adrielle stayed back. "I knew you would bring reinforcements. Raiding our sanctuaries. Stealing fish like the treacherous landwalkers you are. I knew you couldn't be trusted." He aimed his question at Angie, scowling.

"And now they've lured you here to murder you, I presume," Adrielle added, her voice tight.

"Angie, what is he talking about? Sanctuaries?" Mia hissed into her ear.

"You remember when Nick showed up with the fish last night? That's where he got them from," Angie replied in a murmur, never taking her eyes off the three mer.

Mia sucked in a sharp breath. "They're angry. We should leave."

"Not yet," she said, hopeful. Angie didn't bother to mention how Cyrus almost killed her when they first met. If she did, Mia would try to kill Cyrus herself.

Kaden's voice drew her from her conversation with Mia. "She," he looked to Cyrus, and he motioned with his head to Angie, "isn't directly responsible. I will find out who is. They're not here to murder me."

Adrielle nudged Cyrus with her shoulder and whispered something into his ear. His harsh expression visibly softened. "I suppose the little one doesn't look like a threat. Too small to be a soldier." He jutted his chin toward Rosie who had watched the entire scene by peering out from behind Mia's legs. She appeared both riveted and confused. "Is she the meat shield?"

"They're not, brother." Kaden swam to Cyrus and put a hand on his shoulder. "That's Angie's sister and her sister's child."

"I see." Cyrus tossed a weary look at Mia whose steely gaze pierced through his chest and struck Adrielle behind him.

"Are they—are they safe?" Mia hissed in Angie's ear.

Angie looked to Kaden who looked to Adrielle and Cyrus. They stayed still, but their necks and shoulders appeared relaxed.

Mia crept closer to the shore, and in equal measure, Adrielle and Cyrus approached. Both sides now at the shoreline, no one moved. A tense stillness befell them.

Beside Angie, Mia let out a breath and coaxed Rosie forward. The two bum-rushed the coastline and pelted the three mer with an unending stream of questions. Adrielle appeared to warm to them as she swam closer to shore, and Cyrus followed at her tailfins. His gaze briefly met Angie's, and his head moved into a slight bow. Unlike their hostile, violent first meeting, this time, so close to land, Cyrus didn't seem so threatening.

Mia hovered, watching Rosie like a mother hawk whose chick could be snatched up and eaten any minute.

Adrielle's gaze darted to Rosie's wrist where she had the gold, sea glass-studded bracelet donned. "May I see it?"

"Sure! Angie āyí got it for me a long time ago," Rosie explained. Angie broke into a warm smile. Only a child would think that one and a half months felt like a long time. "She said it came from the sea."

"It did. Because I have its twin." Adrielle held out a wrist encircled by an identical bracelet. Rosie and Angie sucked in a collective gasp. "I had lost it some time ago when I was nearly caught in a landwalker net. Cyrus pulled me out before I was dragged to the surface with it. He crafted it when he was courting me."

"Do you want it back?" Rosie began to slide the bracelet off, and Adrielle stopped her with a hand to Rosie's wrist.

"No, no. Keep it. Think of it as a gift. You're an honorary mermaid now."

Tears gathered in Rosie's eyes. "Oh, thank you! Thank you so much!" She ran forward and threw her arms around Adrielle's neck, tiny feet splashing shallow waters, and Adrielle's slender arms encircled the little girl. Angie's heart warmed at the sight. This time, Mia hung back, her shoulders and neck relaxed.

Cyrus leaned toward Angie and Kaden, keeping his eyes sharply trained on Adrielle and Rosie. "Human children look so bizarre," he mused, cocking his head to one side. "She has such short legs and awkward, ungraceful movements. Are you sure she won't accidentally trip and smack her?"

"They are strange little things, aren't they?" Kaden nudged his brother's shoulder with his.

Adrielle interrupted the reply creeping up Angie's throat with a loud, "We can hear you!"

And Cyrus' chest deflated. "I suppose that one is cute. In her own peculiar way."

Angie stifled a laugh and turned her attention back to Mia, leaving Cyrus and Kaden to their own conversation, they switched to mer language. Angie and Mia sat in the sand, Mia's gaze still glued to Rosie. She switched to Mandarin for her next question.

"Angie, how did this happen? You became friends with the *měirényú*? And one of them is your lover? How come his family didn't try to murder us on the spot?" Mia pinched the bridge of her nose as if trying to snap herself out of a dream.

"I stumbled on a merman who was willing to talk, and I went with it." Angie settled on that explanation for now because Mia pulled her phone out when it pinged. Her eyes grew wide and her shoulders jerked.

"Angie, I'm sorry. We have to go. Nick got off early, and he's asking where we are. I told him we'd meet him at the docks, but I thought we had a little more time." Her voice rose a pitch and her words streamed out in quick succession.

"No problem." Angie couldn't hide the annoyance tinging her words. She never got to leave work a little early. She moved to Kaden and Cyrus and Adrielle while Mia retrieved Rosie. "I'll catch up with you. I just need a minute or two."

"Be safe." Mia's eyebrows lifted slightly and, without another word, motioned for Rosie to follow her, leading them back toward where they came.

Kaden turned and mouthed something to Cyrus and Adrielle who gave Angie one last look that she couldn't read, and they returned undersea.

Once they were alone, Angie clasped her hands together in front of her. His gaze was expectant, and her words came rushing out. She had a minute to explain herself. "My dad had cameras put underwater. They caught me leaving with you, and saw the fish the day you took me there. I swear, I didn't know. I saw a red flash when we were leaving, but I didn't put two and two together." She swallowed hard. "Not until Nick showed up with fish last night."

Kaden lowered his head, the tips of his caudal fins peeking out of the water and flipping forward and backward. There was no indication in his eyes, his expression, whether he took her word or not. Angie ran her hands through her hair over and over, pulling it to one side of her neck, then moving it to the other.

He turned to face the open sea. "I must take my leave."

With one more brief glance at her over his shoulder, his gaze tortured, he left. Kaden would have to see the cameras for himself. He had to. The notion of not knowing when or if she would see him again tugged painfully at her innards.

She didn't have time to dwell on it. Breaking into a jog, she caught up to Mia and Rosie.

They had made it halfway down the path, and once Angie fell in step with them, Mia jutted a finger at her. "You owe me the entire story when we have more time, alright?"

"Of course. And Rosie," her niece looked at her, " If you could please not tell your dad about what you saw today, I'd really appreciate it. He won't understand. Can it be our little secret?"

"Okay. I won't tell Papa. Don't want him to be mad, 'cause I know he doesn't like the nice merpeople," Rosie said, and Angie caught the faintest hint of a flinch.

"Nick lost his temper a couple times because he's so stressed. But he always apologized," Mia added, her words rushed. "It's not his fault. He's so tired all the time, and I know his mind isn't in the right place."

Angie bit the inside of her lip as Mia all but jogged back to where they came, her shoulders and arms visibly tensed.

Another fifty feet and they reached the main dock area where Nick stood shifting his weight from side to side. He broke into a smile at the sight of his family, his gaze averted from Angie. "Hi Rosie! And Mia, my heart." He greeted Mia with a kiss, and Rosie with a big hug. "Where have you two been? I've been looking all over for you!"

"Mia came a little early to surprise you." She exchanged a glance with Mia who nodded her head. "But since you were busy, figure I'd help them kill some time and take them out for a walk on the shoreline," Angie offered, but took back her words at the cold, insincere smile on Nick's face that contorted into an angry sneer. He thrust his chest out.

Mia placed a comforting hand on Nick's forearm. "Please, honey, it was just a walk."

He didn't react.

"Angela, why would you do something so *stupid?* You know there are mer along the shore not to mention traps!" His voice came out in a sudden bellow and blasted into her ears, and Angie staggered backward. Her heel met an uneven part of concrete, but she caught herself.

"I did a sweep to make sure it was safe. I wouldn't bring them somewhere dangerous! You know how much I love them."

Nick folded his arms and puffed out his chest, stance widening.

If he was waiting for her to apologize, he better get comfortable. That wasn't going to happen.

Nick stepped to face her, the tips of their noses nearly touching, and he curled his upper lip. A vein in his forehead pulsed. "Never, ever do that again. Understand?"

For a long stretch of time, neither of them said anything, and Angie refused to budge from where she stood.

Finally, Nick looked away from her with a deep, noisy inhale. "But my wife and daughter look happy, so I'll let it go for now." He grabbed Rosie's hand, practically snatching her, and stormed off with Mia following close behind. "Oh, and Angela?" He yelled back to her, never bothering to turn back around. "Be here bright and early tomorrow."

Angie's hands were still shaking after they disappeared and when Bàba came and stood beside her. "You okay, Beibei? Sounds like you and Nick got into another altercation."

"He asked me to be here bright and early tomorrow. I don't know what that means. I was getting there at five, six in the morning some days." She eyed her bàba. "I think the better question is, are you okay?"

His eyelids were stiff and his eyes red, a sharp change from his joy this morning at the news of another grandchild arriving early next year.

"Yes. Be here at six thirty tomorrow. There's something all of you need to hear regarding the mer and our efforts to fight them and replenish our food source."

Angie's throat went dry and her heartbeat slowed to a crawl.

If the news was coming from Nick, then it certainly wouldn't be good.

Thirty-Two

Nick stood some feet outside the meeting room, his head high and shoulders pulled back. Angie's shoulders inadvertently tightened at the sight of him.

"Angela." Nick's voice was icy.

She swore under her breath and approached him.

"You're buddy-buddy with the mer now?" He flung his accusatory words at her, his posture rigid and tight.

"What are you talking about?" She inhaled so deep that her lungs rammed into her ribcage.

"People saw you talking with a merman." He jabbed a finger toward her face, and she stepped sideways with one hand up, avoiding it.

No point in denying it now.

"I had to find a way to appeal to the mer since nobody will listen to me." She stumbled over her words, but Nick looked too riled up to notice.

"First of all, nobody authorized you to do that. Your dad specifically asked you to stay *away* from them. I sent people to follow you periodically because I had this feeling you were up to something shady." He folded his arms tight across his chest, making his defined pectoral muscles stick out.

Angie thought her stomach had fallen into her intestines, and her hands and feet grew cold even as they stood in the sun's beams. Words escaped her. Nick maintained his glare, shaking his head in disapproval. "That's what I thought. Someone saw you pacing up and down the beach last month, like you were looking for something. He couldn't figure out why you were so close to the beach when we were given explicit instructions to stay far from it, so he came to me. You're lucky he didn't go to your dad first."

She knew what he was talking about. The day where she was looking for Kaden and found his kombu kelp directions stuck in an empty bottle.

"Like I said." Her head weighed heavy, and her words came out in short, quiet stutters. "I wanted to see if I could get them to listen to me."

"Okay, I get it, you had good intentions. But you're real—" She didn't understand his next word, but it was laced with a French accent, and he continued on, "at following directions, you know that? I still don't know what you're up to or what's going on in that brain of yours, but if you don't want me going to Zixin and telling him my suspicions, you'll do what I say, alright? Unless you want Daddy keeping a closer eye on you. Maybe even forced leave." His hazel eyes burned with rage, his eyebrows in a tight V over his eyes. "I have to give it to you though, if it weren't for your sneaking around, we might never have found where the fish were." The smile spread across his face was a mocking one.

Somewhere in his rant, he threw another foreign word at her. Leave it to this asshat to throw what she assumed to be French swear words at her, knowing full well she didn't understand. She wouldn't be surprised if he ran to Bàba the moment he suspected something else.

"Did you tell them to destroy the cameras?"

His question jolted her, and she raised an eyebrow. She didn't even know the cameras had been tampered with. "No!"

Nick snorted, the dubious expression on his face telling Angie he didn't quite believe her, but he didn't press further. It made sense now, the reason he waited for her outside the meeting room was because he was upset that the cameras were damaged and wanted to know how or who was responsible. He wanted to pin the blame on her.

Angie shifted uncomfortably from one foot to the other. Tiān, she wanted this conversation to be over. "What do you want me to do now?"

"You can start by staying away from the mer. Don't let me catch you again," he said, curt.

Angie glared at his retreating back.

Go to the Hells, Nick, and don't come back.

She took a calming breath before following him into the room where the meeting was held. Nick stood whistling, head high and shoulders pulled back. Bàba threw him a fleeting glance from the other end of the room, and then returned to being nose-deep in a large stack of papers.

Angie fingered her watch, twirling it round and round to keep her mind busy for what may come. Her insides quivered.

"Before I start," Nick said after clearing his throat, the sound ringing through the building's high ceilings. "Thank you all for your efforts during these trying times. You come to work and put yourself in danger each day, yet you do not hesitate to contribute. Many of you are even seeking new ideas on how we can end this disaster and get things back to normal again."

Angie recoiled as workers' cheers and whoops erupted around her. She wrapped her arms around herself, a way to shield herself from what he was going to say next.

"We caught another merman, but I decided to keep it alive." Nick paced back and forth, and Angie's hands grew clammy, her breaths catching in her chest.

Please let it not be Kaden. Or Cyrus, or Adrielle. Or the mer-king or queen.

A few confused murmurs rose from the crowd. "Our resident marine biologist, Cam, and his crew noticed a strange blue-tinged vapor coming from the mer's mouth. I was the only one here this early, so I asked him to stay and investigate more. We've never seen anything like it."

Resident marine biologist? Why was this the first time she was hearing about them?

A chorus of hushed voices rippled across the workers beside her. Angie's skin crawled. She had to get out, see who the mer was. She recalled what Kaden had said about the mer releasing their gift to humans. It happened either with their breath or when they were stressed. If she were a betting woman, the blue vapor came from the latter reason.

The other option was upsetting, that the mer had inadvertently released his magic, effectively giving the humans a tremendous advantage, if they found out what it could do.

What Nick said next stopped her from stepping toward the door. "We've sent the specimen to see what the glow is and if it's something we may use to our advantage. We need to maintain our efforts." He pounded one fist into his open palm with a *smack*. "If I must remind you what we're fighting for. Seafood prices have shot up and restaurants are shutting down in droves because of the scarcity. The other day, I had to choose between milk or eggs at the grocery store. If it were up to those beasts, we would starve and die out. We're losing thousands of dollars a day, which means, nobody will have a job anymore if this continues. Do we want that?"

A resounding "No!" came from the workers.

Nick continued, his neck flushed and a frenzied look dominated in his eyes. "Our underwater cameras have been destroyed, but we won't let that stop us." A pause while he swept his gaze over his rapt audience of workers. "Mark my words. We will be hunting down each and every last one of those scaly bastards."

Angie's stomach roiled.

"Those who I spoke with earlier, meet me outside. Zixin, do you have anything you want to add?"

Bàba put his papers down and shook his head. "We will meet again next week. If you're diving later, please follow Nick. The rest of you are dismissed."

Diving? Who was diving now, and why hadn't she heard of it? Her heartbeat raced. Why was nobody telling her anything?

"Bàba." She followed on his heels as they dispersed. "Who's Cam?"

"Oh, we brought him on board to assist us in studying the mer and find a weakness. He came all the way from Anchorage."

"Why didn't you tell me? I could ask him for advice for school. Help him study the mer." A profound sense of rejection overtook her, and she sent Bàba a long, pained look.

She wasn't sure Bàba picked up on it. "I need you to focus on your duties here." His features turned to stone, and Angie shrunk back. "If there's nothing else, I need you to get back to work." He walked away before she asked her other questions.

She crept around the back of the meeting room's building and followed a path to where the dive boats were anchored. There was nobody in her vicinity, and she picked up her pace. Had she missed them?

Stefan and Ken arrived, pushing a cart of oxygen and Heliox tanks down the smooth concrete path, and she flagged them down, waving her arms. Stefan stopped and urged Ken to keep going.

"Angie?" He raised one hand and shielded his eyes from the sun. "Are you diving? They're suiting up over there."

"Where are they going? Sorry, I didn't mean to stop you. Let's keep walking."

Stefan nodded, and they walked side by side. "Nick rallied a group of divers to go out and hunt mer. They bought a whole bunch of camo wetsuits with stealth tech from us recently."

Angie's heart sank as they approached the divers. They wore reef camo wetsuits to help them blend into vegetation on the seabed. They were armed with spearguns and serrated daggers and talked amongst themselves, their words indiscernible and blending together, a fuzzy cacophony.

Stefan announced he'd arrived with extra tanks, and six divers rushed over to retrieve one and thank him. "Look at them. Spent a couple thousand bucks, but it'll keep our shop in business a while longer."

Stefan and Ken had owned the shop for twenty years, and to think of them having to give it up was heart wrenching. Her stomach squelched, imagining what Stefan must be feeling. "What's happening at the shop?"

"People aren't diving anymore, and we were on the verge of having to go bankrupt. I mean, this will help pay our bills for the next month or two, but I don't know what will happen after." Stefan sounded downhearted, and Angie's heart went out to him. "I mean, who can blame people? We even offered to outsource our services, but we can only afford to do so much travel. And only for those few people who aren't too scared to get into the water."

"I'm sorry to hear that the business is suffering." She stepped closer so they were shoulder-to-shoulder. "Do you know where they're going?"

"We'll find a way, even if we have to close up shop for a while." Stefan shrugged. "I heard they were going to go out a nautical mile or two in different directions." His attention turned to Ken, approaching from the side. "Anyway, I'll leave these here for the divers. I have to let Nick know they're on their way onto the boats, sign the tanks out, and make sure they get back to us at the end of the day. It's good to see you, Angie."

Ken joined him and put his arm around his husband, and the two walked away after saying their goodbyes to her.

Three boats pulled out, each stationed with divers armed with spearguns, aiming down at the water.

Her legs shaking, she peered over the seascape, toward the direction where she saw Kaden the day before. She had to warn him. The mer wouldn't be expecting humans in camouflage. Angie waited, eyes scanning the surface, sweeping from one end of her field of vision to the other, desperation rising.

Minutes passed, and nothing. Not a glint of a mer tail, or a head poking out of the water.

Tāmāde. Where was he?

She knew when they had last parted ways, it wasn't on favorable terms. Still, she held onto a strand of hope. That he realized she was honest about the cameras, remembered the usual time she was off work, and would be waiting so they could clear this misunderstanding.

What if he was the merman who was captured and was now left to rot in a facility while they poked and prodded at him? Maybe he was caught after their meeting yesterday?

She tightened her jaw and rushed back to the divers. There was one dive boat left, the captain waving at her. "Hey! Are you the last diver? Because if you are, you should have been here fifteen minutes ago. The others already left!"

"Y-yes. Give me a minute to suit up!"

Angie booked it back to her storage room to get her gear. There was one black-and-bronze camo suit left, and she donned her outfit as quickly as her hands would work. Stefan and Ken's tank carts were still there with two tanks of Heliox left, and she grabbed one, hauling it over to the boat. Then she settled in with her fins in hand and out of breath.

She put the diving mask on her forehead and gave him a thumbs up. The captain pulled away from the dock.

Angie stared out toward the calm seas, unable to stop fidgeting with the things closest to her: the pressure gauge and the air valve on her BCD. In her mind, she willed the captain to hurry. She didn't want to be too late.

Thirty-Three

The boat stopped, and Angie slid her flippers over her booties and pulled her dive hood over her head. She stood and waddled to the dive exit point, and with a giant stride, splashed into the ocean.

The icy waters pricked and stung her exposed cheeks, and her teeth chattered.

Her ears and sinuses filled with pressure after descending two feet, and she equalized.

She certainly missed how graceful, quick, and smooth she felt with the mer magic. As she kicked her feet, her body bobbed up and down with her inhales and exhales.

Angie didn't have the first clue where the other divers were. If they were looking for mer, they'd likely be going deep, and wearing silent, bubble-free rebreathers. She kept moving toward the direction of the palace.

Without the mer magic, she wouldn't be able to spot the mer queendom, but she would see the mer coming in and out of there.

Crippling darkness surrounded her, and she turned on her flashlight to help her see. Red illumination shone before her. It wouldn't startle nearby deep-sea creatures, who couldn't see red colors.

Twenty more kicks led her to where the palace should be. Only a plain, empty seafloor lay before her, and shining her flashlight into the area revealed small groups of mer swimming and floating around, some armed, some not.

Angie kicked her way to the tall stone formation on the other side, keeping watch, using her hands and heels to grab onto the stones' uneven edges, looking for Kaden, or even Adrielle or Cyrus.

Ahead of her, across the seafloor, four white lights appeared.

The divers were here, but Angie couldn't pinpoint where exactly they were.

The sentinels made a dash for the lights. Spears flew from ahead of her and from her right side, spearing both sentinels.

More sentinels followed, all making for the bright white lights the divers waved around to distract them. The speargun group began firing, and Angie's stomach dropped further and further toward her feet with each shot.

She kept moving, crawling across the rocks, looking for a maroon or white tail. Going into the palace area would be too dangerous.

Where was Kaden when she actually needed to talk to him?

Angie had made it to the next rock over, where, if she remembered correctly, the princes' quarters were. She froze.

From the darkness, Mer-King Aqilus emerged, flanked by two sentinels. They moved toward the white lights in front of them.

No. Angie couldn't let him go down. She had to distract him, get him to turn around and go back inside the palace. So she did the first thing she could think of. Shut off her red flashlight and pulled out her white-light one, which she kept stored in her BCD. Fumbling through her dive gloves to turn it to the brightest setting, she crawled sideways on the rock until she could get a closer view of his front side, and flashed the light directly into his eyes.

He turned and blinked, and she directed the light toward the palace.

To her relief, he followed it.

Her plan worked. She turned her flashlight off, stuffing it back into her vest pocket. Thank her ancestors.

Until two spears sailed through the water, moving in slow motion, in front of her eyes.

They struck Aqilus through his side and back. His hands flew to where the spearguns wedged into his skin for a split second, before falling limp.

Angie sucked in a sharp breath. Helium and oxygen from her regulator blasted to the back of her throat, and she gagged.

More sentinels emerged, going for the divers with the lights. In the midst of the ensuing madness, two of the divers sneaked their way in and grabbed the mer-king's corpse, returning to the surface with their prize, leaving her behind.

She caught a glimpse of Kaden and Cyrus and the mer-queen, right before they disappeared again into the darkness. Seeing Kaden was sweet relief, knowing he hadn't been the captured merman being studied.

Her breaths came out short and shallow, and she forced herself to slow down, or else she would burn through her air.

After her breathing slowed, Angie moved toward the surface. The boat which brought her here was gone. Open sea crowded her, waves churning and punching her face.

A Coast Guard ship sailed toward her, and Angie threw her arms up, waving them in the S.O.S. signal.

It didn't stop, and brushed past.

Damn it!

Then she remembered what Beau and Emily had said: that the Coast Guard was prioritizing larger ports' problems.

Is that where this ship was going? Responding to a call from a bigger, clearly more important port?

Cursing in her head, Angie removed her rebreather and replaced it with her snorkel mouthpiece. She unstrapped the neon pink inflatable safety sausage from her BCD, inflating it and letting it hang next to her. She fiddled with her audible signaling device, her last resort in case the loud noise drew the mer's attention.

The dive boat appeared from the fog and sailed toward her. Her eyes shone as she locked in on the approaching vessel, tension seeping from her body. Fortunately, this wasn't the boat carrying Aqilus' speared body. She didn't know if she could handle seeing him until they reached land.

When they docked, she unburdened herself from her weighted BCD and halfway depleted Heliox tank.

Angie fast-walked to the dressing room, and finding her locker, changed out of the wetsuit, dried herself and donned her work outfit. She bunched her wet hair up into a hat to prevent suspicion that she'd been in the water in case Nick or Bàba saw her, recoiling at the chill piercing her scalp when she piled her hair and secured it with a waterproof, phone cord hair tie.

She returned to see a group of divers stuffing Mer-King Aqilus' limp body into a fishing net like he was nothing more than their daily catch. Back when they had a daily catch.

The divers, dressed in their wetsuits and booties and holding their fins, congratulated each other, some shaking with glee, musing over his assumed status because of the pearls and undersea treasures he wore. Their spearguns lay in a row, pointed downward near the small pavilion where they geared up. One diver looked over to them with an appraising nod.

"The camo outfits were key, man," a male diver said, lifting his arm to admire the patterns on his wetsuit. "Never saw us coming."

"They'll probably catch on soon. We'll have to change the colors and patterns for next time," a female diver chimed in.

Angie strained her neck to get a better glimpse of the female diver, whose back was still turned to her. She knew that voice. Celia? She took part in killing Kaden's father?

"By the way, good job with getting those two bodyguards. Beat me to it." She puckered her lips. "I had a clean shot, too."

"You'll get them next time." A different female diver patted her shoulder.

"Yup," Celia said. "I'll make Mom proud. She deserved better than to die by their hands."

Angie's stomach churned and felt like it was folding into itself.

She took another step back so they wouldn't spot her eavesdropping, but stayed close enough to hear them.

Angie wanted to see Aqilus, but wasn't sure she could bear the sight of his speared, lifeless body. Instead, she trained her gaze on Celia, her sandy hair tied into a wet ponytail, and tanned skin glistening under the sunlight. There was a sadness in Celia's hazel eyes that belied her proud smile, and Angie's heart dropped for her. As it did in the photos on Eva's phone, the sunlight created a bright flash off Celia's nose ring, and her wide smile was identical to the picture. On instinct, Angie moved to comfort her, but the divers surrounded her to secure the net. They walked away, still talking amongst themselves.

Angie shuffled her feet on the concrete. Celia approached, carrying two armfuls of empty spearguns. The young woman looked like she was struggling, so Angie held out a hand. "Need help?"

Celia flashed her a grateful smile and shared the spearguns with her.

"How are you doing?" The volume of Angie's voice dropped a notch.

Celia's smile vanished as they pushed open the doors to the storehouse. "It's difficult. Some days, I'm okay. Others, not so much. But I'll make sure Mom doesn't die for nothing."

"I know. It took me a long time to process that my mom wasn't going to be there when I returned from college." Angie held back a sniffle, remembering the first time Māma wasn't in the kitchen when she woke in the morning or in the yard on the rare days the weather was warm enough. Her absence had been stifling and overwhelming, and the Māma-shaped hole in Angie's heart had expanded.

"I know you understand," Celia replied. They dropped off the spearguns, and she took her leave after saying goodbye and thanking Angie again.

"You know." Celia stopped short from opening the storehouse door. "Mom talked about having you over for dinner. You could still come, if you want." Her voice grew thick with emotion. "I mean, so we can talk some more. And the house might not feel so empty. Now that I'm back alone there."

Her last sentence hit Angie like a hard slap. On instinct, she took a step closer, but Celia hung her head and left, the door clicking as it shut.

Angie wet her lips, gaze falling on empty buckets labeled with fish species names and folded fish cleaning tables lined against the walls, unused for over a month. They were too polished. Too clean. Where the storehouse once carried a light fishy stench, now a stale smell permeated the space. The heavy hollowness in her chest expanded.

THIRTY-FOUR

THE DAYS DRAGGED ON WITHOUT FURTHER word from Nick or Bàba. Angie stood by her room's window, staring into the beachfront for nothing in particular.

Lulu meowed announcing her arrival before hopping on her perch next to Angie's head and stared out the window, tail twitching.

Her tail stiffened, gaze plastered on something Angie couldn't see.

"What's the matter, girl? You see a bird?"

The cat jumped from her perch, sprinting out the door in a frenzy. "Hey! Where are you going?" Angie bolted after her.

Lulu darted into the front yard through the ajar screen door.

Bàba must have been out here last night or early this morning smoking a cigar and didn't close the porch door when he left. The man was certainly not in his right mind—with a house full of women, he never left an area unsecured.

She was a terrible sprinter, and when she found Lulu at the beachfront, she keeled over with her hands on her knees, wheezing and panting.

The sun's rays bounced off scales underneath the water's surface.

Fish? How had nobody noticed?

The scales multiplied. Kaden surfaced.

Angie cried out and lost her balance, falling onto her backside.

"K-Kaden? How did you find me?"

He motioned to Lulu, who sat upright with her head tilted to one side. "You were not exaggerating when you said your cat likes shiny things." Lulu hadn't blinked once. "I used my tail to lure her. I had to get her, and by extent, your attention. I wasn't about to try to make it to your home overground."

Angie looked over her shoulder. Thankfully, her village was so sequestered. "Why are you here? It's dangerous."

Kaden laid his chin in his hand. "I wanted to see you. I am sorry for doubting you. About the sanctuaries, that is. The palace guards found cameras near the palace and destroyed them, and we found the two cameras by the sanctuaries where you said they would be."

At his words, Angie pressed a palm to her heart, and then reached for Kaden's hands while settling into a cross-legged sitting position. He clasped them with hers, kissing her fingers, his soft lips a soothing balm on her skin. "I understand. I can see why you suspected that I had something to do with it."

"I also wanted to apologize for not being around. I wasn't avoiding you. I would never. I wanted to tell you about the cameras then, but," his voice thickened, and he forced a swallow, "my father got speared. My family grieves for him, as do I." He bit down on his trembling lip.

She squeezed his hands, running her thumbs back and forth over his knuckles. "I saw the mer-king too. I followed the divers. I wanted to warn you, tell you they were coming. But I couldn't find you, and I even tried distracting your father. I'm sorry." She whispered her apology, wishing it had turned out differently, feeling the sting of Kaden's loss.

"No, do not say that. You were only trying to help." He pulled his hand out of hers, his tail making a gentle splash in the water behind him. "I had just spoken with them minutes before it happened."

"You did?" Angie croaked.

"Yes." He bowed his head. "They were calm. Reprimanded me for neglecting my ceremonies, but I convinced them that I would not marry a mermaid I did not love and did not want to face their wrath. They listened. Accepted my explanation." His chest heaved. "I asked them to release some fish for you, enough for you to cease your attacks, spare our people from more death." His tongue darted over his lips, wetting them. "I tried to get them to see it from your point of view. That of course your people would attack, they are starving. My father agreed, and so did my mother, if begrudgingly."

Shit. Shit. *Shit!* They were so close, and now, it was all going to the lowest level of Hell.

Any hope of a truce between them and the merfolk vanished.

"I can't believe this. This can't be happening." Angie shook her head, as if what she saw, what she heard, wasn't real.

"I wish it was not." Kaden's tone was emotionless. "After speaking with them, sentinels came to inform us of a commotion outside. We sent the sentinels to investigate, but they returned, saying the mer outside wouldn't calm down, and some were fleeing back to the palace. My father followed the sentinels to help." His tail moved back and forth in the water behind him. "Something didn't sit right with me. But he insisted, and now." He trailed off. "I was not close to him. Still, he was my father. And he listened. He just wanted to protect me, and Cyrus, and my mother."

Angie remembered the gruesome scene. How blood puffed out like a cloud from Aqilus' mouth, and she dry-heaved. She let Kaden continue on, remaining silent.

"The one time my father decided to leave the safety of the palace to calm our people. We thought it was simply a sea pig or giant isopod infestation. We never expected humans. I will never know why he did not let the sentinels take care of it." His voice grew thick, and Angie reached over, cupping his cheek. His bright amber eyes shone with unshed tears, and he squeezed them away.

"Kaden, I'm so sorry for your loss. Cry if you need to, alright? I'm here."

"I forget that tears fall on land. They wash off underwater." Kaden took in an audible breath. "But we will grieve for him properly when the time comes." He set his lips in a tight line. "I also came to deliver a warning."

"A warning?" Angie's eyes sprung wide open, a chilly bolt piercing her core.

"Yes. My mother is distraught over my father's capture and death. She will grieve, and then anger will consume her, and there is no telling what she will do in her rage. I urge you to stay away from the seas and the shoreline in the meantime."

She nodded, mute. Those damned cameras. If only she investigated the cameras the first time she saw the red light near the sanctuary. If only she had moved or destroyed them. Told Kaden.

Then maybe their sentinels could have looked for others and found the ones near the palace, and the mer-king would never have died.

If only, if only, if only.

Her belly knotted up. Kaden's voice broke into her spiraling thoughts. "I will let you know where to meet me in the future, at a spot which is safe for both of us."

She looked at him in earnest, and moved closer to him. "You and your people should be careful where you go, too. They captured one of your mer recently. Discovered the blue tinge on his breath, and he's being studied as we speak. They won't stop until they find out what it is. If my father and brother-in-law get wind of the magic, they're going to sack your queendom. They found the mer-king, so they know the general area to look."

"Yes, my mother has sentinels stationed everywhere, and we have reinforcements coming from the central queendom. Thank you for the warning." He gave her hands an affectionate squeeze. "I do feel we are overdue for a proper meeting."

Footsteps trouncing on grass approached behind her, and Angie dropped Kaden's hands. "You have to go."

"Beibei?"

Kaden's eyebrows went up, like he was questioning this name of hers she hadn't told him.

"It's my dad." Angie racked through her upcoming weeks' schedule in her mind. "Thursday night? Three nights from now. I'll be working a shorter shift."

"I will look for you. Come to our regular meeting spot." Kaden blew a kiss at her before returning to sea.

Angie stood as soon as Kaden left. "Over here."

Bàba jogged to her, his eyes creased with worry. "I got worried when I didn't hear you in the house after I woke up. Thought you had left for work, but then I saw the porch doors wide open." He rubbed his eyes. "I realized I hadn't closed it fully this morning, but I knew I didn't leave them like that."

Her voice pitch heightened. "Lulu got out."

Bàba raised his eyebrows, and Angie waved a hand in front of Lulu. Finally, Lulu noticed her.

"Come on, girl. Let's go home, okay?" She made a *psst psst* sound, and Lulu rose to her feet, running ahead of them to the house.

Angie remained silent as she walked beside Bàba.

"I wanted to let you know." Bàba held open the porch door to let her enter the house first. "That I'm going to be back and forth from the docks and mayor's office this next week. We're going to strategize about what else we can do. We have the owners of the Anchorage, Kodiak, Bethel, and Unalaska docks coming throughout the week, too. They still want to help us even if their own docks are shut down."

"So, you're not going to be at the docks most of the week, is what you're saying."

"I still will be, but I'll be in a lot of meetings."

Which meant—

"I'm leaving Nick in charge of operations in the meantime."

Angie gave him a halfhearted nod of assent. She planned to be as far away as possible from Nick until Bàba returned to work full time.

THIRTY-FIVE

FURIOUS WAVES CRASHED AGAINST TRANQUIL ROCKS and shoreline reminding Angie of the ever-growing hostility between the humans and the mer. At first, she likened the waves to the humans assaulting the peaceful mer until they fought back. Now, she was no longer sure which side were the waves and which were the rocks and shore.

Both sides were right, yet they were both wrong.

Storm clouds churned overhead. Without an extra layer underneath her light jacket, a chill pierced Angie to her bones. But when she checked her weather app, it showed clear skies all day with a high of fifty-six degrees, the usual for early August. Which meant one thing. The meteorologists were horribly wrong, or the mer were up to something.

She didn't like the latter thought, not one bit.

"Something's brewing under the surface, isn't there?" Beside her, Stefan leaned against the banister on the raised piece of land overlooking part of the shoreline.

"I hope you're wrong, but this makes no sense otherwise." Angie shook her head, her lips set in a grim line. "Didn't think I'd see you at the docks today."

"We had some leftover inventory in the store. Brought in a few extra pieces of diving equipment to see if it could help anyone here." He chewed his lower lip. "You hear what's been happening the last few days? Lot of accidents."

"Unfortunately, yeah. Horrible." Angie tightened her grip around the banister, the cold metal digging into her palms.

The ocean raged uncharacteristically in the past days, the tide pulling in ever closer.

"Did you hear about the teenager who drowned out here yesterday?" Stefan asked.

"I did." Angie recalled hearing the news early this morning, of a sixteen-year-old boy who disappeared. It reminded her of Luke, and she hung her head, her muscles going rigid. "Did you know him?"

"He had just gotten certified with Ken and I earlier this summer. His name was Yize. He came by our shop yesterday, seemed upset about something, said he couldn't talk to his parents about it."

Angie straightened, turning toward Stefan. "What did he say?"

"That he got into a fight with his boyfriend. He couldn't tell his parents because they don't know about his relationship." Stefan swallowed hard, his Adams apple bobbing. "So he confided in us. We talked a little bit about the sea, and he said that the crashing waves were his greatest source of calm." His voice became thick. "Then yesterday, a dock worker said she saw the boy pulled underwater, and never came back up."

"I'm so sorry, Stefan. And for his boyfriend, and parents." And for all the loved ones, human and mer, of those who lost their lives. Another crash of sorrow hit her. He shuffled his feet across the ground. "Not to mention all those boats further down the coast sinking from violent riptides and the subsequent undertows. Luckily, some were empty, but others had people onboard. Now they're all gone."

"I heard about those boats, too," Angie said softly.

Kaden's warnings about his mother's rage rang loud in Angie's head.

"Hey." Stefan nudged her shoulder with his, pointing to her left. "Look over there."

She followed his pointer finger, and her breaths stilled. A series of waves rocked back and forth, building on each other off a small dock about three miles away, in the next town north, where empty cargo ships were docked. The waves stopped and the water receded from the shore. For an unnerving series of heartbeats, it was quiet. A large wave rose, reaching toward the sky.

Higher, higher, higher.

It raced for the port.

"A tsunami." Her grip tightened around the banister.

"It can't be." Stefan's voice broke.

The tsunami raced for the shore and shattered inland, smashing the structures caught beneath it. Swallowed the cargo ships whole.

In a blink, part of the dock was reduced to splinters and debris.

Stefan murmured a string of curses under his breath. "We have to get out of here." He sounded breathless and tugged on her arm. "Tell Nick what happened."

On the gangway ahead of them, a smattering of dock workers yelled out and ran toward the docks proper, and Angie's chest tightened with a sense of impending doom. Above them, the skies hadn't cleared. The quiet made her arms and legs tense.

"Run!" she yelled to Stefan and to the workers below her.

Following the tsunami, a funnel of seawater rose over the seas, surrounded by splashing, frenzied mer tails at its base. She stared in awe and shock, praying she wouldn't see a hint of Cyrus' or Adrielle's, or worse, Kaden's tail colors in the mix. They weren't there. Only a prism of blues and greens and browns and violets. The beauty in the beast of their creation.

"Angie! Let's go!" Stefan grabbed her wrist.

It rose higher until she had to extend her neck to see its peak. A second, smaller tsunami charged at them. The wave's loud roar thundered in her ears as it raced in their direction, surging fast and powerful as it moved onshore.

Another mer tail, this one maroon and larger than the rest, flipped above the water and swept the wave, surging it forward.

Angie's heart sank, the world moving around her in a slow, agonizing blur.

The tsunami dropped, smashing the gangway in two. A group of dock workers fell with it, sucked into the liquid vortex as it retreated. Two of them escaped, sprinting and screaming.

The banister Angie and Stefan were holding onto broke when the giant wave did, sending a jagged segment flying into their backs. Stefan lost his footing and fell backward, and Angie followed, wincing as the rocky ground dug into her bottom. The last remnants of the wave dotted their heads with seawater, and she climbed back to her feet.

The waves withdrew soon after they came ashore, dragging loose debris out to sea and yanking Angie's footing out from beneath her. The water's force tugged her backward before she climbed back to her feet. She cried out and dragged herself forward, clawing at the ground with futile hands, digging her toes in to stop the pull. Her pulse smashed against the veins in her forehead and behind her eyes, and she coughed after swallowing seawater.

The wave carried her to the broken gangway. Her breathing quickened, and she made one last attempt to jolt forward before she reached the gangway's sawtooth ends.

A hand secured itself around her wrist. The person lost their footing and crashed down next to her, coughing but keeping their grasp on her. They scrambled to their feet before Angie could and hauled her out of the retreating surge.

"Stefan," she choked out. "You—" Angie's words died mid-sentence, and she bolted beside him. Eventually, they were joined by the two dock workers who escaped before the gangway broke. Another wave crashed behind them. The rushing water was deafening.

Once they made it to higher ground and were safe for the time being, Angie collapsed to her hands and knees, taking in a shuddering breath and struggling to rein in her emotions.

She couldn't, and a sob broke from the back of her throat.

Thirty-Six

"It's a mess at the docks. Complete chaos this morning," Angie lamented, putting her chin on top of her knees. She had dragged herself to her and Kaden's meeting spot that night, too close to the docks for her comfort. "Nick wanted our workers to construct a seawall, but we can't afford the materials right now. To defend against further attacks while moving our operations further inland."

Beside her, Kaden shifted.

At eleven at night, the sun was starting to take its leave and make way for the moon.

"I'm not sure a seawall or moving further inland would help. Give the mer, especially my mother, enough time and energy and they will find a way to create a bigger, stronger wave that will bypass any defense in their way. Though, the wall may work to stop an initial attack." Kaden tapped his tail up and down in the water, creating ripples. Angie blanched at the sound, the smallest of splashing noises reminding her of yesterday's two tsunamis and of the funnel. Kaden seemed to recognize her squirming, and he stopped.

"The queendom is rallying around her. Your people killed our king, and they seek vengeance."

"I figured, but some defense is better than none, right?" She blew out a raspberry, putting a hand to her forehead. "There's nowhere safe for us, is there? Is that why we're so close to the docks? Hiding in plain sight?" She rubbed her face in her hands. "When is this craziness going to stop?"

"It should have been tidesdays ago, before my father was speared through his back and side." He clasped his fingers together, squeezing them so tight that Angie thought he might crush his own hands. "I don't know what will end this now. Until one of us is wiped out or one side surrenders. My mother will not. Will your father and mayor surrender?"

Angie shook her head, unhappy. "If I know them, no. Especially not the mayor." Her mind flickered to Beau and Emily, who were still trying to grieve the loss of their son. "Nick's not helping the situation either, my sister's husband. He's the one who ordered the dive team out that murdered your father, though I'm not sure who actually speared him."

She couldn't stop herself from mumbling "stupid jerk" when Nick intruded her mind. Just her luck, he was her boss this week.

"Agree. And you dislike him." Kaden said it like a fact, not a question.

"I do. I don't think he's ever liked me, either," she grumbled.

"Why is that?"

Angie sighed. "We were never close, even though he was with my sister for so long. He didn't really bother me when we were younger, but a few years ago, he mocked my choice of graduate school. Told me I was better off finding some rich guy to marry, that I had the looks, and I might as well not let them go to waste." Ire rose at the memory. "He said I'd never make a decent living as a marine biologist. He's wrong."

Kaden shook his head, his expression flat. "Even if that was truly his belief, he was wrong for saying that to you. What a terrible thing to say to your lover's sister."

"Oh, that's not all." Angie was riled up now, and it felt good to get it out to someone who would take her side on this. Mia had asked her once what her problem was with Nick, and when Angie relayed the story to her, Mia had defended him, brushing it off as him being young and dumb. The second snipe he made at her, Mia couldn't brush off as easily, and had solidified Angie's intense dislike for the man. "When I came home after my mom died, I lost a lot of weight. He called me a twig, and asked me if I wanted a burger or something." She put the "or something" in air quotes, and a surge of emotion rose. Angie gritted her teeth. "He only apologized because my sister yelled at him that our mom passed."

Kaden scowled. "I'm sorry he said those things to you. I haven't met him, but I hate him already."

Angie took in a long, slow inhale, calming her racing pulse and newly emerged headache. "Yup. Thanks for listening."

"Whenever you need to talk about something, I will be all ears." Kaden dropped his shoulders and put one hand on her back.

"Appreciate that."

"Then since we are here together now, I'd like to take advantage of the time we have."

"You thinking what I'm thinking?" Angie scooted to him, and he pressed his lips to her nose.

"Follow me. I want some privacy with you. If you want the same, that is." He quickly added on his last sentence, and she laced her fingers through his and squeezed it.

"Let's go."

"But first, let me kiss you." He trailed a finger along her cheek, and she tilted her chin, parting her lips. His mouth descended onto hers, and he breathed out.

Instead of letting him pull away, she hugged him closer, and he let out a guttural moan. She missed him, kissing him, touching him, feeling his arms around her. The graze of his lips on hers to give her breath ignited a blazing fire inside. His hands rose to her sides, running his tongue over her lips, one hand moving underneath her head, his kisses growing deeper, more zealous.

Then he pulled away, gasping for air, their foreheads pressed together. "Not here. Come with me." He moved his head back, his hand never leaving hers.

"It's not my fault I can't resist you," she demurred.

With a growl, he turned back, kissing her again. His skin heated up under her hands, and his grip on her tightened when their tongues found each other. She moved one of his hands underneath her top, her bra, and then to her breast. Her head throbbed and spun at her breast's sensitivity under his careful touch.

He muttered something under his breath that she couldn't fully hear.

Angie stood. "I'm ready. Let's get out of here." She pulled him behind her as she dove headfirst into the ocean.

Once they were safely beneath the waves, Kaden's hand grazed hers. They traveled for what felt like eons.

"Where are we going?"

Kaden flashed her a sideways grin. "You'll see."

They passed a shipwrecked boat, and the presence of trash lessened as they moved further out. Wherever they were, the water was pristine and crisp. No signs of human interference.

Fish swam around them. So many fish. A school of arctic char swirled overhead and below her, and flounder and rockfish flit about, dusting up sand in their wake. "Where are we?"

"Humans do not venture out this far, this remote stretch of ocean. I also know of a special little nook." He pulled her to him and wrapped an arm around her waist and leaned in close, tip of his nose bumping her ear. "Look up, gorgeous."

A single circle showcasing the night sky sat amidst the dark. Sprinklings of stars dotted the skies, a thin veil over a bright, silver half-moon. Angie stared with unblinking eyes as a sliver of a nearly-transparent cloud moved across, and she pressed both hands to her mouth and nose. It was the famed Snell's Window.

"This is amazing."

"Isn't it? Something beautiful on land lies above." He arched his back and made his ascent, and Angie followed.

She broke the surface to find a stretch of rock shaped like thick fingers reaching high above them, bases interconnected with indentations that passed for undefined stairs, each leading to another ledge. The rocks stretched for miles on either side of them, glistening from residual seawater clinging to its smooth surface.

Kaden pushed his chest to hers and swam forward, pressing her back to a flat piece of cold rock, and she shivered when her wet back made contact with it.

Angie's stomach fluttered when he gazed deep into her eyes, and as before, she crossed her ankles around his tail so she wouldn't have to keep treading water. His eyes lit up like two sparkling jewels underneath the blades of moonlight, looking at her like a lover reunited with their significant other after ages apart.

"Now that we're alone." His voice dropped to a deep, husky timbre. "Did you know it was torture restraining myself from barraging you with kisses and more when I came to see you at your village? I will make up for that now."

"Please do."

Kaden gathered her in his arms and pressed kisses to her neck, trailing up toward her lips. Arduous, sensuous, and fierce. Their tongues entangled. A wave curled over and crashed on their heads, and she pressed herself closer to him for warmth, their heartbeats strong and echoing in her ears. He used one hand to cradle behind her head to create a cushion, kissing her deeper and harder.

His contented sigh buzzed along her lips, causing pleasurable vibrations to rush through. "You are breathtaking. Incredible. You're brilliant beyond words, and I want to call you mine, if you'll have me."

Invisible wings beat against her heart, and she put both her hands on either side of his face. "I am yours. As you are mine."

"I think I can describe what it is I feel for you," he added, and she tilted her head to the side. "Angie, I—I love you. From the deepest recesses of my heart and soul. My heart is so entwined with yours that there is no me without you." He moved his head back an inch, his eyes searching her face, as if edgy at what her response would be.

The reply came easily from her heart to her throat, "I love you too, Kaden." As soon as she verbalized her thoughts, an intense passion swelled and burst.

He beamed at her, part of his face brightened by the moon, his skin lambent and so soft and smooth.

His beauty made her weak in the knees and her heartbeat quicken.

"Would you care to follow me one more time?" He pointed above her head. "We can get to the top of the rocks and get a sweeping view of the seascape."

Angie studied the rocky landscape. It was a far climb, and she swallowed hard. She wouldn't chicken out of this. "Okay. Yeah, let's do it. I can use those edges and nooks. What do you do?"

Kaden motioned toward the smooth, vertical finger-like projections. "I climb those."

"This I have to see." She moved to the solid ground, making her way up. She only ever rock-climbed once in her life when her friends in college had pressured her to go for one of their birthdays, and she hated every minute of it. She never had a strong upper body and still couldn't do a pull-up without assistance.

Angie shook her arms, using the step-like projections and nooks to her advantage, and made her way upward. Two climbs in and her arms and legs began to cramp, but she pushed onward.

Kaden was within her line of sight, his long fingers keeping a secure grip in front of him. His tail tensed, curled beneath him and contracted along with his back and arms, revealing powerful muscles as he made his way to the top. Then, to reach her, he extended one arm out to the stone projection beside him, gripping with his biceps and shifting his other arm and tail over. He was a magnificent sight to behold.

When her muscles fatigued and ached and she felt like she couldn't keep going, she reached a smooth, flat area at its apex.

Kaden joined her shortly after.

"Impressive." She gave him an appreciative nod while shaking out her arms and legs, catching her breath.

He winked. "You liked what you saw?"

"Oh, of course." Angie nudged him with her elbow.

He held out his arm, inviting her to come closer. She snuggled into him, resting her head against his cool shoulder.

Now that they had reached the top and the sky was unobscured, she tilted her head and stargazed. The moon's cast over the sea made it glitter like a million tiny diamonds at the surface. Studying the panoramic view, it struck her that she had no idea where they were.

She was alone and free here with the man she loved. It thrilled her.

Love. It was still so foreign to admit it, but the admission freed her both from the restraints of her own mental block and from the inability to accept her growing feelings.

The night sky enveloped them like a dim blanket, the rushing tides a rhythmic lullaby, and the smell of salt and frosty air lifted her senses. Beneath her hands, the cold, wet slickness of the rocks reminded her of days when she was a kid when she and Mia would go exploring the jetty jutting out into the sea wearing big bubble jackets, and they'd slip because of their rubber boots. Their hands would slap against the mossy rocks, and they'd giggle and get right back up.

A more innocent time.

Another wave broke in the distance, and the events of yesterday came rushing back. She wrapped her arms around herself. "Kaden, I have to ask. The tsunamis yesterday, was that your mother's doing? You said you didn't know what she was going to do in her grief and rage."

Kaden sent his gaze downward. "Yes, it was her. I didn't know, and neither did Cyrus. Though the rest of the queendom approves and lauds her because of it, Cyrus and Adrielle and I did not." His fingers squeezed at her shoulder.

"Should we expect another attack?" Angie shivered, though being next to Kaden kept her warm enough. The docks wouldn't be able to handle another hit. It was already so fragile.

"No. The destruction took a lot out of her, and she is on bedrest. It will likely be a long time before she has enough energy to do something of such a large caliber again." He drummed the fingers of his other hand over his tail. "She was not always like this, you know. So full of hatred and rage."

Curiosity sparked. "What was she like before the war?"

Kaden shifted. "She is not a cruel mermaid, but her hatred for landw—humans stemmed early in her life, and having her lifemate murdered was the last straw. When she was an adolescent, she and her family fled unrest in the East China Sea, by the coast of, I believe what humans call Taiwan.

They fled east, but when they found refuge, they did not realize it was near an isolated cluster of islands. Humans discovered them when they wandered from their queendom, and mercilessly hunted them for food. Cut off their tails to eat and then left them to die."

Angie shook her head in disgust.

"She fled again with her sister, and on their travels for safe refuge, she met my father in the Arctic Sea. He was traveling and seeking a place to settle down. They eventually found their home in the Bering Sea."

"Incredible that they established a queendom so fast," Angie mused.

"Yes. They took in many refugees who were seeking safety. Tales grew of their kindness and the population exploded, eager to follow my mother and father's guidance and rule." Kaden appeared lost in thought for a moment. "You know the wave was meant for the docks. I know that does not make matters any better, but her rage was so intense that the wave grew and grew beyond her control, and caused a chain reaction. It destroyed more than she intended."

Angie tucked her knees under her. "I'm scared about what's going to happen now that everything's gone to shit. Nobody will forgive the mer after the direct hit and destroying another dock." She kept quiet at the prospect frightening her most, choosing between her alliance to her colleagues and her friends or to the mer she'd come to respect. Choosing between Kaden or her family. "The local government is sending more divers and boaters to hunt the rest of you down."

Before her, the sea was tranquil, the unnerving calm before the hurricane would crash in.

Kaden trembled, but said nothing, and held her close.

Thirty-Seven

At daybreak, Angie and Bàba stood at the broken gangway with Bàba's lips thinned, eyes narrowed and hands stuffed into his pockets as he shifted his weight from one leg to the other.

His mouth was set in a grim line, gaze stuck on the wrecked gangway before him. "This is a huge mess. With this, and how to deal with the mer attack. I'll have to call in contractors, we can barely afford to pay them. I'll have to ask Beau to help."

Angie rested a hand on the back of his shoulder. "I can make a few calls for you, take some of the work off your shoulders. Just let me know who. Or anything else I can do to help."

He *hmphed*. "Beibei, I have a lot to do. I'm keeping Nick in charge of the docks and dealing with the mer. I need you to continue following his orders, okay?"

Angie reeled as if he had slapped her. He hadn't even considered her offer to help. "You're leaving him in charge? You really trust he's not going to do something reckless?"

"I know you and Nick don't always see eye-to-eye, but I trust you will work together. I'll still step in periodically, but he knows what he's doing."

"That's not a great idea."

He looked her square in the eyes. "Angela." He bore down sharply on her name, and Angie knew his word was final. "I need you to trust me on this. Please." She said nothing and walked next to him when he made his way back to the dock's main area. "Beau and I are still in talks with other cities to get us some help." Bàba rubbed his chin where he had grown a short beard. He stepped over a piece of wood from the gangway. "Now with the trashing of our neighboring port, they could have killed more innocents. Thankfully, that port was empty. And Emily and Beau demand we step up our efforts to destroy the mer for the harm they've done."

"What are you going to do?" Angie jittered a foot against the floor.

"Keep working with them. They're going to increase our funding." He gave her shoulder an affectionate squeeze. "Nick will take care of things here." He looked to his right, and Angie's stomach performed a somersault. "Looks like we spoke you into existence."

"You did." Nick slapped Bàba's shoulder with a hearty laugh, and Bàba thumped Nick's shoulder in return. "Talking about me?"

"Yes, I'm bringing Angie up to speed."

"I'm still here." She hated it when people talked about her like she wasn't standing five feet away from them.

"Sorry, Beibei, but yes, now that you're all filled in, I have to get started on the long list of things I have to do. Nick, watch over her, okay?"

Angie blanched, and Bàba took his leave.

"Oh, I will." Nick said the words in earnest, but Angie caught the smug smirk when he turned back around to her. The smirk disappeared once they stood face-to-face. "Oh, Angela. An unfortunate day may come when Bàba isn't here anymore, and then you'll *have* to listen to me. Why don't you make the transition a little easier and learn your place now?"

She kept her gaze averted from him.

A wide grin spread over his face. "You can start by scrubbing. There're dried and leftover blood stains on the floors and walls from the mer we've killed so far. But we've been too short-staffed to sterilize it. Lots of the cleaning crew are gone. Taken by the mer, those slimy fucks."

Angie glared at him. "You're kidding, right?"

"Nope." He pulled a sad face, and she knew he was mocking her. "You're also going to help the cleaning crew dispose of the dead mer. You can do whatever you want. Burn them, cut them up, leave them by the coast for the mer to see, feed them to the sharks for all I care."

A web of ice spun through her body, her heartbeat slowing to a crawl. Most of all, she knew Mer-King Aqilus's body was amongst them, and she couldn't bear the thought of throwing Kaden's father away like a piece of trash. "No. That's not what I'm here to do."

"Nobody else refused because they all know we need to work together. What's the matter, Angela? Afraid of a little mer blood? You shouldn't be, given your close bond with them!"

Her cheeks froze.

"Yeah. I know about Kaden. And Adrielle and Cyrus. That you and my family had a nice little meetup with them recently." Nick moved closer so he was inches away, his mouth upturned into a snarl. A blast of overpowering peppermint struck her nose from the gum he was chewing.

"W-what are you talking about?" Angie's mind raced, racking her brain as to how he knew. She hadn't seen anyone else around, made sure of it.

Rosie could have slipped.

Or Mia.

No. She loathed to think of that possibility.

"Don't you know my wife tells me everything?" He jerked toward her, his posture threatening, and backed away, leaving Angie shaking in her boots. "I suggest that if you don't want your father knowing what you've been doing, or for us to hunt down your lover and his family, you'll do what I say."

He spun on his heel and stormed away.

Angie stared after him, holding her head. "Why, Mia?"

She grew hot as her temperature climbed. Nick knew because Mia told him. Begging the question of what else he knew and wasn't telling her. She replayed his words over and over in her head, and she never felt so exposed and vulnerable.

8:15 AM

Mia: Hey Angie, you okay? Call me back when you get this, okay?

Beep

1:05 PM

Mia: Uh hey, it's me again. Angie, seriously, you good? Everything okay? Call me.

Beep

4:27 PM

Missed call from Mia.

Angie listened to their landline's voice messages, for the third day in a row since her confrontation with Nick. She picked up the phone, finger hovering over the numbers, starting to dial Mia's number. At seven in the morning, she would be home getting ready for work like Angie.

She stopped dialing and hung up the phone before completing the number.

When evening came around, Angie stood with six other workers at the main gangway. The sun still beat down on her head, and she took her sunscreen stick out of her pocket and applied another layer over her face.

The dead mer lay in a pile, and a male worker tapped his foot on the ground. "What should we do with them? Nick said we can do whatever we want."

Angie looked to the mer-king's corpse. A pain in her chest flickered. She hadn't wanted to throw him away with the others. At the very least, she could give him a decent burial on the beach.

"We could bury them," she said, looking at the other workers.

"Gross. Why?" A female worker wrinkled her nose. "You know how much time that's going to take? I'm exhausted. I want to get away from the water and go home."

"I'm not even getting overtime pay for this," the male worker grumbled.

"Yeah, like we're going to stand even closer to the water and dig their graves. Great idea." Another female rolled her eyes at Angie, and then walked closer to the mer. "Let's just throw them back in."

"I agree," another male worker chimed in.

Angie didn't think she would get any help from them, so their answer didn't surprise her. Maybe that was for the best. The mer could find his body and bring him home to their proper cemetery.

She stepped forward and helped push the mer into the water.

"Angela!" Nick's voice boomed in her direction not a minute after she stepped foot onto the docks.

Angie clenched her jaw. "What, Nick?"

"You're not easy to find." Nick panted when he caught up with her.

She stared at him like he had sprouted an extra pair of eyes. "I've been at my station all day."

"Oh!" Nick slapped the back of his hand to his forehead in false surprise. "I figured you might be hanging out with the mer again. Maybe even plotting against us, your own people. I went down the seashore to see if you were hiding there."

No surprise that he had to jab at her. He had been doing it nonstop the past three days. "What do you want?"

Nick's expression sobered. "Do you know how to spearfish?"

"Yes." She put her hands on her hips.

"Okay, good. Because you're going with some of my divers to go mer hunting."

"Now?" She straightened up.

"No, tomorrow."

"It's not safe to bring boats out. There might be mer around who could ambush you." She vocalized the first reason that came to her head to dissuade him, futile as it may be.

"That's the point, Angela. And not to worry." He waved a dismissive hand at her. "We found a safe route. These boats are as quiet as they come. Plus, you'll be wearing some nifty equipment on your wetsuit that'll block electrical waves." Nick threw her a look of annoyance. "Have you forgotten you still need to follow my orders? I promise you'll be safe. I wouldn't put my precious sister-in-law in danger." The mocking tone when he said *sister-in-law* grated her nerves.

A sense of unease made her skin prickle. "No, I'm not proficient enough with a speargun to catch them." She stared him down in defiance.

"Is that so?" Nick's foot tap, tap, tapped on the ground. "Then you better learn, fast! You're a smart girl, aren't you?" He raised his voice so it thundered over her head, and nearby workers stopped to stare.

His tone sent a shock winding through her veins. Nick waved the other workers away, and they scattered. "Be up bright and early tomorrow morning. Nobody is to come back without at least one kill or capture. We'll show those fish that they can't attack us and think they can get away with it." He threw her one last pointed glare before he checked his watch and jogged off.

She had to do something. A plan began to take hold in her mind, and she walked in the opposite direction of him and made her way to the warehouse, where the spearguns were stored. After a glance around to make sure she was alone, she made quick work of jamming the safeties.

Tomorrow, the divers, and likely Stefan or Ken would inspect the spearguns before they went out, and finding them out of order, would delay the hunt while they worked to procure more. It was futile to think that it would cause Nick to call it off, but at the very least, it would give her time to think of something else in the interim.

Angie leaned against the railing by the shoreline later in the evening, staring out to the open sea. The destroyed gangway below was under repair, but the construction crew took their time. Only a smattering of gangplanks had been put down, filling in the broken spaces closest to the docks. She wasn't to meet Kaden today, but she still hoped he'd come by so she could tell him about tomorrow, and he could give his people fair warning.

He never came.

"Look who washed up from the high seas."

Stefan approached, and her wide smile conveyed her happiness as she slapped hands with him in greeting. "We're going to run into each other every time we're in this spot, huh?"

"Yep. One of my favorite places to go. Best view from the sea is from here. Before the mer tainted it, I mean, but it's still beautiful." Stefan shrugged one shoulder.

"Came for another stroll?" Angie cast a sideways glance at him.

"Well, Nick asked me to come out on this hunting trip tomorrow morning. I got here an hour ago making sure there was enough gear to go around. Make sure the suits were fitted with the electrical impulse inhibitor. This way nobody has to bring anything tomorrow. We got some extra funds from our mayor, so we could get some upgrades and newer equipment." He rolled his shoulders out and shifted his weight from side to side. "Was about to head out, but I wanted to check out the view. Happened to see you here."

"You decided to go out too?" She squeezed her hands tighter together, cracking her knuckles.

"I didn't want to." Stefan sucked in a breath and clenched his fist. "I never like taking lives. Especially something so human like the mer."

"Then why do it?"

"Why are you going?" His voice raised a notch, a slight tremor arising.

"I didn't have a choice. Nick said he needed my help. I *couldn't* say no," she muttered.

"I wasn't thrilled, but Ken persuaded me. We can't keep letting the mer push us around like this."

"Yeah, okay. Um, look, I have to get going. I'll see you tomorrow," Angie choked out, keeping her head low and taking her leave.

She quickened her pace to make the ferry, and her stomach clenched and contracted, threatening to upchuck the tea and half cup of bitter melon soup she had for lunch.

Thirty-Eight

ANGIE SAT WITH A SLUMPED, DEFEATED pose when they set out on the boats. Her plan to delay them hadn't worked. They'd taken the sabotaged spearguns with them after the previous group of divers, including Celia, informed their group that the spearguns were inspected recently and were in good working order. Then Stefan and Ken had brought along another half-filled crate of them, the remainder from their shop.

Nick informed them of the game plan before dividing the thirty of them into groups of four or five and setting out on different boats. They were to be dropped off on a remote stretch of water where mer had been spotted. Then they would spread out and dive down in pairs to seven hundred feet. She and Stefan asked to be grouped together.

Angie scanned the other eight divers on their boat. "Where did all these people come from? I've never seen half of them."

"Oh, the local government is also paying divers to come out and hunt mer. So we've got people coming from Homer, Kodiak, and Dutch Harbor."

The boat's mortar quieted to a low hum and the vessel slowed to a stop.

Angie's heart rate spiked, hoping nobody noticed her incessant fidgeting with her diving gloves. Pulling them on and off, twisting the fingers together, and squeezing her BCD's weights with a grip so tight she constricted the blood flow to her hands, the bristly texture grating against her palms. Her temples pulsed when she thought of seeing Adrielle or Cyrus or the mer-queen.

Or worse, Kaden.

She was indiscernible from the other divers holding a speargun, but she couldn't imagine him recognizing her in her diving getup and killing her. Or watching Stefan spear and kill the man she loved. Her heart splintered into pieces at the notion. She prayed they would be in the palace and not out fighting this battle.

Their captain gave them the okay sign to don their tanks and begin their dives.

Moving at a deliberate pace, she let the other divers go ahead of her while she dropped weights into her BCD and strapped on her tank. The diving pair ahead of them left a red and white diving flag pinned to a buoy, jostled along by the small currents.

She and Stefan were the last to go. Angie took a deep breath, bracing herself and rolling backward into the water after him.

They descended, lower and lower until they reached four hundred feet, once more encircled by stifling gloom. Stefan turned his flashlight on first, and she followed, hanging back so she swam by his feet.

A beam of light nearly blinded her, and Angie held up one hand. The other two divers from their group approached, and one pointed to their left.

For a time, they found nothing.

Angie's breathing slowed. Maybe they would make it out without any casualties and then report that they found nothing. Then Nick might stop his crazy venture.

A long, graceful form darted from the void, the flashlight beam illuminating bright lavender scales. Stefan and the other two divers stayed as still as the rock and coral formations around them.

It was too late.

The form came into view, a disembodied, pale face and tattooed shoulders appearing, and the merman stared them down. Waving their flashlights around revealed three more mermaids and mermen wielding golden lances and tridents.

They were surrounded.

Each mer wore markings on their faces, chests, or shoulders, designating them as royal sentinels.

One diver from the other pair made a hand motion, holding up four fingers, pointing to the divers, and then the mer, followed by an okay sign. Angie suspected she knew their meaning. Four of us, four of them, perfect. An agonizing stillness befell them, as if each were waiting for the other side to strike first.

Stefan floated frozen beside her, sucking through his rebreather in hitched inhales and exhales.

One diver raised their speargun with slow, controlled movements, and pulled the trigger. Did the mer want them to attack? Angie figured there had been enough time that they could have stopped the driver from pulling the trigger.

It failed. The diver looked around and attempted to pull it again, and again. No use.

The mer struck.

Without Angie's help, it was three against four, and the mer were in their element. She shrank back, watching in horror as a mermaid grabbed one of the divers, her tail wrapped around his body like a snake strangling its prey, and snapped his neck. The diver went limp, speargun floating away from his hands and drifted down into the depths. The mermaid released him, leaving his body to the deep-sea creatures' mercy.

The other diver speared that same mermaid and shot their speargun at another, killing two, but not before he took a trident in the stomach. The diver's hand flew to their abdomen, blood appearing as a sanguine algae bloom.

One of the two remaining mermen struck at the dying diver's Heliox tank with a thick lance, puncturing a hole in it.

Stefan raised his speargun, one that Angie had jammed, and attempted to fire at the merman. His trigger stuck while the merman stabbed the other diver again with the lance before letting them fall, still flailing, to the depths, where they would bleed out. If they didn't suffocate to death first.

Angie's head pounded. She knew she should help, but paralysis seized her. Two more divers, likely from the one of the other groups, approached behind them and one fired a spear, ending the merman, and before the last merman struck, he fired a well-aimed shot while the merman rushed for them, trident out.

Another merman came into view, at first a disembodied head and shoulders, before a maroon tail came into view. Stefan raised shaking arms, aiming his speargun at his heart.

If he'd taken one of the jammed spearguns, the merman could kill him. If it wasn't, he would kill the merman. Angie didn't know which was the worse option.

The merman stopped in front of Angie, eyes flashing in recognition.

Cyrus. He darted side to side, up and down, preventing Stefan from getting a clean shot, but he did not strike at them.

Angie had to act fast. With stiff, quivering hands, she reached into her pockets and dropped the weights from her buoyancy vest. Used her respirator to inflate the vest by a breath, enough for her to start floating upward, slow and safe.

She held one palm upward and placed her other fist over it with her thumb pointing up. Then she moved both hands upward, signaling an emergency and to end the dive. Stefan nodded and lowered his speargun, letting Cyrus get away. He grabbed her D ring, and she grabbed his, and together, they kicked their way upward.

Stefan removed his rebreather as soon as they were back on the boat. "Are you alright? What happened down there?"

"She good?" The captain eyed her.

"There's something wrong with my BCD's valve." She went still, letting relief sink in that Cyrus escaped.

And yet, she couldn't stop the guilt that crept into her mind, staring at her feet and focusing on her knees. If she hadn't compromised the spearguns, perhaps the divers that held them would have had a chance to defend themselves.

Fuck, it was her fault that the divers died because their spearguns were jammed. If only they had stopped to inspect them, like they should have.

The extras from Stefan and Ken wouldn't have been enough on their own to arm all the divers.

"Okay, good. Thought I was going to have to take you to the hospital, and then explain to your dad why I let you get hurt." Stefan took a seat. "I'll stay with you until the others get back." He swallowed hard. "Whoever's left."

A pain emerged in the back of Angie's throat, and she removed her Heliox tank and set it in the corner with Stefan's. The captain set to work on pushing them against the side of the boat and standing them flush against each other.

Minutes later, three haggard-appearing divers climbed aboard with them. Two dragged a large net onto the deck, and then climbed back down the boat ladder. The next two nets required the strength of all three people to bring it aboard.

In the first net, a mermaid struggled, curled into a ball in the net that was too snug for her. Another net held a merman, his tail the same tangerine shade as the mermaid's, and Angie's eyelids grew stiff at the sight. Lifemates.

While Stefan and the three divers talked of the other two they lost, Angie craned her neck to see what was in the third net.

She wished she hadn't looked.

A maroon tail peeked through the gaps in the second net and Cyrus lay still, his chest rising and falling with each weak breath. Angie stared, one hand covering her mouth as she struggled to hold back dry heaves. Her eyes teared up, and her chest tightened.

The boat lurched forward and took off. Cyrus' eyes fluttered open and hands slapped on the floor. He made eye contact with Stefan and the two divers who caught him, and last, with her. His eyes were haunted, lips parted as if he was going to say something, but never did.

Angie couldn't take her eyes off him, her hands clasped together in praying position, praying to her ancestors, to Buddha, to whatever other deities dwelled around them that he would survive this ordeal.

At the same time, her muscles tightened with dread, and hopelessness immobilized her.

More bodies awaited them when they got back to the coast. Angie wasn't ready to see the strangled and speared bodies, some left a fair distance from the shoreline, begging the question of how the mer had gotten so far inland. Behind her, the divers dragged the nets to the beach with the mermaid and Cyrus inside.

Stefan walked ahead of her, and Angie's feet weighed a ton. She dragged behind him. It tormented her, and she replayed the scene over and over in her head. Letting Cyrus escape. Seeing his captured body dragged onto the boat, the fear in his weary, rugged face when their gazes locked.

Now, Nick and his crew would take him and do with him what they would. Would they realize he was a prince? The thought sickened her to her core, and she put her hands on her knees, breaths heavy and labored.

A raucous voice snapped her out of it. "Angie, is that you? Oh, thank God you survived!" Ken staggered toward her, appearing breathless, his bright umber eyes wide with fear. "I heard the screams earlier, came down to investigate. Saw them all, dead or dying." He screwed his eyes shut and opened them again. "Nick is coming too. He's bringing some others with him."

"H-how did they end up so far from the beach? Did the mer come ashore?"

"Yes, but not in the way you think. They climbed the rocks, the pillars under whatever's left of the gangway. Brought them even closer." Ken shuddered, wrapping his arms around himself.

"Damn," Angie muttered under her breath. She saw the way Kaden scaled those rocks that night they stared at the stars. A strength the mer could use to their advantage.

"Okay, good, you're all here." Nick panted, approaching the two of them with a gaggle of armed workers around him, Bàba trailing behind, each donning their trusty handguns or pistols. Nick visually scanned the periphery, his lips forming silent numbers as he counted the bodies. "How many are dead?"

"Six total." Bàba shook his head, lips tight and expression grim.

"Yes." Ken hung his head.

"Angela, you saw what happened?" Nick's voice was taut.

"No, I was with the other divers, like you asked." She scowled at him, her words slicing through the air as they left her mouth to reach his ears.

"Oh, right. You did go. See these?" He raised his black semi-automatic pistol, pointing toward the sky and waving it around. "You all have one. All employees will keep their guns with them at all times. Got it?" Nick faced Angie. His eyes narrowed into warning slits. "Even you, Angela. Since you're the boss' daughter, you *especially* have to protect yourself."

"Oh yeah? What are you going to do if we don't comply, fire us? Please do," one dock worker grumbled, drawing some cackles from the crew who'd come with Nick. Angie had to hold herself back from chuckling with them.

Beside them, Bàba appeared to stare over their heads at something indiscernible.

Nick's nostrils flared, and his biceps bulged underneath his long-sleeved top. He turned a harsh glare to each worker, finally landing on Angie. "Yes! You will be fired. Or, I will throw you to the mer myself because I won't have your stupidity on my hands and bringing us down!"

"No. I don't feel safe carrying my gun on me when I'm at work. I'm sorry. Too many things could go wrong." Angie thought of Kaden.

She had to find him and tell him his brother was in their custody. Surely, he and the mer-queen and Adrielle would be beside themselves fretting over him. She knew she would be, if it were Mia in Cyrus' place.

Mia. The betrayal still stung like a swarm of angry wasps. She still hadn't spoken to her sister, but Mia hadn't reached out again since yesterday, either. Angie told herself she needed more time, wait until her head cooled.

"Beibei," Bàba cut into her thoughts. "You will bring your gun with you. That is an order." His voice burst forth, a foghorn tearing through the air between them. She looked to him, aghast, and his countenance softened. "I refuse to leave you vulnerable. Do it, or you will not come near the docks again."

Angie steeled herself and forced the word out. "Okay."

"Good. Now if there is nothing else, we should go. Order the cleanup crew to move our fallen crew and pay them some respect." Bàba motioned at them to leave with a swift wave of his hand.

Angie waited for them to walk ahead of her and dragged her feet behind them, unease sticking to her like double-sided tape underneath her skin.

Thirty-Nine

Angie arrived at the docks at six in the morning the next day, two hours before her shift started. Early enough so she would have time to see Cyrus, but not too early that she would stumble across the night crew.

She'd overheard Nick and the other workers talking about a large outhouse in the docks' center where they were keeping the trapped mer. It held voluminous tanks they once used as temporary holding places for their fish before selling them to the local grocery store and restaurants.

Ten steps from the outhouse door and Cam, the marine biologist, flung the door open and stormed out, wiping his glasses over and over on his shirt. "This is crazy. I didn't sign up for this," he was saying under his breath, rubbing his cheeks and forehead.

"Cam?" she called, but he didn't turn around. "Cam!" He disappeared into the distance.

What freaked him out?

She shuffled back as soon as she opened the outhouse door.

Nick, flanked by two men, had the mermaid by her shoulders. The same one caught with Cyrus, and her lifemate yesterday.

He had just pulled his face away from hers. She looked anywhere but at the men, visibly shaking, her wild braids undone.

Tāmāde, Nick!

Angie ran for her brother-in-law. "What did you do?"

"Oh look, new girl's here to save the day." The stocky man drew his eyebrows together, and moved to block her path to Nick.

Angie recognized him and his blond friend with a weathered face and a grizzled beard. Ian and Marc, the same two who'd mocked her during one of their earlier meetings, and gotten kicked out by Bàba.

When in the eighteen levels of Hell were Ian and Marc allowed to come back? She hadn't seen them since Bàba suspended them.

"Get out of my way." She tried to sidestep around Ian, but Marc blocked her.

"Or what, you're gonna fight me? There's three of us versus you," Ian sneered.

Angie glanced toward Nick. They didn't like each other, but would he really fight her? Before Angie could make another move, the merman beside them jumped out of his tank, his long arms reaching for Nick and clutching him around the throat. He pulled Nick into his tank so Nick was submerged beneath him, his glare murderous and his knuckles turning white as he tightened his grip.

"Boss!" Ian lost interest in Angie as he and Marc rushed to the tank.

Good, maybe the merman would finally drown the life out of Nick.

But Nick fought, grabbing at the merman's fingers and trying to pry them off. His chest still heaved with inhales and exhales, and Angie knew. He'd breathed in the magic from the terrified mermaid.

From next to him, the mermaid pulled herself halfway out of her tank, screaming in Renyuhua. She spoke so fast that Angie couldn't understand a word she was saying.

Ian and Marc jumped to the merman's tank and dragged the mer out of it, throwing him to the floor on his back. He struggled briefly before flipping himself over. "You try to kill our boss? You don't get to live, scaly scum." Ian sneered, and after another brief glance at Nick, who gave him a firm nod, he pulled out his pistol.

"No!" Angie charged him. To do what, she couldn't decide, but she could knock him off balance, knock the gun out of his hand. Anything so the mermaid wouldn't have to watch her lifemate murdered.

Before she reached Ian, he shot the merman at point-blank range.

The mermaid's mournful scream pierced through Angie's ears and into the core of her being. The merman went still, lying facedown, his blood pooling on the ground.

Angie felt cold. The sound of the gunshot ringing in the enclosed space and resulting in the merman's death stunned her into silence.

"You okay, boss?" Marc asked. "Really scared us back there. Thought you were a goner." He and Ian helped Nick out of the tank, but Nick waved them off.

"I'm fine. Throat hurts a little, but that's it. I tried breathing underwater after you pulled that fucker off me. And you guys, I could breathe. I could see. It's amazing." He finally seemed to notice Angie. "Angela. Is this what you've been hiding from us all this time? Sneaky, sneaky." He wagged a finger at her. "Let's go, boys. I have to get dried off. We need to tell the others about this. And how the merman tried to kill me."

The three men brushed past Angie without another word, leaving her inside with the mer. She walked to the mermaid's tank, whose head and shoulders were above water, her shoulders racking with anguished sobs. She dug her palms into the top of the tank, trying to hoist herself out. It was too high, and she slid back into the tank, never taking her eyes off her lifemate.

Angie reached for her hands when she crawled back up, and drove her heels in, trying to pull her out.

The mermaid was waiflike in her frame, but she was heavier than she looked. After two more tries, pulling with all the strength she could muster, Angie's arms gave out, and for the third time, the mermaid was left hanging partway out of the tank.

What could she possibly say to the mermaid? She wasn't sure the mermaid would understand her. So she stood with her side to the tank, and took the mermaid's cool hand in both of hers.

The mermaid didn't fight. Didn't try to pull her hand from Angie's. She cried and cried, her tears forming a puddle around Angie's work boots.

In the tank behind the mermaid, Cyrus hung still and limp, but the movement of his gills told Angie he still lived.

"I'll come back for you," she said to him. He didn't stir.

Angie stayed until the mermaid's tears had dried, and left when her shift started an hour and a half later.

Angie returned to the outhouse when her shift was over, and most of the crew had gone home for the night.

What she had seen that morning struck deep into her being.

The mermaid was on her back in the tank, unmoving, her gills flaring open and closed. The merman's body was gone, leaving only a patch of dry blood caked into the wooden floorboard.

The sight of Cyrus broke Angie in two. He was conscious, but floated aimlessly in the water with his tail curled, the horizontal tank hardly large enough to fit his length. His eyes, once so full of life and fire were now flat and dead.

"Cyrus." Angie put her palms flush against the tank's glass. Cyrus perked up when he saw her, and he wrapped his hands around the top rim of the tank, pulling himself up, his arms shaking, before they collapsed under him. He folded his arms and rested his chin on them while taking in a large gulp of air.

"Angie?"

"Tiān, what did they do to you?" She scanned him up and down, stopping at small lacerations on his chest. "Did they—?"

"Since your people discovered how to steal our magic, a good ten or eleven of them came in shortly after I woke up. Cut Aurora," he motioned to the trapped mermaid, "and I. Forced us to release the magic to them. They've all but drained the life out of me, and I imagine her as well."

"That's why you're so pale?" He looked like he hadn't rested in a hundred years. "I thought the magic only helped humans breathe underwater."

"My brother did not tell you all of it, then? It is also part of our lifeforce." Cyrus shook his head, his expression downtrodden.

"So, when Kaden gives me the magic, he's impairing himself?"

What had she done, gleefully taking his magic every time they explored the undersea?

"No, when we give humans magic, only a miniscule part of us is lost." Even his voice sounded more strained than she remembered. "Each breath, or an equal amount of energy exerted or drained when we bring forth our Goddess' gift, forces us to withhold from utilizing it again for a full tidesday to replenish it." He took in a shallow breath and parted his lips.

"You don't have to explain. I think I get the gist of it. You should rest," Angie said, but Cyrus kept going.

"The more we use, the more fatigued we grow until we're so weak that we cannot move."

Her heart ached, and she clasped Cyrus' hand between hers. "I'm going to get you out of here."

Aurora was heavier than Angie thought, and if she couldn't manage to drag her out of the tank, then there was no chance in getting Cryus out either. After all, it took multiple men and women to pull Cyrus aboard in his net, she didn't stand a chance alone.

Finally, Cyrus spoke, his words carried on labored breaths. "I appreciate the thought, but the shore is too far from here. I would help more had I the strength. I am sorry."

"No, don't be sorry. I'll find a way to get you out, I promise, but I have to tell Kaden. Tell him you're alive, warn him that my people are using your magic." Her words came out faster and faster until they formed a verbal mountain. After their time on the rocks, she'd agreed to meet Kaden tomorrow evening, but it was another day and a half that Cyrus might not have.

"Yes, you must." He squeezed her hand. "The humans have left me alone for most of today, and I replenished a touch of my magic. I can give you what I still have so you can make it down to the queendom. My mother may not take too kindly to you being there, but try to find Kaden or Adrielle. Neither of them should be venturing out far."

"Alright." Angie grabbed a nearby step-stool and stood on it to be level with him.

"Do you know how to get there?"

Angie wrinkled her forehead. She'd been there once with Kaden, and had been dropped off by the dive boat, but she still didn't think she could make it there on her own. "I have a general idea. Can you help me plot a path?"

"Of course." Cyrus nodded. "I will give you directions toward the back of the palace, where less sentinels are likely to see you."

With a focused ear, she listened to point by point of what Cyrus told her, committing his directions to memory until she could transcribe them to her dive compass later.

Cyrus motioned at her with his head. "Part your lips."

She did, and he brushed his lips gently over hers, exhaling a slow trail of warm, steadying breaths into her mouth. "It's done." He turned his lips into a grim smile. "I'll be here."

Angie gave him a reassuring squeeze on his shoulder. "I'll be back as soon as I can." She checked her watch. Angie's gaze trailed down to Cyrus' tail before she left. It was no longer maroon, but a soft, subtle rose.

FORTY

TWENTY PADDLES SOUTHEAST. THEN FOUR KICKS north, fifteen kicks south.

Angie consulted the dive compass on her left wrist, where she'd transcribed Cyrus' directions, using one finger to trace the path she'd followed. So far, Cyrus had been good to his word. She hadn't seen one mer on her way down.

Her clothes created drag, causing her to exert herself more with each swim stroke and paddle. If she knew she'd be going underwater today, she wouldn't have put on heavy cargo pants and a long-sleeved cotton shirt. She would feel like a soaked dishrag when she eventually got back to the surface, and muttered curses to herself until bright lights emerged from the fathomless deep.

She consulted her dive compass to get her bearings. Less than a quarter nautical mile to go until she reached the throne room, and she kept her head low. When she arrived, she slowed, her hamstrings and calves cramping from the ceaseless flutter-kicking.

She circled the seamounts surrounding the palace. The front and sides of the palace were covered with floating sentinels, weapons at the ready. The palace's flank, facing another seamount range, was barren of guards. She reached the back windows facing the throne room and took the moment to stretch out her legs before continuing.

Tiān, this was exhausting.

The back of Queen Serapha's head came into view, as she gestured with exaggerated motions while speaking to Kaden. He floated upright with his hands behind his back, his handsome face holding a somber frown and fraught eyebrows. Two sentinels and Adrielle were on either side of them.

Angie pressed her lips together and shot one arm up high, waving with large arcs, fighting the water's resistance. It took Kaden a minute to notice her flailing, and once his eyes locked with hers, his jaw slackened. Serapha and the sentinels turned around to see what he gawked at, and Angie darted underneath the long window and away from their sight, heart pounding.

More curses wove through her mind, and she didn't have the first thought of what she should do now. She circled the pillar, hiding on the other side and pressing her back to the curved surface. Compared to the neutral temperatures this far below, the building radiated a dull warmth on her back.

A disturbance in the water alerted her, and she lifted her head. Kaden approached, and Angie relaxed her shoulders and arms.

Except Serapha and one of the sentinels were in hot pursuit, faces marred with fury. "Landwalker." The word was notched with hate. "A spy? How did you—"

"Mother!" Kaden grabbed her arm when she passed him, preventing her from advancing further, and signaled the sentinel to hold back.

"What?" Serapha jerked her arm from him, her tail twisted upward and pointed at his chest, as if she were going to jab it at him.

"Wait! I have information you'll want to hear. And you, too." Angie raised her voice. "Let me say what I have to say. If you find that I'm lying, kill me. I won't try to escape."

"You will not be able to escape." Serapha's voice was cool and emotionless.

"It's about Cyrus. And the humans are stealing your magic."

"Did you say Cyrus?" A soft lilting voice joined the fray. Adrielle, with her rose-colored tail matching Cyrus'. Her voice quivered, but rose with hope. "Where is he?"

"How in the black fathoms do you know Cyrus?" Serapha barked.

"That's what I came to tell you. No one is listening to me, and I need you to hear me out." Angie kept moving her arms and legs to keep in place against the currents swirling around her.

"You can trust her, Mother," Kaden said quietly.

Now Serapha looked as if she would murder them both. "How do you know?"

"Because I–I love her."

Angie stared in shock, though a rush of heat jolted through her to hear Kaden say it to the queen.

"You. What?" Serapha spoke through a clenched jaw. Realization flashed. "That's why you were going to the surface? For a landwalker?"

"Yes. I didn't expect it to happen, but she's been trying to help us. I swear to Sanyue." The words shook, but Kaden held himself upright.

Adrielle nodded quickly. "Please, hear her out. If she has news about Cyrus, it may be our only chance to save him." She looked to Angie, and put a hand over her belly. "I can vouch that she can be trusted."

"Both of you?" Serapha looked like she was going to implode, and Angie didn't blame her. It was a lot of news, all at once, and Angie was technically her enemy.

The mer-queen's fists were clenched at her side, and her cheeks and neck flushed red. "Fine," she said finally. "You get one chance. You're lucky Kaden and Adrielle convinced me not to kill you where you float."

When they reached the throne room, Serapha moved to wrap her tail around her throne, and Kaden, Adrielle, and the sentinel flanked her on both sides.

It looked so ominous, like she was facing judgment for a heinous crime.

She supposed that wasn't too far off.

"How are you here?" Serapha asked, leaning forward, her tailfins grazing the coral pillar.

Angie took a deep breath.

Stick to the facts.

"Cyrus gave me his magic—"

"Why would he do that?" The queen's eyes narrowed.

Angie wiggled her fingers and toes, growing uncomfortable. Serapha must suspect that Cyrus knew her, given Adrielle and Kaden's defense of her. Still, she didn't want to be the one to implicate him.

"They are familiar," Adrielle spoke up.

Angie's shoulders collapsed with sweet relief. She told herself to keep breathing, to keep her voice steady, and especially not give away the terror she felt inside at facing Serapha.

The mer-queen's eyes softened in an instant. "So, he lives?"

Angie bowed her head in a show of respect. "Yes. And the mermaid, Aurora. Though, her lifemate is gone. I also have to warn you, my people found a way to take the magic, and they've been draining it from the mer they've captured. My people have discovered what it could do for them." Angie paused for a breath. "Once the word spreads, they'll gather an army and kill all of you."

Serapha gave a harsh bark. "They can certainly try. They think to invade our territory and survive to tell the tales?"

"They found Father here. If they take our magic and return, they'll be able to see the palace," Kaden interjected. "We don't know when they will strike. Or where. And they may kill Cyrus."

Serapha thinned her lips, a crack in her hardened veneer.

Angie squeezed her eyes shut and took the plunge with her next, impassioned plea. "Will you consider negotiating with my father?"

The mer-queen chewed on her lower lip.

Angie raked her hands through her fanned-out hair, awaiting her decision.

Serapha stayed quiet for a torturous moment.

A halibut skittered under Angie's feet, and she pumped her arms in a reverse breaststroke, moving her back to give it room.

Angie's breaths became shallow. Kaden looked from Adrielle to Serapha, to Angie, to the sentinel.

"Your father is willing to negotiate?" Serapha finally asked. "How do we know that Cyrus will return to us alive? That they haven't killed him already?" Her melancholic tone struck Angie's heartstrings.

"He was awake before I left. And they're intent on keeping the mer alive until they've learned all they can from them, and drained their magic. I'll come up with a plan to help him escape." Her mind worked to come up with possible solutions. "Even if it means I have to break him out myself."

"I'll consider it. Why are you so invested in helping us?" The question Angie dreaded.

There was no hiding anymore. She told the truth, speaking slowly, deliberately. "We've lost a lot of people. Some were my friends. So, I would be helping my family, too. And I love your son. With everything I have."

Another long stretch of silence ensued. Angie's head pounded, her neck sore from tensing her shoulders.

"We'll see what your father says, and I will determine if what he says is acceptable," Serapha said, through gritted teeth. She presented herself as an impenetrable fortress, but her posture was rigid, her back pressed flush against the pillar. "I assume he runs the dock."

Angie nodded.

Serapha motioned for Kaden to lean in, and they talked amongst themselves. Back and forth, eventually bringing the sentinel into their conversation. Angie kept turning the watch on her right wrist, over, and over, until Serapha faced her again.

The sentinel left the throne room, returning a moment later. He carried a bottle with a piece of kombu kelp inside. Similar to what Kaden had done for her earlier that summer.

"I asked him to write the letter. Give that to your father. Before I change my mind. I expect an answer within the day." She pushed the bottle at Angie, and Angie swam forward, holding it like it was treasure. "If he agrees, we'll immediately uphold our side of the terms. What I'm asking is fair: Cyrus back and well, my lifemate's body, and you stop polluting our home. In return, we'll supply your village with enough fish to sustain you, and we'll stop killing you. And you will stop courting my son."

Angie hesitated, rubbing the bracelet on her wrist. She could feel Serapha glaring at it as if she wanted to rip it off and scatter the beads across the sea. Angie's gaze flickered to Kaden. His jaw was clenched. Turning back to Serapha, she gave a slow bow.

Serapha gave her a brief nod. "Kaden, see her out. You and I will talk later."

Kaden led Angie away from the throne room, and Adrielle made her way out after them.

"Tiān, I'm so glad that went alright." Angie let out a long, relieved sigh.

"She can be talked to when the time is right," Adrielle said.

"She's already sorrowful this has led to the loss of her lifemate and capture of her oldest son, and she cannot bear to see it be the end of me or Adrielle and the grandbaby, too." Kaden's eyes glistened with hope. "The hope of having Cyrus back alive and knowing that we may no longer be hidden to humans was motivation enough for her to agree to negotiate. Thankfully you came when you did, dangerous as it was. I'm glad Cyrus helped you."

"Adrielle, why did you tell her that you knew me? I thought you and Cyrus didn't want to get involved with our relationship."

"Because she didn't seem fully convinced when it was just Kaden speaking in your favor. I do not care about any punishment she may inflict on me. Cyrus' life is at stake," she replied.

Angie forced a small smile. "His tail color is the same as yours."

"Because I am expecting. I learned of it during low suntide." Adrielle looked toward her still-flat abdomen.

"My sister is expecting, too."

"Then this is joyous news." Adrielle gave her a warm smile. "When will you be able to save Cyrus?"

"By tomorrow, I hope."

"Then I will wait for you by the shore. Take care of her, Kaden." She turned tail and swam in the opposite direction.

"Ready to go?" Kaden asked, clasping her hand.

Angie nodded, her free hand clutching the bottle. "Yes."

Angie and Kaden burst from beneath the waves, and Kaden kissed her before Angie climbed out of the water, pulling herself ashore.

She stopped dead halfway standing up. Four pairs of booted feet greeted her, and Kaden sucked in a sharp breath at her back.

"Mer!"

It was Nick.

A sharp gunshot tore through the air, making her ears ring and pound, and Angie's heart all but stopped. Air caught in her lungs.

When she spun back to face Kaden, he was gasping, holding a hand over his upper arm. He faced Nick and Bàba, the fingers on his free hand fanned across his breastbone in an expression of shock. His biceps were contracting, protection from the pain.

"Kaden!" She rushed to him and fell onto her knees, blocking Nick from getting another clear shot. "Oh, tiān, are you okay? Can you still swim?"

"Yes," he rasped.

"Then you have to run. Now."

"No." His chest heaved with labored breaths. The edges of his hand were covered with blood. "Not until I know you're going to be okay."

"Angela, get out of the way." Nick warned.

She turned to see him raising his gun again, this time aiming it at Kaden's head. "I need you to get out of here!" When Kaden still didn't move, she shoved his shoulders, hard. The bottle with Serapha's message inside flew out of her hand, landing in the sea behind him. "He'll kill you!"

At that, something seemed to snap in him, and he fled back into the sea without another word.

"Nick!" Angie rose up to her full height, looking around for the bottle. It was nowhere to be found, and the currents must have carried it somewhere unknown.

She mentally cursed.

Bàba and Nick stood before her, flanked by two other workers. All four were armed.

The passing breeze was colder, and the fine hairs at the back of her neck stood at attention.

Nick's eyes met with Angie's, his expression stony. He lowered his gun.

"Angela," Bàba said, stepping forward. His tone was eerily neutral and measured. "What is this?"

FORTY-ONE

NEXT MORNING CAME AND BÀBA STILL hadn't said a word to her about what he and Nick saw yesterday. Dread clenched at her chest and gut. It was only a matter of time.

But for now, she had work to do.

A commotion ahead of Angie drew her attention when she stepped onto the docks to start her shift, and she quickened her pace. A group of male dock workers gathered outside the east outhouse, steps away from the shoreline, Marc and Ian among them.

She walked closer, brow furrowed. "What's going on?"

"Couple divers got us some more mermaids late last night. Cam and his guys are gonna come and get them later and harvest their magic. Said we weren't allowed to help, though." Ian replied with an obnoxious laugh.

"I wonder why." Angie let out an exasperated sigh, and her stomach contracted as she pushed her way through and into the outhouse. She finally saw what the crowd was gaping at. Nick stood amongst them with his back turned to her.

Two mermaids languished in large tanks, banging on the glass and trying to climb their way out, their eyes bulging with fear. In the tanks beside them, Cyrus and Aurora floated, both pale and limp. Angie's heart wedged in her throat and both hands flew to cover her mouth. Her stomach heaved at the sight of them.

"Hey man." Ian nudged Marc. "Check 'em out."

Marc leered at the frightened mermaids. "Which one would you pick? The one with the long or short hair?"

Ian pretended to study them. "Give me the one with short hair. Less hair in the way, the better."

"Nah, but with long hair, you can pull it," Marc replied. He licked his lips, walking closer to the tank holding the long-haired mermaid. She shrunk back, and he grabbed his crotch, making thrusting motions while jeering at her.

"Yeah, but how you gonna stick it in a fish?" Ian snickered.

"Who cares? Her mouth works, right?" Marc laughed again.

"Damn right." Ian nodded in approval. "You know what we should do? Kill the mermen and capture the mermaids. I bet the females sell for more on the market, anyway."

"Big boys, aren't you? Talking about violating trapped, helpless women. Pathetic creeps," Angie snapped. "You give men a bad name." She faced them, the question she had been wanting to ask bursting forth. "And when the Hells were you two allowed to come back, anyway? Weren't you suspended?"

The two men stared at her, agape. Marc's expression hardened, and he snarled. "For your information, little lady, Nick asked us to come back because we're short-staffed."

The two sauntered away, whispering amongst themselves. Angie twisted her face and approached Nick, tapping hard on his shoulder. He turned from his conversation, jovial smile fading when he saw her.

"Release those mermaids, and all the other ones you're imprisoning. We've already killed their king and caught one of their princes. If we continue this, the mer will never agree to peace."

"But you forget something." Nick paused for dramatic effect. "What does it matter at this point? We don't need them to agree to peace. We'll keep taking whatever sorcery they have and we're going to use that to kill them where they live."

Angie held up her hands to stop him from continuing. "You're okay with them killing us, then?"

Nick grabbed her arm, his fingers pinching her skin, and dragged her out the back entrance. She stumbled to keep pace with him. "You haven't learned your lesson yet, fish-lover? You going to run back to fishboy and tell them what we're doing? Oh, wait!" He flexed his arm and kept her still so she couldn't walk away from him. "You can't."

"Get off me." She tried escaping, but Nick was stronger, yanking her back into the outhouse with him.

"You." He pointed to a scruffy-appearing man that Angie hadn't seen before. "Take one of those fishes and show the boss' daughter how our enemies are treated."

"With pleasure." Scruffy motioned to several of his colleagues, and they gathered the rolling work table with Cyrus' tank atop it. Angie lunged for them in blind fury, but Nick held her back. Her heart raced and jolted like a tuna fish chasing its prey as they pulled the tank to a corner. A group of other workers rushed to surround them in a frenzy.

She couldn't see what was going on, but Cyrus' screams and wails ripped through the claustrophobic space. Some workers bolted, but a handful stayed to watch.

The mer-prince's pained cries shattered Angie from the inside out.

Time passed in a blur, and when the workers made a move, Nick tightened his grip on Angie's arm, forcing her to follow them.

Cyrus came into view. He laid flaccid in two of the men's arms, on the brink of unconsciousness, his body mutilated with lacerations and bruises, blood trickling down his muscular arms and torso.

Angie desperately wanted to go to him, to treat his wounds and throw him back into the ocean. Like she had with Kaden, what felt like so long ago. The memory of the gunshot wound on Kaden's shoulder, the one she had caused, came back to her. Her stomach burned with guilt, and she took a deep, pained breath, closing her eyes.

Helpless and still restrained by Nick, her eyes snapped open. She watched the men walk back to the tanks and, with their collective strength, slide him back in. Tiny crimson streams snaked out from the cuts on his body. Through hooded eyes and with slow, languid motions, he put one hand over a laceration on his abdomen, and his free hand over a slice on his opposite arm.

"Nick, how can you allow this?" Her entire body shook. "This is barbaric. You're sick."

Nick ignored her and stopped his men on their way back. "Keep the two new mermaids alive and healthy, and don't drain them too fast. And make sure at some point today, you take inventory and check on the other mer we have. I want a full report by close of business."

"You got it, boss." The men ambled away with Scruffy at the helm.

Angie jerked from Nick's grasp one last time, but he threw his free arm around the front of her shoulders, keeping her back flush against his chest. "I want you to behave, Angela."

"Don't tell me to behave. I'm not a child." She clenched her jaw and clutched at Nick's arm, but he didn't budge.

Giving her a hair's width of space so he could spin her around to face him, he continued his diatribe, his face flushed and eyes manic. "You're a race betrayer, and you're crazy. No wonder your mom didn't want you and offed herself. I can't wait until your dad finally punishes you."

His last words ignited a blazing fire in her.

"Fuck. You." Angie widened her stance and rammed her shoulder into his chest as hard as she could. When he staggered, she reared her head back, driving her forehead into Nick's nose. He stumbled into Cyrus' tank, and with a violent sway, the worktable rolled backward, the back of the tank slamming into a protrusion from the wall behind it. A loud *crack* filled her ears, coming from the tank. With a loud yelp, Nick failed to regain his balance and teetered before falling to his hands and knees. Angie glared at him as he began to stand.

Sharp pain detonated behind her eyes and bright white stars filled her vision, but she ignored it. What was that saying about never kicking someone when they're down, because karma will find a way to turn things around?

"Consider this your karma, asshole." Fueled by fury and vexation, she gave him a final, swift kick to the stomach with a loud *thump*. "And this is for hurting Cyrus." She delivered another blow, her foot slamming into his crotch. He fell back to his side and Angie fled, face flushed and hands trembling.

"Angela!" he screamed followed by a stream of what sounded like French curses. Her last glimpse was of him clutching his crotch.

From his lips to her ears, Angie stumbled on a piece of gangway debris sticking from the pebbled ground. When she was safely out of Nick's earshot, she leaned her head against the warehouse's wall, tears pricking at her eyelids. This time, she allowed them to fall.

His words cut deep, like a freshly sharpened knife slicing her heart into tiny, tiny pieces.

——— ☬ ———

After a half hour, Angie's forehead still throbbed as she sat in Bàba's office, waiting for him. Her fingertips and toes were numb. Nick's cruel words stung as if a man o' war had brushed its poisonous barbs along her naked limbs.

He had messaged her minutes ago, asking her to meet him in his office. Saying he wanted to give their high emotions a chance to settle before they discussed what was to happen next. Her feelings were far from settled in light of everything that happened earlier today.

Nick strolled through the door first, one hand over his stomach, and the other holding an ice pack to his nose. Angie stood straight up. "The Hells are you doing here?"

He lifted one shoulder in a casual shrug that infuriated her, and he pointed behind him. "Dad asked me to join." He sat in the office chair next to Bàba's desk. "Think you got away with what you did to me?"

Bàba strode in soon after, and took his seat. His usually warm brown eyes were cold as if she were simply an unruly worker he had to deal with instead of his daughter.

The notion was a forceful gut-punch.

It reminded her of sitting in her high school principal's office when she was fourteen, after she had called Angie's parents to tell them she skipped school. The dread as she waited for Bàba and Māma to arrive. Angie had wanted to scuba dive on the nicest day of summer that year, and hadn't thought skipping one day of classes was a big deal. Her parents understandably did, and after berating her for her irresponsibility, took away her scuba gear for a month and made her stay in her room for a week, only to come out for meals and school. She never skipped school again.

"Nick, why don't you start? You wanted to be here too, right?" Bàba motioned to Nick, and Angie kept her posture tall, her hands on her lap, staring him dead in the eyes.

She swore Nick flinched a smidgen at her hard stare.

Good.

"So, what do you have to say for yourself after you attacked me?" He spoke with spite, but avoided her stare.

"You started it." Angie kept her angry glare fixed on him.

"Beibei, what has gotten into you?" Bàba cut in.

"Wait, what?" Angie threw out her hands. "He was holding me down and saying horrible things in French."

Bàba's face remained stony. "A few other workers who witnessed the altercation confirmed Nick's story. You attacked him."

Angie suppressed a groan. Of course, Marc and Ian took his side.

Nick sighed. "This is what I get for worrying about you."

"What are you talking about?" Angie's hands balled into tight fists.

"About yesterday. I had to go out of my way to find out where you were. Make sure you were okay."

Liar.

"I think we have seen enough, yes? Angela, I got worried about you when you didn't show up for your shift on time." Bàba looked at his watch, as if to make a point. "So we went to look for you."

Figures Nick didn't tell Bàba the real reason, that he wanted to catch her red-handed with Kaden.

He shook his head slowly, a move he was fond of when he was upset with her and Mia. "But it didn't look like you needed help."

The undercurrents of his disappointment in her ran deep. This was one of the few times he didn't call her by her nickname.

He hadn't changed in that aspect from when Angie was a child.

"But how–how did you know where I was?" Angie's voice was small, and she hated how meek she sounded at that moment. Her posture wilted.

"That mermaid told me. Didn't even have to force it out of her." Nick leaned back and kicked his feet straight, crossing his ankles over each other, clearly relishing the moment.

Angie's blood boiled.

Bàba narrowed his eyes at Nick. "So how *did* you get it out of her?"

"I didn't."

Kaden had told her that most non-royal and non-noble mer didn't speak human languages. "But how did you understand her? I couldn't." Angie couldn't imagine why Aurora would tell Nick, after his cronies killed her lifemate in front of her.

"Well, once I got her to kiss me, I could magically understand her. By the way, not a fan. Breath was a little fishy. How do you bear it with your fishboy?"

"They don't smell fishy. You were probably sniffing your own stank breath." Angie clenched her fists. "Wait, you kissed her before you knew about their magic?" She could kick him in the crotch again.

Nick's mouth snapped shut, as if he realized what he just admitted.

"You went behind my daughter's back?" Bàba asked through clenched teeth.

"N-no, I knew about the magic, I was t-taking it—" Redness crept up to Nick's cheeks from his neck.

Angie crossed her arms over her chest, leaning back in her chair and glared at Nick.

"That's not what you said." Bàba pointed at him. "We're not done discussing this, and I'll deal with you when we've settled the war. But that is a separate matter. For now, continue with what you were saying."

Nick was now the same shade as a red sea star. "So, I realized that when that merman tried to drown me. He said a lot of awful things about humans. Oh, she got into a little fight with that merman next to her. I guess he's some prince, or something." Nick pursed his lips. "So long story short, he tried to stop her, but she told him she didn't care. That the royal family caused her lifemate to die because of this war. So, my gain."

Angie stared at Nick, unblinking, like Lulu had been when she saw Kaden.

"But, Angela." The initial smugness on Nick's face had become replaced with hints of regret and guilt. "I wanted to believe you weren't a traitor. I hoped I was wrong. Yes, I told your dad that I was worried about you. I had my suspicions for a while, though I kept them to myself because I wasn't sure what you were up to. I wanted to see for myself." He turned to Bàba. "Sorry. I should have told you earlier. Who knows what kind of information she's given to the mer?"

"No." Bàba shook his head. "I appreciate you bringing it to my attention."

"So, you ratted me out, Nick. I thought so. I talked to their Queen. I had a letter from her." Angie spat out each word, sharp and spiteful. "She wants to negotiate with you, Bàba."

"Then where's the letter?" Bàba asked.

"I lost it when I was trying to stop Kaden from being shot again. But if you're willing, I'll find a way to relay the message to them." She would tell Cyrus or Adrielle, but Bàba and Nick couldn't know she was planning to sneak him out.

"Don't blame Nick. He was trying to do the right thing." Bàba's timbre was so sharp it cut right through her. "I'm not negotiating with them, after they destroyed part of our docks and that merman tried to drown Nick."

"Nick was hurting the mermaid he loved." Angie's shoulders and limbs shook at the memory.

Bàba held up his hands, and she stopped talking. "They're violent and unpredictable. And you betrayed *us*. Defied my orders, which were for your safety! For a merman?" He looked down at his hands, and took in a shaking breath. "He could have hurt or killed you, and I would never have known what happened. I already spent too much time away from you and Mia when I was deployed. I will not lose you to our enemy."

"Kaden would never—"

"How do you know what this Kaden will and will not do? You've known him for what, three months? Two months? I don't even know when you met him." Bàba lifted his head, and an angry flush colored his face and neck.

Bàba's desk phone rang, vibrating on the desk. The sudden sound broke the silence, and he picked it up, listening to whoever was on the other end. "Okay, give me ten minutes." He dropped the receiver with a *clang*, hanging up the phone. "Trouble at the warehouse. Some supplies are missing. Now we have a thief. But we're not done yet. Both of you will come with me." He motioned for them to follow, and they did. Bàba continued once he had locked up his office. "Angela, I don't think we can trust you to be around here."

Her fingers gripped hard at her cargo pants, bunching them up.

"You're fired."

Two words were all it took for the blood to drain from Angie's face and a ghostly fist to punch the wind out of her. The air around her turned to piercing ice, ripping and numbing her skin.

Her voice dropped to a whisper. "I need these last thirty hours or they won't let me start my grad program. These last couple hundred so I have enough to pay off my entire tuition. I have a few weeks left, there's no way I can find another job and make that much that fast. You know that. Can't you—"

"You put us in danger." Bàba's authoritative tones carried over her protests. "Our people Nick sent to check on you reported that you told the mer-prince about us. Meeting him here, at the docks. Who knows what he's learned while in our docks? What you told him of our plans?" The vein in his forehead engorged. "And you broke my trust. You knew where the fish were, and you kept it to yourself." Bàba shook his head. "I expected better from you."

Angie drew her head back, speechless. In the course of hours, she lost the man she loved, her job, and her family's trust. To her, it was everything.

He continued. "Actions have consequences. You know that. And we were about to finish this once and for all. We know where their palace is."

"How do you know that?" she whispered, fearing the answer even as she knew what it would be.

"Divers used the mer's magic to investigate. Saw their palace. Reported it back to us," Nick answered for Bàba.

Angie's feet went cold.

"Oh, come back, and you'll never see Rosie again, and I'll make sure of it." Nick's self-satisfied smirk returned; his glare fixed on her.

"No, you can't." Her voice dropped to a whisper. "Mia won't allow it."

"You're concerned about what Mia will think? She'll do what I ask her, and she'll do anything to keep her family together. Whose side do you think she'll be on? Her deceitful sister who bailed out on the family as soon as she was old enough, and can't even be bothered to return her calls the last few days while she worried sick about you?" He put his hands on his hips, fingers tightening and forearm muscles bulging. "Or her husband, who's been by her side this entire time?"

Angie bit back tears. "She wouldn't," she said, trying to convince herself more than Nick.

"And I will not allow it. Nick, she's been punished. Leave her alone." Bàba's authoritative tone shut Nick up.

Nick grumbled, "Yes, sir."

Bàba turned back to Angie, and his angry glare pierced into the corners of her heart. "They are starving us. Killing our men and women. Killed the *mayor's* son, killed more innocents with that reckless wave they caused, and you ran into their arms?"

Not theirs. Just his. Kaden's. Yet protesting it would make no difference, she was sure.

The slow, controlled inflection when he spoke struck Angie with dread. Bàba walked away silently, leaving her alone with Nick.

Nick folded his arms and puffed out his chest.

Angie straightened up. "What the hell is wrong with you? Threatening to never let me see Rosie again? Not telling my dad the truth about why you wanted to come with him and look for me? How about stealing that mermaid's magic, and that your buddies shot her husband right in front of her? Also, you cheated on my sister, you piece of shit."

"It wasn't what it looked like with that fishy chick. And I'll talk to Dad when he's calmed down." He waved her off.

"You're not talking your way out of this."

"Yeah, I will. And what does it matter to you, now that you can't go anywhere near those goddamned fish, anyway?" Nick's foot made a rhythmic tap, tap, tap against the concrete. "I could ask the same about you. The mer have killed men and women I call lifelong friends. They killed Eva, who was *your* friend, and left her daughter an orphan. Still, you went, what, gallivanting around with one of them?" He closed the distance between them, his upper lip curled and exposing his top row of teeth. She held firm in her stance, even as his next words sent a sickening wave through her limbs. "But it doesn't matter now. We'll hit them right where they live, and show them who the dominant species is on this Earth."

Forty-Two

After sending her paystubs to her personal email for her records, Angie moved her mouse cursor to the "Off" button on the public-use work computer. She didn't click it yet.

"*You're fired.*"

It was surreal, and she covered her face with her hands.

She wouldn't have enough hours or money before she set off for school. But she deserved it. Should have left Kaden before she got herself in too deep. Everything she worked for. Gone.

Before she hit the little semi-circle icon, a new email came in.

Mia: Hey, sorry to email you at work. But I haven't heard back from you at all, and I can't stop thinking about you. Please call when you get this. I know you haven't answered me so far, and I think I know why. Let me explain?

Angie fiddled with the email and sent her a message back, asking her to meet her at work. Mia agreed, and she shut off her computer.

Nick and Bàba's cruel words assaulted her, her mind an echo chamber, their threats spinning round and round in a never-ending loop. She walked outside the business room. While waiting, she kicked a loose rock across the floor, and it soared into the main outhouse's tightly shut door.

Cyrus. She promised him and Kaden she would try her damndest to get him out tonight.

Shit, she should have asked Mia to meet her another time, or even later tonight.

Mia arrived on time and not a moment later, and Angie yanked her into a hug. Mia squeezed tight in return. "Nick told me he tipped off Bàba. That they fired you. I hope you know I would never turn my back on you, I would do anything for you." Mia spoke her entire spiel in one breath and pulled back, gulping in a breath of air. "You know that, right?"

A group of dock workers walked past, led by Nick. He gave Mia a brief wave before walking off, ignoring Angie.

"I have to tell you something," Mia began once Nick and the workers were out of earshot.

"Yeah?"

"Nick threatened me, the day we met with the mer. He kept asking me where I had gone for those two hours. I told him I took Rosie for a walk, but he didn't believe me. He screamed at me, threw things, made me tell him." She sniffled. "Rosie was scared out of her mind. I didn't want to tell him, I swear. But he threatened to divorce me and take Rosie, saying I put them in danger, so I caved and told him. I wish I hadn't."

"I'm sorry I didn't call you back. I should have known." Another thought came to her, gripping her insides. "Mia." Her voice dropped low. "Did he hit you? Or Rosie?"

Mia swallowed hard, grunting with effort as they kept moving. "He was just mad we went behind his back. He's never done it before, he couldn't control himself—" She broke off, eyes growing wide and mouth dropping open.

"I'm going to kill that asshole," Angie said through gritted teeth. "And while you're pregnant with his baby? How dare he."

Mia scoffed. "Hopefully you won't have to. Once we get a chance to breathe, if we make it through this war. I'm leaving him. He's not the man I fell in love with and married. He's changed this summer."

Angie swelled with pride for her. "You have to do what's best for you, jiějie. I'm with you, whatever you decide." She thought of telling Mia about Nick and the mermaid, but decided against it. Choosing to leave her husband couldn't have been an easy decision for her sister.

"Thanks."

"Mia, honey, I know I just didn't hear what I thought I did." Nick had returned with the group of workers, and the group of men stood over them, Nick's arms crossed over his chest, tight enough so his forearm muscles bulged.

Mia stiffened, and Angie's next words died in her throat.

"You three. Stay right there." Nick ordered his men, two of which were Marc and Ian, and they stayed put.

Mia hadn't moved a muscle beside her. Angie's breaths burst in and out. She wasn't afraid of what Nick would do to her, but to Mia.

"Did I just hear that you were planning on leaving me?" The timbre of his voice had become low and menacing.

"You can't do what you're doing. To me, to our daughter, treating my sister the way you do. It's not right." Mia stood straighter, her glare never leaving Nick, and Angie wanted to hug her.

"She. Attacked. Me." Nick jabbed a finger to his sternum and moved closer so that he was nearly chest-to-chest with his wife.

"Because you started it. I know her. She's not a fighter unless you push her into a corner."

Angie saw the pulsing in Mia's neck and temples, heard the slightest tremor in her voice.

Come on, Mia. Don't crumble. Stay strong.

"Oh, is that what she told you?" Nick threw back his head and laughed, a harsh, angry sound. "After all I've done for you, for Rosie, for our second child." He pointed to her stomach while tapping his foot against the wooden-planked ground. "Newsflash, hon. I won't let that happen. My family and I were the only ones here for you when your own family wasn't. There's no you without me."

Tears gathered at the corners of Mia's eyes, and her cheeks paled.

The workers behind Nick looked shell shocked, their gazes constantly darting to each other.

"Uh, maybe we should let you two figure this out. I don't wanna get in the middle of no domestic dispute." Marc took a step back and looked as if he was about to bolt.

"No, you're staying." Nick's order was sharp and final.

Angie couldn't take it anymore. She couldn't stand there and listen to her sister publicly berated by the man who supposedly loved her. "She made her choice. You brought this on yourself." She jabbed a finger in his direction. "Come on, jiějie, let's get out of here." She reached a hand for Mia's forearm, but Nick's hand came down hard on her shoulder, stopping her.

"I don't give two shits what you think, Angela. After today, you're gone. Never to step foot back here again." He waved his fingers in her face and scoffed under his breath. "I, for one, won't miss you. Neither will most of the people here. You're not wanted."

"You hurt my sister. You let your men tear the mer-prince up. And all you do is kiss my dad's ass." Angie was yelling now, but she didn't care.

Mia put a hand on her forearm, her grip tightening.

"You really want to pick a fight?" Nick yelled back in equal measure. "Because this time, I won't hold back!"

"Nick, stop it! Just, we'll talk about this at home, okay?" Mia cried out. Nick lunged for Angie in tandem with Mia throwing herself at him, and with frantic shouts, Nick's three men rushed for them.

"Nick! Nick!" Marc stopped short, grabbing Nick's arm.

"What?" Nick's spittle flew in the man's face, and with a shaking hand, Marc pointed toward the water.

"We gotta get out of here. The water. The mer are here."

Nick yanked his arm out of the man's grasp. "This is between me and my family. Go get some guns, if you're so worried. I have more important things to deal with here."

From her peripheral vision, Angie watched the three men dart into the storage house. They returned a moment later and readied themselves at the shore.

"It's some kind of vortex!" a different man called out, pointing to it.

"What the hell are you talking about, a vortex?" Nick threw his hands up in exasperation, and moved to join them.

Angie stood on her tiptoes to look at the seas. The tides and waves were swirling, slow and calm. The mer must be rotating the waters. Had Serapha's sentinels come to retrieve her? Had she run out of time to get Bàba agree to the peace agreement?

The men held their weapons, trying to get a good aim. If the mer took down Nick, Ian, and Marc, she certainly wouldn't cry over them. The fourth man was a stranger to her, however, and she wished no harm on him.

The four men hadn't moved from their spot at the beach, still talking amongst themselves.

An idea flickered into Angie's mind. They were far enough so Angie and Mia could slip away and buy some time while the men looked for them. If they did.

Angie took advantage of Nick and his men being distracted, and curled her fingers around one of Mia's wrists. She clicked the outhouse door open and shut it behind them. Once they were inside, one of Mia's eyebrows raised and the other lowered in confusion. "Angie, what—?" She jumped back and gasped. "Is that Cyrus?"

"I promised I'd get him out tonight. I'm so sorry, I forgot when I emailed you. Do you think you could give me a hand? Get him back to the sea? He doesn't look like he can hang on much longer."

"I don't think that's a good idea." Mia held up her hands, taking a step back.

"I *have* to. You don't have to help if you don't want to. I owe Kaden this much."

Mia paced around brow puckered in thought. Angie scanned the outhouse for something large enough to hide Cyrus in. No nets to be found.

An industrial-sized, empty mobile garbage bin was clear in sight, and Angie scrambled to take the large black bag out. If they could fit Cyrus into it, and she and Mia combined their strength to carry him, it could work.

"Oh, it hurts my heart to see him like that." Mia's loud declaration jolted her. Mia walked up to Cyrus' tank, never taking her eyes off his limp form, and put her hands on the tank. Then she looked at the bag. "You're putting him in a garbage can?"

"Better than nothing. And we could roll it. He's heavy."

Aurora, and the three, recently caught mer looked equally as lifeless, but their gills still opened and closed with a lethargic rhythm.

Glistening tears streamed down one side of Mia's face. "No one deserves this. Bàba and Nick let this happen?"

Angie nodded, mute.

"Makes me sick." Mia clenched her fists at her side. "Let's make this fast. Are we getting the others out too?"

"I don't think we can," Angie whispered. "We won't have enough time to come back before Nick and those guys come looking for us. The others, I hope they won't suffer much longer. I'm sorry." She directed her apology to Aurora and the other mer, before approaching Cyrus' tank and grabbing the stepstool. "Can you lie the bag on the floor? We can pull him out and into the bag. Then slide him into the bin and roll him out."

After laying the bag flat, Mia grabbed a second stepstool to stand next to her at Cyrus' tail end. "Ready? One, two…" Angie reached over the tank to grab Cyrus under the shoulders, and Mia grabbed the end of his tail.

He was dead weight, too much for both of them to lift from their angles, and he slipped back into the tank. This wasn't going to work, and Angie raked her mind for what to do next. Mia looked equally at a loss for ideas.

More shouts came from outside, and Angie opened the outhouse door to see what the clamor was about.

The whirlpool grew in its diameter, its edges dangerously close to the gangway, and she sucked in a sharp breath. Nick and the workers were gone.

The mer had come for her.

Trying to contain her panic, Angie's gaze drifted to the spiderweb crack on the back of Cyrus' tank. She put a finger on the site of the impact, and gave a gentle push. It felt thinner than the rest of the tank.

"Did you find something?" Mia asked.

"I think so." Angie turned the worktable around with Mia's help. She eyed the crack, and then at her stepstool.

Bracing herself, and picked up the stool and with all the strength she could summon, swung it at the crack. It gave, more thin lines spreading from its center.

Two smashes later from her and Mia, and the glass shattered. The force of the water rushing forth nearly knocked Angie off her feet, and she threw her hands over her head, widening her stance.

Cyrus rolled out like a ragdoll, landing atop the garbage bag they laid on the floor earlier. Avoiding the glass shards that had been sprayed around them, Angie and Mia used their collective strength to turn the forty-pound garbage bin over on its side. They grabbed the bag on each end, holding him like he was a hammock and they were trees. He felt lighter, looked smaller.

"Angie? You came," Cyrus murmured, his eyes batting open for a brief moment. "And Mia. Thank you." His head fell back, eyes closing again. After exchanging a knowing glance with Mia, they used the bag to slide Cyrus into the bin.

"What are we doing with him now? Throwing him back in the water?" Urgency spiked Mia's voice. "Is he even going to live?"

"At least whatever happens, he'll be home. Not trapped here." Angie shook her head in disdain. With Cyrus secured and hidden, she peeked out the back entrance and motioned to Mia. She pulled and Mia scrambled to the other side and pushed, grunting and wincing. "Sorry. You don't have to push so much. I'll take more of the weight." Angie tightened her core and used both hands to pull the bin and they scurried to the shore.

They inched closer to the coast. Fifty feet, give or take, and they would be close enough to toss Cyrus in.

Adrielle appeared at the shoreline, tail flicking with anxiety, sunlight bouncing off her sepia skin. Angie came to a dead stop, but Mia lagged, nearly rolling the bin into Angie. Inside, the mer-prince didn't stir.

Almost there. Ten feet more.

The whirlpool had become a raging maelstrom, just feet away from where Adrielle was. The angry sea swirled, the sound of loud rushing water pounding into Angie's ears.

Was Adrielle doing this as revenge for Cyrus? Angie didn't think Adrielle would hurt her or Mia, but the other dockworkers could be fair game.

They stepped onto the sand, and Angie braced herself to maintain her balance. Mia grunted. "I'm going to have a chat with them later. About them firing you." When they were inches from the sealine, Angie and Mia overturned the bin once more.

Two armed sentinels floated next to Adrielle, keeping watch on her. Her eyes, the color of burnished leather, went first to Angie and Mia, and then to the bin. Hope brightened her exquisite features. "Cyrus?"

"Yes." Mia reached inside for Cyrus, and Adrielle helped to pull him out.

"Here, he's yours." Mia motioned to him.

"Oh, my love." Adrielle's voice was hushed as she cradled him in her arms. She leaned in to kiss him and brush the hair out of his shut eyes, and then kissed one of the lacerations on his arms. "He lives, but needs attention. He has lost a lot of blood, and does not have much life left in him." She pressed her forehead to Cyrus, stroking his cheek. "I will do everything in my power to ensure you live and meet your baby."

"Congratulations, Adrielle. I'm expecting, too." Mia put a hand on her stomach.

"Oh Goddess, that is wonderful." Radiance glowed on Adrielle's features, her gaze aimed at Mia's midsection. "Thank you both so much. I hope I can repay you someday."

"You don't have to, but maybe when our babies are born, they can play with each other? So, they can learn to respect the land and sea," Mia said.

"I would love that." Adrielle gave her a single nod, and then murmured something to the sentinels that Angie couldn't understand. "We should go. I also hope we will cross paths again when we are no longer fighting. And Angie, I will tell Kaden and Queen Serapha that you and your sister returned him to us."

A buzz lapped through Angie, her stomach constricting at the mention of Kaden's name.

She had to know. "Is he okay?"

"Healing. The Queen is quite upset with him, though." The mer-princess' brow furrowed. "And you."

Angie wanted to ask more, but the growing maelstrom didn't escape her. "Adrielle, you need to stop that. It's coming much too close to the docks. Cyrus is safe with you now."

"I didn't do that. Whoever's responsible, I cannot stop it. I've tried." Her voice lowered, and her lips parted. The maelstrom grew wider, eating away at the already fragile gangway. Wood splintered and slid into the maelstrom's gaping maw. Without a foundation, the rest of the gangway began to collapse.

It crept ashore with the force of a devastating tornado.

Her gaze frantic, Adrielle looked back to Angie and Mia. A single word left her lips in a whisper.

"Run."

Forty-Three

ANGIE GRABBED MIA'S HAND AND THEY sprinted inland. Sometime in the last five seconds, the maelstrom had doubled in size, a violent tornado consuming everything in its path. Water levels were rising much too quickly, consuming the rest of the gangway, the smaller buildings in its path, and the handful of workers caught in it.

Their screams as the sea harpooned them into her watery grip haunted Angie.

It was strengthening. Still moving toward them.

More buildings crumbled in their path, the maelstrom shattering their very foundations. Their staff break house. The outhouse that had held Cyrus and the other mer, and nearby storage shed. The building where they held a staff meeting what seemed like a lifetime ago. When Luke and Eva were still alive.

Angie was breathless. She didn't loosen her grip on Mia's hand, but they couldn't outrun the furious tides that charged at them, like aggressive whitetip sharks chasing down its prey.

"I can't run anymore. I'm exhausted," Mia whimpered from behind her.

"We have to keep going. We'll get sucked in and drown." Angie panted, her legs like jelly.

The water reached them, and Angie pitched forward with Mia in tow, narrowly escaping the frantic spinning tides that would have sucked them both in.

She tripped on a piece of driftwood, and her knees smashed into the pavement. Losing her balance, she pulled Mia down behind her, one arm across her stomach. Stabbing pain raced down Angie's shin, and she winced.

They'd made it halfway into the docks. As inexplicably as it had appeared, the maelstrom seemed to settle, the waters receding.

The world slowed, bleary voices coming through in buzzes. Angie stayed on her bruised knees, hands to her head. Her head spun and spun, breaths catching in disbelief. A high-pitched ringing struck her ears, a perpetual siren that all but deafened her.

The voices came together into a coherent noise. Male voices. Bàba and Nick's, in the midst of a cacophony of others.

"Shut it down! Shut everything down, NOW! I repeat, CEASE ALL OPERATIONS."

"Everyone, pull back! Get out of the docks!"

Frantic footprints stampeded past her, and a hand gripped her wrist, pulling her to her feet. "That includes you, Angela and Mia!" Nick's sharp voice cut into her ears, and she snapped out of her daze, allowing him to pull her up by her forearm. His palm grazed a deep scrape on her arm from when she fell to the ground earlier, and she gritted her teeth through the searing pain.

"Are you two okay?" Bàba joined them, helping Mia up.

Nick let go of Angie once she was upright, running ahead to corral workers on the dock's outskirts.

"Y-yeah. I'll live," she whispered, quickening her pace to join the others. Mia gave him a silent nod of assent. "Where are we going?"

"Home." Bàba lengthened his strides, his grip firm on his older daughter.

Around her, people lay hurt and groaning on the ground, others were dead, clothes and hair doused with water and clinging to the ground. Debris littered the docks. Wood planks with their sawtooth edges, crumbled buildings, and in the distance, boats and yachts floated upside down, some in pieces trailing out to sea.

Angie stopped walking when she came across Ian and Marc's dead bodies, Marc lying on his back, and Ian lying on his side. Both appeared to have drowned, their eyes wide open and glassy, and foam trailed from Ian's mouth. As if the sea had swallowed them, and then spit them out in disgust.

Workers around her were screaming, scattering to help the injured, searching for their colleagues and friends. Angie struggled to make out the other terrified, frantic raised voices around her.

She couldn't. It was a blur.

Bàba and Mia left her behind when a group of men toward the dock's entrance grew rowdier. Angie stepped on the small wooden bridge overarching a narrow body of rushing water as she moved closer to the crowd.

A violent splashing and a scream beside her caught her attention, and she stopped to look. If someone had fallen into the water, or the mer had crept closer to shore, in the middle of the docks—

A piece of thick rope lassoed around her ankle and tightened. She lost her balance and shrieked as the floor rose up to meet her. Several workers heard and ran back to grab her.

One man's fingers grazed Angie's as a large net landed on her head, enclosing her and sweeping her off her feet. Her chest smacked the bridge's edge, and she cried out, limbs flailing as she crashed into the water below. Voices above yelled her name, and she clawed at the net to no avail.

Her screams faded into incoherent muffling once her head went underwater. Saltwater rushed into her open cut, and her lips parted in a soundless scream.

The net slipped off and a pair of strong arms wrapped around her from behind, pinching her shoulders into her chest. "You almost escaped. Stupid landwalker." A disembodied voice came from next to her, thin lips pressed against her jaw. The marks on his arm stood out to her. No matter how she struggled, the sentinel's ironclad hold prevented her from budging.

Her lungs protested, and her chest ached. The merman dragged her further to the depths. When she accidentally swallowed a mouthful of water with a frantic breath, the merman pinched her chin between his thumb and forefinger and turned her face upward, his mouth descending on hers. With no other choice but to drown, she accepted his kiss, and he breathed down her throat.

When he pulled away, her lips were sore. His kiss was rough and forceful, laced with hatred. A sharp contrast to Kaden's sweet and passionate kisses, laced with love.

The palace came into view, and abject fear struck.

Her captor took her around back, through the palace. Two sentinels swam up to join them, grabbing each of her legs, fully restraining her.

A carved out, large rock face entered her gaze, covered with sea glass circles, like a rocky honeycomb.

They stopped along a row of prison cells, and he threw the sea glass door open, shoving her inside face-first and slamming it shut again. Angie threw her hands out before her face smashed into the opposite wall.

"The landwalker leader's spawn." The merman's lips curled in contempt. "By order of Mer-Queen Serapha, you will answer for your attempted murder of Prince Kaden. And dishonoring your end of the agreement you made with her." His brows drew together, obsidian eyes drilling holes into her, and Angie cowered. "We will return when we have word from her."

Attempted murder? Dishonoring their agreement? No, no, no!

Then he was gone, leaving her alone and pressed against the glass door, pounding in useless desperation.

Forty-Four

Angie pressed her back against the ceiling, extending her arms. The cell was shaped like a cylinder, twice as long as she was tall, the ceiling low, designed to hold the lithe, agile mer in a horizontal position. She could only log roll to face the ceiling or the floor, no way to stand upright.

She'd been here overnight, and her back ached from the constant arching. What she once thought was a vibrant, glittering palace was now a menacing and oppressive prison.

Angie faced the small, circular window on the opposite end of the cell, the view leading to the vast, unending sea.

Looking for help that never came.

Two glistening emerald eyes appeared in the dark open sea, moving forward to form the shape of a great white's silver nose, followed by colossal jaws.

A beautiful sight, but in her predicament, she couldn't properly admire the animal.

Futile as it might be, she searched for an escape. Angie had looked all over the cell, even pushed against the door with all her might when a sentinel wasn't present, but it was sealed tight.

Yet she'd seen the sentinels opening and closing other prison doors with ease. It must only open from the outside, and the notion made her sick with anxiety.

Her vision blurred, salt stinging her eyes. Her lungs strained to expand as she inhaled, creating tightness in her chest. The mer's magic was fading, and she would drown. None of the patrolling jailers came to check on her, and she suspected they'd forgotten about her. She swallowed a mouthful of saltwater with her next breath, and she clutched her throat, feeling like the walls were closing in, about to crush her like she was nothing more than a boneless jellyfish.

The magic dissipated, and she held her breath. She was going to die here. Bàba and Mia would never find her. Even if they knew where the palace was, they wouldn't make it before the mer swarmed and killed them. She wouldn't see Rosie again or meet her unborn niece or nephew. Never realize her dreams as a marine biologist.

Angie was fading, flashes of black burst into her vision.

She pressed both hands under her breasts, pushing down the pain. She sucked in another gulp of water, retching at the briny taste and gritty texture.

Tiān, she could use one, or three or four of those damned air bubbles right now.

The cell door swung open and a pair of hands grabbed her, pressing strong fingers on both sides of her jaw and forcing her mouth open. The touch of lips came next, and then a rush of soothing breath from their throat to hers.

The world cleared and her breathing resumed. Angie's head still pounded, but she lived. Her eyes met Kaden's, his hands still clutching her shoulders as he floated above her. She gasped in relief, putting both hands on his chest.

"Kaden. Oh, I'm so glad it's you." Her head tilted back to rest on the floor.

He touched her cheek. "I feared I was too late." His words came out rushed and panicked. "I couldn't escape the infirmary any sooner."

"No, I'm sorry too. I didn't expect my dad and brother-in-law to be there, waiting." Her eyelids burned with hot tears, and she released them, letting the sea wash them. "I didn't know."

"I know you didn't." Kaden's easy chuckle was a sweet harmony to her ears. He pressed his forehead to hers, and Angie curled her fingers around the back of his hand.

"Then why am I being kept here?"

He moved his head back, his features grim. "My mother still had her reservations about you. So she sent two sentinels shortly after us to keep an eye on me. They saw me return to the sea with a bleeding tail, and after sending me to the infirmary, reported to her that you had led me into an ambush."

"You have to tell her it was a mistake. Have you talked to her?"

"I will. Now that I know you're okay. I heard rumors about a landwalker in our prisons. Somehow, I knew it was you."

She raised a hand and brushed a lock of hair from his face. "There was a maelstrom. I thought you said your mother was bedbound?"

He fiddled with her fingers, still entwined with his. "She recovered much faster than I expected. A blessing from the Sea Goddess, perhaps. And, I visited Cyrus. He lives, though I suspect his consciousness is elsewhere."

"Thanks for the update. Will he recover?" Angie watched him carefully, waiting for his answer.

"Yes, but it will take some time. Three tidesyears. One for every tidesday that your people trapped him and drained him of his magic." He rolled his lips between his teeth. "Our energies are not meant to be drained so quickly."

"Three years. I'm so sorry." Angie shook her head.

"The healers will take good care of him. Thank you for keeping your word." His gaze locked on something behind her head, and he let go of her. "The sentinels are here. Stay alive, and I'll come back for you as soon as I can."

"Stay alive, huh? I'll do my best."

His fingers peeled away from hers as he swam out of the cell. She rolled so she faced the door, both hands flying to cover her mouth when the merqueen approached, flanked by two armed sentinels, cutting Kaden off.

Serapha faced her first, then sent a glare set on fire to Kaden, her fists and torso held tight, as if stopping herself from strangling him with her bare hands. "Kaden." Her voice trailed out in a low growl, like her son's name was a word she had to force out. "What are you doing here? This landwalker tried to have you killed."

"Mother." Kaden held up a hand. "She is innocent and brought your message to her father, but they were awaiting us at the shore. The bottle was lost while she tried to save me. I bled too much to try to retrieve it."

"I knew I didn't have a good feeling about her, but I took yours and Adrielle's word for it because Cyrus was in danger. How do you think those landwalkers knew exactly where to await the two of you?"

The thunder in Serapha's tone struck fear into Angie's core.

"Aurora told them! The mermaid that was trapped with Cyrus," Angie burst out.

"You expect me to believe that one of ours would turn on us, while under capture from your *revolting* species?" Serapha snarled at her. "You must think me a brainless barnacle."

Kaden said nothing, gaze unflinching as he floated eye-to-eye with her. Serapha swam upward so she towered over him. He didn't move to meet her level.

"I want you to stay away from her. She cannot be trusted, and neither can you, for putting your naive trust in a landwalker in the first place." Her lips morphed into a scornful twist, the venom in her eyes pierced Angie through the chest. "I will use her to make the landwalkers back down. And you." She jabbed a finger into his chest. "If I catch you around here again, or going near the surface, you will be exiled. Understood?"

Kaden's arms slackened at his sides. "Wh-what?" He looked with wide, frantic eyes in Angie's direction. "You cannot simply exile me–"

"I can, and I will. I am the ruler of this queendom, and you are still my subordinate." Serapha's expression hardened.

Angie pounded on the cell door to protest, but the mer ignored her.

"Get out." Serapha pumped her tail and swam in a circle around him.

Kaden didn't move, and something in his face snapped, shock giving way to defiance as he stared her down. Serapha met his gaze, inching closer. In turn, Kaden moved toward Angie's direction, his back to her.

Angie pressed her palms to the cell door. Kaden kept his eyes on Serapha and the sentinels.

As soon as he made for Angie's cell, hand outstretched, the sentinels grabbed him by his arms. Kaden escaped their grasp. She didn't know what he had been planning. Get her out, and then leave her to her own devices while he dealt the Queen and her sentinels? Attempt to escape with her?

One sentinel with a sapphire tail clutched Kaden's, violently pulling Kaden toward him. The other sentinel, with a golden tail, approached him from the front. Serapha's steely gaze tracked them, never making a move to help either the sentinels or Kaden, or stop them.

Kaden twisted his upper body and contracted his tail, wrestling his way out of the grasp of the sapphire-tailed sentinel. Their scuffle and resulting chase were a dizzying dance to Angie's eyes while her stomach fluttered and arm muscles twitched. He slithered away each time the sentinels attempted to grab him. Then he fought back, striking at the sapphire-tailed sentinel like a venomous snake, causing the sentinel to flex and wiggle backward, clutching his abdomen in pain, and Kaden took his lance, holding it to his chest with a clenched jaw and wildfire in his eyes.

Angie shouted Kaden's name, but only Serapha acknowledged her with a glare like winter's ice.

Finally, another sentinel, this one with a prismatic tail, arrived from outside Angie's immediate vision. Together, the three restrained Kaden, one holding fast on his tail, another clutching his upper body, and they swam him back to Serapha.

Serapha gave her order once they were close enough. "See him out. I don't care where he goes, as long as it's not anywhere in this vicinity."

She left, and the sentinels, one keeping her trident pointed at his head, led Kaden away and out of Angie's sight, taking with them any hope of escape or seeing him again.

"And as for you." Her words pierced Angie's very being, as cold as the deep sea. "One of my messengers is drafting a missive to your landwalkers.

If they do not give me an answer when the next low noontide comes, I will have you executed and thrown ashore."

Angie wanted to shrink into a ball at Serapha's commanding presence.

The Queen turned to leave, stopping short when a group of sentinels sprinted into her and Angie's presence.

"My Queen." One sentinel paused, pointing toward the prisons' exits. "Landwalkers have been spotted!"

FORTY-FIVE

ANGIE SPUN AROUND AND BANGED INTO the narrow walls, and she flinched. The mer swimming guard outside moved into formation and darted out, leaving her with Serapha and the group of sentinels.

One sentinel's voice drifted to Angie. "We must keep the Queen safe!"

Angie struggled to make a U-turn in the cell so she faced the back window. She was at the palace's flank, and divers approached in droves, dressed in red scuba outfits effectively camouflaging them in the deep's darkness. Mer approached from the left, right, above, and beneath them. Spears, lances, and tridents struck. Blood flowed and formed sanguineous clouds around them until Angie couldn't differentiate between tail, blood, human, or mer.

She hoped one of the divers wasn't Stefan or Ken.

When the blood dissipated, it revealed the dead. Their bodies sank to become food for the sea's scavengers, littering the ocean floor around the palace. The cell blocked out much of the sound, so she watched the goings-on outside with rising terror, a silent, deep-sea horror movie.

Tiān, if one of the mer was Kaden—

Her cell door burst open, and a pair of hands grabbed her ankles, pulling her out. The blood-curdling noises came. Screams from the mer as they were impaled. The divers too, with their mouths free of regulators with the mer magic in them. Screams, yells, and battle cries rang through her skull.

The sentinels escorted her out with Serapha at the helm.

They fled from the carnage outside.

This time, it wasn't only the sight of blood striking at her. It was the stench. Even diluted, the thick, ferrous odor assailed her nostrils and made her want to heave had she anything in her stomach to throw up.

The mer and humans were still fighting around her.

Fighting, fighting, fighting. Tiān, she wanted this to end. Wanted to go home. Wanted to be with Kaden in peace.

A brief thought of escaping their grasp crossed Angie's mind. Anything was better than what the mer-queen and her group of armed sentinels had in mind for her. Yes, Serapha had said she would use Angie to make the humans surrender, but she didn't say how, or whether Angie would live or not.

Though, if there was the miniscule chance of escape, she'd take what she could get.

Desperation clawed at her, and she broke away, kicking and cycling her legs and arms as fast as her fatigued body would allow. Every stroke felt like torture, her muscles screaming in pain, but she pushed through, fueled by adrenaline. Angie had made it three kicks before arms grabbed her ankles and dragged her back down, and she shrieked.

"What are you thinking?" Serapha hissed, flanked by one sentinel while the other brought a still-struggling Angie back to them. One of the sentinel's arms squeezed around Angie's shoulders, and he held his trident to her lower back.

Though her mind refused to quit, her body gave up the fight, and she went limp in the sentinel's strong arms.

She should have squashed the notion, knowing it would never work. They swam much faster than she could ever dream to, and her body remained fatigued from not eating and drinking anything but sips of seawater for a day. Her lungs and skin were tight from dehydration, and she suspected Kaden's magic was the only thing keeping her conscious.

They stopped briefly when another sentinel swam up to them, her long braid swaying on her back. "Your Majesty. The messenger you sent has been slain."

"Black trenches." Serapha set her jaw, and the sentinels moved to surround her, their weapons pointed outward. "Bring me one of the cursed landwalkers, then."

The mermaid sentinel gave her a single nod, and turned away.

They moved through one tunnel, then another, and then a third, until they were out in the open sea. No fighting, no dead bodies, no blood, no weapons.

Only chilling silence.

Their path took them through a sanctuary, and a melancholy wave draped over Angie's head as the fish inside darted out of their way.

"Here." Serapha waved them over once the sanctuary had vanished from sight. She pointed to a giant rock cluster before them, and they ducked underneath, entering the littoral cave from the bottom. Inside was a passage sandwiched between thousands of cenotes, stretching an endless distance ahead.

Vibrant sea sponges and soft coral dotted the walls around them. A sight Angie likely would never have seen if she wasn't the mers' captive. Though the situation struck fear, she relished this picture of beauty.

A sentinel held out her arm, barring Angie's chest when they reached an open space with a single, large, flat rock formation. The male sentinel pointed her to the rock.

"Wait there." If Angie could sweat underwater, she would have been doing so profusely by now. She swam to the rock and brought her arms upward to lower herself onto it. Clutching at the edges, driving her heels into the sandy ground, and pushing her calves against the rock kept her from floating.

The mer-queen paid them no attention, her back turned to her.

For a tortuous stretch of time, the four remained in silence.

Angie slid her gaze to Serapha again. She had her head bowed, murmuring what sounded like a prayer, or mantra under her breath. Angie's heart softened, knowing she must be grieving her comatose crown prince and her mer-king.

The mermaid sentinel from earlier returned with a male sentinel, and a struggling, kicking person held by his armpits as they dragged them in.

"Here. We found this one swimming around aimlessly, away from the intruders." The male sentinel braced himself with his tail, and swung the human around to face them.

Angie gave a small yelp. "Stefan?"

Stefan looked up and stopped his kicking. "Angie? Oh my God, you're okay."

"You—what are you doing here? You came to attack the palace?" Angie still couldn't believe he was here. Wearing only a crimson scuba suit. "You took the mer magic?"

"Oh, so you two know each other. Makes this much easier," Serapha sneered.

Stefan floated with the sentinels binding his arms behind him. "The others came to siege the mer, and I said I wanted to join them so they'd lead me here. But I didn't attack. I heard you had been captured. Your dad sent me to find you. Figured with the camouflage, the mer wouldn't find me."

"Then you go and tell your leader that they have until low noontide to meet at the shoreline. If they do not agree, or if they attempt to attack us again without speaking, she dies." Serapha tossed a haughty glance to Angie.

"Okay. Okay. I will. Just, how do I get out of here? I'll tell your dad, Angie. I promise." Stefan winced, then gritted his teeth as he rolled his shoulders out. "God, it hurts. My shoulders don't have that kind of flexibility anymore."

"Escort him. Make sure he reaches the surface." Serapha dismissed the two sentinels, and they turned and left with Stefan.

Angie watched after them, and let a stretch of time pass before addressing Serapha. "Your Majesty?"

Serapha turned her head in Angie's direction, but didn't bother to rotate her body enough to face her. "Do not call me that." The sentence came out abrupt and snappy. "You're not of my kind. You're a filthy landwalker, and you caused my people to die in droves." Unmistakable hatred coated her words. "Then you led my son into a trap."

Angie flinched, but kept her eyes trained on Serapha's back and contracted tail. "No." Her exhale carried the word. "Kaden and I were trying to stop this. I swear, I didn't lure him. Why would I? I just returned Cyrus to you."

Serapha's hands curled into fists at her sides. "Keep Cyrus out of this."

Angie set her jaw. "Your people have died, and so have mine. They're killing each other in the palace as we speak. Can't we come to an agreement, for both of our sakes?"

"I've heard nothing from you about whether your leader had agreed to negotiate in the first place. I was still open to talking of peace, but then your divers sieged us. Clearly peace is not what you landwalkers want," she sneered.

Angie held her breath for several seconds before letting it go, slowing the pounding pulse beating through her veins and arteries. "Your Maj—Mer-Queen." She hoped the title wouldn't offend her. The Queen said nothing, didn't move, and Angie took it as her cue to continue. "I'm sorry about King Aqilus. But I heard Prince Cyrus still lives. I kept my promise, didn't I?"

"His heart still beats, but he is far from alive." At last, Serapha faced her, and Angie sat at attention, her hair fanning around her head. She eyed a coiled, striped nautilus drifting by. "I have already lost too much."

She turned her back to Angie again, and she took the hint and stopped talking.

——— ꍙ ———

Angie didn't have the first idea of how much time had passed, and she was numb from sitting in the same position for so long. She longed for a way out, but with the cave's single entrance and the sentinels never leaving her side, it left her no choice but to sit and wait for what happened next, much as she loathed not knowing what was to come.

A second attempt at speaking with the Queen yielded stony silence, and Serapha hadn't deigned to turn around to face her.

Finally, a lone sentinel entered the cave. "It's safe to return. The landwalkers are gone."

Serapha raised a hand and gave them a nod. Without a word, the sentinels took Angie by the upper arms and traveled back to the palace.

A small group of haggard mer greeted them at the palace gates. Mer and human corpses littered the courtyard floor, and salmon and Greenland sharks were closing in. "My Queen, you are safe. Thank the Goddess." The mer lowered their heads in a bow to her. Then their gaze moved to Angie. "This is the human captive?"

"Yes."

Many of the mer glared at Angie, but the one who had addressed the queen continued, "A small landwalker group flanked the rear. Entered one of the sanctuaries, stole a netful of fish. We've lost fifty soldiers, but we took their lives in equal measure."

"This is how they wish to try to end this? By attempting to steal the fish back for their own terrible use? I will not let this come to pass," Serapha said, her silvery voice full of resolve.

"What do you propose?" One of the sentinels escorting Angie asked.

Serapha tilted her chin upward. As they inched closer to the surface, dread unfurled in Angie's innards.

"We follow them," Serapha ordered. "They cannot outswim us. Call what sentinels and soldiers you can. We will make for the shore. I wish to end this on this tideday. The landwalkers will cede to me or see their end."

Forty-Six

ANGIE WENT LIMP ONCE SHE SUCKED in her first breath of fresh air. Sunlight hitting her face disoriented her. The grips around her arms tightened, and she felt herself being dragged forward, the sea's peaks smacking her face.

They stopped short, and she blinked, her vision clearing. They had reached the delineation between sea and land, before the water grew too shallow.

What was happening?

The beach stretched end to end with people, including Nick, Bàba, and Stefan. Behind her, a large gathering of mer. There must have been over a hundred on each side facing off with each other. The mer had their lances and tridents raised, and the people with their guns in hand. Stefan must have informed them the mer were coming.

"Motherf—" Nick raised his shotgun, but Bàba moved to stop him.

"Beibei? No!" Bàba gaped, horrified when his and Angie's eyes met.

Angie wanted to call out to Bàba, but her voice came out as a croak, her throat too scratchy and dry to produce a sound that would travel far enough to him. Instead, Angie tried raising a hand to greet her family, but the mers' unyielding clutch stopped her.

The tension hanging in the air was so thick Angie thought it would suffocate her.

"Landwalkers! You will surrender to me, or lose her. Stealing from us once wasn't enough?" The spurts of wind carried Serapha's voice, amplifying it. In response, Bàba held up a loudspeaker.

"Let my daughter go, and I'll consider it." Angie heard the quiver and worry coating his voice. "Please."

Nick whispered something to Bàba, and Bàba handed him the loudspeaker. Nick yelled into it. "Why should we surrender? After all the horrible things you've done? You stole from us. Starved us!"

The seas swirled around them and the skies darkened as Serapha's face pinched as if struggling to hold in her rage.

"How dare you!" Serapha shouted. "You humans, all you do is take and destroy!"

The seas spun to form a vortex, sinking Angie and the mer into a shallow whirlpool. Angie pressed herself against the sentinel holding her, kicking her legs with whatever feeble strength she mustered up so she wouldn't be dragged in the undertow.

"You think you can take our food? Our livelihood and think we would roll over and take it?" Nick yelled. "You're wrong!" He walked closer to them, a swagger in his step. He leered at Serapha and sniggered. "We are all on this Earth to survive!"

Angie willed Bàba to speak up, but he appeared too shell-shocked.

Then Nick whispered in a dock worker's ear, and they pulled out a revolver.

The whirlpool stopped, and Angie found herself swaying with the currents.

"Wait! No, stop!" Angie choked on her words and held up her hands, but the worker pulled the trigger, striking true at the sentinel that held Angie captive. A funnel of blood spurted out from the sentinel's chest, and she fell limp with a quiet splash. Meanwhile, the dock worker who shot her raised his free arm in a cheer, and Nick patted him on the shoulder while Bàba looked on in horror.

"They want a fight? They will have one. Kill her! Then kill them all."

Once Serapha gave the order, the second sentinel seizing Angie tightened his grip, making her feel as if her wrist bones were being crushed under his strength. He twisted her around to face him, and with a raging maelstrom in his bright umber eyes, he reared his arm back.

Angie gasped sharply.

His lance's serrated tip ripped through her abdomen. Her eyes popped wide and her jaw dropped open. Pressing her hands to her stomach, she looked down. Her stomach leaked a slow trickle of blood, the saltwater in her wound rendering her speechless and dizzy with excruciating pain.

The sentinel who struck her pulled the lance out, and if the pain intensified any more, she was going to pass out. He reared back as if to strike her again, but a gunshot struck him in the head, and he fell dead before her.

"That's it. You're all dead, you filthy fish!" The fury in Nick's voice rang in Angie's ears.

Gunshots tore through the skies, striking the mer around her. Lances and tridents flew through the air, spearing the humans and bringing them to their knees. More people appeared on the beach, and more mer appeared from behind her.

Angie didn't know where to go, trapped within the mer horde. Brine swarmed into her mouth, and she spat it out. Warm mer bodies trapped her, screams and shouts conglomerating into a dissonant melody.

Her abdominal muscles contracted over and over. With the mer occupied, she summoned what was left of her strength and dove underwater, only to become tangled in a mess of tails slapping at her.

A bullet pierced the surface, embodied in a trail of white and slowing down as it brushed the corner of her eye. She turned her face, wincing, keeping one hand pressed over the gaping wound in her gut. More blood bloomed in the water, and she let out a shocked, muffled cry.

Two dock workers' bodies tumbled into the water and sank like they were weighed down by boulders. Beside her, another mermaid descended to her death.

Below them, gray and white shapes appeared, snatching up the dead and dying mer and humans, a veritable buffet. She knew her hand was coated in blood.

Please let the sharks stay busy, and leave her alone.

Angie swam past the feeding sharks and re-surfaced, the gunshots' thunderous booms blasting her eardrums. The mer appeared to notice the sharks' feeding frenzy below them, and swam closer to the shoreline.

More sentinels moved to Serapha's side, speaking to her. Angie couldn't make out their hushed words, except for one: *tsunami*.

The utterance of the word kept Angie's body still, even as her eyes roved to absorb the sea around her. Watching for rising waves, disturbances in the water, the arrival of dark storm clouds.

Nothing.

Serapha was shaking her head no, sorrow in her eyes.

Another round of gunshots rang through the air.

The mer closest to her took the hits, their bodies jerking and warm blood splattering on Angie's cheeks and neck. With a shaking hand, she wiped it off, numb to any revolt she would have normally felt. She put both hands to her still-bleeding stomach, pressing and pressing, numb to the pain now.

"Tiān, please stop. Stop," she choked out, her throat catching from the salt stuck in it, and she let out a dry, hacking cough. She didn't know how many had died. How many more had to die to end this?

Serapha and her sentinels swept their tails forward, moving the tides closer onto the surface. It reached the dock workers, gripping their knees. The water receded, pulling the workers out to sea.

The mer took their chance. Neither the mer nor the humans that went under came back up unless they floated lifelessly.

Shots resumed. Lances and tridents flew.

More blood, more dead bodies sinking into the water. A handful of humans fell, bodies collapsing into the sand and staining it with ichor.

With each fallen mer, Serapha's face fell further and further, eyes widening until her eyelashes reached her eyebrows.

Angie bolted. Ducked underwater, repeatedly waving one arm over her head so she would descend beneath their tails and then swam in breaststroke, breathing hard and fast as she made for the shoreline.

It was so close. She could see it. Had to take advantage of the adrenaline spike.

She prayed that Serapha was dealing with the deaths of her people to give chase to a wayward human.

Hands grabbed her ankles and pulled her back, and they surfaced.

"Beibei!" Bàba cried out. Now that she was close enough to shore, Angie heard him clearly.

With a low snarl, Serapha grabbed Angie and pressed her back to Serapha's chest.

Angie shrieked as Serapha's scaly tail moved around her waist and chest, starting to squeeze. Tighter, tighter.

In one hand, she held a trident. Serapha pierced the small of her back, and a scream tore from Angie's throat. Any deeper, and it would reach past her muscles to the organs beneath. Serapha moved the weapon—slow, methodical, torturous.

"A shame my sentinel didn't finish the job. I'll ensure your death is slow and painful so your family can see what happens to landwalkers," Serapha hissed in Angie's ear.

Angie's lower back muscles screamed in agony, and she forced in her breaths. She couldn't take in enough air to retort something to Serapha. Water swirled beneath her feet, binding her ankles together. The trident peeled out of her back, and seawater seeped into her open wound. Tears sprung to her eyes, the pain returning and setting her on fire.

Bàba hollered a string of words, but they sounded muffled.

Nick's words were clearer, somehow. "Move! She's close enough. I can get a clear shot."

On the verge of blacking out now, a sound like an exploding bomb rang through the open skies, a supersonic crack as a bullet ripped in their direction.

A mer cut out from the water beside her, taking the bullet, and crumpled like a rag.

Time seemed to still for a moment.

Angie recognized the maroon tail. The beautiful, thick dark hair.

She mustered enough energy to cry out, reaching for him. Heart split in two. "No, no, no."

Serapha let out an ear-shattering scream, her hands flying to her mouth and releasing Angie. Tears fell from Angie's eyes, and she suppressed her sobs, taking the opportunity to swim to safety before Serapha could finish her.

As she swam, Angie kept her head above water, looking to her family, her colleagues. Nick had lowered his gun, his eyes wild with rage. He lifted his shotgun, poised to shoot again.

A flurry of lances sailed over Angie's head and impaled Nick. His eyes wide, he stumbled backward and fell flat on his back, unmoving.

Mia shoved her way through the wall of dock workers. She shrieked and rushed to Nick, catching him before he crashed to the ground.

Had Mia been here the whole time?

More yells and screams. The dock workers kept shooting. Hands grabbed Angie's ankles, pulling her back to the mer horde so that she was side to side with a sentinel. A water wall came up around the surviving mer, growing thicker and thicker. An awesome, terrifying sight to behold. The mer swam closer and huddled together, keeping Angie close. Some shouted to Serapha, and when no more bullets came through, she allowed it to lower.

"Stop this madness!" Serapha cried out.

Salt burned Angie's eyes, and through the haze, Bàba raised an arm, signaling the others to stop. The mer had crept closer to the shore, and now, both sides stayed at a standstill.

"I do not want to see more death." Serapha sounded breathless. "You landwalkers may take the fish you need to survive. Only what's needed for survival. As long as you stop this bloodshed. Decline, and I will kill her. Just like you killed my son and my lifemate." She put an arm around Angie's neck.

A silence befell them as Bàba stood stock-still like a wooden doll, his eyes still bulging in horror. Standing as if in a trance, until Mia nudged him hard with an elbow and broke him out of it.

When he spoke, his voice quivered in a way Angie hadn't heard before. "We agree to your demands, Mer-Queen. If you will release a few more fish to us so we can financially survive. And if you let my daughter go."

Please, Serapha. Say yes. For your people. For your son.

Beside her, Kaden floated like a dead man, blood trailing from the gunshot wound she couldn't locate. His abdominal area was fogged with thick, serosanguineous fluid.

No, she couldn't lose him like this. She wouldn't accept it. Had to come back for him.

Serapha spoke. "I agree. Take her back." She pushed Angie into the arms of a sentinel, who escorted her to shore. Once she met with sweet, sweet sand, gasping for air, she crawled ashore with her hands over her wounds. Bàba rushed to her and lifted her by the arms until her feet were planted on the ground.

Behind them, the mer retreated into the sea, their forms disappearing one by one. Angie's throat grew thick, and she fought to stop another waterfall of tears tumbling from her eyes. She couldn't stop to grieve now, and wanted to be home. The tears could flow then, and she could weep to her heart's content.

Serapha and two mer sentinels surrounded Kaden, one sentinel cradling his upper body, the other cradling his tail.

They dove back underwater, and he too, disappeared with the rest.

Mia appeared from behind Bàba, her face ghostly white, one hand over her mouth. "Angie? Oh, you're okay!" She grabbed Angie and hugged her tight, burying her face in her hair. Bàba put an arm around both of them, his body and hands trembling.

Angie licked her dry, chapped lips, cracked from dehydration. "Water. I need water."

"Here." Bàba held out a half-drunk bottle of spring water, and Angie swiped it from him, drinking it in one large gulp.

She felt alive. "Thank you," she whispered.

"Why are you here?" Bàba asked Mia, his breath hitching.

"I couldn't just stay home and hope that you would live. I stayed behind everyone. What if you all died?" Mia's lower lip quivered. "Like Nick."

She eyed Nick's still body, blood still trickling from his mouth, and sank into a cross-legged sitting position beside him.

"Let's get you home. It's over." He put an arm around Angie, holding her close to his side as they walked together. Then he stopped, looking behind him. "*Doudou*, are you staying?" Again, Bàba rubbed at the stubble on his chin, calling Mia by her childhood nickname, *Little bean*.

"I want to stay with him a little longer." And with thickness in her words, she said, "*Qǐng ānxí ba,*" a wish for him to rest in peace, and hung her head.

FORTY-SEVEN

KADEN MAY HAVE DIED TRYING TO defend his mother and possibly Angie. She might never know, and it killed her.

"Beibei." Bàba approached Angie, and she turned to face him on the couch, gasping as her wounds contracted. Each time they stung it reminded her of Kaden. The slim hope that he still lived drove her through the past several days, willing her wound to heal as fast as possible. She had to see him again, dead or alive. Her heart clenched that she didn't have a chance to say goodbye before Nick shot him down.

And Nick. As much as she had hated him, he had died trying to stop the mer from killing her.

Lulu circled around her ankles. The cat had stayed glued to Angie's side the past several days.

Bàba sat down at the other end of the couch with his tea mug in hand. He offered her a drink, setting it in front of her. He'd always been a quiet man, but he had hardly spoken a word in the past six days. "Yes, Bàba?"

"I'm sorry."

Angie did a double take, and sat herself upright. She couldn't remember the last time Bàba apologized for anything. "You're sorry?"

"For firing you. I understand now. You were trying to help." He rubbed his face, sniffling. Angie remained silent as she reached for her mug with slow, cautious movements, waiting for him to continue. "I know you're leaving soon, but you can return to the docks anytime you like. I'll also have our secretaries write a letter that you completed your hours. I'll loan you the rest of the money that you need. Take your time returning it."

Angie's mouth went dry. She brought the mug to her lips. He'd made her oolong, the floral aromas dancing in her nostrils. "Thank you, Bàba. I appreciate that."

"Yes, of course. Because if it weren't for you, this might not have ended as quickly as it did. We thought about it, and striking at their queendom, in their territory and with them outnumbering us, would have been too much for our men and women. The failed ambush on the palace proved that. The mer-queen would never have agreed to negotiate otherwise, I'm sure." Bàba's eyebrows pinched together.

"No. She was going to kill everyone with another tsunami." Angie shuffled her feet on the ground, looking at her toes. "With how many people we have left, it just might have worked." No matter how she racked her mind, she couldn't think of why Serapha didn't throw one final tsunami at them and decimate the rest. Whatever her reason, Angie was grateful that she chose to hold back.

"Beau and Emily are not happy with me that we agreed to peace."

Angie grimaced. "They weren't the ones fighting at the front lines. They'd rather see the rest of us dead? If not from the mer, then withering away from starvation?"

"I would not think so. But, dealing with them will be for another day." Bàba leaned his head over the headrest. "Brokering peace was the right thing to do. I only wish it had not come to you being captured or losing your mer-prince in the process." His voice pitch dropped another notch, and he shifted his weight from side to side.

"Please don't remind me of that, Bàba." A fresh wave of tears rose to meet her eyelids, but she wiped them away with the back of her hand.

As much as she thought of Kaden and how Mia was dealing with being a single parent, another question gnawed at her.

"What were you going to do with Nick? After you found out what he did."

"Demand he tell Mia, or I would. And that I would stand by whatever Mia decided. Then demote or fire him, I hadn't decided." Melancholy haunted his eyes. "He's not the man I thought he was."

Angie stared at her lap. "She all but told me he abused her, and she was going to leave him."

"I would have funded her divorce." Bàba rubbed his temples. "Your Māma and I did not raise you two to tolerate that sort of behavior."

She sat upright at Māma's mention. It was time to tell him.

"I saw Māma."

The teacup slipped from Bàba's hand, and the bottom met the saucer with a *clack*. He rolled his lips between his teeth, and his eyes were wet. Time stretched and stretched until he responded. "What do you mean?"

Angie's lower lip trembled. "Kaden took me to her resting place almost two months ago. She's buried with the mer. Looked so peaceful. Kaden said they found her floating, but I thought she had a diving accident." She blinked, trying to stop the tears from falling. "I didn't know how to tell you." Bàba nodded his understanding. "Did you know what happened to her?"

Bàba gripped the arm of the couch hard. He dropped his head and Angie stayed glued to her spot.

"Yes. I knew Ning wanted to die with her first love, the sea. Her sickness was terminal by then, and she didn't have much time left. She didn't want to live out the remainder of her days in hospice or a nursing home." Bàba took in another shaky breath, and Angie put a hand on his forearm and willed him to continue. "I tried to stop her. Suggested home hospice so you and Mia could be with her. She agreed."

He took a tentative sip of his tea.

"But when I came home from work one day, she was gone. I never saw her again. Could not reach her." His voice thickened. "I suspected she went diving with the intent to die, but I could not believe it. What you told me, you confirmed what I had thought all these years."

Angie swiped away the tears falling from her eyes. "Why didn't you tell us? We spent so many years wondering and grieving and not having closure. If you knew, you should have told us." The timbre of her voice came out laced with invisible flames.

Bàba scooted away from her. "I couldn't burden the two of you with simple suspicions! You had to focus in college and Mia was raising a young child. How could I explain that I suspected your māma took her own life?"

"I wish you told us the truth. It's better than hiding it from us for so long," she insisted, closing the distance between them. It was the same thought she had about Kaden and the mer, when she found out they had buried Māma.

"She didn't want to strain us and her parents financially, and she didn't want to live in pain until death finally took her. She did not want the two of you to worry." Bàba didn't move.

Angie swiped at the stream of tears that escaped one eye. She should have been there with Māma on the day she went into the sea, for the last time. Angie would have stopped her, or insisted on diving with her and forced her to come back. She could have given Māma her supplemental oxygen.

Angie inhaled a shaking breath and exhaled slowly, silencing her rabid thoughts.

She could have saved Māma, but for what?

So, she would suffer an even longer, more painful passing?

Māma made her choice a long time ago. She must have known that her daughters were in good hands with Bàba, and she spared them from watching her wither.

A flood of emotion threatened to swallow her whole, and she thanked him. "Thank you for telling me. Will you tell Mia too?"

"Yes, I will. She deserves to know. I will tell her when enough time has passed. She lost Nick, after all."

"That's a good idea. I'll check in on her too."

Angie had been calling Mia daily, talking as much as she wanted to. With Angie's injury, Mia and Rosie had come to stay with them for the first four days after Nick's death. Yesterday, Nick's parents and brother and sister arrived at her house, and Mia and Rosie had left to be with them.

She reached for Bàba. With his teacup still in one hand, Bàba wrapped his free arm around her and enveloped her in a comforting hug.

Angie relished this moment with him. Tomorrow, they had a lot of work to do.

FORTY-EIGHT

"Aㄴɢɪᴇ ᴀ̄ʏɪ́?"

Angie looked down, dusting off building debris from her arm from sweeping the residual parts of the dock's gangway.

Rosie ran up to her, her sneakers tap-tap-tapping on the boards. Gasping, Angie knelt and gathered her niece in her arms for a long hug. "Oh, tiān, what are you doing here? Are you alright?"

Rosie broke away, fidgeting with the friendship bracelet on her right wrist. "Māma took me to come see you because you're leaving next week."

Angie squeezed her niece's shoulder. "Yeah, I have to go back to school."

School. With the events of the last several months, it was the last thing on her mind. Now she only had ten days to pack up her things and Lulu and get her materials ready, while consoling Mia and joining Bàba on the dock cleanup crew. She had written to Pacific Grove asking for a deferment several days ago, and had yet to hear back. There was also the matter of bringing the last of the captured mer back to the sea, dead or alive. That task had started the day after their truce, with Aurora and her lifemate the first to be released by the dockworkers.

"I know. But I won't see you as much." Rosie dug her small foot into a gap between the wooden planks and sniffled, wiping her nose.

"Hey, sweetie. What's wrong?" Angie put a hand on Rosie's shoulder.

"Māma is so sad cause Papa is gone." At the mention of Nick, Rosie burst into tears. "And I am too. I wish he was still here."

"I know, my love. I know." She took Rosie's hand in hers, closing her fingers over them. "If you or your mom ever want to talk, you can call me anytime, okay? And I'll come back and visit as much as I can."

"Okay." Rosie rubbed her eyes. "But um, remember that mermaid we saw like a long time ago? She wanted me to tell you something."

"What?" Angie loosened her grip, searching her niece's bright eyes, still wet with tears. "Adrielle?"

"Yeah, her. Adrial!" Rosie mispronounced her name, but she looked so proud of herself that Angie didn't bother correcting her.

"Wh-when? How?"

"Well, I *am* an honorary mermaid." Rosie fiddled with her bracelet.

"That you are." Angie couldn't help but smile.

"I couldn't stop thinking of her, so Māma took me back to look for her. She wants you to meet her at the place from last time."

"Where's your mom?" Angie looked, but found no sign of her sister.

"She's coming with Gōnggong. They stopped to talk to some people."

"There you two are," Bàba said, Mia beside him, her face and lips pale and undereye shadows dark as ink. "Beibei, we have to keep going. The docks aren't going to rebuild itself."

"Rosie, next time, wait for me, okay?" Mia said with an exasperated sigh, before turning to Angie. "But I saw she found you. So I let her be."

"I know, I promise I will, but I have to talk to one of the mermaids. I'll be right back."

Bàba looked at Mia and Rosie, and then back at Angie. "Mind if I come with you? I have not seen a mermaid up close. Alive and healthy, that is."

"Definitely." Angie waved goodbye to Mia and Rosie.

Stefan walked by then, giving her a wave and stopped to talk to Mia and Rosie, putting a hand on Mia's shoulder.

Angie traced her steps to where she'd met with Kaden, Adrielle, and Cyrus with Mia. A small pocket of happiness in an otherwise turbulent time.

As Rosie said, Adrielle awaited them, her long arms folded on the shoreline and rose tail breaking the surface. She brightened when their eyes met. "I'm glad you came."

"Me too. How's everything been? Cyrus? And Kaden? Have you done the burial ceremony for him yet?" Angie settled herself on her knees.

"Burial ceremony?" Adrielle's features marred with confusion. "He's not dead. He is temporarily infirm, but he will recover shortly. He wants to see you, if you would see him and asked me to fetch you."

"I would love to." Angie's hands flew to her chest, heartbeat pulsing strong.

Bàba finally spoke. "May I come as well? I would like to see my wife one last time. If you can wait, I will retrieve my gear."

"No. I can give you both breath. Come."

"Will that be okay? It won't make you too tired?" Angie wrinkled her brow.

"I will be more tired, yes. But just give me some extra time while we swim." Adrielle beckoned them closer, and Angie went first, parting her lips and gently met Adrielle's, and the mermaid exhaled deep into her. Bàba followed suit after a moment of hesitation. He winced after Adrielle pulled back.

"I feel hot." Bàba put his hands to his face and neck. "What's happening?"

"It's normal," Angie said, and together, they followed Adrielle undersea.

He didn't appear nearly as excited as Angie was when she first dove underwater with the mer's magic, not speaking a word while they approached the palace. Angie would pay to know what went through his mind.

Adrielle was noticeably slower, and they paused every few paddles to let her rest. When they reached the infirmary full of injured mermaids and mermen, Angie searched for Kaden. She found him in the far corner beside his brother, who still appeared to be in a deep sleep. Adrielle swam to Cyrus's side.

Serapha floated upright at the foot of both their beds, and after her eyes met with Bàba's, she tensed.

"Mer-Queen," Angie whispered. "I know you don't want to see us." She gestured to Bàba. "This is my father. He only wants to see my mother. His uh, lifemate. And get closure. Then we'll leave."

Serapha's shoulders dropped an inch, crossed arms loosening. "Just as well, but only because you've shown you are on our side. And because he has agreed to peace." She jerked her head toward Bàba.

"Appreciated, Mer-Queen," Bàba said, tone level.

Serapha motioned with her hand. "I will take you, with one of our sentinels."

Bàba bowed his head, and left the room. A sentinel followed, and Angie watched them leave. She had questions and hoped Serapha could spare her some minutes to ease her mind. It could be her only opportunity to get her alone.

"Mer-Queen, can I ask a question before you go?"

Serapha stopped, circling around. "Ask."

"When we faced off. You and another sentinel were talking, and I heard the word *tsunami*. But you were shaking your head. You could have ended my people right then and there, turned the tide in your favor." Angie licked her salty lips. "Why didn't you?"

A flash appeared in Serapha's eyes, and she folded her arms, appearing to close herself off, and Angie worried that she might have inadvertently angered her.

Serapha smoothed her long, thick braid over one shoulder. "I did not have the strength to create one without it killing me." She carried herself tall and unapologetic. "I created two too close to each another, and then the maelstrom, draining too much of myself without time to replenish. I would have gladly given my life to destroy my enemies, had I somebody to rule in my place. In that instance, an offering of truce was the clearer option."

Angie did appreciate her brutal honesty, and she bowed. "Thank you, Mer-Queen. For answering my question."

Serapha lifted her chin, then turned and left after her sentinel and Bàba.

Angie passed Cyrus' bed on the way to Kaden. Adrielle had her tail curled under her, seated on a flat rock, Cyrus' hand clasped in hers.

She saw Angie and gave Cyrus a gentle tap, awakening him. His eyes fluttered open, and he gave Angie and Adrielle a faint smile before falling back into his slumber. "He will be fine, after some time." Adrielle sighed deeply, her gills flaring, and then relaxing. "You should go see Kaden."

"Wishing a fast recovery for him." She didn't understand the sudden bout of awkwardness.

Adrielle gave her an encouraging nod. "He awaits you. You were the first person he asked for when he awoke."

Once Angie reached Kaden and touched his hand, his eyes opened and lit up. A jelly-like wrapping rested around the wound on his abdominal region. He opened his arms, and she pulled herself to him and rested in his tender embrace.

"Why were you at the surface?"

"You were still being held hostage when I left. I wanted to see you, take you away from my mother, but I was too late. Saw the gun aimed for the two of you. Better my life than yours and my mother's. Losing her would be too much. For Cyrus, for the queendom, for me."

She gazed into his eyes. He lived, and nothing else mattered. She knew she would never find anyone else like him.

Small creatures wiggled in her hair, coupled with tiny pecks on her scalp, and she jolted, searching for whatever bit her.

"What the Hells?" A smattering of longfin smelt the size of her hand, fled.

Next to her, Kaden's cheeks were puffed and his lips tight, his eyes holding back laughter. "Remember how I told you to keep your hair tied back? Now, there's fish wandering around the sea, and they will seek to make a temporary home in your long flowing hair. They think it's seaweed."

Angie laughed with him then, burying her face in her hands. "Alright, smartass. Tying my hair was the last thing on my mind when I heard you were alive."

"Ah, I jest." He grinned, and she laid back down, pressing her chest to his so she wouldn't float. "I thought I lost you. That I would never see you again, and that's the way I had to see you go." Her voice laced thick with emotion, and he stroked his knuckles along her spine, her nerves awakening and sending warm, comforting signals to the rest of her body.

A low chuckle sent a rumble through his chest, tickling her cheek. "You think I would leave you without telling you I loved you one last time?"

She pushed herself up onto her forearms, gazing into those striking amber eyes she'd missed seeing. "I love you. I love you so much." She leaned in and kissed him, and he put one hand behind her head, drawing her in closer. The tension she carried melted with the undulating, caressing deep, and she lost herself in him.

Angie pulled back, breaking their embrace. Adrielle had been watching them from the corner of her eye, but turned her attention back to Cyrus with a lowered head and a smile after her gaze connected with Angie's.

"We will have to make up for lost time." Kaden reached for a lock of her hair and smoothed it. "When I'm better."

"I'd like that." Angie wound her fingers in between his.

"You know, my mother said my love for you cost her her lifemate. Sent her oldest son into an infirm state, and she thought her remaining son was mortally wounded. She held a grudge for some days, but—"

"But because of you, my sons live to see another tidesday."

Angie hadn't heard Serapha approach them from behind. "Mer-Queen," she said at the same time Kaden said "Mother."

Serapha gave them both a head bow of acknowledgment and swam aside to reveal Bàba behind her. His eyes were swollen, his nose red, his cheeks puffed. He approached Angie to hug her, and then moved to Kaden to shake his hand.

"Kaden, I want to tell you. What happened to you that day at the shore, should not have happened," Bàba started. "I was only looking for Angie. I did not expect to see the two of you together, and Nick fired before I could stop him."

"I told you, Mother," Kaden added. "She wouldn't set a trap for me after agreeing to rescue Cyrus, and then keeping her word."

"I was doing exactly what I promised. Getting your message to my dad. I mean, before I lost the bottle," Angie said. "I also helped get King Aqilus back into the sea. I figured at least he would be home."

"Yes. Sentinels recovered him recently, and we've provided him with a burial. That still doesn't explain how you knew where to find them," Serapha cut in, the second part of her statement directed at Bàba. "It seemed much too coincidental."

Angie listened as Bàba filled Serapha in on what Nick had said about the mermaid, Aurora. When he was finished, Serapha thinned her lips. "I see. It is certainly a shame she felt that way. But she would not be the first. War will divide even the most united of mer."

Bàba clasped his hands behind his back, his legs scissoring under him. "I have seen war in my past, and now this. It divides humans, as well."

Serapha gave Bàba a nearly imperceptible nod in response. "I would have felt similar in Aurora's position. My lifemate was taken from me, as well." She went silent, gaze dropping to the seafloor.

Perhaps if Serapha had listened to her that day in the mer prisons, the bloodbath at the shoreline would never have happened. Yet Angie understood. Losing her lifemate, having one son injured and her other son tortured and drained to the point of unconsciousness by the same enemy would cause rational thought to flee her mind, as well.

"Mother." Kaden reached toward her.

She shook out her shoulders. "He will be properly grieved, once we have a moment to breathe. And he will be taken care of in the afterlife. I will await him when he reincarnates."

"I am waiting for that day with my wife, as well," Bàba murmured.

"Did you see Māma?" Angie studied his still face.

"I did. It has been so long. To see her face again," he said, his voice breathy and his hands clasped over his chest. "Thank you, Queen Serapha, for bringing me to see her." He looked at Angie. "Beibei, are you ready to go back?"

"Yes, I think so."

Kaden put one hand on his heart and inclined his head toward Bàba, who bowed in return.

She let go of Kaden's hand and swam back to the surface with Bàba.

FORTY-NINE

ONE YEAR LATER

Angie stepped out from her beachside Seattle apartment, reciting fishes native to the Salish Sea and murmuring under her breath. Two weeks into school, and her Biology of Fishes professor had already announced a quiz next week.

"Coastrange salmon, *cottus aleuticus*. Lobefin snailfish, *liparis greeni*. Queenfish." She drew a blank on its scientific name.

Damn. What sadist gave their class a quiz on the third week of class?

Her phone pinged with an incoming text from Mia, and thanking her ancestors for the distraction, she opened the message. It was coupled with a photo of Mia's four-month-old little boy, Jacques, but they called him Jack. His middle name was Nicholas, in honor of her father. Jack's complexion was fair with eyes reflecting copper, his hair of golden brown and slender lips. He looked like Nick, and even as an infant, his personality was already as big as his father's. Angie knew it comforted Mia that her son mirrored her late husband. Jack was laying on his back, his chubby legs and arms splayed. One hand toward the camera, a wide, toothless smile on his face.

Despite looking like Nick, he was much too adorable for words.

Angie grinned and texted her back, and continued making her way toward the shoreline.

Then another text came in, this one from Celia.

Celia: Hey Angie! Thanks for checking in on me. I'm okay. I miss my mom, but I know you understand. Let me know when you're back in Creston. We'll meet up.

Angie replied in kind and slipped her phone back into her pocket. She had been in Seattle three weeks, having moved here a week early to get acclimated. With the whirlwind of school starting, moving into her apartment, and getting Lulu settled in, it felt like only days had passed.

Ten paces more, and a glint appeared out of the corner of her eye. Then another.

She turned her head and squinted. What could that be?

Several more steps, and colorful gems spelling out her name came into view.

Angie stopped short and kneeled. Cobalt, gold, copper, and graphite crystals as small as her pinky nail and as large as her hand greeted her. She began to gather them into her hands.

"Do you like them?" Kaden's voice came to her, carried on the breeze. Her next breath caught in her throat, and she met his gaze.

Angie stopped halfway in her quest to gather all the gems. Adrenaline spiked and rejuvenated her, and the blue-gray seas and skies, golden sun, and sandy shores brightened. "Kaden! You're here." She ran to him and fell to her knees, and he rose to meet her height, drawing her into a tight hug.

"Did you doubt me? I told you I would follow where you went. And I had good reason to hasten my trip." His lips on her neck emitted sweet vibrations, and she pulled back, keeping her hands on his forearms.

"Oh, and yes. Of course I love them, they're from you. But where did you get them from? These are worth a fortune to some people." She fell to her backside and sat cross-legged, pocketing the precious gemstones.

"Hydrothermal vents are rich with minerals. Exhausting, and hot, but it's worth it to see your joy." Kaden shifted backward so that everything but his upper arms and shoulders were obscured by the moody sea, and rested his chin in his hands.

"Thank you. I'll keep these safe." Angie closed her eyes and inhaled the invigorating, refreshing sea breeze. "How was everything at the docks? I mean, I know you probably left a week after I did, but still."

"All was well. The repairs are moving along, and I've been helping where I can. Especially when they needed structures placed closer to, or in the water." Kaden shifted, his elegant dorsal fin peeking over the surface, swaying with the waves. "I think your dad is warming up to me."

"If you've managed to impress him and Mia, you're good in my book," Angie said, full of mirth.

Kaden pushed himself up on his hands, and put one hand to his chest, his eyes growing wide. "Well then, my love. I'm glad to hear it." He laughed and looked away when Angie flicked sand at him.

A fishing boat appeared from the horizon, bringing Angie back to last summer. She instinctively drew her shoulders to her ears, as if expecting the boat to be taken down by mer.

But the war was over. And the central queendom had pulled their reinforcements back when the humans and mer reached a truce.

Kaden had already turned his head to look.

"Incredible." The word carried on a long exhale, and he jutted his chin in the boat's direction. "This never gets old. I still am in awe of their size."

"Yeah, we like them big." Angie grinned, moving backward to avoid an incoming wave, breaking at the shoreline. A futile motion, because the seafoam still splattered onto her jeans.

The boat disappeared into the blue horizon, likely heading for the nearby docks some miles away.

The early fall sun beat down on her face, and she didn't even care that she'd forgotten to apply sunscreen. The welcome smell of a clean sea breeze filled her nostrils, and she took it in, savoring the smell and brisk warmth.

The past year had flown by, like a black marlin sailing the seas. She had written to Pacific Grove University after the mer and humans had reached a truce, and asked for a deferral simply due to extenuating circumstances. They'd granted her permission to start one year later without asking further questions, and she couldn't have been more grateful.

It had taken Kaden another month to fully recover from being shot, and when he'd regained his strength, he explored the undersea with her, and Angie kept current in her studies, helped Bàba rebuild the docks, and comforted Mia while she grieved Nick.

Kaden reached for her and put his hand over hers. "Come for a swim with me? Three weeks is much too long to not have you at my side."

"Sure. Let me go change. I'll be back." She fed Lulu, stored the gems in her jewelry box, dressed in a crimson tankini and shorts, and returned twenty minutes later. Excitement skittered under her skin.

Kaden's gaze hungered as he eyed her, and when she was close enough, she jumped into the blue.

Angie shrieked, the high fifties temperature water shocking her system.

"If you would have waited one minute," Kaden chuckled and pulled her in, pressing his lips to hers. First a kiss, and then breath.

Her body warmed in an instant, and she followed him beneath the waves. They passed through a kelp forest, leaves tickling her bare arms and legs. Beneath her feet, halibut and flounders darted about in the sand.

Halibut, *hippoglosus stenolepis*.

The olive flounder? Angie raked her mind. *Paralichthys olivaceus*.

Okay, so maybe the first quiz of her PhD program wouldn't be too bad.

"How's the family?" Angie asked once they cleared the forest and entered the darkened deep.

"Mother is doing a fine job of ruling on her own. The mer are more sympathetic to her than ever. Cyrus is still recovering. But Libbi and Hadrien are doing wonderfully. Getting bigger by the day, I feel."

Adrielle had borne her twins shortly before Mia had her baby, with a promise to bring them closer to shore once they were older and their lungs were more developed.

"I look forward to meeting them one day." Angie tightened her hand around his. "Where are we going? You seem like you have someplace in mind."

"I do." Kaden turned right, ducking beneath a bluntnose sixgill shark sailing overhead, wiggling back and forth.

He led her to a spacious, empty grotto and leaned in to whisper in her ear. "Now that you're all mine, I'm going to enjoy tasting and feeling every inch of you on my lips and fingers."

"Oh, please do, Mer-Prince." Angie backed into the wall behind her and trailed a finger toward her cleavage, maintaining eye contact with him. She shivered with desire, despite the feverish rush bursting from her core.

Kaden watched her a moment longer through hooded eyelids and closed the distance between them. A gasp escaped her lips as he leaned in to kiss her, dotting his lips down her neck, her collarbone, and her shoulder. Each kiss sent a pleasurable electric jolt down her arms and legs.

One arm wrapped around her waist, and his other hand moved to help her remove the bottom piece of her swimsuit.

He pulled her flush to him, and pulled back, his eyes dancing. "Ah, Angie Song, how I love you."

"Mm. I love you too, Prince Kaden."

"Oh, stop it with the *prince* title." Kaden bumped his nose to hers. "Now, where were we?"

"I think you're right where you're supposed to be," Angie replied. She buzzed with happiness and passion as he kissed her again, and trailed his lips further down her body.

"That I am." Kaden's voice sounded more distant when he was at her bellybutton. A wicked grin was on his handsome face when he glanced up at her. "Now lie back so I can hear just how much you love me."

His tongue traced a line along the inside of her thigh, and he pushed one hand against her hip to prevent her from floating away. Her breath hitched, and she let her head fall back, her racing pulse reaching a breaking point, and did as he asked.

It felt like an eternity and a fraction of a minute passed while they were wrapped up in each other.

Angie had slipped her bottoms back on and followed Kaden as they made their ascent back to the surface so she could prepare for tomorrow's classes, pausing every few feet to exchange kisses.

They had made it three hundred feet, with no sign of moonlight or sunlight filtering through. Kaden kept his arm loosely wrapped over her waist, as if he couldn't bear to let her go. If she had calculated right, they still had another hundred feet to go before they reached the light zone.

"Doing alright?" Kaden looked over to her.

"Yeah, I'm peachy." Angie grinned at him. She yelped when something cold, solid, and sharp slapped to her bare thigh. "Shén me guǐ?" Looking down revealed a dead, nearly footlong, blue-gray fish with a dark horizontal line running along the length of its body.

Where did that come from?

Kaden reached for the fish and peeled it off her leg, inspecting it. "Looks like she was caught and released." He examined it closer, brow furrowing.

Angie leaned in. A silver hook wedged through the fish's mouth, and protruded from her gills. She grimaced. The tip of the hook had scratched her leg, but fortunately, not deep enough to break skin. "These fucking fishers. Couldn't even be bothered to take the hook out of her mouth."

Kaden shook his head in disdain, still holding the fish by her caudal fins.

Angie kept her gaze trained on the fish, its appearance striking a familiar chord. She racked the back of her mind.

"A queenfish." She hadn't meant to say it aloud, but the words left her lips of their own volition. The scientific name came to her as if she'd never forgotten it. "*Seriphus politus.*"

A passing, inexplicable sense of dread filled her, and she locked eyes with Kaden. His lips were parted and eyes unblinking as he stared first at her, then at the fish.

In a flash, strong currents swept through, snatching the queenfish from Kaden's grasp. She tumbled away into the blackness and out of their sight.

Kaden licked his lips, his shoulders dropping. "You okay?"

Angie gave him a firm nod. "Yeah. So um, I'll see you tomorrow, right?"

"Of course." Kaden took her face in his hands. "And the day after that, and the day after that, and after that. Until you're sick of seeing my face."

She looked toward where the dead queenfish had been swept away, then relaxed her pose, her mood brightening. "That would be never."

"I feel the same about you. Until tomorrow, then." Kaden kissed her forehead and took her hand, motioning his head upward. "But for now, let's get you home."

ABOUT THE AUTHOR

C.W. Rose is a Fantasy and Romance author who writes about ordinary Asian women in extraordinary situations, about the cinnamon roll (not always human) men who adore them, and how they find themselves and sometimes—okay, usually—love along the way. She is also a certified scuba diver and lifeguard with a deep love for the world and animals around us, though she hasn't spotted any mermaids yet.

Outside of writing, you can find her buried in a great book, learning to sing in different languages, and finding any excuse to spend time outdoors. She's also a third culture kid who grew up in Singapore and currently lives in New York City with her family, working as a Physical Therapist.

Find all of her socials, website, and newsletter sign up at http://linktree.com/cwrose

ACKNOWLEDGMENTS

Whew, where do I start? I have so many people to thank who helped to bring *Oceansong* to life. It took me nearly six years of querying, one shelved manuscript, and over two hundred rejections (and a lot of heartbreak) to get here. A massive thank you to the team at Hey Hey Books: my editors Jordan and Caitlyn and my cover designers Jenny and Gianni. You are all amazing, and I had the best time working on this book with you all. I knew you were my champion the moment you called us both "mermaid-loving lifeguards."

Of course, I also wouldn't be here without my family and friends' support. To my brother, Kevin, my oldest best friend, you've wholeheartedly supported me and were never afraid to be frank and real with me in the choices I made. And you were the first person I told when I found out I was going to be a published author after nearly six years of trying and decades of writing. To my Xiao Gugu, Mama and Baba, your support has meant the world while I stumbled for a few years trying to figure out my career path, and while I wrote one manuscript after another, hoping the next one would be the one that would meet the world. You may have been tough on me growing up (and sometimes even now!), but I never doubted your continued support of my endeavors. For my best friends, Emily and Jenny, two amazing women, your unwavering and enthusiastic love and support have meant everything to me. I miss both of you so much. I love all of you.

And where would I be without my amazing author friends? Ana, Daphne, and Deborah (I mean, nothing beats our epic WhatsApp novels!), you three were some of the first people I connected with when I started querying *Oceansong*. It's been a joy to navigate the querying trenches with you, and getting to know you on a personal level. Even though we live in different states and countries, I sincerely hope that I get to meet all of you one day. To my Elemental ladies, Kassidy, Erica, and Courtney, I adore our group texts and as we all now navigate the publishing world together. I couldn't have asked for a better group of people to have connected with. I'm so proud and elated to call all of you my friends, and of course some of my favorite fantasy and romance authors.

I also have to thank all my beta readers and everyone in Twitter/X's Writing Community who have supported me during pitch events, during the highs and lows of querying, and of course, read any part of the book. Whether it was part of it, the whole book, or just my query letter or synopsis, all your feedback has helped immensely in making this book better with your feedback. So, to Virginia, Kylie, Michelle, Haley, Debbie, Sarah, Paul, Lilly, Amanda, Antoinette, Bee, Ashley, Abby, Madelyn, Anna, June K., Hanna, Nicole, Shalini, Kit, and Emma, thank you so very much for your time and sharp eyes.

To the authors who generously gave their time to read and blurb *Oceansong*: Thea Guanzon, Ben Bishop, Melissa Karibien, Deborah Wong, Kassidy Coursey, Paulette Kennedy, Desiree M. Niccoli, Erica Eberhart, Courtney Collins, Mariet Kay, and Chantal Gadoury, thank you so much! Your kindness and generosity mean the world to me.

Okay, second to last mention. I want to give a huge shout-out to the character artists who brought my characters to life: Nikolai Espera, Jackie Moss, Marcella W., and Alli. Your artwork is beautiful and brought me to tears when I saw Kaden, Angie, Zixin, Mia, and Adrielle and Cyrus as I imagined them in my head.

Finally, thank you, the reader, for taking a chance on *Oceansong*. None of this would be possible without you. I'm truly grateful for your time, and I hope you enjoyed joining Angie and Kaden on their journey. If you did, please consider leaving a review on your preferred site.